D0362566

A woman of flame hides
   beneath the streets of the city...
      and only a man of fire can save her.

"I was sent to find you. To protect you. And I will do that. You run and I will find you. Again, and again, and again."

She believed him. And it enraged her.

Ten years on her own, and she'd made it—hammered out a life that was quick and dirty but hers. And now this man, a stranger, was telling her he was in her life?

You need help, whispered her rational side—but it was too late. The dragon inside her had never been rational. "Get away from me," she growled.

"Lyssa," he said, reaching for her.

She whirled, lashing out with her fist. Eddie twisted, clamped his hand around her wrist. She grabbed his throat, but not before his hand slid forward—and touched her bare skin.

The contact burned. Burned to the bone. A roaring sound filled Lyssa's ears and her vision brightened in a haze of golden light, until all she could see was Eddie's eyes.

Smoke rose from beneath her hand.

Everything exploded.

———

"Readers of early Laurell K. Hamilton, Charlaine Harris, and the best thrillers out there should try Liu now."
Publishers Weekly

By Marjorie M. Liu

WITHIN THE FLAMES
IN THE DARK OF DREAMS
THE FIRE KING
THE WILD ROAD
THE LAST TWILIGHT
SOUL SONG
EYE OF HEAVEN
DARK DREAMERS (anthology)
THE RED HEART OF JADE
SHADOW TOUCH
A TASTE OF CRIMSON (Crimson City Series)
TIGER EYE

Marjorie M. Liu

Within *The* Flames

A DIRK & STEELE NOVEL

AVON

An Imprint of HarperCollinsPublishers

This is a work of fiction. Names, characters, places, and incidents are products of the author's imagination or are used fictitiously and are not to be construed as real. Any resemblance to actual events, locales, organizations, or persons, living or dead, is entirely coincidental.

AVON BOOKS
An Imprint of H arperCollins*Publishers*
10 East 53rd Street
New York, New York 10022-5299

Copyright © 2011 by Marjorie M. Liu
ISBN 978-0-06-202017-8
www.avonromance.com

First Avon Books mass market printing: December 2011

Avon Trademark Reg. U.S. Pat. Off. and in Other Countries, Marca Registrada, Hecho en U.S.A.
HarperCollins® is a registered trademark of HarperCollins Publishers.

Printed in the U.S.A.

10 9 8 7 6 5 4 3 2 1

ACKNOWLEDGMENTS

Heartfelt thanks to my lovely editor, May Chen, and all the hardworking souls at HarperCollins who have been so very kind and supportive. I'd also like to thank my wonderful agent, Lucienne Diver—as well as friend and publicist, Elena Stokes.

To my readers, who are delightful and magical, a mighty thank you.

PROLOGUE

I T began as a game. Death was always a game, under civilized circumstances.

Tea was served. Tea and sandwiches, accompanied by glistening cakes and sugared cookies. The guests fidgeted inside the small room with its stone floor and hard wooden chairs: rare antiques made for kings and queens, in older, darker, years.

In all, six women were present. Three were in their early twenties. Strong girls, with clear skin, bright eyes, and rosy cheeks. Good girls, chosen for their good hearts.

The two women who had lured them here were older, though only just. The woman in charge had chosen *them,* years ago, for reasons that had *nothing* to do with goodness.

Which was why they were still alive. Whether or not they stayed that way would depend on how the wind blew. The woman in charge had trained them. She knew what they were capable of. She knew the precautions necessary when dealing with them.

"So," said one of the newcomers, a lanky brunette with an unseemly penchant for gum chewing. "This is just like a sorority, right?"

The woman in charge set down her tea. "It has been called such, though I prefer to think of our organization as somewhat more . . . mature."

"I'm a Kappa Kappa Gamma," replied the girl, smacking her gum. "We're very mature."

"Indeed." The woman smiled. "I think you will be happy with us."

"And the networking opportunities are good?" asked another girl, a blonde, as blithely oblivious as the rest but with a great deal more intelligence in her eyes. "I suppose you've seen my résumé. A computer science degree was supposed to be a sure thing, but no one seems to be hiring. At least, not people they don't already know."

"Or who don't have experience," added the last of the new girls, also fair-haired, though certainly from a bottle. "It's worse in the legal field. They're telling me they need at least two years of prior work at a firm. Christ. Where am I going to get that if no one will even *talk* to me?"

"That is why we are here," said the woman in charge. "Bright Futures is an organization dedicated to promoting the advancement of promising young women such as you three. Think of us as . . . headhunters."

"Yeah," said the sorority girl, giving one of the older women a cheerful look. "That's what Betty said."

Betty wore jeans and a velvet blazer, and lounged like a cat with her arm thrown casually over the back of her chair. Her hair was black, and so were her eyes.

"I told Hillary that we have contacts in the fashion industry," she said crisply. "Here in the city."

"Not just New York. Paris, too," added Nikola, the other girl whom the woman in charge had trained. Dark-skinned, with lush copper-toned hair, and a sensual mouth that always distracted men. She wore a long red dress that clung to her curves, and her golden earrings fanned downward against her throat.

"Cool," said the sorority girl, though her companions seemed less impressed. Not that it mattered. The woman in charge thought their color was growing worse, and she had to hide a smile when the young lawyer swayed, blinking hard.

"Is there a bathroom?" she asked, with a touch of embarrassment.

"We're almost done here," said the woman in charge. "Can it wait?"

She kept her tone polite but with an edge, a hint of disdain.

The young lawyer stayed seated but gave her a defiant look that under other circumstances might have made the woman in charge think twice about using her as a candidate.

"You don't look so good," said Hillary, who had eaten less than the others and had hardly touched her tea.

"I don't feel well," said the young lawyer, swaying again, her hands white-knuckled as she gripped the edge of her chair.

"Neither do I," said the computer science major, who was having trouble keeping her eyes open. "Oh, wow."

"Wow," echoed Hillary, her own eyes getting big. "Yeah, maybe you should both find that bathroom."

"Air. Air would be . . . better," said the young lawyer, trying to stand. "I think we . . . we should get out of here."

"Mmm," said the other girl, covering her mouth with a trembling hand. "Mmm . . . God."

She pitched forward, landing hard on her knees. She

tried to hold herself up, hands braced on the floor, but her elbows quivered so violently it was only seconds before she lost the fight and was curled on her side, panting. The young lawyer fell beside her moments later.

Hillary shot off her chair, gasping when her knees almost buckled. Swaying, swallowing hard, she managed to straighten and shot a concerned look at Betty, who hadn't moved and was watching the two fallen girls with a faint smile.

"I think they need help," Hillary said.

"Do you?" replied Betty, glancing at her with that same sharp amusement. "You should be more concerned about yourself, sweetheart."

Hillary frowned. "Why?"

Nikola sighed, examining her nails. "Well, you're going to feel *everything,* for starters."

"What does *that* mean?" Hillary asked, but the woman in charge had risen while the others were speaking, and unsheathed the obsidian blade hidden inside her leather jacket.

She stood behind Hillary. Betty and Nikola smiled.

"Answer me," said the girl.

"As you wish," murmured the woman in charge, and stabbed the dagger into the girl's side, in the kidney. It was a soft spot, easier than trying to cut her throat—or wound her in the back and risk the blade bouncing off bone.

Hillary shrieked, twisting. The woman muttered a sharp word, power tingling over her skin—and the sorority girl froze, her voice choking in her throat.

Betty and Nikola moved in like vipers. But not toward Hillary.

Betty rolled the lawyer over, and knelt hard on her

chest. The girl tried to struggle, but it was a feeble effort that bordered on dreamlike. The computer science major wasn't moving at all. She barely breathed. Nikola crouched beside her and removed a dagger from within a slit in her long red skirt. Betty held her own weapon. Both she and Nikola looked at the woman in charge.

"Begin," she said softly.

And so they did.

LATER, AFTER THE POWER HAD BEEN DRAINED FROM the blood, and all were full and sated—sprawled upon the sticky floor beside three cold corpses—the woman smiled to herself.

"Now we're ready for her," she said, closing her eyes and seeing fire. Old fire, old screams.

She would find the dragon. Finally.

Betty and Nikola laughed.

CHAPTER ONE

A DRAGON slept beneath New York City.
    Her dreams were fitful. Her dreams always
were. She had been hiding a long time and had run a
great distance with no home, no place to rest her head.

Her home now was humble and small, but it was
hers. Filled with light and color, and glass. Small jars
of paint, and a canvas to stretch her wings upon.

Others shared her underworld. Men and women,
and children. The dragon protected them, when she
could. Some, she considered friends. But always from
a distance, where it was safe. Safe, for them.

Safe meant being alone.

The dragon had been alone a long time.

But sometimes, like tonight, she dreamed of a man.

And he was made of fire.

MORE THAN TWENTY-FIVE HUNDRED MILES AWAY,
Eddie knelt on the polished concrete floor of a glass-
walled cage, trying very hard not to catch fire.

The cage was an eight-by-eleven block of concrete
and fire-resistant glass, and the door was made of thick
steel, framed in that same concrete. No furniture. No

blankets. The space had once been part of the dining room, and the double-paned glass wall usually offered Eddie an unobstructed view of the kitchen. There was, however, a privacy curtain that he could draw over the exterior of the cage.

He had used it tonight. There was a guest upstairs.

It was over, thought Eddie, putting his back to the wall as sparks danced off his clothes. *I was sure it was over.*

He had not lost control in almost a year.

He had not needed the cage.

Until tonight.

You know why.

Eddie closed his eyes, haunted. Every inch of him, so tender that the softest touch of his clothes hurt as though he were being dragged naked, on gravel.

Breathe, he told himself. *Breathe.*

Eddie breathed, but each breath was hot in his lungs—the same heat burning in his bones, rising through his skin. Smoke rose off his body, singeing his nostrils. He tried to think of cool water, ice, this morning's silver fog around the Golden Gate Bridge. He imagined the flow of the salt-scented breeze on his face as he'd walked to his favorite coffee shop . . .

Everything, good and normal. Part of the life he had made for himself.

But it meant nothing. His mind kept returning to his mother's sobs, the broken rasp of her voice—the sound of his grandmother in the background, trying to calm her. Trying, and failing—because she was crying, too.

Tears sizzled against his cheeks. Eddie held his stomach, overwhelmed with grief and anger. So much anger.

He pushed it down. Then he kept pushing, and *push-*

ing, methodically bottling his emotions: frustration, unhappiness, regret. He hid them all in a cool dark place inside his heart. He buried them, far away and deep, until he felt raw, empty.

Empty, except for the loneliness. An isolation so profound it bordered on despair.

Flames erupted against his legs and hands, flowing up his arms to arc over his shoulders—down his back like wings. Eddie tried to stop the fire—struggled with all his strength—but it was like trying to catch the wind. The flames slipped around him, through him, and all the control he had so carefully cultivated once again meant nothing.

He was powerless. Helpless. And he hated himself for that.

His spine caught on fire, a deep burn born in his bones, born deeper, rippling from his heart. Eddie closed his eyes, listening to the crackle of flames eating through his jeans and T-shirt, turning them to ash.

He didn't make a sound, not even when the burn of his skin made him feel as though he would split apart. He pretended not to feel the soaring waves of heat moving around him, wrapping him in a nest of fire that brushed against the walls of his cage.

He tried so hard not to think about his sister's murderer walking out of prison.

But in the end, it was easier just to burn.

WHEN EDDIE LEFT THE CAGE, A WOMAN WAS WAIT-ing for him.

He happened to know that she was in her early fifties, though she hardly looked it with her loose red hair, creamy skin, and long, supple body clad in black. A patch covered her right eye, and the other was golden, pupil slit like a cat's. She leaned on the kitchen counter, arms folded over her chest—and even standing still, there was a lethal, inhuman grace about her.

Eddie froze and clutched the curtain around his waist. None of his clothes had made it through the blaze.

"Ma'am," he said, a little too hoarse.

Her gaze traveled down his body, cold and assessing. "You make me feel so old. How many times will we meet, Edward, before you call me Serena?"

Eddie waited. Serena gave him a slow, dangerous smile and picked up a cloth bag on the counter behind her. She tossed it to him. When he looked inside, he found sweatpants and a T-shirt.

"Roland told me where you keep your things," she said. "He also mentioned that your skin is sensitive . . . afterward. I chose what seemed soft."

"Thank you," Eddie said. "Ma'am."

Serena tilted her head, golden eye glinting. Eddie stepped back into the cage, letting the curtain fall behind him. The process of dressing made him feel more human—more grounded in his own body—though his skin still ached, and when he moved too quickly, lights danced in his eyes.

When he reemerged, Serena stood at the foot of the stairs.

"They're waiting," she said.

Eddie did not move. "No one mentioned that you would be here."

"Shocking, I know."

"Yes," he admitted. "It's a bad sign. What else has happened?"

"I don't know. Yet." Serena gave him a faint, mocking smile and turned to climb the stairs. "If it's any consolation, no one told me I'd be in San Francisco to-night. But here I am. I go where there's trouble."

"You make trouble," he replied. "With all due re-spect."

She laughed, quietly, and kept climbing.

Eddie did not follow. He watched until she disap-peared around the landing, then looked down at his hands. Small, circular scars covered his skin. He rubbed them and shivered.

He was always cold after he lost control. Cold as winter, in his bones. When he felt like this, he couldn't imagine losing control ever again. Drained of fire, burned out. Safe.

If only.

Eddie took a deep breath and climbed the stairs.

He entered an immense room filled with over-stuffed couches and low tables sagging with books and newspapers. The top floor, the penthouse suite of an entire building owned by one man, one organization—converted into a home and office. Nine floors that could be traversed by stairs and hidden elevators.

It was night outside. Only a few lamps had been turned on, but the floor-to-ceiling windows let in the scattered light of downtown San Francisco, and that was enough to illuminate the room, softly, as though with starlight.

Two people stood near the windows. Serena still had her arms folded over her chest. The man who stood beside her was taller by half a foot and broad as a bear. His rumpled flannel shirt strained against his shoul-ders. Thick brown stubble, peppered with gray, cov-ered his jaw. The scent of whiskey clung to him, but that was no surprise. Not for months.

Roland's bloodshot gaze was compassionate and sad as he studied Eddie. Edged with doubt, too. And pity.

Eddie tamped down anger. "Don't look at me like that."

Roland grunted. "Like what?"

"Like I'm broken," he said hoarsely. "Like I'm you."

Low blow. Eddie received no satisfaction from the surprise and hurt that flickered across the other man's face—but he wasn't sorry, either. He had never thrown a first punch, hardly ever used his fists at all, but for the last year he had wanted to—against the man in front of him. Words were a poor substitute.

And he needed to hit someone right now. Right now, more than anything, he needed to inflict some pain.

Roland cleared his throat. "You little shit."

"I only look like shit. Don't confuse the two."

"In your case, it's the same thing." Roland tilted his head, watching him. "Are you going to be able to do this? Handle New York?"

Eddie hadn't told him about his mother's phone call. He hadn't needed to. Roland had known from the moment Eddie entered the penthouse, heading for the cage. Some telepaths were like that.

"According to you," Eddie said, "there's no one else."

"That's not an answer."

He set his jaw, warmth finally trickling back into his hands. "It's the only answer I need. You taught me that."

Roland stilled. Serena murmured, "Generous praise. Given that you're speaking to a man who hasn't left his home in over a decade."

Roland blinked hard, tearing his gaze from Eddie. "*You're* certainly free to go."

"I wish I could. I have a grandchild I could be visiting right now, and you smell like a drunk." Serena swung away from Roland to stare out the window. "But the new alliance stands. *A Priori* wants me here, and I work for *them*. Not Dirk & Steele."

Eddie was already tired, but hearing those words stole the last of his strength—whatever was left in his heart. He couldn't keep the bitterness off his face, and it made him feel like a different man. A worse man. Too much like the man who had burned those scars into his hands.

"It's all the same," he found himself saying, even though he wanted to stay quiet and hold in that bitterness and bury it, again and again, as he had been burying it for months. "*A Priori*. Dirk & Steele. It's just family."

Family and lies. And that was hardest of all to reconcile.

A Priori was one of the largest, most powerful corporations in the world. Run by a tight-knit family of men and women who possessed singular gifts of a paranormal nature, gifts that had been used almost exclusively for material gain.

But more than sixty years ago, members of that same family had broken away to form another, much smaller organization, one founded on values that had nothing to do with money or power . . . but instead, helping others.

That organization had become Dirk & Steele. To the public, it was nothing but a high-powered detective agency—but in private it functioned as a refuge. For people like Eddie. And others, who weren't human by any stretch of the imagination.

Until recently, however, almost no one at Dirk & Steele had been aware that *A Priori* existed, or that its connections to the agency ran so deep.

And *no* one, certainly, had known that Dirk & Steele's worst enemy, the Consortium—responsible for human trafficking and experimentation, bioterrorism, mass murder—was part of that same family.

Your brother, Eddie said silently, looking at Roland, knowing he could hear his thoughts. *Your brother runs the Consortium. You knew all along that it existed, and why. You never warned us, not even after it was too late.*

Too late for me.

Roland flinched, but his bloodshot eyes showed nothing. And Eddie felt nothing except a dull ache when he looked at him.

At the other end of the room, a shadow detached from the wall: a slow, sinuous flow of movement made of perfect, dangerous grace.

Eddie had been aware of that presence from the moment he entered the room, but he still tensed; and so did Serena and Roland. It was impossible not to. The old woman who emerged from the shadows was deadly, in more ways than one.

Little of her face was visible, but her eyes glowed with subtle, golden light. She was Chinese, but so old—and so inhuman—that definitions based on ethnicity held no value.

"Ma'am," Eddie said, with careful respect.

"Boy," she replied, and the air seemed to hiss across his skin with power. "I've met immortals with younger eyes than you."

He said nothing. Roland muttered, "Long Nu. Get on with it."

The old woman's hand flashed out, trailing light, and touched the corner of Eddie's mouth. Not with a finger, but a claw—cool as silk, sliding across his lips, down his jaw. He smelled stone and ash, and a hint of sandalwood.

"You know what you have to do?" Long Nu said to him quietly.

"You want me to find a girl. A girl who can control fire."

"A shape-shifter," she murmured, as golden light continued to shimmer over her hand, and her flesh rippled with scales. "A dragon."

Eddie reached up, very slowly, and pushed her hand away from his face. "I don't understand why you don't go yourself. One of your kind to another."

"It would draw the wrong kind of attention. More than what is already focused on the child." Long Nu glanced at Roland. "She is being hunted."

Hunted. A girl, hunted. Eddie felt a cold, visceral disgust when he heard that. It made him think of his sister.

"No one told me," he said.

"We were not sure. Now we are."

"Who's after her?"

Long Nu hesitated, and that was enough to convey to Eddie just how bad it was.

"They are called the *Cruor Venator*," she said, in a cold, heavy voice. "Blood Hunters. Witches who steal power from blood."

Serena sucked in her breath, a startling sound because it was filled with fear, dismay: two emotions Eddie had never, once, associated with her.

Eddie shared a quick look with Roland. "Witches?"

"Not just any witches," Serena said sharply, continuing to stare at Long Nu. "Killers. Vicious, ruthless. They live for death. It's their first, and only, pleasure." She moved even closer to the dragon woman, as though stalking her, hands flexing at her sides. "But it's impossible. That magic hasn't been seen in a hundred years."

Long Nu shook her head. "I know what such a death looks like. A shifter in Florida was lost to a group of them only two weeks ago. The same shifter who contacted Dirk & Steele about the girl."

A hard knot of unease hit Eddie's gut. "I didn't know he was dead."

Roland rubbed a hand through his hair and closed his eyes. "I only just found out. Long Nu discovered Estefan's murder through different channels. When he stopped e-mailing me, I thought maybe he'd changed his mind about asking for our help in finding the girl."

"I suspect he reached out to you because he had an idea of what threatened her. Except the *Cruor Venator* got him first," said Long Nu in a cold, blunt voice—looking directly at Eddie as she spoke. "Estefan was ripped apart. Drained of blood. Part of his heart eaten. Skinned. It was a very bad death."

Eddie did not blink or flinch. Long Nu, still watching him, added, "His wife is human, and was away when he was murdered. She explained that just before her husband died, Estefan told her that three women had been asking locals about a girl with golden eyes. It concerned him a great deal . . . especially when he learned that they were using her real name."

"You think those women are witches," he said, "and that they found the shifter, and murdered him, because they were looking for the girl."

"I know it," Long Nu replied, with chilling certainty. "And even if I am wrong, the mere possibility makes it urgent that we find her as quickly as possible."

Serena's eyes narrowed. "Did he know that she was headed to New York?"

"Yes. And everything he knew, the *Cruor Venator* now knows."

Deep, dangerous, waters, thought Eddie, feeling that old familiar shift inside his skin, as though he were a shape-shifter himself, transforming into a different person.

That transformation had begun as soon as Long Nu said the girl was being hunted. After all these years, it was natural as breathing. Part of him was always quiet, always waiting, beneath the fire. A mind-set, where nothing could be depended on, where violence was expected, promised, and always lethal. He had the scars to remind himself if he ever forgot. But he never had.

His heart donned a cold armor, where he would feel nothing. Nothing, until the job was done.

Because it was obvious the job was going to require doing things he was going to regret.

"Just find the girl," Roland said heavily, clearly reading his thoughts. "Serena, talk to your contacts. I'll do the same here."

Eddie didn't need to hear more. He didn't want to.

He turned and walked away, descending the stairs to the kitchen. He did not look at the cage. He strode down a long hall, then took another flight of stairs to the seventh floor.

He had an apartment half a mile away, but a spare room had been given to him several years ago, after he had contracted an artificially constructed virus: the prototype of a bioweapon. The infection had almost killed him, with one additional side effect.

Eddie had lost all control over his powers. All those hard-earned years of focus, sacrifice, and isolation— gone, meaningless. Literally, up in flames.

The way he lived his life until then had revolved around his ability to protect people from himself. Suddenly, in an instant, that was no longer possible. For almost a year he had needed to live in that glass cage, where he would be safe from others.

Confidence, shattered. Heartbreakingly alone.

Those first few times venturing beyond its glass walls—terrifying. After that, months where Eddie did nothing but stay indoors or sit on the roof of the building, staring at downtown San Francisco. Watching people. Watching the world.

It had taken another six months for his confidence to return . . . but only because he'd had no choice. A friend needed help. That had been motivation enough for him to test the limits of his new control, and after that . . . it had gotten easier.

Taking back his old life had felt like a miracle.

Now he wondered if he needed to return to the cage again.

The spare room that Roland had given him was nearly a thousand square feet in size and full of windows, overlooking the city. His bed was a mattress on the floor, and his clothes were stored in plastic bins. Stacks of travel books, language study guides, and science magazines surrounded his bed, along with a small lamp and a box full of bottled water.

Eddie found a backpack and began stuffing it with underwear, a pair of jeans, and some T-shirts.

He found a small leather wallet, covered in stains and worn so thin with age it almost broke when he handled it. No money inside. Just photos. He hesitated but placed it in one of the bins, carefully. He had enough distractions.

Free. He's free. Good behavior. They let him out because he was a model prisoner.

Oh, my God.

Oh, my God, baby.

He's free.

Eddie closed his eyes, and focused on his breathing. With a great deal of effort, he pushed away the memory of his mother's stunned, grief-filled voice.

But there was another voice inside his head. His own.

Don't go to New York City. Go after Malcolm Swint, instead.

Kill him.

For Daphne.

It would be so easy. All it would take was a thought. Just one, little, thought.

Eddie shook his head in disgust. No. This was the *perfect* time to leave San Francisco.

He kept the lamp off. Old habit. He preferred working in the dark, unseen. The city lights were more than enough for going through the motions. He had packed this bag so many times, he could do it in his sleep. It gave his brain time to sort through everything he had been told.

Find the girl.

Air moved across his neck. Eddie turned. Long Nu stood behind him, silent as a ghost. He was too surprised to speak—and then he was too busy keeping himself calm as heat flooded his bones and muscles, rising through his skin. The air warmed around them.

"One more thing," she said.

Eddie never saw the old woman move. Suddenly he was falling, falling and falling until he hit the mattress so hard he bounced. Golden light flashed, and he heard a rough, rubbing sound, like the belly of an alligator dragging over the floor.

A huge clawed foot settled on the mattress beside his head. Heat washed over his body, but it was not from him.

"Look at me," Long Nu whispered, her voice deeper now, almost a growl.

Eddie turned his head. It was too dark for details, but he glimpsed scales rippling over the muscles of a long, serpentine throat . . . the hard line of a jaw, the shine of a sharp white tooth. Golden eyes shone like fire.

"The *Cruor Venator* don't just take the blood of shape-shifters," she said, each word softly hissed. "Any blood will do. But yours . . . your *fire* . . ." A deep rumble filled the air, caged thunder, born in her throat. "Fire is elemental. Only dragons have fire in their blood. You will stir their hunger."

"I'm no dragon," Eddie whispered. "I'm human."

Long Nu leaned away from him, a slow retreat, revealing a massive body that in the darkness resembled a sinuous coil of muscle and claws, and draped leather. Eddie did not look too closely. He began breathing again. His heart pounded so hard he was dizzy—and that was dangerous.

Staying calm kept him cool. Staying calm was the key.

"You're wrong," said Long Nu. "What you bury only grows stronger, in time. This is true of what sleeps in blood."

Eddie swallowed. "Stay out of my head."

"I can't," she said simply. "You hide so much of your heart, even from yourself. Hide too long, and you will forget it's there."

He sat up, but had to shield his eyes as golden light flared bright as the sun, blinding him.

When he could see again, he found Long Nu on her knees, human and mostly naked. Her clothes were torn, hanging off her in rags. Eddie averted his eyes and dragged the blanket off his bed. He handed it to her.

"Ma'am," he said quietly.

Long Nu's hand touched his fingers as she took the blanket. Her skin was hot—just as hot as his. Even hotter, when she grabbed his wrist with her other hand and held him tight. Smoke rose between them. Eddie set his jaw and met her golden gaze.

"There are so few left of my kind," whispered Long Nu. "Find the girl."

"I will," Eddie promised, and found himself adding, "Whatever it takes."

Long Nu gave him a mirthless smile, and the smoke between them suddenly became fire. It did not burn him, but the flames flickered up both their arms, like tiny deadly fingers.

"If the *Cruor Venator* is hunting her," she said softly, "it might just take everything you have."

CHAPTER TWO

WHEN Jimmy screamed, Lyssa was holding a warm teacup in her gloved right hand and shading watercolors with her left: ungloved, her skin pale and oh-so-human. A mild headache had been brewing all morning. Not enough sleep. Too little sunlight and fresh air. Bad premonitions.

Lyssa jumped when she heard the boy's voice, jumped right to the edge of her battered folding chair, knocking her knees on the plastic table. Everything slid sideways. Tea sloshed over her wrist, onto the painting—and the brush tumbled from her hand, hitting the concrete floor. Cold sweat broke against her back, followed by a wave of heat that made all the burning candles flare with a massive, crackling hiss.

They found me, thought Lyssa, and all her careful planning went out the window. She sat, paralyzed, even when the boy cried out again. Her body just wouldn't move.

Until, suddenly, it did.

And she ran.

It was black as a cave outside her nest, which was at the farthest end of the unfinished subway tunnel, at the spot where construction had stopped, many years ago. Nothing there but the old worker's station she'd moved into, built inside a massive concrete wall. Outside— scattered, shoveled up against the damp walls—was loose rock, unused iron rails, and old electric cables that draped in snakelike piles. In some spots, garbage still remained from the previous resident: plastic cups and rotting clothes, a hollowed-out mattress that was home to rats.

Desolation, in the dark. Her apocalyptic garden.

The cool air was heavy with the scent of rust and cement, and stagnant water; and the ground was uneven beneath Lyssa's boots: dirt and gravel, and the old train tracks that hadn't ever been used. She raced over them with sure footing. No flashlight, no lamp burning in her hand. Her eyes were good in the dark.

Lyssa tried to stay calm—to *think*—but when Jimmy cried out again, his young voice echoing against the cavernous walls, power poured into her muscles, and her entire body prickled with heat. Sight faded into a golden haze. Her teeth sharpened. Lyssa slapped her gloved hand over her mouth, breathing hard through her nose.

No, she told herself, running faster. *Not now.*

Lyssa rounded a curve in the tunnel, passing tents and lean-tos: small makeshift rooms with no roofs, and walls made from standing sheets of cardboard and plywood; surrounded with folding chairs and other boxes; piles of nameless, unidentifiable *stuff* that had probably served some purpose, once upon a time. Clothes, toys, magazines, broken Styrofoam, metal scrap: rotting in the dark, filthy, smelling vaguely like shit and piss. Or maybe that was the fact that there was shit and piss everywhere, at the edges of the tunnel. Years of it.

She hated the place.

Ahead of her, light glinted: cookfires burning in old stainless-steel pots and deep pits dug in the ground. Lyssa smelled onions, hot dogs, and whiskey; and the air sizzled, smoke rising around the face of a familiar man: Albert, who crouched over the food with a pair of chopsticks held in his trembling grip.

His watery gaze was focused on the boy. On the man holding the boy.

Jimmy. Twelve years old, so skinny he was practically swimming in loose jeans and a zip-up sweatshirt. His hair was brown and floppy, his cheeks ruddy. His brown-eyed gaze, usually so cocky, was lost behind an expression of real fear. He was trying to free himself from the old man standing rigid in front of him.

It was Mack. Which was good and bad.

Bad, because he was nuts. Good, because he was only human.

He held the boy's skinny arm with his right hand—the other raised high, gripping an empty can of SPAM.

"You little *fuck*!" he roared, shaking Jimmy so hard, the boy lost his footing. "Where's your fucking dog, you worthless piece of shit?"

Stay calm, Lyssa told herself, jaw clamped tight. *Calm.*

But she wasn't feeling calm when she grabbed Mack's left wrist with her strong right hand. She held on so tight her claws almost punctured her glove. Her sweater sleeve slid down. Reptilian scales glimmered into view. Just a hint of them, covering her arm.

It was dark. No one was close enough to notice that her skin wasn't human.

But it made Lyssa panic, all the same—and she forgot her strength.

She yanked down too hard on Mack's arm. The old man screamed, and dropped the can of SPAM. He also let go of Jimmy, who scrambled backward, eyes huge.

Mack fell to his knees, groaning. Lyssa released him, ashamed and afraid. Her skin burned, and she lowered her head, long braids and oversized knit hat falling around her face. If her eyes were glowing . . .

Lyssa shut them. "Mack. What the hell?"

She heard him shifting on the gravel, hissing through his teeth. "Bitch. You broke me."

She wanted to be sick but made her voice strong, hard. "No. You'll bruise, but that's all. Jimmy, you okay?"

"Fine," he said, somewhere in front of her.

Lyssa took a deep breath, then another. "What happened?"

Mack's voice quavered with a sob. "His fucking dog stole my lunch. Left the can out for just two fucking seconds."

She finally opened her eyes and looked at the old man. In the three years she had lived in this tunnel, she had never seen him without his gray knit cap, punched with holes and bits of debris. His beard was the same dull color, and so was his skin: ashen, the shadows so deep under his sunken eyes that it was hard to know where one began and the other ended. A skinny, sinewy, cadaverous man—burdened with profound mood swings.

Seconds ago he had been enraged. Now he just looked miserable, and hungry, and very old. Too old to be living down here, too old to be touched so roughly. Too old to be dealing with someone like her. Even if he was an asshole.

"Jimmy," she said heavily, without looking away from Mack.

The boy climbed to his feet, but remained half-crouched, wary. "I'm sorry. *Really* sorry."

He didn't sound sorry. Lyssa gave him a warning glance. "Mack, I've got some food you can have."

"Keep it. You got mean hands." The old man shot Jimmy a hateful look. "I'll kill that fucking dog if I see it again. You hear me?"

"Go to hell," said Jimmy, with all the squeak and snarl of a puppy.

Lyssa rolled her eyes, marched over to him, and grabbed his arm. She didn't have to say anything. The boy looked at her and grimaced.

Albert, who had finally risen from his cookfire, shuffled forward to help Mack stand. Albert was middle-aged, black, with a bad knee that got stiff on rainy days. According to him, it rained every day.

"That kinda talk's no good," said Albert gently, also giving Jimmy a warning look. "Come on, Mack Daddy. I got some dinner you can have."

"Fuck you," Mack said, and this time there was definitely a sob in his voice. "Not hungry. Just surprised I still got my arm."

You're lucky I didn't rip it off your body, thought Lyssa, uneasy. At full strength, she could have. She had done it before, to other men.

Fewer than ten people resided in the tunnel, but it was midday up top, so only a handful of the usual residents were around. Most had jobs—part-time at McDonald's, or working as janitors at Grand Central. Some temped at local businesses that needed muscle for a day. Two panhandled. A veteran who had come back from Iraq only a year before had just landed a job at a construction site—but like Lyssa, had issues with living around people. Nevertheless, she didn't expect him to stay in the tunnel for much longer.

The rest, like Albert and Mack, were alcoholics or too mentally disturbed to function up top. Lyssa didn't care about their problems, so long as they stayed harmless. This was a good tunnel, filled with folk who were desperate but hopeful. Old Mack losing his cool with a kid was a bad sign. Almost as bad as the police sniffing around, which hadn't happened yet.

Lyssa figured it was only a matter of time. Most tunnels were watched by authorities—locked, or rigged with cameras and alarms. No one wanted terrorists slinking underground and setting bombs.

"You shouldn't be here," she said to Jimmy, walking him down the tunnel to her nest. "Forget the fact it's a school day. It's not safe. Your mom got you out of here for a better life. Not more of this."

The boy didn't answer her. His silence was tense, heavy.

"Jimmy," she said, worried. "Why are you here?"

He ducked his head, almost like a flinch, and pulled a flashlight from his backpack. He switched it on. It hurt Lyssa's vision, but she didn't tell him to turn it off. He swung the beam around, and somewhere on their right, she heard a muffled sniffing sound, followed by toenails clicking on stone.

A dog slunk close. A mutt, one of the ugliest animals Lyssa had ever seen. Part Chihuahua, maybe, but there could have been dachshund in it, or some kind of Jack Russell. Lyssa had seen rats that were bigger.

The dog whimpered. The boy scooped him up. Lyssa said, "Mack was serious. He'll kill him."

"I'll kill *him*," muttered Jimmy, hugging the dog even closer to his chest. Lyssa gripped his bony shoulder with her human left hand.

"Don't say things like that," she said quietly.

Jimmy tensed and gave her a sullen look. "I was joking."

"I don't care. You have to think about repercussions."

The boy stared at her, then glanced away. "Did you ever kill someone?"

Lyssa felt cold. "That's some question."

"My mom was wondering why you're still down here. You're not like the others. Which means you're like *us*." Jimmy looked at her again, and the glow from his flashlight cast shadows that made his face look hollow, ghastly. "You're hiding."

It was Lyssa's turn not to answer him.

The tunnel curved. Most of the walls were unfinished, nothing but excavated dirt. The support columns were made of concrete, covered in graffiti. Trains rumbled, sounding so much like thunder it made Lyssa homesick and heartsore. She missed a good rainstorm.

"I'll take you to school," she said. "We'll drop Icky off at your place first."

"They hate me at school," he mumbled.

"Good. Having people hate you builds character."

Jimmy gave her a dirty look. "You're mean."

Lyssa ruffled his hair. "Don't come back here. Not unless someone is with you."

"I had to." Jimmy pulled away from her. "Mandy is missing. Flo, too."

Lyssa missed a step. "What?"

"They're gone. That's what their friends said when Mom stopped by their bench at Grand Central. She had sandwiches from work that she was going to give them."

"They're heroine addicts. Anything could have happened."

"You haven't heard the rumors?"

"No."

"People are disappearing," said Jimmy. "I'm afraid you'll be next."

HE HAD NEWSPAPERS, ARTICLES THAT HE HAD TORN out.

It was an old habit. The boy was a punk, but he was good with words, and his mom didn't read English as well as she spoke it. She depended on Jimmy to keep her updated on what was going on in the city, and elsewhere. Newspapers were cheap. Listening improved her English. And it made Ms. Sutabuhr feel good that her son might be learning something every time he read to her.

Lyssa gave Jimmy a bottle of water from the cooler. He knelt on the threadbare rug, and dribbled some into his cupped palm. The dog, Icky, wagged his tail and lapped at the water. She watched for a moment, amused and uneasy.

You've been alone too long, she told herself. Solitude was easier to accept without reminders of what she was missing.

Lyssa smoothed out the newspaper articles Jimmy had given her. He watched, wiping his wet palm on his jeans. No emotion on his face.

He focused instead on the watercolor she had been working on. The canvas was part of a thick drawing block: a heavy sheet of paper with a prominent tooth, its rough texture creating a grainy surface that captured pools of flame-colored water. Flames, everywhere, twisted in knots and claws, and wings made of sheer, delicate fire—all surrounding an empty white space to the right of center.

A white space that made her heart ache when she

looked at it. A white space that stared at her from the page with its own peculiar, haunting, life. Even when she did not look at it, she felt its presence.

Like now. Heavy, at the corner of her eye.

Lyssa swallowed hard. "You've brought me articles on six different women. Disappearances dating back three months. Only three of them are from New York state. None are homeless, either."

Jimmy shrugged, and bent to pick up Icky, who pawed at his ankle. The tiny mutt got lost in the over-sized folds of his sweatshirt. "Those have to do with something else."

"Jimmy."

"Rumors started a couple weeks ago," he said sullenly. "Maybe earlier. I didn't hear anything until I went with Mom to the church place and helped with the sandwiches. Guys were warning her to be careful. They knew people who knew people who were just gone one day. All girls."

"Homeless? From the city?"

"Yeah."

"How many?"

"Four, five. More if you count Mandy and Flo."

"Maybe they're sitting in jail, some hospital."

"The guys didn't think so. They were sober," Jimmy added, after a thoughtful moment. "One mentioned blood had been found at a Midtown bench, in a station where some girl liked to hang."

Blood meant nothing. Probably there wasn't any blood. Just a crazy unfounded rumor getting larger and nuttier by the minute. But hearing that word—"blood"—sent a chill through her anyway.

Lyssa tapped the newspaper clippings, forgetting herself and using her right hand. The claw on her index finger clicked through the leather on the hard surface: a distinctive, cold sound. Her heart lurched a little, but Jimmy was still looking at the watercolors and didn't seem to notice. The dog, though, twitched.

"These six," Lyssa said, after clearing her throat. "What about them?"

Jimmy hugged the dog more tightly. "No one knows what happened to them, either."

It didn't surprise her that he'd paid enough attention to the news to single out six missing women. Even when the kid was still living in the tunnel, he kept boxes for different kinds of crime. He collected robberies, murder, assault, rape, kidnapping—there was even a box for the elusive and indefinable *miscellaneous*—and he was as careful and obsessive as any detective in poring over facts..

Lyssa wasn't certain his obsession was healthy *or* normal, but she wasn't in much of a position to judge. If it helped Jimmy feel in control of his life—then fine. Maybe he would grow out of it. Maybe she was looking at the future director of the FBI.

She studied those six faces. Besides the fact that their disappearances remained unsolved, the only thing the women had in common was their relative youth— all were in their thirties, or younger. Two were black, one was Asian, and there was a blonde, a brunette—a lawyer, a college student, an accountant, a homemaker, a cashier at Walmart . . .

No connection. The dates of their disappearances were random. Their locations dissimilar.

Lyssa gave Jimmy a careful look, but he was staring at her painting again.

"Is that fire?" he asked.

"It could be," she said. "Yes."

Jimmy pointed to the empty white spot on the drawing block. "What's supposed to go there?"

Dread filled her. With some reluctance, she said, "Eyes."

He frowned. "Why?"

"Because I see eyes in my head," she said, which was the truth but not the whole truth. "And I can't get them out of my head."

Lyssa could see those eyes even now, as though they occupied a permanent spot just to the left of her thoughts: eyes that were dark and masculine, staring into her with incredible intensity.

A *knowingness* . . . leveled at her soul.

Premonition, maybe. Which frightened her. Enough so that she was already considering uprooting her life—again—and running. But that was the problem with premonitions: Running might be the very thing to make them come true.

Lyssa was afraid of what would happen if she ever met the man those eyes belonged to.

Jimmy scrunched up his nose. "You're weird."

She had to smile. "Yeah?"

"Well," he said, hedging a little.

Lyssa shook her head. "Why *these* women? Why did you bring them to me?"

"No reason," he said, after a noticeable hesitation. "I told you . . . they're gone."

She wished he would tell her what was really on his mind. "And nothing in the papers about homeless girls disappearing?"

"Not yet. Probably won't be."

He was right, but it pained her to hear that kind of pessimism in a twelve-year-old. "What does your mom say?"

The dog squirmed, sad eyes watery and huge. Jimmy tucked its knobby head under his chin. "Nothing. I tried talking to her . . . but she got mad. She doesn't . . . want to be afraid anymore."

Lyssa said, "You don't have to be afraid, either, you know."

Jimmy shot her a cold look, then ducked his head, burying his face against his dog. Lyssa also looked down, embarrassed. Of course he was afraid.

She began folding the newspaper clippings. Both hands at first, then just her left.

Her right hand was suddenly useless—seized with a terrible cramp that made her clawed fingers curl inward against her palm. She breathed hard through her nose, trying to control the pain. It was getting worse, every day. Her body, betraying her in so many little ways.

"Okay," she said, hoping her voice didn't sound too strained. "I'll keep my ear to the ground. I'll be careful. I promise. If I hear anything, I'll talk to your mom."

Jimmy shrugged, like he didn't care—but his eyes, half-hidden beneath his hair, lost some of their sullenness. His shoulders relaxed.

And then a smile touched his mouth. "Do I still have to go to school today?"

"Don't even," muttered Lyssa, and bent past him to blow out her candles, one by one. Careful to separate her mind from the silken heat of fire licking at the edges of her thoughts.

Before she put out the final candle, she glanced around her small, dark, nest: with its sleeping bag set on layers of cardboard and swept concrete; and the walls with their scorch marks; and the dirty air that smelled like smoke because of the mattress that had so recently burned beneath her while she slept.

Twenty minutes away, Lyssa had an apartment that she never lived in—and in this same city, an employer, and agent who didn't know her real name or what she looked like—or that she lived beneath their noses. In all this world, she had only one friend who knew who she was—and *what* she was—and Lyssa hadn't seen him in several years.

Because it wasn't safe. Because she wasn't human, and people had died because of that. Because she might die—or worse—if the wrong people found her.

Whatever it takes, you live, her father had said. *Whatever you have to do, don't let them catch you.*

Lyssa grabbed her backpack off the concrete floor. "Better turn on your flashlight."

Jimmy did. She blew out the little flame, and darkness swept in.

CHAPTER THREE

THERE were too many people around him.

Even here, out in the open. It was a problem. New York City was too crowded for fire. One blaze, in the wrong place, at the wrong time, would kill.

If the shape-shifter had had any sense—or cared about people at all—she would have gone elsewhere to live.

You went to Los Angeles, Eddie reminded himself, drinking coffee, watching crowds of people cross the intersection at Columbus Circle. *You ran from home, but you stayed in a city. Because it felt safer to be anonymous.*

Anonymous and lost. Thirteen and terrified. Thirteen and a murderer.

Eddie's foot began to tap. He stilled it. When he realized that he was rubbing the back of his hand, fingering the old scars, he placed his palm against his thigh and kept it there. His leg felt hot through his jeans.

Eddie closed his eyes and took another sip of coffee.

You're so nervous, teased his sister, in his memories. *Take a chill pill, little bro.*

Chill. Chill out. Chillax.

Stay cold. Don't care so much. It'll pass.

Eddie didn't want to remember her voice. He didn't want to think at all about her.

He didn't want to think too hard about any part of his life.

Matthew Swint is getting out of prison. I have to do something.

Like what? Kill him?

Eddie closed his eyes, rubbing his brow with his knuckles. He'd managed to go years without thinking too hard about Daphne's murderer. Once a day, as opposed to all the time. Maybe some people managed to move on, but it was hard for Eddie.

Every time he created fire, he thought about Matthew Swint.

Every time, he thought about Matthew Swint's *brother.* Who had died in a blaze so hot the police hadn't found much except his bones.

I killed the wrong man.

The sun was warm, but the wind was cold. It felt good. Eddie's skin was hot, and so were his insides. He set down his coffee on the stone step he was sitting on and carefully pulled a battered, charred photograph from his jacket pocket. It was in a plastic Ziploc bag, and bits had broken off in large black flakes.

The photograph had burned long before coming into Eddie's possession and looked as though it had been salvaged directly from hot ashes. Not much left except a fragment of a face: a girl with golden eyes, only eleven or twelve years old, thick auburn hair roped over her shoulder. She was grinning, pulling a fuzzy purple hat down around her ears. Eddie glimpsed snow behind her.

"Lyssa," Eddie murmured to himself. "Lyssa Andreanos."

She looked like a goofy kid. Sweet, and very human. Not a worry in the world. He would have even gone so far as to say that she appeared . . . loved.

He was happy for her. But also envious. Of all his family pictures that had survived, only a couple showed him with a real smile.

"You've been on the run for ten years," he murmured to the girl in the photo, wondering if she could still smile. Hoping she could.

The scant details Long Nu had given him hadn't painted a clear picture of the girl. Her father had been a dragon shape-shifter. An old friend of Long Nu's. He and his human wife had died in a fire. Their daughter, Lyssa, had never been found.

Eddie sipped his coffee. It had gone cold. He concentrated, and the paper cup warmed beneath his hand. A little too warm, maybe. When he tried his coffee again, it burned his tongue.

He returned the photo to his pocket and glanced around. Even with the cold breeze, the sun had brought out the crowds. He watched faces, pretending he was thirteen again, living on the street, looking for a mark.

He found three in seconds. Easy targets. Easy cash. New York City was full of people, crammed together, crowded. During those bad years, he would have lived more easily here than in Los Angeles.

Eddie wondered what the girl in the photograph had done to survive.

His gaze roved across the street to the Time Warner Center. The curved sidewalk was crowded. Kids perched on the stone guards, talking and listening to music, while cops sat in the cars parked alongside the cabs—watching the kids, and all the men and women coming and going, past the mall, from the mall, talking on cell phones, or not—gazes on the ground, or stubbornly straight ahead, focused on anything but everyone.

Cabs parked in front of the Time Warner Center. An enormous man got out of one, nearly crawling from the backseat.

His shoulders were broad, his legs long, chest thick with muscle beneath a button-up denim shirt. Like Eddie, he didn't seem affected by the cold. His dark hair was tousled around his craggy face, and his demeanor, his height—his entire presence—was utterly imposing. Women gave him appreciative looks. Men got out of his way.

If only they realized Lannes isn't human, thought Eddie, amused.

Not that anyone could tell. As Lannes crossed the street, Eddie marveled at the strength of the illusion: even up close, the man appeared completely human. No sign of wings. No silver skin. Not a glimpse of horns. The illusion perfectly hid the impossible truth: that the man walking in broad daylight was actually a gargoyle, from a race of winged creatures capable of magic.

And an expert on magic was exactly what Eddie needed.

He walked forward to meet him, extending his hand. Lannes engulfed him in an immense grip that felt different than it looked: Instead of human fingertips, Eddie felt claws scrape his skin—and the carefully restrained strength in that touch was more than human.

"I'm sorry for being late," Lannes said, glancing at the people around them and lowering his voice. "I had to make certain Lethe was safe with her family."

"Safe?"

Lannes grimaced. "We're still not sure we can trust her parents. Lethe hasn't even told them about *me*."

"You're married."

"They don't know it. Every time she goes over there, they try to get her back together with an old boyfriend." His grimace turned into a scowl. "He looks like a Ken doll."

Eddie ducked his head, trying to hide his smile. "Your illusion wouldn't fool them?"

Lannes growled. "Stop laughing. And no, even Lethe can sense it, just with the training I've given her. Her family would certainly know me for what I am. We can't take the risk."

Hearing him say it like that wiped the smile off Eddie's face. "I didn't think *all* witches were a threat. When your brother told me that your wife's family was full of . . . of magic-users . . . I just assumed . . ."

He didn't finish, watching as a cold, humorless smile touched Lannes's mouth. "Lethe's own grandmother tried to sacrifice her to demons. And Lethe was her favorite grandchild."

Eddie held silent. Lannes said, "So, you understand."

"I wouldn't have asked for your help if I'd known," he replied quietly.

"We want to help. And Lethe doesn't think the rest of her family means *her* harm. Her grandmother was an anomaly."

Eddie raised his brow. Lannes said, "Yeah, I know."

"Someone should have told me."

"Why? Your job is to find a girl."

"And *protect* her. But if learning how to do that puts you or your wife at risk—"

"Stop. You're not responsible for us."

"Responsible enough. *You're* not sure she's safe with them."

"I'm biased. I hate witches. I love Lethe. So I compromise. I have to trust her judgment."

Eddie was not comforted. "Could the *Cruor Venator* be members of her family?"

"I hope not." Lannes rubbed his shoulder and winced. "Let's talk in the park. My wings are killing me. I need to loosen the restraints."

As they walked, Lannes did his best to give other passersby a wide berth. Eddie, trying to avoid a stroller, brushed too close and hit something firm and invisible—about eight inches away from the gargoyle's body.

"Sorry," Eddie said.

Lannes grunted, giving him a sidelong look. "It's why I don't like cities. I always get touched in a crowd."

"Your brother doesn't bind his wings."

"Which is why *he* only comes out at night and dresses like a crazy person." Lannes's mouth twitched. "I use a leather strap. Foot wide, cinched around my wings and chest. Imperfect, but it cuts down how often I bump into people when I walk. I hate it, though. I can't take a deep breath."

Eddie studied the illusion but found nothing that would give away the fact that a winged *gargoyle* walked through Columbus Circle, in broad daylight. "Does it ever make you nervous that a trick of light is all that keeps you from being discovered?"

"Used to. Until I realized there were things more frightening than being . . . seen." Lannes gave him a pointed look. "I hope you're prepared for the possibility that you'll face some of those bad things."

"What makes you think I'm not?"

Lannes studied him a heartbeat too long.

"You're right," he said. "I'm sorry."

Eddie pretended not to care. "I haven't said it yet, but thank you. It was good of you and Lethe to come down from Maine for this investigation."

"Witches are hunting a girl," said Lannes simply.

It was a short walk. The leaves in Central Park had turned golden and red, and a long line of horse-drawn carriages was parked alongside Fifty-ninth. Tourists surrounded them, taking pictures. The drivers stood off to the side, in small groups, smoking cigarettes.

Just past Merchant's Gate, Lannes and Eddie left the path and cut between the trees to a small grassy clearing still within sight of the Time Warner Center. It felt quiet. Private, even. Dead leaves crunched beneath them. No one else was around.

"Where will you go after this?" Lannes asked.

"We were given a list of places she likes to visit, but there's a second list that Roland put together, on his own. I have a photo of the girl when she was young. I'll be showing it around."

"Needle in a haystack."

"We're close. That's what Roland and the others say."

"Psychics." Lannes said the word like some would say, *kids*.

He fumbled at a spot above his chest. His fingers shimmered, as though immersed in a heat wave or the watery light of a prism. Eddie watched closely, searching for a break in the illusion.

It never came. He heard the distinctive sound of leather creaking, and the gargoyle's chest expanded several inches—as though he had been holding his breath. He let out a quiet sigh.

"Better," he said, and looked at Eddie. "What did my brother tell you about witches?"

Not enough. His brother, Charlie, was another agent of Dirk & Steele, and lived in San Francisco. Asking about witches had *not* elicited a positive reaction—more like suggestions to run for the hills and never look back.

"A witch imprisoned you and the rest of your family," he answered. "Charlie said he was the only one not turned to stone."

Lannes closed his eyes. "I thought he was lucky at first. But then the witch began carving up his body. Every night, like a slaughtered hog. We had to watch her eat his flesh. There was nothing we could do to stop her."

Eddie didn't speak. Charlie had not told him that part.

Lannes took a breath, then exhaled slowly. "Imagine being imprisoned inside your own skin for years, unable to move or breathe, existing only as a thought. Forced to watch someone you love be tortured, over and over again. And the only way to stop it is to sell your soul."

Eddie didn't need to imagine. All he had to do was think of his sister.

I watched. I was helpless. I couldn't move or breathe. In the end, I sold my soul.

I did something I could never take back.

He remembered, and heat suffused his skin, rolling through him in a slow wave that poured from his head down to his toes. Eddie breathed slow and deep through his nose, trying to maintain control.

Lannes didn't seem to notice. "The witch who captured us was incredibly powerful. And she loved that power. She wanted more of it. She wanted to *flaunt* it."

"You're warning me," Eddie said in a strained voice. "I get it."

"You better." Lannes gave him a flat, empty look. "There's a tipping point. It's different for everyone. I don't know if the witch was born without compassion, but somewhere in her life, she forgot it. She began enjoying the pain she caused. She fed off the agony of others."

"I know the type," he replied, still struggling with the heat gathering beneath his skin. "I won't hesitate."

Lannes paused. Eddie realized he was rubbing the scars on his hands. The gargoyle was looking at them.

Eddie stilled. Lannes dropped his gaze and stared at the ground. "It's been years since I heard of the *Cruor Venator*. I had to ask my brothers about them. I had to go outside the family. Everyone says the same thing."

Lannes finally looked at him. "When they want you, all you can do is run."

"Not an option. And nothing I haven't already heard."

"Then you know their power comes from blood. Blood obtained through death. The slower the death, the better. And not just any blood. A true *Cruor Venator* will absorb the essence of the victim, and so they choose only those whom they perceive to be strong, vibrant. The ones with the most to offer."

"Shape-shifters," Eddie said. "That doesn't explain why everyone is so afraid of them."

Lannes gave him a hard look. "Really?"

Eddie didn't back down. "Really. You talk about magic and witches, and it means nothing to me. Just more people with strange gifts."

"Gifts that alter reality. In small, personal doses."

"So how do you fight that?"

"With luck and a strong sense of free will." Lannes leaned forward, holding his gaze. "What creates a witch is nothing more than desire and power. That, and a particular bloodline that makes it possible to manifest that desire. What makes the *Cruor Venator* different is the way they harness power."

"It doesn't seem as though it should make them special. Anyone can spill blood."

"You're wrong. But that's not something I can explain in words."

Eddie jammed the toe of his boot into the grass, and dug in, frustrated. "I spoke to someone else. Long Nu. She's a very old shape-shifter . . . old enough to remember the *Cruor Venator*. But she didn't explain any of this."

"I've heard of her. Dragons are like that."

Great, he thought. "Do you know how to kill these witches?"

"Maybe. But it's not good." Lannes leaned against a tree and, despite the illusion, suddenly looked tired. "I've been told they can only be killed by one of their own. The magic that gives them power . . . is the only magic that can take their lives."

Eddie didn't immediately respond. He couldn't. It was all too overwhelming and strange.

He listened to the dull thrum of the city beyond the trees, a mix of voices and honking cars and birdsong. He imagined himself younger, hungry and homeless, craving a normal life. Free of violence. Free from the dead.

"Fire," he said. "Will fire kill them?"

"I don't know. It's been a hundred years since the last *Cruor Venator.* A lot could have been forgotten."

"But not the magic that made them. Who killed the *Cruor Venator* a hundred years ago?"

"One of her own kind. It had to be."

"But after that, no sign of them. No deaths."

"The last *Cruor Venator* was famous for her cruelty. She hunted nonhumans specifically, because they made her so much stronger. She could . . . adopt some of their powers. But the one who stopped her was either better at hiding her nature—"

"Or she just wasn't a killer."

"She killed at least once," Lannes replied. "No reason to think she stopped."

Eddie wasn't so sure. "Could she still be alive?"

Lannes arched his brow. "You want to find her, too?"

"Well?"

"Maybe. Witches can live a long time. But there's always a price."

"Someone had to teach the current *Cruor Venator.*"

"Or maybe it's the same witch who killed the last one."

"We need to know."

"You don't *look* for a *Cruor Venator.*"

"Apparently you do if you need one dead."

Lannes stared. Eddie ducked his head and shoved his hands in his pockets. Silence fell around them.

"I'll see what I can find," Lannes finally said, quietly.

"Thank you." Eddie had trouble meeting his gaze, too aware of what he was asking of the gargoyle. It was one thing to put his own life on the line for a stranger, but Lannes and his family had already suffered too much.

The gargoyle bound his wings again, then both men walked from the park. A large group of tourists mingled in front of them. Eddie and Lannes kept their distance. His gaze roved over open purses and backpacks, taking in expensive cameras and other small electronics belted to waists or tucked inside pockets. Out there, exposed. Like blazing targets.

"You're frowning," Lannes said. "Still thinking about witches?"

"I'm thinking that people never expect they'll get hurt." Eddie tore his gaze from the tourists and looked across the street, assessing, watching. His neck prickled. He felt exposed and uneasy, like something big was about to hit him. Big, like a fist. Big, like a wave.

His gaze continued to rove left, where it stopped at the red light just before Eighth.

A boy was marching across the intersection.

Like a little soldier, his legs kicking out, each foot pounding the pavement with hard, decisive, steps. He wore an oversized sweatshirt and jeans and had dark floppy hair that he kept pushing away from his face. With his other hand, he clutched a backpack to his chest. A tiny, ugly, dog with huge eyes peered out.

The boy held Eddie's attention. There was something small and lost about him. The way he held that dog, with tenderness and desperation—heartbreaking. He reminded Eddie too much of himself at that age: clinging to pride, defiance, but always afraid. Always, and doing his best to hide it.

It hurt Eddie to see. He wanted to know if the boy needed help, but there was no way. No way that wouldn't come off as creepy or strange.

And then he realized the boy wasn't alone.

A woman was with him. Eddie couldn't see much of her. From his vantage point, just her profile: pert nose, rosy cheeks, a small, delicate mouth. She was wrapped in an oversized green sweater, patched together with hearts and stars made of multicolored satin and velvet scraps. It stood out, compared to all the black, monotone colors worn by every other New Yorker around her.

The tail of a pink-checkered flannel shirt peeked from beneath the sweater's hem. Her jeans were tight, tucked into heavy boots, and a brown newsboy hat covered her head. Loose strands of auburn hair flew out from beneath the long red scarf wrapped around her throat, a scarf that she kept touching and tightening with slender gloved hands.

Eddie stared.

He couldn't see her face, but the way she moved was beautiful—a dancer, graceful and certain of each light step. Everyone around her seemed like a clod in comparison, weighted down, hard and gray—while she flowed through them, around them, in a patchwork of color. Warm and sublime, and welcoming.

Confident, he thought . . . but a heartbeat later she bowed her head, just so, and touched her covered throat. The gesture was pained and vulnerable, in the same way the boy was vulnerable.

As though she felt lost. Out of place.

It cut Eddie again, right in the heart. Deeper, even. He felt an instant, and inexplicable connection to the woman, as though she was a page out of his own book—someone whose pain mirrored his own.

Which was ridiculous, of course. He didn't know her. She was just one woman out of eight million people in this city—and here he was, making up a story for her. Pretending that he understood her. A stranger.

It all makes pathetic sense. I'll never know that woman. I'll never hurt her, *and she'll never hurt* me. *Of course I'm attracted.*

She's untouchable.

And yet . . . as he watched her . . .

I would take care of you, came the unbidden thought, and the need and hunger that followed rocked him to the core; so overwhelming, his breath caught with the pain of it.

I wish I could.

The woman stumbled. The boy reached out and grabbed her hand. Eddie took a step in their direction.

He stopped, though. He couldn't just run after her. What would be the point?

If I were safe, he thought to himself. *If I were safe to be touched . . .*

He took another step, anyway. And then realized something was wrong.

The woman was staring at Lannes.

The boy stood on the sidewalk, but the woman was partially in the road, one foot on the curb, remaining very still as she watched the gargoyle—who had walked a short distance ahead without noticing that Eddie wasn't with him.

An entire street and heavy foot traffic separated them, but there was no question who had caught her attention.

She's looking at a handsome man. It happens. There was no need to feel jealous about that, either.

But, moments later, it became clear something else was going on. Her face was too pale, jaw slack, eyes wide and stunned. The boy tugged on her sleeve, worried, but the young woman ignored him—staring at the oblivious gargoyle with what seemed to be deep, profound shock.

Too much shock. The first time Eddie had ever watched a shifter change shape from human to animal, he had felt a similar astonishment. No doubt his expression had appeared the same.

She can see through the illusion, he thought, followed by another realization:

She looks like the girl in the photograph. The resemblance was uncanny: in the set of her mouth and the tilt of her eyes.

Eddie ran halfway across Columbus Circle before realizing he had moved. He heard his name called. Lannes. Eddie did not look back to explain but instead watched the woman turn her head, slowly—to stare at *him.*

His world stopped. Everything inside him, around him, suspended in a wash of a terrible heat. Even from across the street, he could see the color of her eyes: golden as the sunrise. Fire licked beneath his skin, inside his heart, in his bones—but it felt transcendent, made of light instead of flame. Light, burning inside him.

It was her. Lyssa Andreanos. No mistake. No doubt. He was staring into the face of a little girl who had grown into a woman.

Strands of hair floated around her face. Her golden eyes were large and sharp with intelligence—tempered with the vulnerability that had haunted him from the first moment he had seen her.

Fate, he thought, stunned she was here. *Fate and magic.*

But his wonderment was smashed to a thousand pieces as her expression turned stark with fear. It cut him, so cold his first instinct was to retreat. Instead, he stayed rooted in place, startled and numb as she fumbled for the boy's arm, frantically pulling him with her as she backpedaled, nearly tripping over the curb.

He fought for his voice, but his throat was so dry. "Wait!"

She ran, pulling the boy after her.

The light at the crosswalk was green. Cabs roared past. He glanced at the road, saw an opening, and plunged forward. He heard honking, felt the rush of oncoming traffic—but he didn't look. He focused forward—blood roaring in his ears, heart pounding, skin hot.

"Lyssa!" he shouted again, his voice breaking on her name. "Estefan sent us!"

She stumbled, turning to give him another shocked look.

But it didn't last. Lyssa tugged hard on the boy, and they disappeared into the entrance of the Fifty-ninth Street subway station.

Eddie followed, desperate not to let her get away. Fire flowed beneath his skin.

You're out of control, he told himself—but he didn't slow. His feet hit the station-entrance stairs, and he flew, down and down, trying not to knock anyone aside.

At the bottom, he hit a wall. No MetroCard. Long lines at the vending machines to buy one. And there were police everywhere, near the turnstiles. Some with dogs. No way for him to just break through. He couldn't afford to be arrested.

The woman and boy were nowhere in sight.

No green sweater covered in patchwork hearts and stars. No boy with a dog. No grace, anywhere. Just tired-looking people in black clothing who kept their gazes down, rushing, lost in the pulsing crowd.

Eddie stood there, staring at everything, and nothing. Disgusted, disappointed, utterly heartsore. He had failed. Fate had given him exactly what he needed—and he had let her slip away.

Police were watching him, but he ignored them and stood a moment longer, making certain she would not reappear—or that he wasn't simply hallucinating.

Lannes was waiting for him up top, standing in front of the display window for the Coach store.

"What happened?" he asked. "Was that her?"

Eddie rubbed his face. His heart still pounded, and his legs felt weak. Heat rolled through him, around him. Losing her should not have upset him so much. Every job had a hiccup, but this one . . .

It felt strangely personal. And he couldn't help but think again about that overwhelming feeling of connection that had flooded him when he first laid eyes on her. It made him homesick for something . . . unnameable.

He took a slow, deep breath, searching for calm. "Yes. Her friend said she liked this area, but I didn't expect to see her here. I screwed up."

"From what little I saw, you never had a chance. I've never seen anyone run that fast." Lannes hesitated. "She seemed to recognize you."

"No." Eddie thought about the way she had stared at him, with so much fear. It made him sick. "You're the one she focused on. She saw through your illusion."

"You're certain?"

"She saw you before me. She seemed stunned."

"A shape-shifter shouldn't be able to see what I really am. Only a . . . ." He stopped, shaking his head. "We frightened her."

Or maybe it was me, thought Eddie, uneasy. Lyssa hadn't run from Lannes. Just him.

But why? He had never met her. Was it because he was a man? A stranger, looking at her? Had she been hurt so badly that even *that* much attention was frightening? The idea made him furious and scared for her . . . but it also didn't feel right. There had to be more to it.

She knows she's being hunted. She doesn't trust anyone.

"We don't have much time." Eddie gave the subway entrance another reluctant look. "She may leave the city after this."

"You won't find her down there. Not now."

"I know." She had been so close. Right in front of him. Staring at him with those golden eyes.

Beautiful eyes. Fearful eyes.

He had seen that expression on other women. His sister. Girls on the street. Fear was a bitter disease. Having a woman look at *him* like that . . .

I will never make you afraid of me, he promised silently. *When I find you again, whatever it takes, you're not going to be scared.*

Ever again.

CHAPTER FOUR

Lyssa did not make Jimmy go to school, after all.
They took a roundabout path to his home, first
on the A train, heading south. But at Forty-second,
she yanked the boy off his seat and forced him onto
the crowded platform—timing it so the doors almost
closed on them.

Lyssa made Jimmy hustle up to the street, where
they caught a cab outside the Port Authority. She had
never ridden in a cab with him because those were expensive. Even though she had the money, money and
the tunnels didn't mix. She hadn't wanted him, or his
mother, to ask questions.

It didn't matter so much, now. It was more important
to make certain they weren't followed.

They exited the cab after ten minutes and walked
three blocks to another subway station, where they
boarded a second train. She didn't look to see where it
was going, but after three stops, she pushed Jimmy off.
He didn't protest until they reached the street, and she
hailed another cab.

He had not said a word the entire time. He had
barely looked at her. But he settled his clear, unflinch-

ing gaze on her face, and his expression was older than his years, and sharp.

"You knew that man," he said.

"What man?" she asked dully, stepping back onto the sidewalk as a cab slowed.

Jimmy gave her a dirty look. "My mom does the same thing. She sees men that remind her of my dad, and she runs. When I ask her why, she plays dumb."

Lyssa frowned and opened the cab door. "Okay, fine. He reminded me of someone."

"He called you Lyssa," said the boy accusingly. "You told us your name is Liz."

She stilled and looked at him. "I'm sorry I lied to you. But don't ever say that name again. I'm Liz to you. If anyone ever asks, I'm Liz."

No twelve-year-old should have been capable of the look that Jimmy gave her. "He hurt you, so you ran away and changed your name."

"No. It's more complicated than that."

"That's what Mom always says when I ask why she didn't leave my dad right away." Jimmy crawled inside the cab. His voice was muffled as he added, "Don't worry. I'll protect you."

Lyssa stared, an unexpected catch in her throat.

It did not take long to reach his home: an old apartment that Jimmy shared with his mom and an elderly woman named Estelle, who worked days in a small store that sold art supplies.

More than six months ago, Estelle had asked Lyssa if she knew anyone nice who might want to share her home. She'd had a scare with her heart and didn't want to live alone anymore. Rent wouldn't be much, and the apartment was roomy. Plenty of sunlight. Near the subway. A laundry room in the basement.

Jimmy and his mother moved in two days later. Lyssa asked Estelle not to tell them that she'd paid for their first three months of rent.

Lyssa entered the apartment first. She heard a kitchen faucet dripping, but that was all. No scents that didn't belong.

"Is Estelle still in Ohio visiting her children?"

"Mmm. We're safe, right?" Jimmy peered around her, fidgeting with the sleeves of his huge sweatshirt. Nervous, she realized with regret.

Of course he was nervous. *She* was nervous.

"Of course," she told him, as gently she could. "Just be careful. Don't go anywhere until your mom comes home. And don't come visit me again. Not alone. Promise."

"Okay."

"Say the words."

"I promise."

"I might not always be there, you know."

"Okay."

"It's dangerous, Jimmy."

"*Okay*," he said. "I'm sorry if I scared you today."

Lyssa hugged the boy. He stiffened, arms hanging awkwardly at his sides.

"It's okay," she said. "I worry about you, that's all."

"Mmph," he muttered.

Lyssa started to pull away. Jimmy surprised her by flinging his arms around her waist and hugging her back.

"I'm sorry," he muttered again. "I'm sorry someone hurt you."

Her heart broke. "Jimmy."

"That's why you live in the tunnel. Because of someone who looks like that man."

She held silent, unable to tell him the truth.

She lived in the tunnel because of a *woman*.

The man, however, was a different kind of danger. He was part of a dream, a portent of profound change . . . and that was why he frightened her. Because he represented the unknown, and she was a coward. Her life was so carefully structured, made up of habits that cut her days into manageable pieces. Structure made her feel normal. Structure made her less afraid for her life.

But surely there's nothing to fear from a gargoyle?

Gargoyles were known for their honor, for their moral strength and trustworthiness. No gargoyle would associate with, or practice, magic of dark intent. It simply was not in their natures.

The witches who wanted her dead would never leave a gargoyle alive.

Which meant that if the gargoyle knew the man . . . that man whose eyes had filled her dreams . . . maybe she had run for no good reason.

No, she told herself. *I'm a danger to be around. Especially for a gargoyle.*

As for that man . . .

Icky whined and pawed at her ankle. The little mutt had never been scared of her, which was more than she could say for most dogs. Lyssa patted his head, then hugged Jimmy again.

"Gotta go," she told him. "Be good."

Jimmy followed her to the door, looking like an urchin from some Charles Dickens novel. Lyssa could barely see his eyes beneath his hair.

"Remember what I told you. Be careful."

He didn't say anything. When Lyssa reached the end of the hall, she turned around one last time. He stood in the doorway, watching her. Icky peered around his legs.

She tried to smile for him but couldn't make it last. She'd never been much of a liar. She didn't want this to be the last time she saw him. She didn't want to live never knowing how he turned out, if he was okay, if he or his mom needed help.

But she couldn't let him get hurt because of her.

Outside, she caught another cab, and told the driver to take her to Midtown, near Fortieth and Lexington. It was a twenty-minute ride, and Lyssa spent the entire time thinking about gargoyles and strange young men with familiar eyes.

Today had been fate.

She loved Central Park, but had not intended to walk down Fifty-ninth to the subway. Something had tugged her there, though.

A nagging instinct that felt too much like premonition. She had *needed* to walk toward the park. When she tried to go a different direction, a sense of profound dread had fallen over her.

Lyssa knew better than to fight her gut. And it had paid off.

Gargoyle.

The memory still thrilled her—despite everything that had followed. A gargoyle in New York City. It was like spotting a dead rock star. Elvis, maybe. Impossible, crazy, and wonderful.

She had seen the illusion first—but the shimmer of light around his body, the otherworldly glow of energy, had made her stop and look deeper. Deeper, to wings. Silver skin. A craggy face and long hair, and a coiled set of horns upon his head.

Lyssa had never seen a gargoyle. Her father had known

them, had a friend who was a member of that race . . . but had not seen him for many years. She remembered that he always seemed sad about that. Regret in his eyes.

He never discussed any of his old friends in front of her mother. It had taken Lyssa a long time to understand why.

But that doesn't explain the man with him.

Lyssa pressed her forehead against the cab window, savoring the coolness of the glass. Memories flashed, a mixture of dream and life, life and the young man, running across the road toward her. Staring at her with those eyes.

His voice, whispering in her head.

I would take care of you. I wish I could.

She knew the difference between reality and fantasy. The man's voice was not her imagination. It was real. A real mind, touching hers for one brief, unexpected— and terrifying—moment.

You're overreacting. What did you hear? Nothing threatening.

No. His voice, inside her mind, had been wistful and sad, and full of compassion. Perhaps, even, wonderment.

He was talking about me.

She'd felt that, too. His focus on her. That was what had made her look around. Only she'd seen the gargoyle first. And thought, briefly, that it was *his* voice inside her mind.

But none of that mattered. She had been found.

Ratted out by her only friend.

I'm gone. Now. Tonight.

Right after she did one thing.

THE CAB LET HER OUT IN FRONT OF BLOOMING Nails, which made Lyssa think of her mother. She had liked to paint their nails crazy colors, different on each finger: glossy purple and pink, turquoise and red, tossed with glitter.

Like jewels, she would say. *Like magic.*

"Magic," Lyssa murmured, rubbing her gloved right hand. No claws, back then. Controlling her shifts had always been troublesome, but at least she'd managed to return fully to her human body.

Starbucks was just a few steps away. Lyssa ducked inside. The place was crowded and hot, and smelled good. Long line, filled with jazzy people her age who were looking down, up, sideways—anywhere, but at each other. No one ever *really* looked, in the city.

She checked her scarf, but it still covered her throat—just like the other hundred times she'd touched it. Her glove was firmly in place. Loose sleeve hanging well over her wrist. Nothing showing.

Lyssa didn't buy a drink. Just weaved to the back of the coffee shop, near the bathroom, and snagged a chair from an occupied table—inviting surly looks from two young men dressed in black, surrounded by laptops, stacked paper, and *Macbeth, Cliffnotes: Macbeth,* and *Shakespeare for Dummies.*

She gave their books a wary look and thought about grabbing a different chair. "I just need ten minutes to check my mail."

"You have five," said the guy on the right, hunching forward to slide his arm across the table—between her and his laptop.

"Don't talk," added his friend, tugging his computer closer to him.

"Mmm," she said, already bent over her worn canvas backpack. She used her right hand to undo the strap, but had to stop when a sharp, stabbing ache flowed from her wrist to her elbow. Her fingers stiffened, paralyzed and hot.

Lyssa gritted her teeth as the muscles in her right arm tightened and contorted, shifting against her will: a fraction, a breath, but enough to make her afraid. She grabbed her shoulder with her left hand, squeezing. Begging her body to listen.

Slowly, it did. Trembling, sweating, Lyssa cast a quick look around. No one was watching her, not even the guys at the table, who were flipping through *Macbeth* and snarling at the pages. She might as well have been alone in her tunnel, in the dark, for all that people saw her.

Good and bad. Lyssa wished she had a friend here. Someone to lean on who wasn't a thousand miles away.

She fumbled one-handed to pull free her laptop, and powered it on, connecting to the coffee shop's free Wifi. She logged on to her Webmail account.

There was a new message from Estefan, as well as one from her editor. Lyssa chose her friend first.

The e-mail said:

When you get this, contact me. I haven't heard from you in some time, and it's important we talk. I know you're obsessed with being on your own, but kid, that can't fly forever—especially now. So I did something you're not going to like.

I found you some help.

And it's coming.

Lyssa leaned back in her chair, staring at those words. Help? What the hell was Estefan thinking? Who could help her? And why would anyone even want to try?

"Shit," she muttered to herself.

Her right hand ached too much to type with. One-handed, pecking at the keyboard, she replied:

> *Got your message. Will try calling later. Does your help include a gargoyle? Because I saw one outside Central Park today. Coincidence or not? Need to know.*

She almost ignored her editor's e-mail, but there was no way to know how long she'd be off-line. The man was already prickly about only being able to contact her via the Internet.

Even if her world was going to hell, she still needed work.

In front of her, one of the guys slammed *Macbeth* on the table. "Unchecked ambition. I say we write the paper on that."

"Bullshit. We need something better."

"Better? This is due tomorrow."

His friend got the middle finger in response.

Lyssa muttered, "Ambition and violence. Focus on that."

Both men stared at her. One of them might have said, "What?" but she was distracted by her editor's e-mail. A note about cropping and deadlines, and an inquiry about the possibility of taking on another illustrating job—this time for a friend who worked at a children's magazine. He wanted some dreamy, surreal image for an upcoming short story. Not a bad gig.

One of the guys rapped his knuckles on the table. Lyssa tore her gaze from the computer screen, annoyed.

"What do you mean, ambition and violence?" he asked.

"Read the play," she told him, looking back at her e-mail—telling her editor that, yes, she was interested in the job—adding that she'd be on the road for a week, away from her computer. She cc'd her agent.

Lyssa began packing up. The guys bounced in their seats.

"I'll pay you a hundred bucks to help us right now," said the one on the right, stabbing his finger at her. Like that would seal the deal.

"Ha," she replied.

"We're desperate," added the other. "We'll love you forever. Just give us something more."

Grow a pair, she wanted to tell them, and slung her backpack over her shoulder. "Fine. Think about this. Once you decide to use violence to get power, it's difficult to stop."

The young men gave her blank looks. She shook her head and left.

A cold wind blew down Lexington, sweeping bits of loose trash against her boots. She walked fast, hat pulled low over her brow. Her right arm was better. When she flexed her fingers, they worked. Not well enough to hold anything, but at least they weren't cramping. She dug her thumb into her palm, massaging her hand.

Not Boston, she thought, considering where to go next. *Philadelphia?*

The idea of leaving made her ill. For better or worse, she felt comfortable in New York. Giving that up, just because Estefan had reached out to find her help . . .

Help for what? Lyssa thought again. *A home I can't use? Money I don't need? Estefan knows all that. So why now? Why after all these years would he suddenly become so protective?*

Lyssa thought again about the gargoyle—but also the man with him. A shudder raced through her, but not one of disgust. Just warmth. So much heat, in fact, that she stopped walking and looked down at her feet and legs to make sure she was not shedding sparks.

A month ago, she had started dreaming of his eyes. Always, during her nightmares. Her mind, wrapped in fire—screaming, terrified—so very alone—until, like a ghost, she would see someone watching her. A male presence, within the inferno. Just standing there: intense and dangerous, and more *real* than the flames.

Focusing on him always made the nightmare go away. Usually. Sometimes, she just needed to burn.

Seeing those eyes today, recognizing them—was like being hit by lightning.

Now, though, with some distance, the memory of that moment inspired a different feeling.

Homesickness.

Fear, she understood. But homesickness was inexplicable, and specific: She felt sick for the old days, when she was safe and loved. It hit her hard, with a fresh, raw tenderness that made her want to press her clawed hand over her heart and dig in.

It's him, she thought, suffering deep unease. *He makes me feel this way.*

No way Estefan could have known. But if that was help . . .

If that's help, I can't take it. . . . no matter how curious I am. Besides, there's nothing anyone *can do to help me.*

Not while I'm being hunted.

Lyssa saw a bank of pay phones near the intersection at Forty-first, and started digging through her pockets for change. She needed to call Estefan and find out *exactly* who he had contacted, and why. He had to have a good reason, after all these years of so carefully leaving her alone.

Her skin crawled when she thought of what that reason might be.

She slipped some quarters into the pay phone, careful to use her left hand—claws not being great for picking up small objects—and dialed his home number, which Estefan had made her memorize before she'd left Florida.

When the call went through, however, all she heard was a busy signal.

Lyssa tried three more times, but the call never connected. She tried the café, but the phone rang and rang—and no one picked up.

Unease crept. Lyssa hung up but didn't move. The heat throbbing through her blood only grew stronger. Pins and needles pricked her thighs and shoulders, between her breasts.

Something's wrong.

But no, that was stupid. Paranoia. Lyssa *always* thought something was wrong. A busy signal and an unanswered call was *not* a big deal. Besides, she never called Estefan. Ever. She didn't know the first thing about his phone habits.

Don't leave the city tonight, she told herself, massaging her right arm. *Take a couple days to plan. Talk to Estefan first. You don't want to run blind.*

But even as that thought passed through her, the prickling in her skin intensified, accompanied by a crawling sensation on the back of her neck. Like spider legs.

Someone was watching her.

Lyssa turned, and found herself face-to-face with the man.

The man from her dreams.

CHAPTER FIVE

EVERYTHING stopped. Heart, lungs, the world. Sounds died. Lyssa went numb.

Those eyes.

In all her dreams—a month of nights, lost in fire— those eyes had been her constant companions. Eyes that belonged to a face she could never see, or remember. Eyes that stared at her with an intensity that burned and made her feel lost, dizzy, as though she were falling.

She was falling now.

Lyssa blinked, and the spell broke. No longer just eyes, but the man from Columbus Circle. She hadn't looked closely at him, before.

He was young, which surprised her. When she looked at only his eyes, she thought of him as old.

Instead, he seemed close to her age. He was tall, but not much taller than she. Lean, lanky, but broad in all the right places. He looked strong, fast. Dressed in black, with scruffy dark hair that framed a pale, chis- eled face that would never be called boyish or weak.

I know you, she thought. *I dreamed you.*

But that was no comfort. Terrible heat burned be- neath her skin, flowing into her right arm in a wild, uncontrolled rush that made her clawed hand close into a fist. Pain tingled, simmering in that heat, and the muscles running from her neck into her shoulder twitched so violently she sucked in her breath and gripped her shoulder hard with her left hand.

The dragon stirred beneath her skin.

The dragon opened an eye within her heart and looked at the man in front of her.

Lyssa felt it, as though she carried a second life within herself. Terror fluttered. The dragon could not be allowed to wake. Not here. Not ever. It had been years since she had felt its presence.

She backed away. The man followed, holding up his hands. "Miss. Don't run. Please."

His voice was soft but filled with a quiet, gentle strength that tugged at her heart. It was the same voice she had heard in her mind, flowing through her with the most intimate of touches.

I would take care of you. I wish I could.

Lyssa didn't trust her voice to speak. Every instinct told her to run. Running was what she knew. Running was safe and empty, and kept the fire at bay, and all those dark memories that haunted, and tempted her.

This was dangerous. This *man* was dangerous, even if he meant her no harm. The harm would come, somehow.

Lyssa gave him a long, searching look. He let her look, though he didn't make it easy. She was used to studying people from a distance, or while distracted . . . anytime, anywhere, so long as no one realized what she was doing.

But she didn't have that luxury with him. He stared back with unflinching eyes, as though taking her measure as much as she was taking his. There was no place to hide in that gaze. Lyssa had never felt more naked.

"Who are you?" she asked.

His jaw tensed. "My name is Eddie."

Eddie. A scruffy name, with an edge. Sort of like him.

Lyssa backed away, wary. "How did you find me here?"

He did not follow, but she sensed that if he wanted to, he could be at her side in a heartbeat. He was just like her dream. Intense, dangerous, and *real*.

Completely real. Flesh and blood, staring at her as though he was ready for her to try and slip away. It unnerved her. Made her feel as though she couldn't trust her own perceptions of dream and waking.

"Estefan sent a list of places to search for you," he said quietly, holding her gaze. "That Starbucks behind us was one of them. He said you like to use the Internet there."

Damn, she thought, giving him a sharp look. "How do you know Estefan?"

Discomfort flickered in his eyes. "I don't. Your friend sent a letter to my employer. He explained you needed help. So I'm here. To help."

It sounded too good to be true. Who was he, a Boy Scout? Like those existed anymore. Lyssa had seen too many good people who needed help, shut out and ignored, treated as though invisible—simply for being homeless, or a little different. Even she, at her lowest, had been an untouchable. Except from those who wanted to use her.

"Estefan shouldn't have gotten you involved," she said, wondering why she was still standing here.

"Miss—"

"I am none of your concern."

"You need help."

"Starving kids in Africa need help. *I* don't. Not even a little."

He studied her—as though actually listening to what she was saying and digesting each word. It set her off-balance. Again.

Frustration warred with curiosity, and a bone-deep need to understand why the hell this man had been in her dreams. Had he dreamed of *her*? The possibility was almost as unsettling as his presence.

"You really came here because you were told I needed help?" she asked him, and what was intended to be a genuine question turned derisive when her voice came out too sharp. "Is that your job? Do-gooder?"

His brow lifted. "What's *your* job? Professional cynic?"

Her mouth twitched. "Something like that."

"That's too bad," he said, then, more softly, "Lyssa."

She was not expecting the sincerity of that answer, or the regret in his voice. Nor could she have predicted what hearing him say her name would do to her nerves.

Like, electrifying them.

I had peace and quiet, she thought, weakly. *I was alone, but that was safe.*

"Eddie," she said, feeling like a coward for not being able to stare as unflinchingly into his eyes, as he could hers. "Go home."

Lyssa pushed through the crowd and walked away.

She turned left at the intersection, walking with long, ground-eating strides. Not running, but almost. A cab passed her but didn't stop when she held out her hand.

Moments later, Eddie caught up.

He remained opposite her on the sidewalk, lanky and graceful. Outwardly relaxed though she sensed a coiled power inside him—and a tense control over that power that gave him a dangerous edge.

Light foot traffic passed between them. She heard

an ambulance's sirens. Maybe the police. None of it felt real. Not the people around them, not the wind on her face, not even the concrete beneath her feet.

Her world had narrowed down to him—and only him.

"Lyssa Andreanos," he said, quietly.

She hadn't heard her full name spoken out loud in ten years. Hearing him say it made her feel crazy. "Did Estefan tell you that, too?"

"First, from him," he replied, with a calm confidence that was assured, and, oddly, gentle.

She shivered. "Estefan shouldn't have told anyone."

"He made it clear he was violating your trust. But he didn't see another way to help you."

In two seconds, frustration was going to become anger. "I told you, I don't need help. So just . . . get lost."

"I can't." Eddie settled his gaze on her. "You're being hunted."

Lyssa stopped and stared at him. He shoved his hands in his pockets and spoke with a grim gentleness that she'd never heard in another man's voice.

"Hunted," he said again, "by witches who call themselves the *Cruor Venator*."

Her heart squeezed down into a vicious lump of pain, and she drew an unsteady breath that was loud and rough, and made her dizzy.

"Not even Estefan knows that," she said, hoarse. "Certainly not that name."

"You already knew they're looking for you?"

She exhaled sharply, wanting to laugh with devastating bitterness. "Of course. But who told *you*?"

His hesitation lasted a heartbeat too long. "Another of your kind."

"My kind."

"You know what I mean. It's in your eyes."

Golden eyes. He knows I'm a shape-shifter.

Of course, if his friend was a *gargoyle,* then it made sense he would know the signs that made a nonhuman stand out. But still, it felt like too much, too fast. The world was too mundane for this conversation.

Lyssa forced herself to breathe. "Does this person have a name?"

Eddie closed the distance between them. As he did, the air warmed. So much, it was like being exposed to the immense heat of a Southwest summer afternoon. A dry, rippling warmth, mirage-inducing.

Her own fire rose to meet that heat, with such power and hunger, she felt afraid all over again. She tried to read his face—as if her life depended on it. But all she could be certain of was that, for the first time in her life, she didn't trust her instincts.

Because her instincts wanted to trust *him.* Her instincts picked apart the way he moved, the way he looked at her, the tone of his voice—his eyes, *those eyes*—and there was strength in his intensity—and compassion, and even gentleness.

She couldn't trust it. She wouldn't let herself.

Her mother's voice drifted like a ghost through her mind.

You can tell everything from a man's eyes, and the way he looks at you. If you're not too afraid to see.

I was afraid when I met your father. He was too good to be true. So I ran, Lyssa.

It's a good thing he followed.

The memory was so strong. Lyssa touched her throat, the scarf wound so tight she could barely breathe. Fire burned in her gut. Her right arm tingled.

Eddie's gaze flicked to her hand. "Her name is Long Nu."

For a moment, the name didn't register. But it sat there, the sound of it ringing through her head. Slowly, so slowly . . . her mind made the connection.

And it was horrible. Terrible, and confusing.

"It's been ten years since I heard that name." Lyssa's voice shook, nerves betraying her. More rattled than she wanted to admit.

Eddie gave her a cautious look. "You don't seem happy about it."

Again, she wanted to laugh, but it would have sounded awful. "She knows you're here?"

"She was one of the people who asked me to come."

Fury gathered in her chest. "*She's* your employer?"

"No," he said firmly. "This was a favor."

"There are no favors with Long Nu. You do or you die . . . and if you don't die, you're punished." Lyssa backed away, wetting her lips. "Why now, after all these years? Why not *before,* when I was a child? I needed help then, and *no one* came for me."

"My impression was Long Nu thought you were dead."

"Wishful thinking," she whispered. "She's probably disappointed I'm not."

Eddie gave her a sharp look. "What does *that* mean?"

Lyssa shook her head and realized she was hugging herself. Hearing Long Nu's name should not have upset her as much as it did.

But it opened old wounds. It made her think of her father.

Straightening, she lifted her chin and looked him straight in the eyes. "Did Estefan know about Long Nu?"

He watched her, so carefully. "I don't think so. My

employer was the one who contacted her after receiving your friend's letter."

"What did Long Nu tell you about me?"

"Not enough." Eddie reached, very slowly, inside his pocket—and pulled out a plastic bag. Inside was something charred. "This is yours."

Lyssa didn't touch it. "What is it?"

"A photo of you when you were twelve."

She blinked, startled. He held up the bag. Inside, she saw a fragment of her face. Young and smiling. Before it all went to hell.

Her right hand clenched into a fist, claws biting through the tips of her gloves into her palm. "Did Long Nu give you that?"

"Yes."

Sorrow burned away into anger. "How dare she."

"What happened?"

"None of your business." Lyssa backed away, that glimpse of her young face burning a hole through her heart. "We're done here. Get away from me."

Eddie's mouth hardened, and in one long stride he stood inside her personal space. Suddenly, he seemed so much larger than her—strong and big, and powerful— bristling with a heat that seemed to shimmer over his body. It took all of Lyssa's strength not to retreat.

"Back off," she snapped.

His eyes were so dark. "No."

No. It was impossible that one word should be laced with so much determination.

"I will kick your ass to Sunday," she told him.

He leaned in even more. "You try. Beat me black-and-blue, if that makes you feel better. I'm not going *anywhere.* I was sent to find you. To *protect* you. And you better believe I will do that. You run, and I will find you. Again, and again, and again."

She believed him. And it enraged her.

Ten years on her own, ten years *alone,* and while some of that time had been shit, she'd made it—and hammered out a life with her own two hands, a life that was quick and dirty, but *hers.*

And now this man, a stranger, was *telling her* that he was *in her life?*

And Long Nu was involved?

No, she thought. *No way.* Not in a million years was Lyssa going to let that stand. It would be like spitting on her father's memory. All the humiliations, his isolation, his *sacrifice.*

Because Long Nu had thrown them to the wolves.

"Get away from me," she growled.

"No," he said again, and there was more quiet power in that one word than in any other she'd ever heard.

She backed away. Eddie followed. She turned, and he stayed right on her heels, terrible heat flowing down her back.

"Lyssa," he said, reaching for her.

She whirled, lashing out with her first: a solid right hook that snapped toward his face. Fast, driven by arm muscles deformed with power.

Eddie blocked her. Barely. Her fist clipped his ear, but he twisted, and clamped his hand around her wrist. She grabbed his throat, but not before his hand slid forward, beneath her sleeve—and touched her bare, reptilian, skin.

The contact burned. Burned to the bone.

Lyssa flinched. So did he. A roaring sound filled her ears, and her vision brightened in a haze of golden light. She tried to let go, but her hand around his throat would not loosen, no matter how hard she tried. The world blurred away in the light until all she could see was Eddie's eyes.

He was looking at her . . . not with fear . . . but that quiet, deadly compassion.

I understand, she heard him say inside her mind. *I'm sorry.*

Smoke rose from beneath her hand.

Everything exploded.

CHAPTER SIX

Eddie knew it was a mistake the moment he touched Lyssa.

Because he was irritated when he caught her wrist—and it didn't matter that she had tried to punch him. He had laid a hand on her, with frustration, annoyance—and it was too close to anger for comfort.

Too close to his worst nightmare.

So Eddie didn't fight when she grabbed his throat. He went still, staring into her glowing golden eyes, taking in her anger and knowing it was fear. The same fear he had felt for years on the street: cornered, forced to look strangers in the eyes and hope it would be okay, without knowing whether or not it would be.

I understand, he wanted to tell her. *I'm sorry.*

A thought that was followed by fire.

When he could see again, when the world stopped spinning, and the heat inside him was nothing but a matchstick, burning—he blinked away tears and found there was nothing left but smoke clouding the air.

Alarms wailed, sounding tinny in his ears. His

clothes were charred, his jeans on fire. Pavement, cracked and blackened. He smelled gasoline and burning metal, and felt terrible heat press against his back.

Cars had exploded, parked at the side of the street. The skeletons of each vehicle burned, pouring off a poisonous cloud of smoke that was thick and gruesome. Eddie didn't see anyone inside, but maybe that was just wishful thinking.

He rolled over. Nothing but broken glass in the office building beside them. Windows had blown in. He heard screams and moans. How many? How many injured? Had anyone died?

Lyssa.

Eddie twisted and found her close, curled in a ball. Her green sweater had been reduced to rags that sparked and glimmered. She was on fire.

Choking, eyes stinging, he crawled to her and beat out the fire with his bare hands. Not once did she move. Grabbing her shoulder, checking her blackened face and arm, he was relieved to find the dark spots on her skin were nothing but soot. The fire had not touched her. Relief made him tremble.

She was like him. Immune.

"Miss," he rasped. "Lyssa."

Still no response. With a gentle push, he rolled her over—and stared.

Her scarf was in tatters, her sleeve mostly gone. Much of her glove had burned away, revealing her neck, right shoulder—her arm, her hand.

Gleaming red scales had replaced human flesh. Large scales, like a snake's, edged in gold. It was like looking at armor made of rubies and precious metal, glinting in the smoke-shrouded light as though lit from within. Beneath that reptilian skin were contorted, sinewy muscles. Golden claws tipped her slender, triple-jointed fingers.

Eddie saw it all too quickly. No time to take it in.

He glimpsed movement on the other side of the dark cloud—people rushing down the sidewalk, pouring from the few office buildings that lined the street. Police would be coming soon, ambulances, fire trucks. Cameras.

Get out of here. Right now.

His ears still rang. Eddie fell the first time he tried to stand, and looked around, wildly, for a way out. Through the smoke, across the street, he glimpsed a parked car: an older model Camry.

Lyssa's backpack was a wreck, but the strap was still intact. He slung her belongings over his shoulder, then scooped her into his arms. He held her carefully, her inhuman shoulder tucked against his chest. Hidden, as best he could. She did not make a sound.

Hunched over, hurting and breathless, he staggered between the burning wrecks. He felt movement from the corner of his eye, heard shouts and more screams as he carried Lyssa across the street. He set her on the sidewalk and pulled a multipurpose folding knife from his charred jacket. One of the tools was a window punch, which he set against the lower corner of the car window. He tapped, hard, and the glass crumpled with a crackling sound. Tapping again, he made a hole large enough for his arm. He reached in and unlocked the door.

Lyssa was so quiet and still. Gritting his teeth, trying to stay calm, Eddie pulled and pushed, and shoved her into the cluttered backseat. Newspapers fell to the floor, along with limp gym clothes and empty cans of soda. He tossed in the backpack after her.

Before he jumped into the driver's seat, he looked

around one more time—and found that they were not
alone.

Two women stood close. The one on the left was
tall, African-American, wearing a cropped red motor-
cycle jacket and a skintight black bodysuit with tall,
heeled boots. Her striking face was dominated by eyes
highlighted in purple shadow and black liner.

The other woman was shorter, but no less beautiful: long black hair, pale skin, crystalline blue eyes.
Dressed in jeans and a white blouse partially obscured
by a heavy necklace strung with chunks of onyx.

They stared at him. Him, and not the blast.

Might as well have been no fire, no screams, no
billowing smoke and burning cars . . . none of that
touched them. They stood eerily still, still as stone,
still as cats waiting to pounce—their eyes narrow and
watchful, their mouths tilted into faint, sly smiles.

And Eddie realized, in one split second, that he was
in deep trouble.

Few people scared him anymore. Most inspired caution, yes—but not fear. It wasn't arrogance that made
him feel that way. Just age and fire, and experience.
Most of the time, he was more scared of himself.

Something about these women terrified him.

It was hard, immediate: a primal fear at the back of
his primitive brain, like hearing a scream in a pitch-
black forest, or the touch of bone fingers in the night.

When he looked at them, he thought *death*. Or
something worse. And for those brief seconds that he
stared into their eyes, the fear made him feel like a kid
again, faced with all his worst nightmares: powerless-
ness, despair, guilt, desperation.

Eddie averted his eyes. He couldn't help himself. It
felt like a matter of survival, not looking at them.

"What a puppy," said the black woman. "Such a handsome boy."

"Adorable," added the other woman. "I want to eat him up."

Their soft laughter chilled him. Because he thought, *yes*, they really would eat him up. And then bury his bones in a ditch.

He shivered. "Who are you?"

"It speaks! How unusual," said the black woman, swaying close. "I am Nikola. This is Betty. And you have something we want."

"Besides your virtue," said the other woman, showing her white teeth. "And here we thought we'd actually have to *work* to snare a dragon. It turns out we just have to follow her until she does something *stupid*."

The meaning of their words was almost lost to him. What mattered was the sound of their voices, which crushed him smaller and harder, like he was nothing but a walnut or little stone.

Each word, a fist. Each word, an iron collar tightening around his soul.

Nikola moved even closer. It was all he could do not to fall on his knees and whimper. Sweat trickled down his chest. His fear was so nauseating, he could barely think.

"Mmm," she murmured, her breath hot against his cheek. "You smell . . . different."

"Like fire," Betty added, with a note of surprise. "Like . . . a dragon."

I'm human, he wanted to tell them.

"It must be *her* scent," said Nikola, suddenly sounding bored. "Open the car door, puppy. Pick up the little lizard and come with us."

She spoke as though she expected him to obey,

without question. Part of him wanted to. He was that
scared of them.

But not scared enough to forget who he was or what
he had come to do.

I'm going to protect you, he thought, toward Lyssa.
I'm going to take care of you.

And just thinking that . . . changed everything.

Another chill raced through him, but this felt like a
splash of cold water: clean and bracing. Suddenly, he
could breathe again, and his spine straightened, and
the nausea faded away.

Eddie raised his head, and looked the two women
dead in the eyes.

"No," he said.

Betty's right eye twitched. "Excuse me?"

Nikola frowned. "Get the bitch out of the car and
come with us, you little fuck."

"Ma'am," he replied, and slipped into the driver's
seat, slamming the door and locking it. He locked
Lyssa's door, too, then pried off the panel beneath the
steering wheel. In ten seconds he had the engine roaring. Just like old times.

The women stood outside the car, staring at him
with stunned expressions.

Eddie accelerated into the road, catching the light just
as it turned yellow. He crossed Lexington, rolling down
his window so that people wouldn't notice the broken
glass. By the time he turned left on Third, the trembling
had begun, deep quakes that made him clench his jaw
so his teeth wouldn't chatter. He felt so cold.

I just met the Cruor Venator, he thought, shakily.

And if it wasn't them, and just some *random*
witches . . . then God, *yes,* he finally understood what
Lannes was warning him about.

Their presence alone had filled him with crippling, nauseating fear . . . though now, with some distance, he couldn't understand why.

Is that what a spell feels like? Or was it just them? And why did they let me leave?

Because he had surprised them, he realized.

Those women were *not* used to being defied. If they could instill that much fear in anyone they chose, then he understood why.

No way in hell could they be allowed to get close to Lyssa.

Eddie glanced into the backseat and found her eyelids twitching. Even unconscious, she grimaced as though in pain. He wondered if that was what *he* looked like after losing control of his fire.

Lyssa had caused the explosion. It had to be her. He had felt none of his own triggers, and the heat that had rolled off her skin in the seconds prior to the blast had been immense. Just standing next to her would have been enough to put a normal person in the hospital for burns.

He recalled Lyssa's hand on his throat, her glowing eyes, the scent of smoke . . .

Someone got injured today. No way there weren't injuries.

Maybe she won't care.

He chanced another look, this time at her exposed arm. Her hand, covered in red scales, rested on her stomach. Claws glinted, razor-sharp.

Seeing her caught in a partial shift was disconcerting. As though it should have been a makeup job, something out of a Hollywood creature shop. It also limited his options of where to take her.

You only have one choice.

But it would be bringing more trouble on their doorstep.

He reached into his pocket for his cell phone. The screen was cracked, but he held his breath, and it powered on.

Lannes answered on the second ring.

"Trouble," Eddie said.

EDDIE PARKED THE CAR ON FIFTY-EIGHTH, IN FRONT of a steakhouse behind a white delivery truck. He wiped everything down with his sleeve. The hunt would have already begun for the cause of the explosion. Terrorists might be blamed. Homeland Security would get involved.

He called Lannes again and gave him the address.

"It's on the news," said the gargoyle. "Just now."

Eddie stopped breathing. "Fatalities?"

"Nothing yet, but the media is going nuts. Were there security cameras in that area?"

"I don't know. There was no way to stop it, Lannes."

"I thought . . ." He paused, his silence heavy and thoughtful. "I know you've been ill. It couldn't be helped."

Eddie stilled. Lannes thought *he* was the one who had caused the explosion?

Of course he does. I'm the one who's been out of control.

It hurt his pride and embarrassed him. He almost corrected his friend, but thought of Lyssa . . . and kept his mouth shut.

"We'll see you soon," Eddie said, and hung up before Lannes could say anything else.

Behind him, he heard a soft whimper.

Lyssa was still unconscious, but her face contorted

with pain, her breathing shallow and fast. She clawed fitfully at her scaled throat. Nightmare, perhaps. Eddie hesitated, unsure whether to wake her.

Until a wave of heat blasted his face. Smoke rose from the charred edges of her sweater, followed by sparks. Another fire, brewing.

He twisted fully around, reaching for her hand. "Lyssa."

She did not wake. But the pain in her face softened. Her breathing slowed. Eddie stroked the back of her hand and watched the sparks fade, along with the smoke and heat. He did not breathe any easier, though.

Her skin was so soft. Eddie rested his chin on the car seat, content to take a moment and just . . . stare. Soot didn't hide her beauty, which managed to be delicate and fierce—vulnerable—and totally, utterly, striking.

She can't be all those things, his sister would have said. *She's a girl, not a laundry list.*

Eddie smiled to himself. Fine. If he had to choose one word . . .

"Fierce," he whispered. Fierce, stubborn . . . but not hard. Not yet.

Their conversation before the blast had told him more about her than perhaps she realized. Her words were sharp, cynical . . . but her eyes had been soft with uncertainty and buried hunger.

Something he understood all too well.

If you get used to having the rug pulled out from under you—or not having any rug at all—you stop trusting anything that sounds like good news.

But that doesn't mean you stop wanting *to trust.*

Once again, Eddie tried to imagine her life. She had dropped off the radar after the deaths of her parents. No other family. No apparent friends—except one dead shape-shifter—and maybe a little boy. Had she been alone all this time? Homeless?

If she had lived on the streets, she seemed to be doing better now. Her clothes had been worn, but clean—and even now he saw the edge of a blackened laptop poking through a charred hole in her backpack.

Everything about her was a mystery.

Eddie let go of her hand as she stirred. Not yet awake but settling deeper into the backseat. The ragged remains of her sweater slipped, revealing the curve of her pale breast. More breast than she would probably be comfortable with him seeing—though he gave himself a few moments to appreciate the sight.

His jacket was charred but mostly intact. He stripped it off, then squeezed between the seats to lay it over her, tucking in the sides as best he could. Eddie wanted, very badly, to wipe the soot from her cheek. He began to. Just one little touch.

Her eyes opened. Golden, hot, staring. And glowing.

His breath caught in his throat, his hand frozen near her cheek. Unable to look away as her eyes shifted from human to . . . something else. Pupils narrowed into slits, and tiny hints of crimson appeared around the rims of her iris—as well as her lower eyelids.

Dragon eyes.

Lyssa did not move, but her golden gaze searched his face with a thoroughness that was alien and cold—and utterly unlike the woman he had faced before the explosion.

"You," she whispered. "You, with fire in your blood."

Her voice was dry and sibilant. Eddie stared. "Lyssa?"

"Lyssa," she murmured, faintly mocking. "Lyssa sleeps. I am her dragon."

He didn't know how to respond to that. He wondered if she was playing games, but he looked closer into those eyes and felt power crawl over his skin. Whoever was staring back at him now was not the same woman. There was no fear in that gaze, no uncertainty.

Nothing remotely human.

He wet his lips. "I don't understand. What does that even mean, you're her dragon?"

She drew in a rasping breath that sounded like the rub of scales. "If she trusted herself, it would mean nothing. But she forgets that human and dragon can be passengers of the same heart. She does not believe that we are one, and that accepting me will not diminish her. So I wait, and protect her when I can."

It sounded like a split personality disorder. He hadn't realized that shape-shifters could be caught between the different spiritual and mental aspects of their existence—independent of one another. It was sort of creepy.

Eddie wanted to choose his next words very carefully. "Were you protecting her today? Were you aware of those women who came for her?"

"I was aware. But *you* protected her. Simply by saying no to them."

"Who are they?"

The corner of her mouth curled. "Prey."

Eddie wondered if she was cocky or just that dangerous. "Does Lyssa feel like that?"

Her smile faded. "She is afraid to."

Based on what he'd seen, Lyssa's anger stood out more than her fear. She had a lot of anger inside her. But he didn't want to bring that up. In fact, he suddenly felt extremely uncomfortable discussing her. "Will she remember this?"

"No."

"Then this conversation is done." Eddie stared into those golden eyes, refusing to flinch when her clawed right hand slipped out from beneath his jacket and slid down his arm. "I mean it, ma'am."

She stilled. "Yes. I can tell you do."

Eddie pulled away, slowly. "You do this often?"

"Never."

Curiosity got the better of him. "Why now?"

She closed her eyes. "Because I wanted to see the man who makes her blood sing."

Eddie exhaled sharply. "Ma'am."

But she said nothing else. After a quiet, breathless moment, her face relaxed and softened. Until then, he hadn't even realized her expression had hardened, but the difference was startling. The weary vulnerability was back.

I wanted to see the man who makes her blood sing.

Eddie fingered the scars on his hands and watched her sleep.

It took Lannes more than thirty minutes to reach them, but it felt longer. He heard sirens wailing—far away, then, once, very close. He watched police and an ambulance speed through the intersection half a block away.

Every time people walked past the car, his throat closed. If vehicles drove by too slowly, he had to force himself to breathe. A litany of excuses flooded his head—*she's drunk, carsick, just sick, we're waiting for a restaurant to open, we're homeless so give us a break*—anything, everything.

He hated being a sitting target. Worse, this reminded him too much of the old days. Always waiting to be caught—if not by police, then by someone worse.

Finally, *finally*, his phone rang. Lannes was on the other end.

"I'm here," he said. "I can see the Camry. Get ready."

Eddie got out of the car and opened up the back door. A black SUV rolled close. No cars behind it. Some foot traffic, but far enough away that very little, if anything, would be seen. He hoped.

He had Lyssa halfway out of the car when Lannes stopped beside them. She made a small sound. Eddie looked down into her eyes.

Human, golden, eyes. No dragon in them. Staring half-lidded and so exhausted he wasn't even certain she was seeing him.

"It's okay," he whispered, smoothing her hair back from her face. "You're safe."

"No," she breathed, eyes drifting shut again. "No, I have to . . ."

Eddie held her as close as he could, pulling his jacket tight around her. She didn't fight him when he piled her into the backseat of the SUV, slumping down into a boneless heap when he let her go.

It took him less than twenty seconds to rub down the Camry's interior and exterior for the second time. He grabbed her backpack, kicked the door closed, and climbed into the idling car.

Lannes accelerated away before the door was closed. "You look terrible."

"Been better."

"And her?"

Eddie touched Lyssa's shoulder and shook her as gently as he could—which was little more than a tightening of his fingers. "Hey."

"No," she murmured, as though dreaming.

"Lyssa."

At the sound of her name, her entire face tightened

with so much pain, his heart broke. "No . . . don't hurt me . . . *please* . . ."

He sagged against the seat, staring. Buzzing filled his ears, along with his thudding heartbeat. Fire burned in his blood.

"Hey," Lannes said in a low voice, sounding very far away. "Eddie."

He wet his lips. "Yes?"

"Take a break. Join me up front."

Eddie flashed him a surprised look, but after a moment's hesitation, crawled into the front. Lannes drove with his seat pushed all the way back, hunched over, his massive hands tight around the steering wheel. Lines of concern were etched in his brow.

"So," he said. "That's her."

Eddie swallowed hard. "Yes. I think she's had a difficult life."

"Mmm." Lannes glanced at his rearview mirror. "I feel like I'm committing a crime."

"Any more news?"

"Still no deaths reported. Everyone's screaming terrorist, though. You need to get out of the city."

"I know." Eddie looked at Lyssa again, who was still unconscious—or seemed to be. Would she leave with him? He very seriously doubted it.

Lannes followed his gaze. "Does she need a doctor?"

"I don't think so. It wouldn't be safe, anyway."

"Her arm," he replied thoughtfully. "It looks as though she's caught in a bad shift. I've never seen it so extreme."

"There's a shifter who was found in a Consortium facility in the Congo. He's part eagle, still. It was forced on him, by scientists."

Lannes let out a weary sigh. "Lethe called. She said something's up with her family. They won't tell her what, but they're talking about leaving the city for a while. They're insisting she go with them. For her safety."

"She won't, will she?"

He hesitated. "I'm thinking of telling her to go."

"She won't like that."

"And she probably won't listen." A faint, worried, smile touched his mouth, but it faded almost as soon as it appeared. "She thinks they know the *Cruor Venator* are here."

Nikola and Betty, thought Eddie, with anger. They had made him feel like he was thirteen years old again, terrified and abused. That was one crime he could not forgive.

Both men shared a long look. Lannes said, "You were lucky to get away from those women. Very lucky."

"Maybe *you* should go. Take Lethe back to Maine."

"Run for the hills? Not yet."

Not yet, but maybe.

It took them twenty minutes to reach Greenwich Village, where Lannes and Lethe had a home. It wasn't just their home, but a brownstone that belonged to the gargoyle's entire family. Eddie didn't know how often it was used, but he'd heard from one of the brothers that it had been passed off to all of them for about seventy years. Gargoyles were long-lived.

West of Seventh Avenue, Leroy Street bent and became St. Luke's Place. Quiet, upscale. Row houses lined the block, brick and brownstone, with arched entries and other elegant details. The trees were old and shedding their leaves. Expensive cars were parked along the street.

He felt out of place. Like a thief.

Lannes found a parking spot about a hundred feet

from their brownstone. Eddie said, "People are going to see."

"Let me carry her. I can spread my illusion."

Eddie would have preferred to hold her, but he couldn't say that. He could barely admit it to himself.

No traffic on the street. Just an old woman walking a dog half a block away. He didn't see anyone watching from the windows, but that didn't mean much. He felt as though a target were painted on his back as he opened the SUV's back door. Lannes loomed over him and bent to pull out Lyssa.

He froze, though—and made a sharp, surprised, sound.

"What?" asked Eddie, concerned.

"I . . ." Lannes stopped, leaning back with a frown. "Nothing. When I touched her . . ."

He paused again. Eddie said, "Spit it out. Is there something wrong?"

"I don't know." Lannes pulled Lyssa into his arms. She made a small sound, but when her head lolled, her eyes stayed closed. Eddie didn't think she was faking it. Whatever had happened in that explosion had drained her completely.

Her, *and not her dragon*, he reminded himself, as his jacket slipped off her body. He tucked it again more carefully around her—heart in his throat when he looked at her face. Heart in his hands when he touched her, as gently as he could.

When he looked up, Lannes was watching him with peculiar intensity. It embarrassed Eddie, but he met his gaze and did not flinch.

"You like her," Lannes said.

Eddie set his jaw. "I can see her. Your illusion isn't working."

"Sure it is. It just isn't working on you." He started walking down the street. Eddie frowned at him but grabbed Lyssa's backpack and shut the car door. When he caught up with them, Lannes said, "It's strange, actually. Even *I* can't see her. It looks to me like I'm holding air."

Eddie glanced around to see if anyone was watching. "Are you sure you didn't do it wrong?"

"It's about *willing* an action," Lannes said dryly. "I don't have a magic wand, or a special incantation. And no, I didn't make a mistake. For some reason, you can see her."

"That doesn't make sense."

Lannes glanced down. Maybe he really couldn't see Lyssa, but Eddie thought that he was looking at *something*. And not anything that made him happy.

"No," he finally replied, in a particularly grim voice. "None of this makes sense."

Eddie moved in so close he brushed against the gargoyle's wings. Lannes gave him a hard look and moved away. Eddie crowded him again, refusing to back down. Concern warred with irritation. "What aren't you saying? What did you feel when you touched her?"

"Let's get inside first," Lannes muttered, as they reached the front steps of a brownstone decorated with carved pumpkins, goofy witch dolls, and stone gargoyles with bunny ears glued to their heads.

"Wow," Eddie said.

"Shut up," said Lannes.

It was quiet inside. No one else home. In front of the door, a set of stairs led up to a second floor—and on either side of the entry were two massive rooms, spacious and furnished with overly large, well-worn blocks of furniture that looked big enough to hold several gargoyles, and maybe a baby elephant, or two. Threadbare rugs covered the hardwood floors, and large black-and-white photographs of mountains and rivers covered the white walls. A long hall led to the back. Eddie smelled cinnamon buns.

Lannes paused. "Here, take her."

Eddie did, cradling Lyssa as gently as he could. She felt light, lighter than she should have, as though her bones were hollow, or she was made of air.

The gargoyle let out an unsteady breath once Lyssa was out of his arms. Eddie said, "What?"

"I don't know if I should have brought her here," he said, then stood there, looking stunned—as if he couldn't believe he had just said that.

Eddie couldn't believe it either. "What do you mean?"

His expression turned uncertain. "She makes my skin crawl."

"I . . ." Eddie began, and stopped. "If you want us to leave—"

"No." Lannes stepped back and pointed up the stairs. "First door on your right. But, if you don't mind—"

"I'll keep an eye on her," he said, a little more sharply than he intended. Irritated at himself—and Lannes—he began carrying Lyssa upstairs.

"Eddie," called out the gargoyle, behind him. "Just because she's a shape-shifter . . ."

He didn't finish. He didn't need to.

Just because she's a shape-shifter, doesn't mean you should trust her.

Eddie continued climbing the stairs, holding her even closer—soft and warm against his chest. Her scent washed over him: indefinably sweet, with a hint of smoke, and vanilla.

Trust. What did trust mean, anyway? There were so many ways to lose trust before it even had a chance to form.

Give her a chance.

Give her the same chance you wish she would give you.

After all, it was only a matter of life or death.

The first room on the right held a bed, a standing wardrobe, and a small desk. One narrow window overlooked the front street.

Lyssa stirred in his arms, her eyes fluttering open. Just a little, then wider. Alert. He froze, staring down at her—and she went still, as well. Both of them, like caught animals.

"Hi," Eddie said, awkwardly.

Lyssa sucked in her breath and pushed hard on his chest with her clawed right hand. He had no choice but to let go, but he tried to do so gently. She fell anyway, though, and he got clipped in the jaw trying to hold her upright.

"Stop," she gasped, as her knees buckled, and she fell back on the bed. Eddie stepped forward, concerned, but she threw up one hand—breathing hard, eyes wide. Eddie held as still as he could, afraid to breathe.

Lyssa did not speak, but the wariness in her eyes was enough. Slowly, with a wince, she tried to sit up—and noticed her exposed right arm.

Fear filled her eyes. Panic.

Eddie said, "Hold on."

His jacket had slipped away. He picked it off the floor and placed it on the bed beside her.

"I had you covered up before." He had trouble meeting her gaze, which was tragic and lost. "Your arm . . . it doesn't bother me."

Silence. Stillness. Eddie looked down at his hands.

He rubbed his scars but barely saw them, his attention focused entirely on the woman sitting on the bed in front of him.

Finally, with small movements, she took his jacket. Eddie did not watch her slip it on. It felt too personal, too intimate.

"Are you hurt?" he asked quietly. "You've been unconscious for more than an hour."

Rustling sounds ceased. "That long? I . . . what happened?"

"There was an explosion. A fire."

Her silence was excruciating. Eddie finally looked up, and wished immediately he hadn't. Her horror overwhelmed him.

"How . . . bad?" she whispered, her left hand white as bone as she clutched his jacket closed.

How had he ever thought that this woman might not care that people had gotten hurt? Her fear, the devastation teetering in her gaze, was almost more than he could bear to see.

"No one died," he reassured her.

Lyssa inhaled sharply. "But people were injured."

"I don't know details. It . . . made the news, though."

She covered her mouth like she was going to be sick. Eddie stepped closer to the bed, moving carefully in case his presence frightened her. She hardly seemed to notice.

Lost. Lost deep, and far away.

Lost in his jacket, even, which was huge on her. Her right arm wasn't in the sleeve. Hidden against her body, out of sight. Covered in soot, her clothing in tatters, auburn hair tangled and wild . . .

. . . and still the most compelling woman he had ever met.

Looking at her even now hit him with breathtaking force, deep in his heart and gut . . . stirring some primal ache that he hadn't realized he was capable of feeling. Not like *this*. It frightened him, a little.

"You didn't tell me if you're hurt," Eddie said, hoarse.

"I'm not," she murmured, voice muffled against her hand. Then, after a moment's silence: "You?"

"I'm fine."

"You don't look like it."

Eddie wasn't sure what he looked like, but he felt battered on the inside. "Fire doesn't hurt me."

Lyssa held herself even tighter. "You're no shape-shifter."

"Is that a requirement?"

"It's what I know." She pushed herself to the edge of the bed, watching him warily. "Are you a witch?"

"No. I'm just . . . me."

"That doesn't mean anything."

Eddie set his jaw. "It doesn't have to. I'm here anyway."

But that doesn't mean anything to me either, he imagined her thinking, and it stung more than it should have.

This was a job, he reminded himself. This was a job, like any other he had been on. He had helped doctors in Africa, mermen in the South China Sea. He had fought mercenaries in Mongolia.

He had lived as a thief on the streets of Los Angeles.

Lyssa Andreanos was just one more challenge.

She looked down at her torn, charred jeans, little more than rags covering her soot-covered legs. Eddie remembered her backpack and slid it off his shoulder onto the bed. When Lyssa saw it, she let go of the jacket just long enough to touch the blackened, burned canvas.

Some tension left her shoulders. "Where am I?"

"The home of a friend. The . . . gargoyle."

Her reaction was unexpected. Eddie saw surprise in her eyes, followed by grief—and a heartbreaking longing that disappeared almost as quickly as it appeared.

She lowered her head until her hair fell around her face, and he could barely see her. "I need to go. You shouldn't have brought me here."

She tried to stand, but her knees buckled again. Eddie let out his breath and went to her. Her hand shot up, and the look she gave him was angry and fearful. "Don't touch me."

"Then don't fall," he shot back. "You need rest."

"I need to get out of here," she muttered, but trying to stand a third time was no better, and he grabbed her waist before she could fall. He half expected her to hit him, but all she did was stiffen and make a muffled sound of protest.

Her body was slender and soft, and warm. Her scent, smoky and sweet. Eddie's nose brushed against her hair, and a deep need sparked inside him, an ache that felt too much like being adrift, lost, homesick.

A need that he knew, in his gut, this woman could ease.

His reaction, and the thought that accompanied it, stunned him. He tried to let her go, but his hands tightened before he could stop them, and it took all his willpower to merely help her sit—instead of pulling her even closer.

When he did finally loosen his hands, and step back—he felt hot, light-headed. Lyssa was not looking at him. Her shoulders sagged inside his oversized jacket as she braced her left hand on the covers. She seemed to be breathing hard. But so was he.

Distance. He needed distance to clear his head. Eddie went to the wardrobe. He didn't know whose room this was, but it looked feminine enough to have *something* around she could wear. His sister—and mother—had always filled every closet in the house with their things, even in rooms that didn't belong to them.

He found summer dresses hanging inside, alongside purses and frilly cardigans. Behind him, Lyssa said, "Who else lives here?"

"My friend's wife. I don't know who else."

"A gargoyle doesn't wear those clothes."

"She's human." Nothing in here was going to work. It was all short sleeves and gaping necklines. Eddie closed the wardrobe door. "You're going to need something . . . warmer."

Lyssa tried to stand again, and this time stayed upright. She swung the backpack over her shoulder and winced. "I don't feel the cold."

"Where are you going?"

"None of your business."

"I can help you."

Lyssa shook her head and moved unsteadily to the door. Eddie crossed the room and planted himself in front of her. She shot him a deadly look, which he easily ignored.

"What happened, with the fire," he told her. "If nothing else, I can help you with *that*."

Distrust filled her eyes. "Don't lie to me."

Anger flared, unexpected and hot. He couldn't push it down. After a moment, he stopped trying.

"I'm not a liar," he said in a deadly soft voice. "Don't call me that."

Lyssa shivered.

That—and the sudden uncertainty in her eyes— made his anger flash away as quickly as it had arrived.

She gets under my skin, he thought, wondering what the hell was wrong, that he couldn't control his emotions with her around.

Bottled up was safe. He needed to stay safe. For her. *No anger means no pain.*

And while I'm at it, best not to feel anything at all.

Uneasy with himself, slightly nauseated, Eddie held up his hand and snapped his fingers. Sparks flew off his thumb.

Lyssa made a small sound of surprise and backed away. Eddie followed her. He was taller, but not by much, and liked being able to look her in the eyes.

He conjured another spark of fire, which shimmered like a star. Then once more, only this time it was an actual flame, rippling from his palm up his wrist, setting his sleeve on fire. He clapped it out with his other hand, smoke rising between them.

The surprise in her eyes turned haunted. Lyssa reached out—slowly, tentatively. Her left hand was pale and delicate, smudged with color.

Inks, he thought. Or paint. His hand seemed so rough in comparison. Ugly and scarred.

Her fingertips hovered close to his. Heat touched his palm, warm and delicious, spreading deep into bone—down his wrist, into his arm. Slow and easy, and strong. A good heat, without the tumult of emotion that usually accompanied the fire inside him. A calm warmth that felt more right than anything he had experienced in a long time.

Do you feel it, too? Eddie almost asked, wanting to touch her so badly. Instead, he held his breath, and remained still. Waiting for her. Waiting for her not to be afraid.

Waiting for himself not to be afraid, too.

Lyssa's gaze flicked to his face, then down again.

Her cheeks turned pink. She lowered her hand, and that good heat faded, leaving him cold. Cold, and so empty, so alone, he had to take a moment to steady himself.

She clutched the jacket closed. "You're not human."

"Not a dragon," Eddie said heavily, watching her flinch ever so slightly. "But human enough."

"You know too much," she whispered.

"Let me help you. It's what I do."

"Who are you, really?"

"I told you. My name is Eddie." He felt at a loss for what else to say. Giving her a bullet point of his interests and hobbies seemed stupid, and he didn't have much of a life outside work. Nothing that mattered here. "I could tell you other things about me, but that probably wouldn't mean anything to you. I wouldn't expect it to."

Lyssa was silent a moment. "Who would do a favor for Long Nu?"

She said the name with quiet bitterness and resentment. Eddie wanted to know what had happened to cause such anger. It made him uneasy.

"The organization I work for helps people. All of us there are . . . not normal. Long Nu came into our lives almost seven years ago. We don't see her often unless she needs something. But let me be clear. I'm *not* here for her. I'm here for *you*."

"I don't need anyone," she muttered, and tried to walk around him. Eddie blocked her again, and she looked at him with a great deal of wariness. That stung, but he buried it, buried his heart, until he felt nothing when he met her distrustful gaze.

Almost nothing.

She was so pale, the shadows under her eyes very deep. But there was defiance there, too—and strength.

Her spine was straight. She would go through him if he didn't set her free.

"Leave me alone," she said.

He didn't bother arguing. Not directly.

"There were two women," he told her. "On the street, after the explosion. I think they were witches. Maybe even the *Cruor Venator*. They knew you were a dragon."

A profound stillness fell over her, and the fear returned to her eyes—along with terrible, haunting dread. He could *feel* her terror, and it was almost more than he could bear. Eddie burned to comfort her. All of him, burned. Being near her set the fire loose inside him in ways he did not understand. He had never felt this way about anyone.

"Describe them," she said, in a low, hoarse voice.

"One was tall, African-American, wearing a red leather jacket. She called herself Nikola. The other was named Betty. A little shorter, with long black hair and very pale skin."

"How much did they say to you?"

Eddie hesitated. "They wanted me to . . . carry you for them."

"And you didn't?"

"You seem surprised."

"I am. If they're who I think they are, you should have been too frightened to resist. That's what women like them can do. Scare you into submission."

"I was terrified," he told her. "I've never been so frightened. All they did was look at me, and I wanted to give up. But that's not the same thing as losing my mind."

Lyssa looked as though she wanted to disagree. "What'd you say to them?"

"I told them no. And then I got into a stolen car and drove us out of there."

"That's it?"

"Isn't that enough?"

"I . . ." Lyssa stopped, staring at him as if he was new and strange. "Thank you."

Eddie felt embarrassed. "They had been following you."

She closed her eyes . . . but when she looked again at Eddie, moments later, her gaze was clear and determined, and hard. "You resisted them. That will make you a target, too."

Cold armor slipped over his heart. The quiet place welcomed him, and all his fear slipped away.

"I know," he said.

She took a breath, blinking.

"Call me Lyssa," she said, and moved around him to the door.

Eddie exhaled, briefly closed his eyes, and followed her.

CHAPTER SEVEN

WALKING, breathing—and seeing straight—were all too difficult. Lyssa had to concentrate just to put one foot in front of the other, blinking hard as lights danced in her vision, and strange buzzing sounds filled her ears. Her lungs hurt. So did her throat, as though she had been screaming.

Her entire right arm felt as though it belonged to a different body. Her forearm was numb, but her fingers ached, and there was a spasm in her neck that made it difficult to turn her head.

All her symptoms were familiar. Losing control always weakened her.

She'd never experienced the aftermath with witnesses, though. Just huddled underground, in some alley, or beneath a bridge. Alone. Waiting out her body. Waiting for her life to change.

She would have lost her life if it hadn't been for him.

Right now . . . she'd be cut open, bleeding out. Bleeding, slowly . . . because the *Cruor Venator* would want to make *her* death last.

Well. The bitch hadn't won yet.

Eddie walked behind her: a slow-burning fire, warm

against her back. Tall, lanky, with a quiet grace that seemed to flow around her each time he drew near.

He looked like hell, though. Covered in soot, his clothes charred and ragged. Her fault. Her weakness. His eyes were even darker than she remembered, intense and thoughtful, and worried.

Of course he is worried, whispered a familiar voice in her head, the voice of her instincts, the voice of her dragon, a voice that she had not heard so clearly in years. *He is worried about* you.

That's ridiculous, Lyssa replied. *He doesn't know me. I'm a job to him.*

No, you are not. The dragon sounded affronted. *Do you not trust me to tell you the truth?*

You're delusional.

I am right. You are in his blood. Just as he is in yours. You have found your mate.

Lyssa's left knee buckled. Eddie caught her arm before she went down.

"Excuse me," he muttered, with an oddly disgruntled politeness. "I need to . . ."

He stopped talking, then, and slid his arm around her waist. She froze. Maybe he did, too. He had touched her like this earlier, and it had felt like being anchored by a mountain: unyielding and powerful. It had stolen her breath away.

She rarely touched people. Habit, instinct, circumstances. So few people were familiar enough to her to even *be* touched, casually or not. The simple contact that most took for granted just didn't exist for her.

So when Eddie put his hands on her for a second time, it was weird and wonderful, and frightening. Even through the oversized jacket, she felt his hard strength . . . and for one moment, she let herself imagine resting in that strength, unafraid.

Lyssa tried pushing him away. "This isn't safe. The last time we touched . . ."

The last time, when I tried to kill you . . .

Her hand, at his throat . . . squeezing . . .

I can't be trusted.

Suddenly, the only thing holding her up was Eddie's arm around her.

"Don't think about that," he said, as if he could read her mind. His voice moved through her, into her blood. "It doesn't matter. Let whatever you're feeling, right now, wash over you. Feel it, put it away. Box it up where it can't touch you."

What she felt was despair. "Boxing up your emotions only delays the inevitable."

"It's control," he countered.

"If you can't control yourself when you're at your worst, then you don't have control." Lyssa pulled at his arm, and this time he let go. Her left leg barely held. All her limbs felt like Jell-O. So did her heart.

Eddie stood back from her, his eyes so dark.

She leaned against the wall, exhausted. "I'm sorry. About what I did to you today."

"You were afraid."

"That's no excuse." Lyssa heard movement below them, near the stairs at the end of the hall. The sound of someone large, approaching slowly. She tried to catch a scent, but all she could smell was the jacket wrapped around her, with its warm dark notes that were masculine and Eddie.

She pushed away from the wall. "I need to go."

"No. You're safe here."

A bitter laugh escaped her. "With the *Cruor Venator* in this city, no one should be near me. If they've been following me . . ."

Her voice choked off with dismay. She couldn't

imagine how they had been following her, but if they
had . . . then she might have led them straight to the
home of a gargoyle.

"Wait," he said, but she had already turned and was
hurrying as best she could down the hall. Each step
unsteady, the lights in her eyes dancing brighter, hotter.
Her blood, which had been cool upon waking, warmed
even more. Fire, filling her. Fire, rising beneath her
skin.

Because of Eddie. All that fire, reaching *for* him.

Don't turn around, she told herself, feeling him
right behind her. *Don't turn around to look at him.*

Even though she wanted to, more than anything. The
compulsion unnerved her. So did her dragon's words,
still rattling around her head. Crazy words. No way she
was right. Like hell. That big lizard was insane.

Lyssa, however, had to stop at the top of the stairs . . .
and she let go of the jacket just long enough to brace
herself against the rail.

A gargoyle stood on the stairs in front of her. No illusion to see through, this time.

Her mouth went dry. He was huge. Almost seven
feet tall, with silver skin and broad, thick muscles that
rippled over his long, powerful limbs. Horns protruded
from his hair, and leathery wings draped over his
shoulders. He wore cutoff jeans and held a giant mug
of some steaming hot liquid.

They stared at each other. Lyssa didn't miss the
flicker of unease in his eyes.

"Wow," he rumbled. "Okay, you're up."

"Lannes," Eddie said, behind her. "Meet Lyssa."

"I . . ." she began, and for some reason tears sprang
to her eyes. "I need to get out of here."

Behind her, Eddie made a frustrated sound, and

she finally let herself look at him. He stood there, skin shadowed with soot, raking one hand through his hair until it stood up—and the only thing keeping him from looking like some dark Sidhe was the curve of his ears.

"Don't say it," Lyssa said hoarsely, as a deep ache burned through her entire right arm. "Let me go. Before you make yourselves targets." She turned to face the gargoyle, who watched her with a frown. "Both of you, get out of this city."

Eddie stepped in close. "I would love to."

Her cheeks reddened, and she backed away from him. "What's the problem, then?"

He gave her a faint, unbearably sweet, smile. "You have my coat."

She stared at him. The gargoyle let out a small, muffled grunt that sounded suspiciously like a laugh.

"Here," he said, taking another step and holding out the steaming mug. "I made you tea."

Those tears were coming shockingly close to burning up her eyes. "You're both idiots."

Eddie arched his brow, and the gargoyle sighed. "You sound like my wife. Please, take this."

Lyssa took the mug, reluctantly. She had to let go of the jacket to do so, and instinctively sloped her shoulders, trying to keep them from seeing her right arm, folded over her stomach. Stupid, yes. They had to have already seen it. But old habits died hard.

The tea was dark and smelled good. The gargoyle stepped back when she took the mug and rubbed his clawed hands together. Uneasy, she thought. Eddie joined her at the top of the stairs and leaned against the opposite wall.

It got very quiet, then. All three of them, just standing there. Both men, watching her.

Lyssa sipped the tea, suddenly shy, and uncomfortable. "I wish you both wouldn't stare."

Eddie's mouth softened. The gargoyle grunted. "I pulled some of my wife's clothes from the dryer. When you're ready to change, come down and get them. There's a bathroom down here, too, with a shower. Feel free to use it."

He turned before she could thank him and walked back down the stairs, silent and graceful, despite his size. The tips of his caped wings trailed against the steps. Lyssa watched him go, feeling as though she were losing her mind.

"I'm losing my mind," she said.

"I felt like that the first time I met his brother," said Eddie quietly. "I never get tired of feeling surprised."

"Surprises are dangerous." Lyssa walked down the stairs, leaning hard on the rail. "I don't like them."

He followed her. "I'm not sorry I found you."

Lyssa wanted to say, *I am, you should be, I wish we'd never met,* but when she opened her mouth, those words wouldn't come out. Apparently, there were some lies she just couldn't tell.

At the bottom of the stairs, she heard a television— the quick sharp tones of a news report. Dread filled her. She went still, staring down the hall.

Eddie pushed past her. "I'll tell Lannes to turn it off."

"No." Lyssa almost reached for him with her right hand, and that shocked her enough into silence. Her right hand, which she hadn't shown another human being for ten years . . . coming out into plain sight as if it were the most natural thing in the world.

She held her hand against her stomach. "I want to listen."

Eddie regarded her a moment, then stepped aside.
When she tried to pass him, though, his fingers grazed
her arm. A tingling shock rolled through her, a powerful awareness of him.

"Lyssa. Whatever you see in there—"

"—is my fault," she interrupted, and his hand slid
fully around her arm, holding her still.

"Look at me," he said in a soft, firm, voice.

She did so, reluctantly. It was very difficult to meet
his gaze. As though she were dreaming again—only
this was real. *He* was real. He looked at her with those
knowing eyes, and it was as though he could see right
through her.

"You're not alone," he said. "Whatever happens, remember that."

Of all the things he could have said to her, that was
the most devastating. It made her feel more alone than
ever, and tears—those damned tears—burned her
eyes, again. She never cried. Never, not in years.

Today, it seemed that parts of her were grieving
whether or not she wanted them to.

Lyssa ducked her head. Eddie's fingers brushed the
edge of her jaw. She flinched, and he made a soft sound
between his teeth.

"Don't," he said. "I'm just wiping off some soot."

His thumb brushed her cheek, and the fire inside her
responded, lighting up her heart like some hidden sun.
With it, she felt a terrible ache that was another kind of
loneliness.

Lyssa had never been touched by a man she wanted.

Actually, "want" was too cheap a word. Every part
of her felt inexplicably, inexorably, *tugged* toward this
man. The attraction was primal, elemental—utterly
beyond her comprehension. She would have blamed

witchcraft if she were susceptible to that sort of thing, but in this case, all she could call it was *insanity*.

She didn't know him. She didn't want to know him. Yes, he had saved her life. She might not have been conscious, but she could smell a lie—and he was telling the truth about those two women. *Two* women. Just the right number. Exactly what the *Cruor Venator* would use.

No, she thought. *No. I can't want this man. Not him, not anyone. I shouldn't even have friends.*

Not Jimmy. Not Estefan. Not anyone who could get hurt because of her.

Lyssa pulled away from him. "Stop. Just . . . stop."

Eddie lowered his hand. "I'm sorry."

"No, I . . ." Regret hit her, as did pain—flowing through her right arm. Bad, this time, a hard spasm that made hand curl into a trembling fist. She sucked in her breath, wincing.

"Lyssa," said Eddie, with concern.

She shook her head at him and walked down the hall, holding herself strained and rigid. The television was loud.

" . . . no word on what caused the explosion, and eyewitness reports are conflicted. Some have indicated that it might be the work of suicide bombers, but we've received no confirmation . . ."

Lyssa walked into a brightly lit kitchen: white walls and counters, and a white stone floor covered in rag rugs. Other splashes of color came from bowls of oranges and grapes, and several potted geraniums. A cozy, elegant space. She wished it were hers, to curl up in, and read, and pretend the world outside didn't exist.

The gargoyle perched on a heavy oak stool made from solid rough-hewn timber. A giant mug of tea was

in front of him, along with a novel that had the words
DEATH and LUST on the cover.

A small television was set to a news channel that
showed overhead aerial shots of firemen putting out
burning cars, and ambulances parked on the outskirts
of a blast zone: a blackened, charred, scorched-earth
circle that made the sidewalk look like the heart of a
meteor strike.

Lyssa's heart stopped. A stool pressed against her
legs. Eddie gestured for her to sit down.

She did, then stood again. Anxious, miserable, horrified. Too many emotions boiling inside her—chief
amongst them, fear.

"Fatalities?" she whispered.

Lannes watched her carefully and hit the mute
button on the remote. Beautiful silence filled the
kitchen.

"Some broken bones. No one died, or will die.
That's been confirmed about a million times in the past
fifteen minutes."

"When I look at that damage, I can't believe it."
Lyssa sat down again. Her jeans were half-burned,
her knees sticking out. Seeing them made her think of
when she was a kid, and for one agonizing moment,
she let herself imagine what her parents would have
said about this.

Wow, her dad might have told her. *Impressive.*

Lyssa sought out Eddie and found him leaning
against the kitchen counter, very still and quiet, watching her with those dark eyes.

"It's not just the *Cruor Venator,*" she told him,
wincing when her voice broke. "I have to get out of
here before something like *that* happens again. I'm not
safe."

Lannes straightened. "Wait, I thought . . ."

Eddie cleared his throat. The gargoyle blinked and shut his mouth.

Lyssa frowned. "What? You thought what?"

Lannes hesitated. "Well, I thought *he* caused . . ."

He didn't finish. Eddie glared at him. "Where are the clothes you promised?"

The gargoyle's wings shifted uncomfortably. "Er, bathroom. Down the hall."

Lyssa stood and walked from the kitchen. She glimpsed a bathroom, door half-closed.

Eddie caught up with her. "Lyssa."

Heat flared, wild beneath her skin. "Why did he think you caused the fire?"

"He assumed. I let him."

"Why?"

Eddie grimaced. "I don't know. I was trying to protect you."

Her heart did a funny little jump. "You didn't need to do that."

"I know."

Lyssa stopped by the bathroom door and made the mistake of looking at him. He didn't appear any different than he had moments before—still scruffy, covered in soot—so handsome dirty, she couldn't imagine how good he'd look clean. But it was his eyes that drew her in. They were her weakness.

His soul was in his eyes. And what Lyssa saw in his soul was mystery, and pain, and shadow. In her dreams, she had never seen such emotions in his eyes: just determination and a dangerous resolve.

He hurts, whispered the dragon. *Like you, his heart has nowhere to fall.*

You could fall together.

Lyssa blinked, swaying. Eddie seemed to sway with her—or maybe that was her imagination.

You are not alone, said the dragon.

"You," she began, but her voice was hoarse, and she had to stop to wet her lips. "You lose control of your . . . fire?"

Regret filled his eyes. "Yes."

"Have you ever hurt anyone?"

"Yes," he said again, and the pain in that one word hurt worse than it should have. She ached to touch him—but he stood so still, and so did she, her right hand clenched in a fist against her stomach, the other white-knuckled as she held his jacket closed.

"I'm sorry," she told him, and found herself adding, "I've hurt people. I didn't mean to, but the possibility I might do it again . . . frightens me . . . more than anything."

"It's the same fear I live with." Eddie hesitated. "But you don't have to be afraid with me."

The truth of that was almost too much to believe—and heartbreaking. He was immune to her fire. She was immune to his. Something she had never dared imagine.

But there were other things to fear . . . that he most certainly would *not* be safe from.

Lyssa pulled away, reluctantly. Warmth faded. Cold crept in. An insidious, bone-deep chill that made her feel as though she had stepped from a warm fire into the old Montana winter, with its hollow winds and ice.

Eddie made a small sound deep in his throat, like pain. It sounded like the same pain she felt, putting distance between them. As though she were stretching some part of her heart too tight—and it might snap.

She was afraid to look into his eyes. Gaze down,

she turned and entered the bathroom. A small part of her hoped he would reach out and stop her . . . but he didn't. She should have been happy for that. Happy to turn the tide on whatever she was feeling.

He was a stranger. She did not know him. Whatever *this* was in her heart . . . it couldn't be real. It just couldn't. She might believe in magic, but not . . . trust at first sight. Or instant, devastating hunger for another human being.

But when the bathroom door was closed behind her, and she gazed at her reflection in the mirror, all she saw was a shadow. The soot didn't matter, or her dirty hair, or the scrape along her jaw.

Just her eyes. Haunted, red-rimmed with unshed tears. Pained and lonely.

"Pathetic," she whispered. "Toughen up, kid. Be tough."

Deep breath. Jaw set. She could do this. Ten years, she'd been doing this. Now was no different.

So why have you not run? whispered the dragon. *Do not deceive yourself, sister.*

Go back to sleep, thought Lyssa. *I liked you better when you were just a feeling.*

I have been asleep too long. You need me now. You need him.

I don't even know *him.*

A pity you are too much of a coward to try.

Lyssa exhaled sharply and spun away from the mirror.

The bathroom was small, white, and very clean. A white basket had been placed on the edge of the tub. Inside were clothes: faded jeans and an ivory-colored cable-knit sweater that was oversized and soft. Socks, underwear . . . and a scarf. A pair of gloves.

She stared at the gloves, then, carefully, shrugged off Eddie's jacket. She hung it on the hook that was on the bathroom door, then stripped off her clothes and placed them in the small garbage bin beneath the sink.

The shower felt tremendous. She slouched beneath the pounding stream, watching hot water hit her right arm and trail in rivers down her crimson scales. Golden claws glittered.

She imagined them around Eddie's throat, and still felt the power of that grip, as well as her inability to let go.

Power is dangerous, she remembered her mother saying. *Power over life and death is the most dangerous thing of all.*

Anyone could kill. But to turn that death into something more . . . to take a life and twist it into the otherworldly . . .

Made her sick.

"Nikola and Betty," she murmured. New women. New servants. As terrified as Lyssa was of having come so close to them, she wished she could have seen their faces.

How did they find me?

Eddie had found her through Estefan.

Lyssa shut off the water and dried herself— shivering the entire time. Not from the cold but from possibilities.

She needed to call Estefan and make certain he was okay. The older shape-shifter had been exceedingly kind to her, once upon a desperate time . . . and for years they had traded e-mails. Not about anything important. Just little stories about life, his family. He loved talking about his wife, who had started out as a waitress and now ran a little café with him in Florida.

That little bit of contact with another of her kind had saved her, in more ways than one. Just a few words, proving to her that someone . . . someone in the world . . . knew who she was. Her real name. Not Liz, but Lyssa.

Never mind that she hadn't told Estefan *everything*. Just the fact that he'd known she was a shape-shifter, a dragon, was enough to make her feel anchored.

How much did I tell him in my e-mails? How much have I let slip over the years?

Favorite coffee shops. That was how Eddie had found her. The fact she loved Columbus Circle and Central Park, which explained why he had been there, as well. She had told Estefan about her volunteer work at various homeless shelters.

Had she mentioned Jimmy and his mother? Yes. But not their address. Not where he went to school, or where Tina worked.

She hadn't told him she was living underground, but he could have probably guessed the general area of where she made a home, just from certain details about places she liked to go. On occasion, Lyssa had even mailed him gifts. Some of her paintings, or little trinkets that could only be found in New York. She'd gone to post offices on the other side of the city, but still . . .

I got sloppy, she decided. And Estefan, with his graying black hair, grizzled, toothy smile—and good heart— had finally gotten tired of just sitting idly by, something she had always known would happen, eventually.

Maybe, deep down, she had *wanted* it to happen. Perhaps she had *needed* for him to take the step she couldn't—and find her help.

Bullshit, thought Lyssa, angry with herself. *Bull. Shit.*

The *Cruor Venator* had found her. And the timing

of that . . . just when Estefan had contacted strangers to locate her in New York . . . was not lost on her.

The witch had never come so close to finding her. Not to her knowledge. Then again, she'd had no idea that two of her servants had been following her. For how long? Had they seen her with Jimmy?

"Fuck," she muttered. "I'm an idiot."

An idiot who had a choice to make. Except it wasn't much of a choice.

I can't run anymore.

It was time to fight and die. Or fight and kill.

And if she killed . . . if she did exactly what needed doing . . . what would she become then?

You'll hate being a coward more than you'll hate being dead, her mother had once said. *Fight your battles. Dig in your heels. What's a little pain?*

Pain leads to death, her father would have replied. *Don't give your daughter ideas.*

And yet, he had stayed and fought. He had dug in his heels. For his wife. For his daughter.

"Be tough," she told herself, staring into her eyes. "Do the right thing."

The problem was how? How, without losing everything?

One step at a time. One step.

Lyssa exhaled slowly and flexed her right hand. Her golden claws gleamed, each tip razor-sharp.

One step. One cut. And once she started . . .

She dressed quickly. Everything fit and felt good on her skin. The scarf was dark green and made of thick cashmere. She wrapped it around her throat, fussing with each fold until she was satisfied that it would hide her scales. Or reveal only enough to make someone think she had an elaborate tattoo.

The matching glove slid easily over her right hand.

Carefully, she took Eddie's charred jacket off the hook and slung the backpack over her shoulder.

She opened the bathroom door, listening.

It was quiet in the hall. On light feet, she made her way to the front entrance. Holding her breath, waiting for someone to stop her.

No one did. Until she opened the front door and stepped outside.

Eddie sat on the stoop. The tips of his hair were wet, the rest of him scrubbed clean. He was just as good-looking as she remembered—darkly handsome, lean—all man. He wore a black sweater that hugged his body and dark jeans that did the same.

He smiled. "Hey."

Lyssa blinked at him. "You're not coming with me."

"Of course not." He stood, slow and easy, and slung a backpack over his shoulder. "I'm going for a long walk."

"How pleasant for you."

"Very."

Her eyes narrowed. "Maybe you could tell Lannes good-bye for me? Thank him?"

"I already did. He just left to go pick up his wife."

Lyssa folded her arms over her chest and leaned against the rail. "Human, you said?"

"More or less." Eddie glanced down, scuffing his boot against the stone step. "Where are you headed?"

"I need to find a phone."

"You don't want to use the one inside?"

"I think . . . the least amount of attention I bring to you and your friends, the better. I don't want my call traced back here. Same with your cell," she said, as he began reaching into his pocket. "I'll find something."

Eddie nodded, looking away. "I'm sure you will."

She studied him, wondering again how he had managed to stand up to the servants of the *Cruor Venator.* No one did that. No one had that much courage, or conviction.

You did. Your parents.

Her mouth softened. "If I ask you not to follow me . . . will you listen?"

He gave her a gentle, sidelong, smile. "What do you think?"

I think you're going to break my heart.

CHAPTER EIGHT

THEY walked. Eddie didn't ask where they were going. Questions seemed to make her prickly. Just being with her now was a hard-won victory.

"You haven't told me much about the people you work for," she said, as they left Lannes's block-long neighborhood and crossed over to Leroy Street. "They sound . . . eclectic."

"I suppose they'd have to be. Some of them aren't human."

She glanced at him. "How many?"

"When I was first discovered seven years ago, there were none. Since then, we've found quite a few. Or they've found us."

"Found."

"Dirk & Steele looks for people who need help. Regular people. And people like you and me. We investigate crimes no one else can solve."

Lyssa frowned. "Dirk & Steele."

"You've heard of us?"

She shook her head. "No. Probably not."

"You don't sound so sure."

Lyssa gave him a dirty look, but that only made him

smile—and suddenly she was smiling, too, just a little. "I'm *incredibly* sure."

Eddie shoved his hands in his pockets and grinned. "Okay, then."

He took a risk as they crossed another intersection and bumped her gently with his elbow. She shot him a look, but he kept his gaze locked straight ahead. Pretending he didn't notice. That it was an accident.

Not every touch is a threat, he wanted to tell her. *Not every person is out to get you.*

A moment later, she bumped him, very lightly.

Eddie's gaze jerked sideways, but she was looking down at his jacket draped over her arm. With a surprising amount of reluctance, she held it out to him.

"Keep it," he told her. "I don't feel the cold."

"Neither do I."

They stared at each other a moment.

"When," began Lyssa, and hesitated. "When did you know? About . . . the fire?"

When I killed a man.

Eddie looked away. "There was an accident."

It was an accident that I killed the wrong man.

Matthew Swint's face swam into his memories, but he pushed it away as hard as he could.

"You?" he asked, inwardly wincing at how sharp his voice sounded.

"I was ten," she said, with particular softness. Eddie finally met her gaze and found her looking at him with knowing, gentle, eyes. His breath hitched in his throat, caught behind a hard, aching knot.

"I got angry," she continued. "I was a clumsy kid and tripped down a couple stairs. I set the whole thing on fire as payback."

"Really."

"I had a temper. My parents were not amused."

He smiled to himself and looked down at his feet. "You could talk to them, though. They weren't . . ."

"No," she finished for him. "They weren't frightened. What about . . ."

"My mother," he said. "No, she doesn't . . . know. I don't think she could handle it."

"Is she your only family?"

"I have a grandmother. I had a sister. But she's not . . ." Eddie couldn't say the words. He never spoke of Daphne.

"It's okay," said Lyssa.

He chanced another glance, but she was looking down at his jacket again. Her gaze lost, thoughtful.

"You could throw that out," he said.

She smoothed her gloved hand down the charred leather. "No. That would be a waste. You really don't want it?"

Eddie shook his head, and she gave him a shy, hesitant smile that made his heart stop.

And then he stopped breathing altogether when she slid his jacket on.

It should have meant nothing. She had worn his coat earlier. He'd had girlfriends who slipped on his shirts. Cute and fun.

But seeing Lyssa wear his clothing . . . even just his coat . . . now, out in broad daylight with the hint of a smile in her eyes . . .

He couldn't think of a word for it. "Sexy" wasn't good enough. A parade of naked women could have been marching up the street, and it would have meant nothing compared to seeing this woman lost in his jacket. The sight hit him with breathtaking force— making him suffer some primal, guttural, ache that he hadn't realized he was capable of feeling.

Not like *this*.

Her hair was still damp, tangled around those intelligent, golden eyes. Everything in her face was smart and alive—and tempered with the vulnerability that had haunted him from the first moment he had seen her in Columbus Circle.

"Thank you," she said.

He blinked at her, unsteady. "It looks better on you."

Lyssa's cheeks turned pink. Eddie wondered when she'd last been given a compliment. Not that he was much better. He suddenly felt awkward and shy—like he was eleven years old with Suzie Mitchell on the school field trip, helping her catch insects while hoping, maybe, if nothing else, she'd say, *I like you.*

It's better if she doesn't like you. It's better if you don't like her. Keep your distance.

Words that Lannes had spoken, right before leaving to pick up Lethe.

She's dangerous, said the gargoyle. *Maybe you can't feel it, but I can. There's something inside her that isn't right.*

In what way?

I don't know. I'm not wrong, though. If my brothers were here, they would tell you the same thing. But not as nicely.

So, what? I turn her loose? I don't help her?

Does she even need your help? Lannes had been so grim. *Let me put it another way, Eddie. I only get this itchy feeling around witches. Lyssa Andreanos is not just a shape-shifter.*

She's something else, Eddie told himself, watching Lyssa check her scarf and adjust it around her throat. Her movements were quick, delicate. An old habit, he thought. Always hiding. Even inside his jacket. She wanted to get lost in things, he thought. Like armor.

Lannes might not trust her, but Eddie's life depended on reading people. Instincts mattered. Small gestures. This woman was hiding something, that much was clear. Was she a danger to be around? Probably.

But did any of that make her a bad person?

She's no Matthew Swint.

Matthew Swint, who was free. Matthew Swint, who was free and knew that Eddie had killed his brother.

He exhaled and rubbed his forehead. "Why are the *Cruor Venator* hunting *you*? There must be other people in the world who would be just as attractive."

She shot him a look he'd seen in the mirror a time or two: afraid, angry, and desperate. But just as quickly as it appeared, the mask fell down, and all that raw emotion vanished—replaced by cold wariness.

"You should be more concerned about *how* they found me. I'm worried they might have gotten to Estefan."

Eddie looked away, chilled. Her friend *had* been murdered. A fact that had been burning a hole in his heart since first invoking the shape-shifter's name. He had wanted to tell her the truth from the beginning, but their few moments together hadn't seemed right.

How could he tell her now? How could he say the words?

The Cruor Venator killed your friend, and that's how they tracked you to this city. They drained his blood, skinned him, and ate his heart. But don't worry, because I'm here to take care of you.

Right. Like hell.

She'll blame herself. She'll run from me. I can't let her do that.

But silence stuck in his throat like a claw. It wasn't honest. She had a right to know.

"Why you, Lyssa?" he asked hoarsely, hating himself. "It sounds personal."

She was silent a moment. "They're hunting me because that's what they do. My . . . blood . . . is valuable to them."

"Because you're a dragon."

She made an exasperated sound. "Don't say that out loud."

"No one's around us."

"It doesn't matter. I don't like you knowing what I am."

"You know my secret."

"I don't know anything about you."

"You've been hiding for years. It's a hard habit to break. I understand that."

"No," she muttered, looking down at the sidewalk. "No, you don't. How could you?"

Because I killed a man when I was thirteen years old, then ran away from home.

Lyssa stumbled. Eddie caught her elbow, and heat roared up his arm. He let go, startled, and she gave him a haunted, troubled, look.

It was so quiet. Every sound, muted. Every car engine, every voice, dull in his ears. His beating heart was louder than it all.

"Why are you looking at me like that?" he whispered.

Lyssa let out her breath. "Like what?"

Like you heard what I thought.

Eddie backed away and shoved his hands in his pockets. "I left home after the first time I lost control of . . . of the fire. I was just a kid. I lived on the streets for years until it was safe enough for me to be around the people I cared about. So I know about hiding. About . . . holding back."

"You were homeless," she said.

"About as homeless as a person can be," he replied. "I think about it every day."

Lyssa swallowed hard and looked away. "Hard not to, isn't it?"

"You have some experience with the street?"

"You could say that. It was the only option for a long time." She spoke with particular brittleness and gave him a lingering look full of doubt. "You said Long Nu told you about the *Cruor Venator*."

"Some. Not enough." Eddie started walking again, needing to move, to focus on something other than her. "I asked Lannes to help me gather more information."

Lyssa matched his pace. "You shouldn't have. You'll make him a target. Maybe I did already, by being in his home."

Maybe, he thought. "I need to know what the *Cruor Venator* are. What they *do*."

Lyssa walked faster. "Witches have the blood of the fae in them. That's what gives them their power, diluted as it may be. Sometimes it doesn't even manifest, or if does, it can be mistaken for intuition or good luck."

Eddie stared. "I . . . the fae?"

"You know." She wiggled her fingers and raised her brow. "Faeries. Sidhe."

He had thought there was nothing left that could surprise him—but he was wrong. Crazy or not, though, it wasn't worth arguing over. Not after all the other strange things he'd seen in his life.

"So why does everyone act as though the *Cruor Venator* are different from other witches?"

"Because they're descended from a specific bloodline." Disgust twisted her mouth. "Not fae. Demon."

"No."

"Yes. If you don't believe me, that's fine. But—"

Eddie touched her arm, stopping her. "I was told the *Cruor Venator* haven't been seen in one hundred years. How come *you* know so much about them?"

Lyssa grimaced. "I don't want to talk about that."

"Can't you just answer the question?"

"No. I shouldn't even be here with you. I wasn't . . . thinking." Her voice was sharp, but he heard a hint of pain that was all too familiar. Before he could say anything, Lyssa walked into the street and hailed an approaching cab.

Eddie stepped in front of her. "Not without me."

She gave him a haunted look. "What is your problem?"

"You," he said, and grabbed the front of her jacket, pulling her close with gentle, firm, strength. Lyssa made a small sound of protest, staring at him with huge, troubled eyes. The cab slowed, then drove past.

"You," he said again, quieter.

Her hands rose to cover his, but she didn't try to free herself. Her touch was soft and warm, and a terrible prickling heat rose beneath his skin, behind his eyes. It scared him, but only because she slipped so easily behind the walls he'd worked hard to build. Years of keeping his heart quiet and calm, segregated from emotions that were too strong.

Because it wasn't safe. Fire reacted to the heart.

His heart reacted to her.

Her gaze flicked to his mouth, sending a bolt of hunger from his throat into his groin. Embarrassing, impossible to control. All he could do was keep his focus on her eyes, but if he looked at her delicate lips, the pale curve of her jaw . . .

"What do you want from me?" she whispered. "Why are you trying so hard for a complete stranger?"

A million reasons tumbled through his head. She was a job, it was the right thing to do . . . if only someone had done the same for him all those years ago . . .

But shining through those thoughts was the memory of seeing her across Columbus Circle—that first sight when he hadn't realized who she was, when *all* she was to him was a faceless, graceful woman—who had sparked a feeling of connection so powerful, so deep inside him, he could barely think about it, let alone try to describe it in words. He had wanted to take care of her, then. A complete stranger.

Now that he was face-to-face with her . . .

I don't care what Lannes says. I don't care.

"I need to do this," he told her, finding it difficult to say the words. "I don't think I could . . . live with myself . . . if I didn't make certain you're safe."

Uncertainty flickered in her eyes. Eddie forced his hands to loosen. "I don't expect you to understand that."

"Just like you don't understand the danger you're in, being near me?"

He gave her a crooked smile. "How many times are we going to have this conversation?"

Lyssa looked away, visibly swallowing.

Eddie let go of the jacket entirely though his fingers ached and felt stiff. "We could be on a plane in two hours."

Her gaze darted toward him. "I thought you were determined to stay here."

"Because of you."

"So if I leave, you'll forget about the *Cruor Venator*?"

He couldn't lie to her, not about that. Lyssa waited a heartbeat, then gave him a bitter smile.

"No, thanks," she said.

"Okay," he replied, watching her carefully. "Does that mean *you're* going after these witches?"

Again, she said nothing. Eddie sighed. "Fine. We go our separate ways. I'll stumble along until these witches find me, or I find them. And you can do the same."

"You're serious," she said.

"Yes."

"You're manipulating me. That's ridiculous."

"We don't have time to fight each other."

She took a deep breath. Both of them, watching the other. Standing so still as the leaves rustled on the trees, and cars drove past. Far away, sirens. Far away, laughter.

But here, between them, it was quiet.

Lyssa's mouth tightened. "The witches you encountered today are not the *Cruor Venator*. They're her servants. But if you thought *they* were frightening . . . if just their *presence* was terrifying . . . then keep in mind that whatever you feel around the true *Cruor Venator* will be a hundred times worse."

Eddie swallowed hard. "Understood."

"No," Lyssa said, with a hint of sadness. "You don't."

She looked away from him and took a deep breath. "Maybe I'll lose my nerve. Maybe I'll run again. But if I do leave New York with you . . . there are some things I need to do first. Or else I'll never be able to live with myself."

"Again?" he said. "Just how long have you been running from these people?"

"Ten years," she said, giving him a flat look. "Since the night my parents were murdered."

THEY WALKED TOWARD WASHINGTON SQUARE Park. Eddie didn't know the way, but Lyssa had no trouble navigating the streets. No one paid attention to them. New York University was close, and they could have been just another pair of college kids.

Few words passed between them. Lyssa hadn't elaborated about her parents and seemed uncomfortable having told him anything at all. Eddie understood her loss, which meant he knew better than to respond with anything more than a simple, "I'm sorry."

Because he *was* sorry. Sorrier than he could express in words.

Daphne, he thought, shivering as old memories filled him. Good and bad.

Lyssa glanced at him. "Are you okay?"

No, he wanted to tell her, but that one little word refused to crawl from his throat. Her problems were big enough without him turning into some emotional victim. Maybe it was old fashioned, but while he could—while he was able—he wanted to be her broad shoulder. Her guy she could depend on. Her wall.

Walls did not hurt. Walls didn't break.

Lyssa needed to feel safe with him. No matter what.

He focused on all the NYU banners hanging in the distance, and said the next thing that came to mind.

"Did you ever try going to school? All these years?"

Lyssa gave him a lingering look as though she knew he was changing the subject. Eddie's cheeks warmed, but instead of calling him out—she hunched deeper inside the charred leather jacket.

"No. I was home schooled, and then . . . later . . . I spent a lot of time in libraries. You can learn pretty much anything you need to, that way."

She sounded wistful. Eddie said, "That's how I survived. My formal education ended when I was thirteen. I never went back. Sometimes I wish I could have had that experience. High school. College."

"You still could," she said. "Maybe not high school . . . but this, college."

He looked at her, surprised. "Would you?"

Lyssa hesitated. "No. I have what I need. I've been . . . educated in my own way."

"Yeah," he said, remembering watching other kids with parents and money, and books—being less envious than sorry that he was not home, where he knew he would be welcome, and needed.

None of which would have made his thirteen-year-old self feel less awful, or frightened.

"After the things I've seen," he told her, "I'm not sure I could sit in a classroom. It might feel like the opposite of learning."

Lyssa gave him a gentle, wistful smile. "And yet."

"And yet," he agreed.

They passed in front of a small café. The door stood partially open. Eddie heard a radio blasting the news and slowed to a stop as a harried voice detailed the explosion off Lexington. A police source had confirmed that investigators were looking for evidence of suicide bombers—a man and woman seen just before the detonation. So far, however, their bodies had *not* been recovered.

"Didn't anyone see me carrying you away?" he asked, mostly to himself. "Or see me stealing that car, or speaking with Nikola and Betty?"

He didn't really expect a response, but Lyssa seemed to seriously contemplate those questions.

"Maybe not," she said. "If the *Cruor Venator*'s women wanted me—and, by extension, you—it would have been in their interest to obscure our presence."

"Like the illusion that Lannes casts on his body, except over a wider area?"

"Exactly."

"But how?"

She frowned. "You imagine and will it to be. It's not quite that simple, but that's the essence. All you need is the power to back up the desire."

"But there are limits."

"That depends."

Eddie's cell phone rang. Both of them flinched.

He checked the screen. The call was from his mother. Another kind of dread filled him. A million little nightmares.

When he answered, she didn't wait for him to say hello.

"I know this is a bad time," she said in a low voice that reminded him so much of his sister. "You're at work."

"It's okay," he said, as Lyssa looked down at her feet, pretending to give him privacy. "What's happened?"

She laughed, but it sounded like a sob. "Nothing new. I just needed to make sure you're okay. Now that . . . *he* . . . is free, I'm afraid . . . I think he might . . ."

"I know." Eddie bowed his head, staring at the scars on the back of his left hand. "I asked some friends to keep an eye on things. But . . . you be careful, okay? Doors locked. Security system on. Tell Grandma the same."

"Yes." She drew in a deep breath. "I'm sorry I did this to you, Edward."

"You didn't." Eddie closed his eyes. "I have to go. Call if you need anything. If it's an emergency, 911 first, then Roland. You have his number."

"Yes, and yes," she said, but with a trace of sadness—and perhaps, disappointment—that made him feel terrible. He was an awful son. He'd abandoned his mother after Daphne's murder, and even if his reasons were good . . . he'd never told her why. She had blamed herself for losing him. Blamed herself for bringing Matthew Swint into their lives.

Deep down, Eddie still blamed her, too.

Hanging up exhausted him. He stared at his phone, heartsore, helpless. What was he doing *here,* with Matthew Swint on the loose?

Lyssa said, quietly, "That was your mother?"

He glanced at her. Embarrassment flickered over her face. "Sorry. I didn't mean to eavesdrop."

He slipped his phone back into his pocket. "I know you must have . . . sharp ears."

"Too sharp, maybe." Lyssa gave him a hesitant look. "Is she okay?"

"Been better."

"She sounded scared."

"There's a man," began Eddie, but after that, he didn't know what else to say . . . how much to tell her. He wasn't even certain he *could* talk about Matthew Swint. Or his sister. The wound was too raw.

"There's a man," he repeated himself, hoping she would understand.

Lyssa gave him a long, thoughtful look. "That's the worst kind."

He swallowed hard and nodded.

Both of them stayed silent for the remainder of the walk. Eddie watched the city: neighborhoods that transformed from one block to another—gritty to chic, to sleek, then back again.

But the people never changed. Everyone walked fast, expressionless, lost in their own worlds. No one looked anyone else in the eye.

He studied them all, and noticed Lyssa doing the same: quick assessing glances that never stopped, never looked down. She was, he thought, completely aware of everything around her. Including him.

Only once did he get an odd feeling. A prickling at the back of his neck. He glanced around but didn't see anything out of the ordinary.

"So these women have been sent to retrieve you," he said, uneasy. "Why not the *Cruor Venator* herself?"

"She'll come eventually."

"That's it?"

Lyssa's silence went as deep as her eyes: reserved and thoughtful. "If you're looking for logic, don't. A *Cruor Venator* lives for death, but the slower the death, the better. The same is true when hunting. Prolonging the chase just means more pleasure in the end. Games are part of it."

"That's sick."

"Yes," she said, and there was no end to the pain he glimpsed in her eyes before she ducked her head, hair falling down around her face and obscuring her gaze.

He had no defense against that. His heart bled for her. But more than that, the mystery of *why* all this seemed so personal, haunted him.

Eddie reached out, very carefully, and grazed his fingertips against her gloved left hand. Lyssa's own fingers twitched, curling toward his. But just before she touched him, she pulled away and shoved her hand in the jacket pocket.

He let out his breath, slowly. "Lannes said he . . . sensed something different about you."

"Did he?" Her voice was strained. "I suppose it made him uncomfortable."

"His wife is a witch," he said, watching her flinch. "Or at least . . . she has that potential. Her family lives in this city, and they're definitely . . ."

"I get it," Lyssa said. "And since the gargoyle brought it up . . . no, I'm not a witch. Not exactly. I suppose I have . . . that potential, too. But it's nothing I'm interested in exploring."

"Why not?"

"Some powers aren't safe to want."

"Specifically?"

"You ask a lot of questions."

"Maybe you don't ask enough."

"Maybe I don't care. Maybe I just want to mind my own business and be on my way before anyone gets hurt."

"Or you get hurt," he said, unable to stop himself. "It's more convenient not to feel anything, isn't it?"

She gave him a sharp look. "Are you talking about yourself or me?"

"Fair enough." Eddie held up his hands as heat shimmered around his skin. "People are fragile. It's easier to be alone than worry all the time about hurting someone. But then one day you wake up, and you realize you've been alone for—"

"Ten years?" she said dryly.

"—a long time," he finished.

Her expression turned disgruntled. "I have friends."

"I know," Eddie said, suddenly regretting saying so much.

He never talked like this. He never asked this many questions. Like her, he minded his own business, except for when it involved his friends. And even then, he preferred to stay silent, to hang back and observe. To be the man everyone could depend on—without their needing to ask.

That had been all he needed . . . until now.

Lyssa stopped at a pay phone near the intersection

of West Fourth Street and MacDougal, on the southern tip of Washington Square Park. Beside them was a clean brick building covered in ivy and bordered by a tall wrought-iron fence. Eddie was pretty certain it was part of the NYU campus, given the university banners hanging from a similar-looking building across the street.

"Are you calling Estefan?" he asked, with dread.

"Yes," she said, searching through her backpack for change. "Did you ever talk with him?"

"No. All I saw were forwarded e-mails."

"E-mail is how we usually communicate."

"How did you meet?"

Lyssa suddenly looked uncomfortable. "It's a complicated story. I'm sure you're getting sick of hearing me use that word."

"You're a complicated woman. That's not something I mind."

She looked at him like maybe he was teasing her, but he was serious—and seriously dreading telling her about Estefan. He had to, though. Right now.

"Lyssa," he began, but her gaze sharpened, and she turned to stare at the park across the street. Eddie turned with her, on guard. His right hand twitched, fire at the tips of his fingers.

He studied the people at the intersection, but all he saw were several Asian girls wearing backpacks, and a man in a suit carrying a briefcase. A biker zipped past, and so did a man on rollerblades . . . but that was it. No one watched them. No sign of Betty or Nikola.

But if they were witches, not seeing them probably didn't mean much, anyway.

"What is it?" he asked quietly.

Lyssa tilted her head, and closed her eyes. "A scent. I smell . . ."

She stopped, and her eyes flew open, stark with surprise. Without another word, she started running.

"Dammit," Eddie muttered, chasing her.

Lyssa was fast, graceful, her feet barely touching the ground as she flew across the street, nearly getting clipped by a cab that swerved into another lane and laid on the horn. Eddie followed, heart in his throat, trying to keep track of everyone around them—anyone near *her* who could mean her harm.

She didn't run far. Just down the sidewalk that led into the park, then across the grass—straight to a slim woman resting on a blanket near some bushes.

Eddie thought at first she was sleeping, curled on her side. He saw a pierced brow and nose, and tight brown curls. Her dark skin held an ashen undertone, and the hollows under her eyes and in her cheeks were so deep she might have been a cadaver.

Maybe she was, Eddie realized.

The blanket beneath her was stained red with blood.

CHAPTER NINE

IF the wind had been blowing in another direction, Lyssa would never have smelled the blood.

But she did, and because it was blood she paid attention—and smelled someone familiar.

Mandy. One of the women Jimmy had said was missing.

Lyssa didn't know her well. A crazy, loud girl, who liked to dance in the middle of Grand Central, and hold signs advertising FREE HUGS. She and her girl-friend, Flo, were inseparable—homeless, sometimes-prostitutes—addicted to heroin.

She dropped to her knees, trying not to panic—and reached out to touch the young woman's face. Her skin was cool, but she was breathing.

The blood was on her clothes. Mandy wore a green army jacket that was three sizes too large, and her clothes beneath were all black. Lyssa had to lean in to see the bloodstains that covered her chest, and reached carefully beneath the girl's jacket to give them an experimental touch. Some of the blood had dried, hardening the sweater.

But most of the blood was wet. The blanket beneath,

soaked through and stained. That metallic scent washed over her, making sweat break out against her back and between her breasts. When she swallowed, her throat burned. When she breathed, her lungs were hot.

"Mandy," she whispered harshly.

Eyelids fluttered. Cracked lips moved. Lyssa listened hard, but all she heard was a quiet hiss of breath.

There was no way to know how long Mandy had been here, but it was long enough to come close to death—without anyone's noticing.

No one ever noticed. No one ever looked. It was why Lyssa had come to this city.

But I don't want to die alone. Alone, in a crowd. Invisible.

Eddie crouched beside her, already on his cell phone. She listened to him speak with a 911 operator, his words less important than the fact that he was there, with her.

"Liz," breathed the young woman. "S'you?"

Hearing Mandy's voice filled Lyssa with terrible relief, though it was short-lived. "It's me."

She let out a strained, shaky, sigh. "God, Flo."

"Flo isn't here."

"No. Gotta get to . . . Flo. 'Fore they kill her." Her face crumpled, tears sliding down her cheeks. "They took me . . . away from her. I tried to . . . to fight. Didn't wan' 'em to make me . . . leave."

Lyssa leaned back, Mandy's grief tearing into her like a knife. She had thought similar words over the past ten years.

I should have stayed and fought. I shouldn't have run.

Heat exploded behind her eyes, but it's wasn't fire. Just tears. Lyssa felt twelve years old again, dying of guilt. She would never forgive herself for that night. Never.

She touched Mandy's hand, wanting to comfort her.

A connection formed, unexpected and instantaneous: a split-second bond, electric hot, tossing her into a mindscape that resembled a frenzied dance floor crowded with memories, fragmented and frozen between rapid pulses of light.

Flo.

Flo, with her ruddy skin and wild blond hair . . . those lips she puckers to blow kisses, everywhere, at anyone . . .

Flo. Smiling.

Flo. Screaming.

Chains. Blood. Sobs.

A knife glints. Wicked blade.

Black blade. Curved. Obsidian.

Etched with runes.

Pain seared: a lick of fire in her head, above her heart. Sharp as a stab.

The connection snapped.

Lyssa tilted, breathless. Floating, flying, falling. Part of her was still in Mandy's mind, listening to Flo scream. Staring at the blade.

She slumped forward, clutching her chest. Blinking hard. Heart pounding with frightening irregularity. The grass came back into view, but it was blurry. Lyssa blinked, and tears spilled from her eyes. She hardly noticed. All she could think about was the obsidian blade.

The weapon of a *Cruor Venator.*

Someone touched her shoulders. Lyssa recoiled, but it was only Eddie. His scent washed over her: a mix of woodsmoke and sandalwood.

It had a strange effect on her. His scent reminded

her too much of warm winter nights in front of a fire. Nights holding hot chocolate and listening to music. Nights that had been home, long ago and far away.

Lyssa rubbed a shaking hand over her mouth, but the scent of blood was so strong on her fingers that she reeled. Eddie immediately pulled her against his chest, and the contact was warm in the most healing way possible, safe and solid, and more real than the grass beneath her.

"Breathe," he whispered, covering her hand with his, and squeezing. "Close your eyes, listen to my voice, and breathe."

She shivered. "Don't worry about me. Just Mandy."

Eddie's hand tightened. "You know this woman."

"Yes," she whispered. "She went missing. A lot of homeless women have been disappearing."

"Was it the *Cruor Venator* who hurt her?"

An obsidian knife flashed through her memories. Mandy's memory . . . and her own, ten years old and still fresh in mind.

Lyssa nodded, as more tears slid down her cheeks. Embarrassed, she tried scrubbing her face with the back of her hand, but it did no good. More tears took their place. It was horrifying.

"Hold on," Eddie said, and reached into his backpack. He pulled out a rumpled tissue and held it out to her. "Here. It's clean."

Lyssa was more surprised by the thoughtfulness of the offer than the possibility the tissue might be dirty. She looked at him, and the kindness in his eyes stole her breath away. No pity. Just compassion and concern.

He pushed the tissue into her hand, and she pressed it to her nose.

"Thank you," she whispered, unable to tear her gaze from his. "Is an ambulance coming?"

"Listen," he said, and just like that, she heard the wail of a siren.

She looked around the park. Mandy lay ten feet off the sidewalk, just one more homeless woman amongst thousands—making her invisible. No magic needed to hide a dying woman in plain sight.

Some people walking down the sidewalk were watching them now, but no one stopped. Their scents filled her nose—body odor and perfume, pizza grease, halitosis. Nothing slick or dangerous.

Her skin prickled, though. As a child, she'd watched a mountain lion stalk a young elk, and that poor nervous creature had sensed the blow long before it happened. It just hadn't known from what direction it would come.

I've been waiting ten years for the knife to fall.

Lyssa should have already been running. This was a trap. Or a message. A homeless drug addict was not the type of person a *Cruor Venator* would choose to kill. And there was no way Mandy could have escaped the witch . . . unless she was let go on purpose.

But I hardly know her. Why would she be a target?

What did that mean for Jimmy and his mother?

And who would stop the *Cruor Venator* and her women this time?

Who, she said to herself, dreading what she already knew. *Who else?*

"You know something," said Eddie.

She shook her head, but only because panic and anger had lodged in her throat, cutting off her voice. The ambulance sirens were closer, and she struggled to her feet—the fire inside her so hot, her skin prickled.

"I need to get out of here," she muttered, staring at Mandy's ashen face. The woman was barely conscious, making soft moaning sounds as her fingers twitched. Blood seeped beneath her on the blanket, inviting Lyssa to make another, different connection.

She backed away. Eddie stood with her. "We need to wait for the ambulance."

A frustrated growl left her throat—followed by the tremendous urge to swing her fists at a stationary target. "I can't. I barely knew this woman, but if they got to *her* . . ."

Mandy was a small target. The next one? Closer, more important.

"There's a little boy," Lyssa whispered to Eddie. "The one who was with me earlier today."

He stared at her for one second, then looked away at the sidewalk. Coiled, intense, his eyes focusing on a power-walking woman in yoga gear, with a tight face, glossy hair, and lips that were plumper than her breasts.

"Ma'am!" he shouted, with a hard authority that Lyssa had only ever associated with the police. The woman responded immediately, teetering to a stop and giving him a startled look.

Eddie didn't give her time to ask a question. Lyssa watched, impressed, as he strode to her and pointed at Mandy.

"That woman has been attacked. An ambulance is coming, but my partner and I have to direct the EMTs to this spot. I need you to stay with her until they arrive."

Her expression crumpled with uncertainty. "I don't—"

"Ma'am," Eddie interrupted. "Do it. Now."

She blinked at him, then crossed the grass to Mandy, rubbing her palms over her thighs—uneasy, still startled, acting on automatic pilot. Lyssa crouched again beside Mandy, whose breathing was shallow, her eyes closed tight.

"You're safe," she told her, hoping that was true. "It'll be okay."

"Lyssa," Eddie said, tugging gently on her shoulder.

The power walker didn't watch them go. She kept rubbing her hands, standing beside Mandy and staring down at all that blood with horror and consternation.

Sirens wailed with ear-screeching strength. The ambulance had arrived. Eddie and Lyssa jogged to the intersection and met one of the EMTs: a burly man with a beard, and a tattoo on his neck.

"What happened?" he barked, slinging gear over his shoulder.

"I think a woman was stabbed." Lyssa pointed at the pathway into the park. "Someone is with her now."

The EMT grunted and helped his partner, a young woman, grab a stretcher from the back of the ambulance. More sirens filled the air. The police would be next.

Lyssa and Eddie looked at each other and started walking.

"YOU MENTIONED THAT OTHER HOMELESS WOMEN have been disappearing," Eddie said, as a police cruiser sped past them, lights blazing. "For how long?"

It took Lyssa a moment to find her voice. "Couple weeks. I only found out today. I didn't even know Mandy was gone. Like I said, we're not close."

"Then they weren't targeted because of you."

Lyssa touched her scarf, pained. "How do you know?"

"You weren't aware they were missing until today." Eddie glanced at her, his eyes dark and serious.

"What's the point of a message if the intended recipient isn't even aware there's one in the first place?"

He had a point, but it didn't make her feel any better. "Finding Mandy in that park was not a coincidence."

"So they carry an injured women with them *all the time,* just waiting for the right moment to spring her on you?"

Lyssa blew out her breath, frustrated. "I don't know."

"They must have a van," he muttered to himself. "Especially if they're kidnapping women off the street."

"That part doesn't make sense," she admitted. "Mandy is a heroin addict. Not the kind of person the *Cruor Venator* would kill."

"She only goes for doctors and lawyers?" A hint of sarcasm touched his voice.

Lyssa shrugged and nodded. "Something along those lines, yes. And kidnapping? Not her style, either. She likes to play games and pretend she's dignified. She'll lure the victim—or stalk, attack, and murder on-site. But throwing girls into a van . . . is beneath her ego."

Eddie stared. Lyssa's cheeks warmed. She had said too much, again. And the way he looked at her . . .

She couldn't hide from his eyes. First in her dreams, and now here in broad daylight. If running from the *Cruor Venator* had been difficult all these years . . . running from this man's gaze would be impossible.

No doubt, too, he was going to ask, *again,* why she knew so many details about a race of witches that hardly existed anymore. What was she going to tell him this time? Too complicated? Shut up? Go away?

Go away, she thought. *That would be the smart thing.*

But the idea of speaking those words out loud filled

her with a shocking amount of pain—as though part of her heart would be ripped to pieces. How the hell had that happened? Why him?

Because he is the right one, whispered the dragon. *Have faith, for once.*

Faith. What was that, again?

But Eddie surprised her.

"Okay," he said. "What made you think, initially, that Mandy had been hurt by the *Cruor Venator*?"

Lyssa hesitated. "It'll sound hokey."

His mouth twitched. "Try me."

"I had a vision when I touched her. I saw the blade of a *Cruor Venator* cutting her body."

Amazingly, he seemed to take her seriously. "Did you see anything else?"

"Her friend, Flo."

Eddie was silent a moment. "Let's say all these homeless women *have* been taken by the *Cruor Venator,* and not some other crazy person. If they aren't the typical target, then why bother?"

Lyssa said the first thing that came to mind. "Training."

"What?"

She felt ill having to explain. "People aren't born knowing how to kill."

"That's disgusting." Eddie looked away, swallowing hard. "But if you're right . . . is she training more like Betty and Nikola?"

"I'd be shocked if she was."

"But?"

"But it's possible," she admitted reluctantly. "I don't know why she'd want to. A *Cruor Venator* doesn't keep more than she can control."

Eddie was silent a moment. "I was told they . . .

absorb things . . . from blood. If one of them . . . tasted Mandy . . . could your connection to the woman have been found that way?"

"Maybe. I don't know. Something stinks about this."

"Besides the obvious?"

Besides everything, she wanted to say. *Including what I should do about you.*

Lyssa had never let anyone slip under her guard as quickly as Eddie. Here she was, telling him things no one else knew . . . revealing her problems, her *life* . . . letting him *risk* his life . . . and she barely knew him.

She just . . . couldn't help herself. The need to share with him, to *be* with him, was overwhelming. Beyond instinct. Natural as breathing.

Could she even trust him?

Yes, whispered the dragon. *I would kill him for you if his heart meant to hurt yours.*

No, Lyssa replied. *I wouldn't let you.*

As if you could prevent me, it replied, with such chilling certainty she had to stop walking and hold her head.

"What is it?" asked Eddie. His voice was low, thick with concern, and sent an aching rumble through her heart.

"You ever feel like you have a split personality inside your head?" Lyssa tried to make it sound like a joke, but he gave her an odd look that made her feel embarrassed. "Never mind."

Eddie's mouth softened into a faint smile. He took her right hand in his, holding it loose and warm—and then, as if that wasn't shock enough, he kissed her palm—with breathtaking gentleness.

The heat of his touch soaked through the glove. Muscles she hadn't even known were tense seemed to relax, and a tight knot buried deep in her chest unwound, just a little. No one had ever held that deformed hand of hers. It felt strange and good. Too good.

"I know what you're talking about," he said.

Hard to breathe. Lyssa felt naked in his gaze but anchored, too. More safe, more *accepted,* than she had in years—right now, in this moment. She didn't know if that made her a fool or naïve—or very lucky—but it scared her enough that she pulled her hand free and backed away from him.

"Lyssa," said Eddie, but she stepped out in the street in front of an oncoming cab. The driver barely stopped in time and leaned on his horn. Lyssa ignored his ire, slid around to the side, and got in. So did Eddie before she could shut the door.

"What are you doing?" he said to her, angry. "Running again?"

"Screw you," she replied, even though he was right. "Get out of this cab."

"No," he snapped. "Forget about that. And next time, try not to get yourself run over."

"Hey," said the driver, flicking his fingers at them. "Take it outside or give me a place to drive. I don't got all day."

Neither did she, unfortunately. Eddie stared at her challengingly, and she shook her head, heart aching as she gave the cab driver the address. He accelerated so hard she slammed backward.

"Women," he muttered, and turned up the volume on his radio—and kept turning it up—until reggae music seemed to flood every molecule of her body with the not-so-relaxing urge to claw through the divider and rip apart that radio. Her eardrums vibrated. So did her teeth.

Eddie grimaced. Moments later, she heard a loud click, and the radio quit.

The driver said, "Shit, man."

"Check your wiring," he told him. "Sometimes it burns."

Lyssa stared, and he gave her a disarming smile that made all her anger at him feel petty and misplaced.

"Well, it does," he said.

She shook her head, planting her feet on the floor, so they wouldn't start bouncing nervously. "I need your phone."

"You're using it now, but not earlier?"

"Circumstances have changed. I don't have time for pay phones, and it's clear I'm not protecting anyone by trying."

"So who are you calling?" Eddie gave her a surprisingly wary look as he placed the phone in her hand.

"Jimmy," she said, wondering why he seemed relieved by her answer. "The little boy."

She dialed his number, but the phone rang and rang. He didn't pick up.

Icky probably needed a walk.

Maybe he went back to school.

He's in the bathroom.

Taking a nap.

"If that kid's not hurt, I'm killing him," she muttered, trying again—still receiving no answer. There was no machine to leave a message. The phone rang twenty times before the call was disconnected.

"Jimmy seemed like a good kid," Eddie said. "What little I saw of him."

"The best. I've known him and his mother for about a year." A year too long if this ended badly.

But what was I going to do? Turn my back on them?

Pretend they didn't need my help and protection in that underground hellhole? I couldn't do that.

There are some things you can't run from, she thought.

I wouldn't want to, she realized.

Lyssa made another call and suffered another endless round of rings, each one driving into her skull with the same hammering force of that reggae music—only much worse. Eddie watched her with concern but kept silent. Just there. Strong, and there. Which she appreciated more than she cared to admit.

She tried Jimmy's mother, who worked at an upscale deli in Midtown.

"Tina's not back from her lunch break," said the girl who answered. "Our boss is *pissed.*"

"How long has she been gone?"

"An hour. Bitch," she murmured, and then, louder: "If you get hold of her, tell her she better get her ass back, like now. Dishes are piling up, and the bathroom needs new toilet paper."

Lyssa hung up, her head pounding. "Dammit."

"Talk to me," Eddie said.

She glanced at the cab driver, but he was on his cell phone, making an angry speech about his radio.

"Jimmy's mother isn't back from lunch. That's not like her. She takes her job too seriously. Something's wrong. If the *Cruor Venator* got them . . ."

Her voice choked off, her throat closing up as if actual fingers were squeezing the life out of her. Lyssa clawed at her scarf, uncaring if anyone saw her dragon scales. She couldn't breathe.

Eddie reached out and wrapped his hand around her wrist, stilling her. No words. Just his touch. Heat seeped through her skin, deeper into muscle, bone—

soothing, embracing, a sweet fire that once again made her think of kinder days, softer memories.

The knot in her throat loosened. Lyssa drew in a deep breath.

"Thank you," she whispered.

"Of course," he murmured. "We'll find them, Lyssa. That's what we do."

She took another breath. "I'm afraid that knowing me is going to ruin their lives."

He squeezed her wrist, very gently. But there was *nothing* gentle about the way he looked at her.

"I've seen lives ruined," he said in a too-soft voice. "I've seen people hurt in unspeakable ways. I know what that looks like. I know what it feels like. So when I tell you, Lyssa, that you've ruined nothing . . . I know what I'm talking about."

He let go of her. "Don't blame yourself for things that are out of your control. The world is unforgiving enough."

It was still hard to breathe, but for a different reason. "Jimmy and his mother are beneath the contempt of women like the *Cruor Venator*. If those witches have hurt them . . . it's because of me. To hurt *me*."

"Sounds like it would be easier to kill you."

"Yes," she agreed.

But "easy" wasn't the point. Death would be the last on a very long list of things that the *Cruor Venator* would do to her.

If you let her, murmured the dragon. *You have a choice.*

My mother had no choice, replied Lyssa.

You are wrong. She chose your father. She chose you. Your survival. That was a good choice. What you choose is cowardice. Because you do not trust yourself.

So true. How come, then, she was finding it easier to trust a stranger than her own heart? Why did she *want* to trust him . . . even more then she wanted to trust herself?

It made no sense. It felt crazy.

Crazy and right.

If I could tell you my secrets, she thought at Eddie, but there was no way to explain just one part of the story without spilling the whole thing . . . and that was something she could not do. Not yet. Maybe not ever.

Eddie filled up his side of the backseat, exuding calm and strength, and resolve—though the hard light in his eyes made all of that seem dangerous. "Is this another trap?"

"I don't know." When Lyssa dialed the phone again, her hands shook. Only this time, she got a busy signal.

"Someone's there," she said.

FIFTEEN AGONIZING MINUTES LATER, SHE WAS racing up three flights of stairs—oozing sweat, sick to her stomach. The elevator was too slow coming to the lobby, and she didn't fancy the idea of being stuck in a metal box.

Eddie was right behind her, moving just as quick and silent. Waves of heat pulsed off his body—or maybe that was her, suffering the wild rise of fire in her blood. Her mouth tasted sour. Her head hurt. So did her right arm, muscles burning from her fingers to her neck.

When they reached the fourth-floor landing, Eddie grabbed her shoulder.

"Slow," he whispered. "Don't lose your head."

Too late, she thought, hearing a muffled, distant scream. It sounded like Tina.

Lyssa did not run, though—not when Eddie opened

the landing door and entered the corridor, not when she followed him—staring past his shoulder at the apartment door. No more screams, but she heard Tina sobbing.

Another door cracked open. A middle-aged black woman peered out, holding a cigarette between her fingers. A phone was in her other hand.

"Calling the cops," she muttered. "Can you hear that? Quieting down, but it's been crazy for the past hour. I like to mind my business, but that don't sound right."

"Ma'am," said Eddie, in that low, quiet voice. "We are the police. We'll handle this. Just go back inside and stay there."

"Don't come out, no matter what you hear," Lyssa told her, and whatever the woman saw in her eyes made her nod real quick and close her door.

As they neared the apartment, Lyssa heard glass shatter—and a man's muffled voice through the door.

"I fucking bought you, bitch. I married your worthless ass, and you run from me? You take my *son*?"

Each word was filled with venom and hate. Lyssa couldn't imagine listening to that vomit day after day, chained to a man who treated her like garbage. It hurt. It was horrible. And she wasn't even the target.

Lyssa glanced at Eddie, and a chill swept over her. His eyes were flat, dead, his mouth little more than a compressed line.

"That doesn't sound like Betty or Nikola," he said, and the barely controlled rage in his voice touched a part of her that was rough and primitive, and hungry for blood. "Is he her husband?"

"Used to be," said Lyssa, feeling grim as death. "Tina left this piece of crap. His name's Aaron Roacher. He likes mail-order brides who don't speak English."

And then it got worse.

"Don't you touch her!" screamed Jimmy, and the rawness of his voice hit Lyssa's heart like a hammer. "I'm not your son! I'm not!"

Tina let out wordless cry, and Aaron roared.

Lyssa closed the rest of the distance in one long stride, and slammed her right fist hard against the door. Again and again, raining down blows as inhuman strength flooded her arm. The old door shook and rattled. It hurt her hand, but she didn't care. She was too angry.

"*Hey!*" she roared. "*Open up!*"

Dead silence. Then heavy footsteps approached.

Eddie nudged Lyssa to the other side of the door. She tried to stay focused, but her heart was pounding, a golden haze falling down over her vision. Her teeth felt sharp. The low rumble of a growl filled the air, but it wasn't until she noticed Eddie watching her that she realized it was coming from *her*.

"You're a wild woman," he said.

"Just wait," she muttered.

From the other side of the door, a man said, "Who's there?"

"Police," replied Eddie. "Someone reported a domestic disturbance."

"Like hell. Nothing's happening here."

"Open the door, sir. Now." He sounded cold, professional, and not one to be fucked with. Right then, he looked like it, too. Lean and dangerous, with shadows in his eyes.

I'm glad you're here, she thought.

It was quiet for a moment. Until, slowly, the locks turned. Lyssa steadied herself. Eddie got even more still—and then, in a blinding flash of movement—slammed his shoulder into the door just as it cracked open.

He crashed inside, and without missing a beat reached around the door and grabbed the other man— who was still trying to recover from being knocked back into the wall. Lyssa caught a glimpse of him— huge as a football player, with fatty muscles and a thick neck, and beady eyes that looked like blue peas tucked in slabs of white meat. He had a hundred pounds on Eddie, and a good six inches—but he wasn't as fast.

Eddie lashed out with a solid right hook, snapping Aaron's head back. He had no chance to recover before he was slammed again in the face, again and again— and it was so quiet except for the thud and crack of Eddie's knuckles, and the other man's pained grunts.

Vicious. Brutal. Beautiful.

Aaron recovered enough to take a swing, but Eddie easily dodged it and kicked out hard. His boot struck the big man in the groin with enough force to make a wet, squishy sound. The man went down on his knees.

"Nice," Lyssa said, when what she really wanted to say was *Oh my God, that was incredible.*

Eddie wasn't even breathing hard. "My pleasure."

Lyssa heard a small squeak and found Jimmy standing behind them, staring. His bottom lip was split, and there was a bruise on his face. Huge eyes. At first, filled with fear . . . and then awe, as he looked at Eddie.

"Wow," he breathed.

Eddie drew in a deep breath and went to the boy. "I'm sorry you had to see that."

"I'm not. He deserved it." Jimmy looked at Lyssa, and suddenly he was all kid again, vulnerable and upset. "My mom."

My mom. Just two words, saying a million different things.

She followed him into the living room and found Tina on her knees, trying to sweep broken glass onto a newspaper. A mug had been smashed on the floor, along with several framed photos of Jimmy.

Her arms were scratched and bleeding, and covered in bruises. No other visible signs of injuries, but Lyssa knew how deceptive that was. She was a small woman, birdlike, maybe only a hundred pounds dripping wet. No match for her husband. One blow from Aaron's meat-hook fist would probably send her flying.

Tina didn't look up when Lyssa walked in. Her small hands were a blur as she tried to clean the glass. Tears raced down her cheeks, but her face showed no grief, no pain. Just resolve.

Glass crunched beneath her boots as Lyssa crouched. "Tina."

"Got to clean this," she murmured. "I don't want Jimmy to hurt himself."

Lyssa stared. The fight between Eddie and Aaron had been quiet, yes . . . but it was almost as though she didn't realize at all that something profound had changed in her home. Or that another person was standing there. Tina's focus had only one note, one beat, one destination.

How many times had she been in fights like this, where her only survival mechanism was to clean up afterward, and sweep away the evidence as though it had never happened?

Worse, she had probably thought the abuse over, that she had escaped. She had let down her guard, only to have her peace and safety ripped from her.

Just like Lyssa.

Everyone runs from the pain, she thought, watching Tina sweep up that glass as though her life depended on it. *I ran from mine. This is how she runs from hers.*

Jimmy stood beside his mother, watching her with

terrible helplessness. "It's okay," he said, voice break-ing a little. "I have shoes on."

At the sound of his voice, Tina shuddered and bowed her head. Her hands stilled. Lyssa held her breath, afraid to make a sound.

"I'm sorry," his mother whispered. "I'm so sorry, Jimmy. I didn't know he would find us."

The boy's face crumpled. "It's not your fault."

Tina finally looked at him, and tears slid down her cheeks. Her eyes were hollow, filled with despair. "You're hurt."

Jimmy shook his head. "No."

She reached for him but pulled back at the last moment, like she was afraid to touch her son. Instead, she looked at Lyssa, and her gaze sharpened, as though she was only *just* realizing that the two of them weren't alone.

"How did you . . . ?" she began, and Lyssa said, "I happened to be in the neighborhood."

Tina frowned and rubbed a shaking hand over her face. "If you're here, Aaron must be gone. We need . . . we need to get out of here before he . . ."

"No," Lyssa said. "Stay right there."

Terrible, pained resolve filled her eyes. "You don't understand. I won't let Aaron hurt my son again. I can't."

"Mom," Jimmy said, with the kind of restrained breathlessness that only a twelve-year-old boy could muster. "It's okay. Lyssa's friend knocked him out in the hall."

Tina stared. "What?"

Lyssa jumped in. "It's okay, Tina. I promise."

"Aaron's still *here*?" She tried to stand, but her legs almost folded. Bits of glass were embedded in the knees of her slacks though she didn't seem to notice. Her hands bled, too, and that bruise on her face had darkened.

"Ma'am," said Eddie, behind them. Tina let out a small, startled gasp. Jimmy grabbed her hand tight in his.

Eddie stood just inside the living room, his face nothing but hard lines and shadows as his gaze roved from Lyssa to Tina with the same dangerous intensity that had drawn her to him in dreams.

Until, as if it was her imagination, all that power in his eyes faded away and was replaced with a deceptive softness that seemed calculated not to threaten.

"Ma'am," he said again, with that old-fashioned, disarming politeness that he seemed to practice on every woman, despite her age. "Your husband will not bother you or your son, ever again."

Tina blinked. "Is he dead?"

Eddie's jaw flexed. "He'll wish he was."

"Wow," said Jimmy.

Lyssa heard a faint whimper. The living room had been trashed, but she straightened a chair and found Icky hiding, his tail between his legs—and a little puddle beneath him.

"I don't blame you," she muttered, picking him up. Jimmy made a small sound and reached for the dog, which started wriggling with joy.

"He tried to squish him," muttered the boy. "With his boot."

"*I'll* squish him," said Eddie, and took Lyssa's hand. "Excuse us for a moment."

He pulled Lyssa across the living room, backing her against the wall. Over his shoulder, she watched Jimmy lead his mother to a chair, his every movement filled with tenderness. It broke her heart, especially when Tina gave the boy a tremendous hug that made him wriggle like the dog trapped between them.

Lyssa's mother had hugged her like that, once upon a time.

"She needs a doctor," she muttered.

"What she needs is to get out of this city," Eddie replied in a quiet voice. "Right now. For your sake, and theirs."

Lyssa exhaled slowly, and nodded. "You're right. But they have no money."

Eddie's eyes softened. "My employer will take care of everything. But they can't come back here. Forget the *Cruor Venator*. This place, this city, is poison for them. And so is that man."

She glanced down the hall and found Aaron Roacher on the floor, tied with duct tape. His mouth had been covered—and his eyes, as well. He resembled a pig.

"That man deserves jail," she whispered. "If they leave town . . ."

"Nothing will change. Did Tina ever testify against him? Did she go to the police?"

Lyssa hesitated. "Not that I know. She ran when he started hitting Jimmy, but technically, they're still married. She may not even have a green card."

Eddie rubbed his knuckles. "If you're worried about him getting away with this, he won't."

"You're not going to . . ."

"Kill him? No. I don't need to."

But you *could*, whispered the dragon. *It would solve so many problems. No one would miss him.*

No one. But the idea filled her with revulsion.

Your life or his. The lives of your friends . . . or his. Or someone like him. There are so many cruel people in this world to choose from, sister. Kill just one of them . . . and you'll save your friends, and yourself.

Eddie touched her arm. "You went away for a moment. I'm sorry if what I said bothered you."

"It's not what you said, but what I was thinking." Lyssa glanced at Aaron, who was twitching now, trying to pull his arms loose. "It wasn't good."

"It doesn't have to be good if there's a good reason."

Lyssa gave him a startled look, and he smiled. "Try to make Tina and Jimmy comfortable. I'm going to make a few calls."

He turned away, but she grabbed his arm.

"Eddie," she said, but words failed her. All she could do was kiss his cheek, her lips lingering on his warm skin.

"Thank you," she whispered in his ear.

Maybe it was her imagination, but he seemed to sway a little.

"I'm your guy," he said, and before she could respond to *that,* he pulled away and walked back down the hall to take care of Aaron Roacher.

CHAPTER TEN

THE man reminded him of Matthew Swint.

Eddie dragged him into the kitchen on his belly, ignoring his grunts of pain and fear. Blind, powerless, stinking. Not so strong now. Not strong enough to beat his wife or hit his boy.

"I've had a lot of years to think about men like you," said Eddie quietly, dumping Aaron by the stove. "About the things I'd like to do."

The big man wore a mustard yellow polo shirt, wrinkled and dotted with blood that was not his.

Eddie pulled out a pocketknife and cut the man's shirt open. Aaron writhed when the steel nicked his skin and made high-pitched whining sounds that would have been pitiful coming from a puppy—but that only made *him* sound pathetic. His cheeks bulged red over the duct tape.

"If you're complaining already," Eddie said, "you're *really* not going to like what happens next."

He pulled out his cell phone, but before he dialed Roland, he placed his bare hand on Aaron's chest, above his heart. The man's skin was clammy with sweat—and he had breasts, which made it especially disgusting.

Eddie's hand began to heat. Slowly, at first. He wanted it slow.

He called Roland, his palm still pressed flat on Aaron's heaving chest.

"Fuck," said his boss, when he answered the phone. "What the hell are you doing?"

"Maybe, just this once, you could turn off the clairvoyance?" Eddie suggested. "I don't think you want to see this."

His hand was much warmer now. Aaron squirmed.

Roland said, "It doesn't work like that, and you know it. Who is that guy, and what the hell did he do to you?"

"Nothing. But he beats his wife and terrorizes his kid."

"Ah," said the other man. "Well. Happy trails, man. What do you need?"

Eddie smiled. He had problems with Roland, but the man had always been practical to a fault, and efficiently ruthless.

"One of those expensive private doctors who knows how to keep his mouth shut. Plus garbage bags, bleach, and a good saw."

Aaron moaned.

Roland chuckled. "Now you're just fucking with him."

Eddie smiled. "The doctor comes first. We have a woman here who was beaten, and her son suffered some injuries, too. Cuts and bruises, mostly, but I want to make sure."

"Okay." Roland's voice was soft. "And?"

"I'll text you the details, but they need to leave this city in the next couple hours."

When Aaron heard that, he strained against his bonds, making a strangled sound.

Eddie put down the phone and dug his fingers into the man's throat until he started choking. Just a couple seconds, but it was enough to make him obedient again.

"Jesus," Roland said, when Eddie picked up the phone. "You're torturing that man."

"When did you start caring about things like that?" He was silent a moment. "Did you find the girl?"

Eddie's hand was very hot now. Aaron cried out: high, sharp, his chest heaving for air.

"Yes," he said, above the man's sounds of pain. "The situation is complicated. The *Cruor Venator* has been following her and might be targeting acquaintances. That's the second reason we need to move this boy and his mother. Lyssa is friends with them."

"Consider it done. But kid . . . what you're doing *now*—"

Eddie hung up on him.

What you're doing now isn't like you, Roland would have said. But he didn't know everything about Eddie.

He hadn't seen Jimmy's eyes when he looked at his mother.

Aaron screamed beneath the duct tape, twisting wildly on the floor. Eddie moved with him, though his hand stayed in the same spot—hot with fire, burning the man as flesh sizzled. Smoke rose from between his fingers, and the scent of cooked meat filled the air.

Finally, Eddie let go.

Leaving behind a brand over Aaron's heart, shaped like his hand.

The man curled on his side, shaking uncontrollably— his sobs muffled, wracking. His pants were wet. Eddie smelled urine.

He waited until the man quieted just enough to hear him, then straddled his body, grabbing his left ear and wrenching up his head. He leaned close, heart thundering, anger making his words thick and hard in his throat.

"I want you to remember this moment for as long as you live," he whispered. "You were helpless and blind, and you had no voice. And I laid my hand on your heart, where you would never forget me. Where you would never forget the pain I caused you, and the terror. Because that's *your* gift to your son, and your wife. That's your only legacy . . . what you did to them. Only it was a thousand times worse because you were supposed to love them."

Eddie heard the rasp of feet coming down the hall. He tossed the remains of the polo shirt over Aaron's chest and straightened as Jimmy entered the kitchen, clutching the small ugly dog to his chest.

Someone, probably Lyssa, had washed the boy's face. The evidence of tears wasn't entirely gone, and the bruises were turning purple . . . but there was a fresh-scrubbed quality to Jimmy that made him look a little less miserable.

Jimmy held back near the kitchen door and looked at his father with big, pained eyes. Eddie crossed the room and stood in front of him.

"You look better," he said. "No blood on your face."

He peered around Eddie to look at the blubbering man. "What did you do to him?"

"We had a talk. I made sure he listened." Eddie steered him from the kitchen. "Why don't you show me your room?"

Jimmy's room was about the size of a closest, with barely enough space for a skinny mattress that hugged the wall beneath the window and a stack of clear storage tubs that held his clothes. There were other boxes, but these held newspaper clippings gathered together in paper-clipped packets, and there were other stacks of newspapers on the floor, along with a couple robot action figures. Beside the bed was a cleared-away area for a bowl of water and dog food.

"What's your friend's name?" Eddie asked, gesturing to the little dog shaking in Jimmy's arms.

"Icky," he said, standing in his room and looking lost in his sweatshirt and big jeans, with his hair flopping over his face. "What's your name?"

"Eddie."

"Are you a police officer?"

"No. I'm a detective."

Jimmy gave him an interested look. "Really? That's what I want to be." He pointed at the boxes full of clippings. "I've got cases. Murders, kidnappings, robberies . . ."

Eddie was impressed. "Have you solved any?"

"I've got suspects," he said proudly, but some of his energy seemed to fade, and his shoulders hunched again. "What did you want to talk about?"

"I think you know."

Jimmy sat on his bed and hugged the dog until he whimpered. "My dad found Mom at work. I dunno how. He made her come home, then they started fighting. He was . . . really mad."

"How long had you been away from him?"

"Almost two years. We had to move around a lot."

Eddie knew what that meant. Homeless shelters, doorways, alleys. "How'd you meet Lyssa?"

Jimmy gave him a wary look. "Are you friends?"

"I'd like to think so, yes."

"She saw you this morning, and it scared her. I thought she'd go away, and I'd never see her again." Spoken with a hint of accusation, and fear.

Eddie looked him straight in the eyes. "I would never hurt Lyssa. I'm here to protect her."

Jimmy studied him. "You're a good puncher."

"I've had to be," he said. "And I'd punch a lot more people than that to keep Lyssa safe. And you, and your mom."

He swallowed, and rubbed his eyes. "Lyssa found us. We were looking for a place to sleep, and she showed up and took us with her into this abandoned subway tunnel. My mom was scared at first. She thought we'd get killed, or something, but I liked Lyssa. She helped us live down there for six months, then my mom got a job and Lyssa found this place for us."

Jimmy's voice dropped, and he gave Eddie a pleading look. "Don't tell my mom, but the lady who owns this place . . . she said Lyssa paid our first three months of rent."

Eddie wasn't surprised. "That's sounds like something she would do."

He looked worried. "I dunno how she afforded it. I don't think she should be homeless when we're not."

You are a good kid. "She won't be homeless anymore, Jimmy. You and I need to talk about that, too. But first, your dad."

The boy hunched over his squirming dog. "I don't want to talk about him."

Eddie sat down on the floor in front of him and held up his hand. "See these marks?"

The boy stared. "Were you born with them?"

"I wish. They're scars. When I was your age, I knew a man like your father. He hurt my sister very badly, and he did this to me, and other things."

Jimmy stilled, and in that stillness there was a world of pain, and nightmare, and old wounds. It hurt Eddie to see. It hurt more than he imagined it could; because even after all these years, he was that kid . . . suffer-

ing . . . and it made him angry to think that Matthew
Swint continued to have that much control over his life.

"You're never going to see your father again after
today," Eddie told him. "Not unless you want to."

"Okay," whispered the boy.

"But you're going to think about him a lot. I spent
years thinking about the man who hurt my sister and
me. I still think about him."

"Is he alive?"

"Yes."

"I'm sorry," said Jimmy.

Eddie let out his breath, slowly. This wasn't as easy
as he'd thought it would be.

"So am I," he replied. "But I want you to listen to
something, okay? Every minute you spend thinking
about that man is a minute wasted. He's not worth your
time. He's not worth your resentment, or your fear, or
any emotion at all. He's too *stupid* for that. He could
have had a son who loved him. He could have had a
wife who loved him. He had *the both of you,* who any
man with a brain in his head would be *proud* to call
family, and he . . ."

"Threw us away," murmured Jimmy, tears spilling
down his cheeks.

Eddie rested his hand on the boy's shoulder. The
dog peered at him from the folds of the sweatshirt, and
whined.

"Hey," he said, hoarse. "Look at me."

Jimmy raised his eyes, and it was like looking into
the face of heartbreak. So much pain and grief. Eddie
tried to corner his own emotions, but it was impossible.

"Jimmy," he said. "There are a lot of good people
in this world. You're going to meet them, and they're
going to love you. And you're going to grow up to be

a good strong man . . . the kind of man who doesn't throw people away. Okay?"

The boy nodded, face crumpling on a sob. Eddie swiped his own eyes and pulled him close for a hug.

"It'll be fine," he whispered raggedly. "I promise."

"I'm scared," he said in a small voice. "My mom's going to be scared."

"I know. But you're going far away from here, for a new life."

Jimmy leaned back, staring. "Where?"

"San Francisco. It's a great city."

"How do you know?"

"I live there."

"What about . . . Liz?"

Eddie hesitated. Behind him, a low voice said, "Maybe I'll be there, too."

He found Lyssa leaning against the doorway. Her hair tumbled around her face, and her golden eyes were warm, thoughtful. A faint smile touched her mouth.

But deeper than that, he sensed sadness. He wondered how much she'd heard.

"Why do we have to go?" Jimmy asked. "Is it because of my dad?"

"No," Eddie said.

"This is my fault," Lyssa told him, walking into the room and sitting on the edge of the mattress. "Remember this morning, how crazy I acted? Well, you were right. There's a good reason. People who want to hurt me."

"But not him." Jimmy glanced at Eddie. So did Lyssa, and the look she gave him shot heat from his heart to his groin.

"No," she said, very softly. "Not him."

"Then . . . why?"

"Well . . ." Lyssa hesitated. "I'm part of a . . . Witness Protection Program."

Eddie bit the inside of his cheek. She frowned at him, and he had to look away fast before he blew it.

"Wow." Jimmy sounded breathless. "What happened?"

"I saw something involving a . . . a Bolivian drug cartel. And now they've found me. The problem is, they may know we're friends."

The boy bounced a little, and the dog groaned. "They could try to use my mom and me to get at you."

"You've got it. I made an arrangement with the Feds, and Eddie is helping."

"You're flying out today. Private jet," Eddie said.

She glanced at him with surprise. "You and I need to help your mom pack, then we're going to put your things together. You can't take much."

"But you'll be able to get whatever you need when you arrive in San Francisco," added Eddie.

"I need Icky."

"Of course."

"And my case files."

"Absolutely," he said, smiling.

Lyssa kissed his head. "Go sit with your mom. I need to talk with this guy for a minute."

Jimmy ducked away from her, wiping her kiss from his head. But instead of leaving, he hesitated in front of Eddie.

"I'm glad we talked," he said, sounding completely grown-up.

"If you need to talk more, I'll always be there."

The boy chewed on his bottom lip. "I'll be here, too . . . if *you* need to talk."

Eddie blinked. Jimmy ran from the room.

"What a kid," he murmured, then stopped breathing when he looked at Lyssa and found her staring at him with soft, haunted eyes.

"What you did for him . . ." she said.

"You heard."

"Everything." Her gaze flickered to his hands. "I hadn't paid attention. I thought it was just a birthmark."

"He needed to know."

"You helped him more than anyone could have." She was quiet a moment. "I went to the kitchen."

Eddie looked down. "And?"

"I hope it's a long time before he hurts someone else, but I'm not an optimist."

He sighed, rubbing his hand. "I called my boss. He's finding a private doctor for Tina, someone discreet."

"Discreet as a private flight?"

"The agency has resources. Might as well use them." He chanced a look at her. "How are you holding up?"

"I don't know. It was . . . strange. As awful as it was that Tina's husband found them . . . when I realized it was *just* him . . ."

"You were relieved."

"Yes," she whispered. "That's horrible, right?"

"No. Aaron Roacher is only human." Eddie rubbed his eyes, tired. "After the blast, and I put you in that car . . . I turned around, and Nikola and Betty were standing there. Just being near them was terrifying. It was worse than fear." He met her gaze and found it solemn and thoughtful. "Can they turn that on and off?"

"Sure," she said. "It's a projection, but the darkness you feel is also part of them."

"You told me those two women are servants. Not the actual *Cruor Venator*."

"They're as close as you can get without actually being part of that bloodline. And that's close enough if you ask me."

"So it doesn't take another *Cruor Venator* to kill them?"

Lyssa gave him a sharp look. "Where did you hear that?"

"Lannes. Why?"

"That's . . . not common knowledge outside certain communities."

"But *you* know it." Eddie held up his hand. "Right, you can't tell me anything."

She looked down, flexing her gloved right hand. "My mom was a witch."

He had suspected as much. "Did the *Cruor Venator* murder them?"

Her nod was small and pained. "It was horrible."

"You saw it happen?"

"I was the bait," she whispered.

CHAPTER ELEVEN

T HE doctor never did give his name, but he was a stout Chinese man in his forties who wore a dark gray jogging outfit and a baseball cap that he tugged backward while working on Tina's face. He liked to whistle, but he hated Icky on sight and made the occasional stupid joke about falling down stairs. It was tolerable the first time, but by the third, Lyssa was ready to strangle him.

He did a good job cleaning Tina's cuts, though. Jimmy pressed his cheek against her arm the entire time and squeezed her hand. Lyssa retreated to the hall, where she stood with her back pressed to the front door, hugging her stomach.

She heard Aaron Roacher whimpering in the kitchen but felt only disgust for him.

Eddie found her there. When she looked at him, all she could think about was the kindness of his voice as he'd talked with Jimmy, the sincerity and strength. Even she had felt better listening to him, as though the world would be okay, no matter what.

She didn't look down at the scars on his hand. She could picture them perfectly, and now that she knew what they were, she couldn't imagine not having realized before.

Someone had repeatedly put out a cigarette on his hand.

I killed a man when I was thirteen years old.

Words from his mind that had slid through hers, a million years ago on that sidewalk. It hadn't frightened her then . . . maybe because it didn't fit her image of him, which was calm, in control, and gentle.

But now she had a clearer understanding of what might have happened. And it broke her heart for him.

He gave her a reassuring smile, and it made him so handsome she had to look away or risk staring.

"A car is coming," he said. "The driver does some jobs for the agency every now and then. Tina and Jimmy will be safe with him. We've got a private jet waiting for them at LaGuardia. One of my friends will meet them in San Francisco. They've got a room at the St. Regis, and we'll rent an apartment for them before the end of the week."

"I hate to ask for anything else, but . . ."

"She'll have a job," he told her. "Though she may have to go to school at the same time."

"Tina will love that." Lyssa's voice barely worked. "But this apartment will need to be cleaned, too, before their roommate comes home from vacation. And then there's Aaron . . ."

"It'll be taken care of." Eddie leaned on the door beside her. Heat rolled off his body, surrounding and soothing her. "We need to worry about other things. If the *Cruor Venator* can only be killed by her own kind, then we need to find one who's on our side."

Lyssa said nothing, but Eddie didn't seem to notice.

"Lannes told me a *Cruor Venator* was murdered a hundred years ago. She was supposed to be bad news, but the witch who stopped her . . . never seemed to kill again. Not that anyone knew. If she's still alive . . ."

"No," she said, more sharply than she intended. "I wouldn't count on that."

"There can't be that many witches in the world. One of them must know something."

"You'll get yourself killed asking."

"Not every witch is bad. I don't believe that."

"You're right. But power does weird things to people. There's no middle ground I've found. You're either extremely good with it . . . or you're a supreme jackass."

He made a frustrated sound. "We have to do something."

Again, she kept silent.

Fear has its use, but cowardice has none, her mother had once said. Quoting Gandhi, no less.

But Lyssa's father, who was Irish, had replied, *It's better to be a coward for a minute than dead for the rest of your life.*

Which was Lyssa's philosophy, most of the time.

Eddie studied her. "You want to run."

He didn't say it like he was accusing her of cowardice, but hearing those words out loud, from him, made her ashamed.

"I'm afraid," she said. "I told you I might buckle."

"Okay," he replied. "I also told you we could leave."

"But you'll be back, won't you?"

"I have to. People are getting hurt."

Mandy used as bait—with other women gone missing. And even if those women weren't the typical prey of the *Cruor Venator,* she was certain it was related. Jimmy and his mother were still at risk.

And Eddie.

"You should go," he said. "Anywhere in the world. You choose."

"You're nuts."

"Maybe." His voice broke on the word. "I'll find you again."

She grabbed his wrist. "You can't find me if you're dead."

He gave her a sad, crooked smile that broke her heart. "Doesn't matter. I can't just walk away. They'll come after you eventually, right? I'd rather try to stop it now than later."

He freed himself from her grip, but instead of letting go, his fingers wrapped around her left hand, sliding under her glove to stroke her skin in a touch so light and gentle it could have been a kiss. It felt like one: sweet, on her soul. He didn't look at her. He kept his gaze down, on her hand.

A connection formed between them. Sudden, bright, hot. Flooding her with emotions not her own but that suddenly mirrored her heart, in so many unspeakable ways. His voice filled her mind.

Please, God, keep her safe.

He was praying for her.

Praying. For her.

It stunned Lyssa, who listened to his voice rumble through her like thunder, accompanied by an overwhelming, heart-shattering torrent of concern and affection, and fear.

Fear, for her.

Please, she heard him whisper, and that fear faded into longing, and heartache, and loneliness. *Please watch over her.*

Please watch over him, she thought, holding tight to his hand. *I don't want to lose him.*

The realization staggered her. She did not want to lose him. Not yet. Never seeing this man again—the very real chance—made her heart break in ways she hadn't thought possible.

Let go, she told herself. *It's better this way.*

But when his hand slid from hers, and he turned away—it was not better. It was horrible. Lyssa watched him walk back down the hall to the kitchen, every nerve in her body electrified.

What would you sacrifice to keep him safe? asked the dragon. *What price is worth paying?*

I don't know, she thought.

You lie, it whispered.

"Wait," she croaked, and he stopped just at the doorway of the kitchen, watching in silence as she walked to him.

"I'm not going anywhere," she said, and the tension leaked from his shoulders and eyes.

"I'd miss you," he said, and looked down. "But I want you to be safe."

"I won't be safe anywhere I go. I'd rather be with you."

He still did not look at her. "You can depend on me."

"I know," she said. "I hope one day you feel the same about me."

Eddie finally met her gaze, and the intensity of it made her breath catch. "Lyssa."

"I'm a coward," she went on, needing to say the words. "If killing one person in cold blood could stop the *Cruor Venator* . . . it would be worth it, right?"

"What's this about?"

"Just answer me."

He touched her shoulder, sparks dancing from his fingertips. "I don't know."

Her throat knotted up with self-disgust. "But if it could?"

"I don't know," he said again, more firmly. "That's murder."

"That's what it takes."

Eddie leaned back, studying her. "Why?"

Good question. "There's a spell."

"That wouldn't require another *Cruor Venator* to kill the witch who's hunting you?"

She closed her eyes and gave him a barely imperceptible nod of her head. A little lie. Maybe not saying it out loud didn't count.

Eddie sighed. "You're thinking of Aaron Roacher, aren't you?"

"Yes," she whispered.

"I can't do it. Can you?"

Tears burned her eyes again. "I told you . . . I'm a coward."

"God." He enfolded her in his arms, holding her close and tight. "No, you're not. How could you think that? You're a good person, Lyssa."

"Good won't win this."

Eddie's low laughter sparked fire in her blood.

"Okay," he said, with a smile in his voice. "But good can try, right?"

Lyssa was quite comfortable being held against his broad, hard chest—but she pulled away to stare at him. "This is not funny."

His eyes were so warm. "Of course not. But it *is* ridiculous."

"You're saying there's no such thing as magic?"

"I'm saying," he said in a soft voice, brushing his thumb against her mouth, "that there's no such thing as absolutes."

He dipped his head and kissed her. No warning, no long looks. Just a light, gentle, stroke of his lips against hers—with such softness she should have felt nothing. Instead, an ache jolted through her, wild and cresting over her heart in a wave of sweet heat and pleasure.

They swayed apart, staring at each other. Eddie looked just as stunned as she felt, but there was also hunger in his eyes—and that affected her almost as much as his kiss.

In your blood, whispered the dragon. *He is your mate. Your father knew this when he met your mother, and that is why he never let her go.*

Never let him go.

Lyssa reached for him, but Eddie was already leaning in, and this time the kiss was harder, deeper, stealing her breath away in a dizzying rush of desire. He hoisted her higher against him, and a gasp escaped her, laughter. He started laughing, too, against her mouth. It was better than any music, better than anything she had ever imagined.

His kiss, his voice, whispering in her ear, "I do believe in magic."

His phone began ringing. Eddie sighed, but instead of letting her slide away, he kept one arm around her waist and held her close as he took the call. Lyssa allowed herself the moment, pressing her forehead against his chin, soaking in his heat, savoring the rise and fall of his chest.

What was she doing? This was nuts.

But she couldn't let go. She didn't want to.

She heard a smooth male voice on the other end of the line, but his words were muffled.

"Okay," Eddie said, and his voice sounded different, hearing it like this, with her body against his: deeper, rougher. "They'll be down in ten minutes. We'll need the chloroform, too, and the wheelchair."

He hung up. Lyssa raised her brow. "Chloroform and a wheelchair?"

"Well," he said, "there's only so many ways to kidnap a grown man."

—

THE LAST TIME LYSSA HAD SEEN JIMMY WITH HIS suitcase was underground, in the tunnels. Seeing it again seemed like a return to the old days, and that hurt.

The driver was a white man in his thirties, short but thick in the shoulders, with strong arms, strong legs, and a jutting jaw. His fists swung when he walked. He wore jeans and a T-shirt, and when his jacket came open for a moment, she saw a shoulder rig holding a gun.

He helped Tina into the back. The doctor had Aaron in the wheelchair, unconscious and drooling. No shirt, but a bandage had been slapped on top of the brand in his chest. He and the driver rolled him into the front seat. No one walking past seemed to pay attention. It was early evening, the time of day when shadows rolled in and lights turned on, and all anyone wanted was to get home from work.

The driver stomped into the building, where Eddie and Lyssa waited, watching. Maybe they hadn't been followed here, maybe it didn't matter if they had, but it seemed to Lyssa that being seen out in the open with Jimmy and his mother might classify as bad luck for them. Just in case it mattered.

"Where do I dump the trash?" asked the driver.

"Someplace frightening," replied Eddie.

The man thought for a moment. "Yeah. He'll be terrified."

And then he grinned, and Lyssa saw that all his teeth were capped in gold.

Lyssa hugged Jimmy and kissed Icky on the head.

"You be good," she said. "Take care of your mom."

"I will," he replied. Eddie crouched and shook his hand, giving the boy a steady, warm look.

"Remember," he said.

Jimmy swallowed hard and nodded.

Five minutes later, the boy and his mother were gone, along with the doctor. Eddie and Lyssa watched the street, the slow flow of traffic, women chatting on phones. It was all so normal. She didn't know how the world could be so normal when everything she understood was just the opposite.

"Now what?" asked Eddie. "What are we doing?"

I'm falling in love with you. I'm getting my heart broken.

"I need to do some magic," she told him.

"Magic?"

"Don't get too excited," she told him dryly, though on the inside the butterflies were already forming. "I made a mistake when I was with Mandy. I could have done something then that might have let me track back to where she had been taken. It's been so long since I even thought of using . . . magic . . . that it didn't cross my mind until it was too late."

"Is there a risk to you?"

"Why?"

"Something in your eyes when you talk about it." He reached for her left hand, stripping off her glove and tucking it into his back pocket. His skin was smooth and warm against hers, the heat between them instantaneous. "If there is, don't do it."

"I have to," she said, and then, softly: "You'll stay?"

Eddie leaned in and kissed her, with a sweet hunger that made her sag against him with a sigh. How many times had she been kissed in her life? So few, and she had never enjoyed the experiences. Felt so little, in fact, that she had decided that it was lies, lies, and more lies that a kiss could rock a person to the soul.

But she was rocked—and now she understood.

"Come on," he said, against her mouth. "I still have the key to the apartment."

They went back upstairs without seeing another person. The apartment felt hollow, ugly, without anyone else there. Furniture overturned, glass still on the floor. Eddie closed the curtains and turned on the lights, while Lyssa knelt, away from the wreckage.

She began stripping off her right-hand glove, but stopped before her deformity was completely exposed.

"I've never . . . done this," she said, not quite looking at him. "Shown this part of me . . . on purpose."

Eddie was silent a moment. "How long have you been . . . caught in a bad shift?"

"Ten years."

"It must have been difficult on you."

"Summer is a pain."

"I can look away."

Lyssa wondered how long it would take her to finally put on her big-girl panties and not care about this sort of thing.

"You know," she said, "I once read a magazine article about loving your true self. But I don't think looking like something out of a freak show was what they had in mind."

"You're stalling."

"I'm on a twelve-step program to self-discovery. This is not easy."

"Just rip off the glove, Lyssa."

"I suppose it would be silly to pretend you hadn't seen . . ."

"You," he said, gently. "I've seen you."

She sighed and stripped off her glove.

Lyssa expected him to stare, and he did. It was okay. He didn't act weird about it, just curious. Maybe, after all these years, she didn't find her own hand entirely freakish . . . but it was so far away from human, it created a disconnect even inside *her* mind.

Golden claws curved over the tips of her slender, scaled fingers: red scales, crimson as rubies, catching light as though burning from within.

"Boo," said Lyssa.

Eddie tore his gaze from her hand. "Sorry."

"At least you don't need smelling salts."

He smiled. "What next?"

Next I do something crazy.

Lyssa let out her breath—and before she could change her mind, raked a claw over her left palm, cutting it open.

Blood welled. Eddie muttered a curse and reached for her hand. She pulled back, but he still managed to grab her wrist.

Heat flared between them, wild and throbbing. He let go, but that warmth remained, sliding down her spine into her stomach: liquid sunlight or lava. A slow fire, burning.

Lyssa shuddered. "Why does that happen when we touch?"

"You can't really control fire," Eddie murmured. "All you can do is focus it. Give it a direction."

"You didn't answer my question."

"I don't know. I've never been around anyone who does this to me." He cleared his throat. "Your hand."

"It's part of what I need to do." She tore her gaze from him and, with a great deal of trepidation dragged a claw through the blood dripping down her palm. It had been more than ten years since she'd done anything like this, but she remembered exactly what to do as though it was only yesterday. That frightened her almost as much as casting a spell.

Her mother had always called her a natural.

Her skin tingled, like pins and needles. Lyssa hesitated for one last moment, asking herself what the hell she was doing . . . but again, before she could change her mind, she opened her mouth and placed a drop on her tongue.

It was like being swallowed up in acid. Not drugs, but real acid. Her entire body burned away—the first flash of pain so intense her voice broke before she could scream. All she managed was a rattling sound that made her feel as though she were choking on her own breath.

The tremors began—first in her shoulders, wracking the rest of her so violently her teeth clacked. A golden haze fell over her vision, and she squeezed shut her eyes—burying her head against her fists, rocking, rocking.

This isn't even the real reason I hate magic, she thought, as the air warmed, and a wave of heat pulsed off her body. A whimper escaped her, long and pained, pulled from her with such force it scared her.

But with the pain, tremors, and the heat—came power.

It trickled into her veins, as though she was hooked to an IV of pure sunlight—dripping into her system with a slow burn that went deep as her soul. It felt like being alive on the best day of her life, only *more,* more alive, shining and brilliant with the world at her feet.

You could have the world, whispered the dragon. *The world is in your blood.*

No, thought Lyssa . . . but for a moment, she couldn't remember why she was doing this. Only that it felt so good, so wonderful, she couldn't imagine living without it.

Suddenly, she could hear her own heartbeat, thundering, and the hard beat steadied her focus.

Where are you? Where the hell are you hiding, Georgene?

It was no good focusing on the *Cruor Venator*, so Lyssa concentrated on Mandy instead. She had touched the woman earlier—connected to her mind—and she focused on those memories, letting herself sink into flashes of Flo and obsidian, and screams.

Where? Lyssa asked again. *Where* were *you?*

As if in response, she glimpsed sunlight, blue sky . . . a river and the glitter of glass . . .

. . . flowing into a room made of stone, where women slumped in chains, faces sunken and slack.

Horrific. Stunning. Part of Lyssa felt removed, as though she were watching some movie . . . but another part of her was there, viscerally, feeling every moment as if it were her flesh, her wrists heavy with bands of iron.

The women had been drugged. Lyssa saw Flo amongst them, then Mandy—who was tied to a stone slab. A beautiful black-haired woman stood beside her, dressed in stylish jeans and nothing else. The obsidian blade in her hand sliced through Mandy's chest.

A woman with a muscular, slithering voice said, *"Little lives, little pleasures. You must learn not to be choosy, Betty. When the world as we know it ends, you will then be forced to take what is at hand."*

Lyssa knew that voice—and it cut her cold, straight into the heart. She choked, trying to claw free of that suffocating presence, feeling as though she were trapped in a garbage bag that was being sucked down her throat.

Until, suddenly, she burst free—able to breathe—and found herself elsewhere, in another world. In a different time.

She sat in snow, and it was night. The moon hung bright in the sky. A thick forest surrounded her.

A girl who wore her face ran between the trees.

Lyssa saw her, and a split second later was running

at her side, behind her, all around her—flying over the
snow like a ghost, her heart pounding in her chest. She
could see the girl's tears, glittering on her cheeks like
diamonds.

Behind her there was no forest, only darkness.

She smelled blood.

You run, whispered a sibilant voice. *But you do not
run from those who would harm you.*

You run from yourself.

The forest disappeared, and so did the girl. Lyssa
floated, struck with terror as she scrabbled at the darkness . . .

. . . clawing at the floor, in a cold apartment where
broken glass glittered on the floor like small stars.

She panted, blinking hard and shielding her eyes
from the dim light flooding the room from the window.
A low voice said her name, but it barely registered until
she heard it again, louder, and felt a tug.

"Eddie," Lyssa croaked, and found him holding both
her hands tight within his own. She felt very far away
as she looked at his skin against her scales, his fingers
wrapped around her fingers, claws gleaming near his
nails. Human, alien . . . but for a moment, their hands
together looked natural, right. And it felt like that, too.

"Lyssa," he said, and just like that, everything
crashed. Her body ached, and her muscles were almost
too weak to hold her upright.

But that was nothing compared to the hole in her
heart, and the emptiness. It was not just the vision
she'd had that made her feel so drained and gray. That
was bad enough, on its own.

This other sensation of barrenness was the product of
magic itself. A placeholder for that sunlit rush of power
that had pumped through her for a glorious few seconds.
It was like being a bird and having her wings chopped

off in the middle of flight, or losing her legs when the only way to survive was to keep running. She had experienced something essential and wonderful, and *freeing*— and now it was gone, in the most absolute way possible.

This was the reason she hated magic. *This* was the reason she never touched it.

Because it would be too easy to never stop. Too easy to do terrible things in order to keep the power burning—and never suffer this crushing loss.

Lyssa choked down a sob. Eddie slid his hands— awkward and careful—over her back. Humiliation wracked her, but she didn't pull away. Just leaned in even closer, her face buried against his chest.

"Shhh," he murmured, and rested his hand against her neck—warming her cold muscles and skin. "I've got you."

She could barely look at him. "Thank you."

"What happened?"

"Power is a drug," she whispered, closing her eyes. "That's what happened."

"You're not crying because of power."

A tense, bitter smile touched her mouth. "No."

Eddie wiped away her tears and kissed her cheek. A small, lingering gesture that was sweet and gentle.

"What do you need?" he whispered, and there was such compassion in that one question.

I need a home, she wanted to tell him. *I need to know that I don't have to run anymore.*

I need you. Whoever you are, I need you.

You're in my blood.

"Just be here," she told him.

"I am," he said. "I'm here."

Lyssa shivered, hunching deep inside the charred leather jacket. "I had a . . . vision. I didn't see much that would help us find anyone, but there was a room.

Women there, drugged and bound. What I was seeing was in the past. It was awful."

Eddie was quiet a moment. "I'm sorry."

"It had to be done."

"You look so pale," he said, then, after a moment's hesitation: "This may not be the best timing, given what you just saw . . . but when was the last time you ate?"

"I . . ." Lyssa hesitated. "I don't know."

He grimaced and gently untangled himself from her. "Wait here."

She sat back on the floor, watching him walk to the kitchen. The apartment felt too quiet and lonely without him near, and even the sounds of his rummaging through the refrigerator sounded muted.

Time helped, though. She was able push away the bad memories, focusing instead on thoughts of her paintings, sunlight, Jimmy.

Eddie.

He returned less than a minute later with a jug of milk, an aluminum tray of chocolate cupcakes, and some paper cups.

"I hope you like sugar," Eddie said. "This is all I found that's easy."

"Rawr," she replied, and he laughed softly.

They poured the milk and sat on the floor, side by side, making a mess of the cupcakes and licking frosting off their fingers. She hadn't done anything in years that could remotely be called companionable, but this . . . felt good. The silence between them as they ate was comfortable and safe—exactly what she needed.

Lyssa let herself imagine doing this over other meals, or—hell—a weekend on the couch, in front of a television. Like normal people lived.

And she could totally see it. It didn't make her want to run. Just the opposite.

"This reminds me of when I was little," she found herself telling him; and then, with that much already said, she added, "My dad was the cook in the family, but my mom could handle box mixes. So we always kept a lot around, just in case."

"Sounds like my mom." Eddie smiled, but his gaze was distant. "We had this thing. Every Friday and Saturday, we'd choose a movie. My sister would get one day, I would have the other. And my mom would bake us something from a box." He glanced at her, and his smile deepened. "It was a big deal."

"Yeah," she agreed. "I loved it . . . but in hindsight, I wish I had loved it a little more often."

He looked down. "I know what you mean."

His sudden vulnerability called to her as strongly as the need to breathe. Lyssa reached for him with her left hand, unable to help herself.

Eddie closed his eyes as her fingers touched his throat, sliding up against the strong lines of his jaw. Hot skin. Hot as fire. Her right remained curled in a fist against her stomach.

She brushed some frosting from the corner of his mouth.

"Got it," she whispered.

"Maybe you missed a spot," he replied, softly.

Lyssa scooted closer, rising to her knees, and studied the hard lines of his face, the slight curl of his dark hair over his forehead. His eyes opened as she stared at him—and as always, she found herself caught in the intensity of his gaze, which was becoming as familiar as her own.

"I dreamed you," she told him, unable to stop herself. "For a month, I've dreamed of fire. And inside the fire there was always a man. I could never see any part of him clearly, except his eyes. Your eyes."

Eddie made a soft sound. "That was why you seemed to recognize me."

"It shocked me," she told him. "And it was frightening."

"Are you frightened now?"

Lyssa shook her head. "No."

He slid his arm around her waist, pulling her tight against him in one smooth, hard movement. Instead of feeling as though she was going to topple over, his strength filled her, warm and light, and the emptiness inside her chest no longer felt so vast and hollow.

Eddie bent his head, only a breath from kissing her.

"Good," he murmured, and closed the distance, drawing her lips between his. She sighed against his mouth, and his hands tightened with a crushing strength that felt as good and safe as his kiss.

"Closer," she breathed, and he laughed softly, curling his broad, hard frame around her body, tangling his fingers in her hair while his other arm squeezed them together in a devastating embrace that still was not near enough for what she needed.

In your skin. In you, thought Lyssa, reaching beneath his shirt to slide her hand up the lean, straining muscles of his back. Eddie grunted and kissed her harder. Fire licked the tips of her fingers—real flames, skimming his skin and hers. She didn't need to see the fire to know they were burning. It felt as though she held her hand against the surface of a swift-moving river of lava, molten and throbbing.

Eddie broke off their kiss, both of them breathing so hard it sounded as though they were in pain.

I am, she decided, burying her face against his throat. *I'm in agony.*

His hand tightened in her hair, and he murmured in a deep, rumbling voice, "I have to tell you something."

Lyssa started laughing. "That is the worst thing you could say to a girl at a time like this."

Eddie laughed, too, swaying them as if a slow song was playing. "No, it's nothing . . . nothing like that. I'm not married. If I had a girlfriend, we wouldn't be . . ."

She smiled, nipping his throat. "I get it."

He shivered, breath hitching when she scraped her teeth over his skin a second time. "I just . . . when you asked me before about whether I ever lose control of my fire, I told you yes. Just now . . . it was going to happen again. When you . . . touched my back."

She was still touching his back. "Are you okay?"

Something pained entered his eyes. "I don't want to be."

Lyssa understood what he meant.

"But that's . . . not me," he went on. "I never let myself feel anything . . . that might make me lose control. I just don't. I can't."

Some of that cold emptiness returned. "Oh."

Eddie leaned back, forcing her to look at him. Lyssa was shocked to find his eyes, those dark and dangerous eyes, filled with a sorrow and hunger that wrenched her soul.

"No," he said quietly. "No, you don't understand. I don't know how to be . . . normal with someone. I've tried. I managed to pull it off a time or two, but I always had to hold back."

"Because of the fire," she murmured, aching for him.

"Not just that," he said, and held up his hand, showing her his scars. Something old and weary entered his gaze, making Lyssa dig her fingers into his shirt to hold herself—and him—steady.

"This is a longer story than just a couple cigarettes," he whispered.

Lyssa reached for his scarred hand and kissed it. Eddie's chest rose and fell.

"You and me both," she said, hoping he would understand what she was trying to tell him.

His other hand touched her cheek. His fingers trembled.

"Lyssa Andreanos," he whispered, saying her name with such tenderness. "You're going to break my heart."

"Funny," she whispered. "I've thought the exact same thing about you."

He leaned in with excruciating gentleness to kiss her cheek. His scent washed over her, as did a slow-burning heat that poured through her muscles, into her heart.

Just a little kiss, but it felt amazing.

Lyssa grabbed the front of his shirt when he began to pull away. Eddie stilled, watching her with those dark, knowing eyes. She wanted to speak but had no words. Or maybe too many words. Too much fear, and uncertainty.

But loneliness was the most powerful of all.

She swayed closer, and he met her halfway, sliding his other hand into her hair as she pressed her mouth against his, soft at first—then harder—falling into his embrace as though she were drowning for his arms, his heat, that kiss.

Before Eddie, Lyssa hadn't been kissed much in her life. She'd met boys while living on the streets, formed strong attachments and crushes when she'd banded temporarily with other children. But there'd always been a law of diminishing returns when it came to kisses. She'd feel nothing. Nothing but empty on the inside.

The opposite was true with Eddie. Every glance, each touch, was electrifying. His kisses, the same—times a thousand—growing more intense with each

caress. Caught in fire. Burning in light. His mouth
hot on hers as he buried his hands in her hair, dragging her tight against him. She felt like a fool to be so
easily swept away . . . but not being here, the idea of
not knowing this man, or being held by him . . . set a
stranglehold on her heart that refused to ease.

He is yours, whispered the dragon. *You are his. Stop
fighting what must be. You were born for each other.*

That doesn't happen, she replied. *Does it?*

Someone knocked on the apartment door.

They flinched apart.

Lyssa glanced at Eddie and found him transformed.
He gave her a cold, hard look that reminded her again
of how he had reacted to Aaron Roacher—with pure
ruthlessness and no hesitation.

Again, more knocking.

Eddie helped Lyssa stand, but her knees almost
buckled, muscles aching as though she'd climbed a
hundred flights of stairs. He caught her easily, both of
them silent. He moved with the same effortless grace
as a shape-shifter, coiled with power.

She fumbled for her glove. Her hands shook too violently to put it on. Eddie took it from her and slid the
soft knit over her fingers. When he was done, he laid
his hand on top of hers and squeezed.

"Yo, messenger service!" came a muffled male
voice from the other side of the door. "Anyone home?"

He put his finger over his lips. Lyssa didn't move.
A minute later, that same voice muttered, "Fuck," and
she heard a thump. Then, receding footsteps.

Eddie waited another minute before going to the
door. After listening carefully, he undid the locks. A
brown paper parcel was in the hall on the floor.

He picked it up, very carefully. "It has your name on
it. And this address."

"What?"

Eddie gave her a disgruntled look. "We were tracked here. But how did they know this exact apartment? I was sure that no one followed us to this floor."

Lyssa felt chilled. "I suppose . . . a spell? But nothing they've used before, or else they probably would have caught up with me long before this."

He hefted the parcel. "Another trap?"

It's like cats playing with mice. "I don't know. But whatever's inside won't be good."

"Right," he muttered, and began tearing the paper, carefully. Lyssa edged closer, trying to see.

Suddenly, Eddie stopped. "I don't . . . know if you want to see this."

Fear clutched her heart. Lyssa steeled herself, and held out her hand.

Regret passed through his eyes, but he gave her the torn parcel. It was heavy, the contents soft, uneven. She took a deep breath, wobbly and sick, and finished opening it.

When she saw what was inside, though . . . she didn't understand. Not at first.

There were four strips of what looked like leopard hide, skinned from the legs. She knew it was the legs, because the knobby portions of the paws were attached, as well.

There was a handwritten note. It read:

Say hello to Estefan.

Lyssa stared in horror, a scream rising in her throat.

The *Cruor Venator* had skinned her friend.

And sent her his legs.

CHAPTER TWELVE

A LL Eddie saw, before Lyssa took the package, was the edge of a sleek, spotted hide. That was enough. He knew, in his gut, what it meant. But when he saw the horror and devastation that spread over her face, he was unprepared for his own reaction.

Rage. Pure, unbridled fury.

Those women who had murdered her friend, and probably others . . . who were hurting Lyssa with these terrible games . . .

. . . they were going to die.

No, he told himself. *No, don't think that.*

But it was impossible not to. He knew what else had been done to Estefan, but seeing that fur . . . holding it in his hands . . . made the cruelty and horror of his murder viscerally real in a way that it hadn't been before. The idea of those same women coming close to Lyssa strained his control to the breaking point.

She threw the parcel to the floor and turned away, gagging. He pressed to her side, holding back her hair—holding her—as she sank to her knees. She tried to push him away, but he didn't budge.

Her grief killed him. It was too familiar.

Lyssa kept trying to grieve in silence, but he was wrapped so tightly around her that every shudder filled him—each heaving breath that shook her body, shaking his as though she were going to break apart against him.

Eddie remained quiet as long as he dared, but he watched the door the entire time—straining to hear if anyone was outside.

Finally, he murmured, "Lyssa."

She buried her face against his chest, momentarily stilling.

"We have to go," he told her quietly. "It's not safe here."

Her fingers tightened around his arm. "Okay."

Her voice was so soft and muffled, he barely heard her. Eddie helped her stand, but she shook so badly, her teeth chattered. Her skin was cold, and he slid his hands beneath her sweater, pressing them hard against her waist and back. He focused on bringing heat into palms, even more heat than he had used on Aaron Roacher.

Fire flowed through his blood, fire that sank from his body into hers, as easily as if it were the same body, same blood, same life. Golden light streamed from her eyes, mixing with her tears.

He kissed her. "Can you stand without me?"

Lyssa nodded, face crumpling as she pressed her left hand over her mouth. A sob broke, and she turned from him, choking.

Eddie took a deep breath, then another—fighting to focus past her heartbreak—but when he started wrapping the shifter's skin in the parcel paper, she turned and watched. It was difficult to work, feeling the heat of her gaze on his every movement.

He tried to be careful, respectful, but there was only so much he could do.

Eddie placed the remains in his backpack, then picked up Lyssa's bag, slinging everything over his shoulder. He found her wiping tears from her cheeks. Grief was raw in her eyes, but her breathing was steadier, and there was a new hardness in her jaw that made her look almost . . . cruel.

"Estefan," she whispered. "He was a good man."

I know, Eddie wanted to tell her, but a strong sense of self-preservation kept his mouth shut. Eventually, she would discover he had known the shifter was dead—and kept it from her. But not now.

"I can't take this anymore. I'm done."

"Lyssa," he said.

Her eyes glowed. "I'm going to kill them. I'm going to rip their guts out."

Anger was better than misery . . . but Eddie felt cold when she said that. He knew she meant every word.

What kind of stain would that put on her heart? He knew killers. He knew men who killed to protect the people they loved. He had known people who killed just because they liked it.

Murder always changed the eyes. Lyssa didn't have those eyes.

But I do, he thought, filled with dread and fear—for her and himself.

"Your friend," she said, her eyes bloodshot, bright. "I wasn't certain Lannes was safe before . . . but now? If Betty and Nikola have been following me, then they must know about him. A gargoyle . . . would be as attractive as a dragon."

Eddie reached for his phone. "If we could find a way to keep them from tracking you . . ."

"I think I know how they did it." Her voice was

ragged, hoarse. "When she . . . when she killed Estefan . . . she stole the essence of a shape-shifter. Same essence as mine. It's no exact science, but with enough power . . . power she certainly has . . . she could take that essence and use it to find any shape-shifter near her."

"And then make Betty and Nikola do her dirty work? Why these games? Why is this so personal?"

She closed her eyes, swaying. "Call your friend."

"Lyssa."

"I can't—" She stopped, and softened her voice, though it broke with grief. "It has to do with why she murdered my parents, but that's . . . that's all I can tell you. For now. Please, Eddie."

Her plea bought his silence but did nothing to ease the ache. He felt too much around her, too much that was reckless and dangerous.

Eddie stepped close, staring into her eyes—trying to harden his heart. But it was impossible when she stared at him with those golden eyes, tear-struck, and glimmering with light.

"They'll come after you," she whispered. "They'll go after the people I care about before they come after me."

He tucked a strand of hair behind her ear. "I'm not that easy to kill."

Lyssa stepped back from him and looked down. "Better make that call."

She really was going to break his heart. Eddie found Lannes's number. On the third ring, the gargoyle answered.

"Eddie," he said, sounding breathless. "I'm glad you called."

Dread filled him. "What's happened?"

"Lethe's family is in some kind of uproar. They won't let her go."

Eddie was silent a moment. "What does that mean?"

"It means I need to face a household full of witches to get my wife back."

"Have you talked with her?"

"Barely. There's too much going on in the background that I don't understand, and she's furious." Lannes hesitated, his voice dropping. "She also sounds scared."

"Hold on." Eddie pressed the phone against his chest and looked at Lyssa, who watched him with stark concern. "Did you catch any of that?"

"Some. His wife is being held by witches?"

"Her family. For some reason, they won't let her leave." He hesitated. "None of them know she's married to a gargoyle."

Understanding entered her eyes. "If he goes to get her, they'll see he's wearing an illusion. And Lannes isn't sure he can trust them."

"It's more than that." Eddie's voice dropped to a whisper. "He has a bad history with witches. He and his brothers were imprisoned and tortured by them."

Lyssa paled. "He can't go in there."

"Not alone."

They stared at each other.

"My presence will only cause trouble," she said, rubbing the heel of her palm against her tear-stained cheek.

"I need to help him."

"God," she said brokenly. "This is going to be a mess."

"LETHE IS NOT HER REAL NAME," EDDIE TOLD Lyssa, during the stop-and-go cab ride to the Upper East Side address that Lannes had given them. "It's Alice. She had amnesia and doesn't remember her life from before a couple years ago."

Lyssa glanced at the cab driver, but he was holding a loud conversation in Arabic over his cell phone, and ignoring them completely. "How did she meet Lannes?"

"Accident." Eddie turned off the touch-screen television embedded in the divider. If he had to hear another ad for daytime television, he was going to throw himself into traffic. "They found each other not long after she lost her memories."

"Lucky." Lyssa plucked at the backseat's peeling black vinyl and dragged down a shaky breath. "Some things I'd like to forget."

He hesitated. "How long did you know Estefan?"

"Three years, but only six months of that was face-to-face. We met in Florida. It was an accident. Going there was stupid because of the heat and how I have to cover my body. But I missed the sun and ocean." Lyssa rubbed her face. "Do you have more tissues?"

Eddie reached into his backpack and found one.

She blew her nose. "There was a waitress he liked to flirt with at this little café near the water. We happened to be there at the same time. It had been years since I'd seen another of my kind, and the same was true for Estefan. I couldn't help but talk to him."

"He was a good friend."

"So good. I was skittish at first, and he had such patience. I can't tell you what it meant to me that someone knew . . . what I was. He made me feel less alone."

"There wasn't anyone else you could have gone to? Your father's family? Your mother didn't have relatives? No friends, even?"

"No one. No one wanted anything to do with my family. My father lost his friends when he married my mother."

Eddie stared, baffled. "Why?"

Lyssa looked down at her gloved hands, but he knew she was seeing past cashmere to scales and claws. "Ignorance and fear. Not that it matters anymore."

It mattered to her, and to him. "Because your mother was a witch?"

"Yes."

"That doesn't make sense." When she didn't take his invitation to explain, he added, "Is that why you're angry at Long Nu?"

"She sent you to deal with me instead of coming herself. I think that says it all."

"She told me it would draw the wrong kind of attention to you."

A bitter smile touched her mouth. "You believe that?"

Eddie leaned back. "You think Long Nu was afraid that she would become a victim."

"For all her power, she is still vulnerable to the *Cruor Venator* and her women. You, on the other hand . . ." Lyssa gave him a curious look. "Why were *you* able to resist them?"

"I had a priority more important than fear."

"Must have been a good one."

"It was you," he said. "So yes, it was."

Lyssa stared, and his cheeks heated—especially when a faint, warm smile broke over her face.

"You should use that line in a bar. It would get you laid, like, a thousand times a night."

Eddie smiled back. "That sounds exhausting."

"What are you, eighty?" Lyssa closed her eyes, leaning against him. Her smile faded. "Long Nu doesn't want to end up like Estefan. He's dead because of me."

He felt like an asshole. "Maybe it was a coincidence. The *Cruor Venator* found him, then realized the connection afterward."

"Maybe. But I didn't hide myself in that town. Everyone knew he was looking out for me. I stayed in his home. If the witch tracked me there, and asked questions . . ."

That was exactly how it had happened. Again, Eddie kept his mouth shut and hated himself for it.

Lyssa shoved her wet tissue into the jacket pocket—and an odd look passed through her eyes. When her left hand emerged, it was with the plastic bag that contained her charred, flaking photo. It was slightly more ragged than he remembered, but her young, smiling face was still intact.

Eddie thought about his sister and felt a pang in his heart.

"You were happy then," he said quietly, thinking that was something he should remember, too. "Don't forget that, no matter what happens."

Some of the tension left her shoulders—but when she glanced at him, her eyes were red-rimmed again, and bright.

"Seems like since I met you, I've been crying non-stop," she said, and stroked the bag covering the photo. "You're right. I was happy. If there was a kid who had a better childhood, I'd like to meet her. My parents were the best. There was so much love in our family."

"I'm sorry you lost them."

She gave him a heartbreaking smile. "I was going to have a brother. My mom was pregnant when she died."

Eddie's breath caught. Lyssa looked again at the photo, and her smile faded.

"Sometimes . . . I think my mom knew she wasn't going to last long. Or maybe she was just paranoid. She tried to teach me as much as she could, even when my dad thought she went overboard." Her hand began to shake, and she set the photo down in her lap. "I miss them."

I miss my sister, he wanted to tell her. *I miss her every day and think about all the ways I could have done things differently. If I could turn back time . . .*

Eddie carefully took her hand in his. He felt wounded, touching her. Heartsore, grieving for his losses . . . and for hers.

She snuggled closer, without hesitation, resting her head against his chest as though she'd done so a million times before. The familiarity of that gesture, the trust in it, made tenderness burst inside him in a rush of heat that went deeper than any fire.

No person had ever *done* this to him. He wasn't even sure what *this* was . . . except that it wasn't *just* infatuation. It wasn't just his lonely self, reaching out to the first woman who could meet and withstand his fire.

Fire was nothing but a chemical reaction releasing heat and light. Fire could be struck with a match, or lightning. Fire was *common.*

This . . . what he felt when close to Lyssa . . . was something else entirely. Losing her would mean losing his life. As ridiculous as that should have been, it was truer than anything in his life.

How was he going to protect her? Was there *any* way to keep her safe that wouldn't end in killing?

She made a small hissing sound and touched her nose. Blood dotted her fingertips.

"Are you sick?" he asked, alarmed.

"Side effect," she muttered. "Don't worry. I haven't done any magic in almost ten years. It puts stress on the body."

Anger made his voice sharp. "Anything else you want to tell me?"

The cab driver swerved to the right and braked hard, nearly sending them into the divider. But Eddie never took his gaze off Lyssa, who—for one moment—gave him a haunted look that chilled him to the bone.

"We're here," announced the cab driver. "Close, anyway."

Close enough to see Lannes, less than half a block away. Even though it was dark, his size made him stand out. The gargoyle, clad in his illusion, waited on the Central Park side of Fifth Avenue, leaning against one of the old, slightly bent trees growing from the sidewalk. Dead leaves littered the ground, and the park woodlands stretched behind him on the other side of the wall. It was all very idyllic—except for the worry on Lannes's face as he spoke into his cell phone.

Eddie and Lyssa slid out of the cab. The gargoyle strode toward them, and they met beneath another tree—a tangle of hearts and initials carved into the bark.

"They're here," Lannes said into the phone, his massive frame strained and rigid. "No, I'm coming for you. It doesn't matter anymore, baby. Just . . . hold tight."

He did not hang up but tilted the receiver from his mouth and gave them both a sharp look—especially Lyssa. "There are eight people up there, ranging in ages from twenty to seventy. All family. All upset."

"Not because of Lethe?" Eddie asked.

"No. I *think* it has to do with the *Cruor Venator*." He gave Lyssa a significant look, and she raised her brow.

"In a perfect world," she told him, "you wouldn't even know I exist. Don't think I wanted this."

Lannes grunted. Eddie stepped closer to her. "Lethe can't tell them she needs some fresh air?"

"She tried that. They're being especially protective."

Lannes pressed the phone to his mouth again. "Okay. I love you."

They waited for traffic to pass and crossed the road to an elegant building constructed from pale stone. On the other side, though, Lyssa held back and flagged down a cab.

Eddie watched her pass him a twenty.

"I'll give you another forty, plus fare, if you wait here," she told him. "We shouldn't be more than ten minutes, and we'll want to leave fast."

"Gonna rob a bank?" teased the man.

"Family reunion."

"Holy shit," he said. "I'll buckle up."

Eddie gave her an amused look. Lyssa shrugged, rubbing her eyes. "What? You think I want to be stuck here?"

Lannes grunted. "Come on."

The doorman eyed their faces but didn't give them any trouble going in. Lethe's family lived on the top floor. The elevator ride was short, and claustrophobic. Lannes took up most of the space and kept fidgeting.

All while staring at Lyssa. Not with a pleasant look on his face, either.

"There's something different about you," he said, just as the elevator reached the tenth floor. "You've done magic, haven't you?"

Lyssa tensed. "Does that bother you?"

He frowned. "Let's get my wife, then I'll let it bother me."

There was only one door on the tenth floor. Eddie heard shouts on the other side.

"What a crappy day for visiting people," Lyssa muttered.

Lannes dragged in a deep breath, and banged his fist

on the door so hard, the entire frame shook. Silence fell on the other side.

And then, very distantly, they heard a woman shout, "LET ME GO!"

Lannes's entire frame shuddered.

Eddie reacted instinctively, grabbing Lyssa and pulling her out of the way—just as the gargoyle stepped back, his massive hands flexing with loud cracks of bone.

The look in his eyes was pure death, and, with an ear-deafening roar, he slammed his foot into the door—and kicked it in.

Wood splintered everywhere. Eddie heard shouts and gasps of surprise, and followed Lannes into the apartment—fire already burning in his hands. He checked for Lyssa and found her behind him, her eyes glowing, mouth set in a hard line. Fresh blood dotted her nostrils and upper lip.

Five men and women were ranged around the room, all tall, fair-haired, with chiseled cheekbones and slender bodies. None wore bright colors, which reflected the apartment—decorated in white, black, and gray. Books lined tall shelves, and a grand piano sat in the corner. Suitcases lined the wall.

All those people looked stunned, and not at all dangerous. Three more women came running from the hall, of such similar appearance they could have only been sisters. Lethe was behind them, slender and blond, and very pale.

She was the only one dressed in color: a sea-blue silken blouse, with dark jeans and emerald green ballet flats. Golden earrings dangled. Her face was flushed, furious. Eddie had only met her once before, the previous year, during a rooftop barbecue in San Francisco.

Sometimes shy, but with a wicked sense of humor, and deep, deep love for the gargoyle who rarely left her side.

When she saw Lannes, a tremendous smile broke out on her face.

"Oh, my God," said an old man, staring at the gargoyle with disgust. "What is that *thing*?"

Lethe burst out laughing, but it was sharp and hard, and brittle. Some of her family flinched, but not one took their gaze off Lannes—or him and Lyssa.

"Uncle Douglas," said Lethe, pushing around the women surrounding her, "that *thing* is my husband."

Finally, the entire room *did* look at her.

"Oh, my *God*," said the old man, again.

"I apologize for breaking your door," rumbled Lannes, with an incongruous politeness that Eddie, under other circumstances, would have found amusing. "I'll pay for the damages, but my *wife* is coming with me now."

No one said a word.

Lethe, who had been running toward Lannes, stopped moving—so suddenly, it was as though her feet were caught in quicksand. Eddie didn't understand at first why she seemed to hang forward, as if on puppet strings.

It wasn't until outrage flickered over her face that he realized it wasn't her choice. Lannes growled, and strode toward her—or tried to. He took one step, and the same thing happened.

His illusion disappeared, as well.

Stripped into nothing but air, revealing his silver skin and massive bound wings. His eyes glowed red, and the tips of his fingers were sharp. His entire body was rigid and straining.

The men and women in the room leaned forward and stared at Lannes as though he were some circus freak.

Eddie scanned their faces. The old man was rubbing his jaw, clutching a cane between his knees, and the middle-aged woman seated on the bench beside him held a glass of red wine in a white-knuckled grip. The three sisters pressed closed together, noses wrinkled as though they smelled something bad and wanted to say, "Ew."

An elderly woman stood behind Lethe. She was dressed in a loose black dress, and gold bangles jangled on her birdlike wrists. Elegant, graceful, with silver hair tucked up in a small bun. She placed a gentle hand on Lethe's shoulder.

But that was all. If there was a fight, and magic was involved . . .

An odd chill raced over Eddie, as though he stood in an ice-cold river, waters rising over his head. A rippling, lapping sensation.

Energy, came the unbidden thought. *This* is *magic.*

Lannes's muscles strained, and he edged forward another step—though it seemed to cost him a great deal of strength. "You don't want to do this."

One of the woman, tall and dressed in black, folded her arms over her chest. She was extremely thin, more so than could be healthy. Eddie hadn't seen anyone that close to starvation since looking at pictures of concentration-camp victims in World War II.

Her collarbone protruded at painful angles—so did her cheekbones. If her body was cadaverous, however, her eyes were a brilliant shade of green and the most alive and vibrant part of her. Loose blond hair flowed down her back, so perfectly styled she might have just come from a hairdresser.

She gave Lannes a piercing look. "It has been fifty years since I saw one of your kind. I heard rumors that you still existed, but frankly, I thought the world had become too small for gargoyles."

"Not yet," he muttered, but there was a note of strain in his voice that made Eddie recall his stories of imprisonment: locked in his body for years, unable to move. "Let my wife go."

"Wife," said the woman heavily. "You cannot possibly be married to my daughter."

Lethe made a furious sound. "Mother."

"Shut up," she snapped—and the young woman's jaw shut. Muscles worked in her throat, and she made a choked, snarling sound that was short and furious. But her mouth . . . her mouth would not open . . . and it was clear that she was trying.

Her mother swayed, staring at her. "How could you be so *stupid*? Don't you know this is impossible? Even . . . thinking about it . . . God. It's an *anathema*."

The old woman standing beside Lethe stepped forward with a disapproving frown.

"Take care with your temper *and* insults, Morgana," she said in crisp, quiet tones—and then, much to Eddie's surprise, she stared directly at Lyssa. "Your power in this room is infinitely small right now."

"Don't lecture me, Ursula." The woman's pale features smoothed into a cold, hard mask—and she focused that heavy, glinting gaze on Lethe. "I understand now why you wouldn't give me a name, why you refused to say a word. *And* why you were so shocked." She took a deep breath, pale hands smoothing down her dress. "Tell me honestly. Is it really his?"

Lethe gave her a hateful look. A trickle of understanding filled Eddie, but it was so unexpected, so entirely impossible, he wasn't sure he could be right.

"Yes," she said, growling the word.

The old man muttered to himself. The sisters exchanged disgusted glances. The elderly woman, Ursula, only sighed—and watched Lyssa with puzzlement and sadness. Eddie's gaze slid to Lyssa, but she was studying Lethe and didn't seem to notice the others' scrutiny.

"God," said Morgana, closing her eyes with visible revulsion. "How could you? I thought, at least, your baby was *human* . . . but this?"

Eddie's gut clenched. Lannes sucked in his breath with shock and stared at Lethe. His wife's eyes were filled with determination—the answer *there* as she stared back at him.

She was pregnant.

"Lethe," whispered Lannes, and the reverence in his voice should have melted even a stone heart. But Morgana's mouth twisted with disdain, and a shudder raced through her that was pure revulsion.

"Her name," she said in a clear, granite tones, "is *Alice*. And she will never bear your child. Not now. Not ever. I will rip it from her myself if I have to."

Lannes said nothing; he might as well have screamed, given the crackle of raw, pure energy that suddenly coursed through that room. He lurched forward one step, and the three sisters winced and touched their heads. He took another step, muscles straining, gaze burning with disgust and resolve.

And then Morgana made a slashing motion with her hand, and he stopped, again.

Lyssa cursed to herself, but Eddie stayed quiet, burying his heart so deep he could barely feel it. Lethe was quiet, too, but it was a deadly, simmering silence that was murderous, and cold.

Morgana said, "If you leave now, gargoyle . . . I will not hurt you."

"Keep him," muttered the old man, tapping his cane on the floor. "In case the *Cruor Venator* finds us. Perhaps we can trade his life, or use him as a distraction. It might make all the difference."

"You don't bargain with the *Cruor Venator*," murmured Lyssa, but no one seemed to hear her but Eddie.

Ursula stepped forward, golden bangles chiming. "You can't be serious, Morgana. This is absurd."

"It's survival. And not a bad idea."

"It's disgusting. She loves him. It's obvious he loves her. If you kill her child . . ."

"No," Lannes spat, while Lethe made a furious sound, deep in her throat. "Don't you *touch* her—"

"—you might as well kill Alice," finished the old woman. "I won't let you do that."

Morgana gave her an icy look. "Are you going to stop all of us? With what? A sharp word?"

Eddie listened, sickened. Were these people actually talking about his friends as though they could be imprisoned and sold? Were they really discussing whether or not to kill their child?

He tested his hands and found he could still move. Fire filled his fingertips, hot, mixed with anger. He was just about to speak, when sharp laughter filled the room.

It was Lyssa.

She stared at Morgana—at all of them—with pure, rock-hard disdain. It took Eddie by surprise because up until then he hadn't imagined her confronting these witches, not when she'd been so hesitant to come in the first place.

Her scorn, however, was a shocking, beautiful thing.

"Look at all of you," she said, with withering contempt. "Look at how ridiculous you are. You think a

little power means something? You think it gives you
the right to control another living being?"

Morgana narrowed her eyes. "Who are *you*?"

Ursula shook her head, looking at the other woman
as though she was a fool. "Morgana, be smart. Don't
say another word."

"Why?" She waved a bony hand at Lyssa. "She's a
little girl. Nothing but a shape-shifter. Give me a *real*
challenge."

A slow smile touched Lyssa's mouth, and it was
dark and chilling, and reminded Eddie too much of
that cruel hardness that had transformed her face when
she talked about killing Estefan's murderers.

"A challenge?" she echoed, too softly. "You will
not keep this woman against her will. And you are *not*
touching her baby. Over my dead body."

Everyone but Ursula shifted—sideways and forward, at the same time—though not with quite the
same movements. Close enough to be eerie, though.

Morgana unfolded her arms, staring. "I can rip you
apart with my mind."

"Then why do you need *six minds* to hold one gargoyle and your daughter? I can feel the link among you
all. Without it, you could never hold either of them."
Lyssa shook her head and stripped off her glove, exposing her right hand. "No. You can't touch me."

She walked toward Lethe, and Eddie fell in beside
her, silent as her shadow.

She gave him a brief, startled look. He didn't understand why, and he didn't care. Everyone in that room
was staring at them with the same surprise—though
their gazes were equally torn to her hand, with its
glinting golden claws and crimson scales.

Morgana stepped in their path. Again, a wash of air

rippled and undulated against his skin, but the fire rose from his heart and consumed the cold—swallowing that watery sensation until it was nothing. Lyssa stepped up to his side. Both of them faced the witch.

"Ma'am," he said. "Move aside."

Morgana frowned. "No."

Eddie gritted his teeth and strode toward her, fire sparking off his hands, flames licking his wrists and threading into the air. He never engaged in deliberate displays of power, but his anger was too rich.

And power, it seemed to him, was all these people understood.

Lyssa moved with him, silent and graceful—deadly in her grace. No fire, but heat throbbed off her body, shimmering around them both.

Morgana's eyes widened, and she slid sideways, almost staggering in her haste to keep him from touching her.

"Impossible," she murmured, staring at him—and then Lyssa. "You can't be immune to our power. Not both of you."

She said it as if a blob of mud had just started quoting Shakespeare. Eddie was pretty certain he should feel insulted.

Lyssa squeezed his arm as she passed him. "Maybe you're just that bad at magic."

Morgana choked.

Lyssa ignored her and stopped in front of Lethe. Eddie protected her back, waiting for someone, anyone, to finally react. No one did. Just that one act of defiance had broken something in them. He could see it in their eyes.

Everyone, that is, except Ursula . . . who gave him an oddly knowing look that was surprisingly kind, and resigned.

"I apologize for what I'm about to do," Lyssa said to Lethe, then scratched the woman's hand. Blood welled, coating her claw.

Lyssa placed it in her mouth and licked.

Everyone in that room sucked in their breath, as though punched. It was the kind of sound Eddie heard in theatres, watching horror movies. An uncontrolled reaction of shock and revulsion.

Morgana seemed the most undone, hands pressing down hard on her bony chest, as if she were trying to hold herself together.

"Oh, my God," whispered the old man. "God save us."

"Hey," Lyssa said in a tense voice, and suddenly Lethe fell forward, staggering into Eddie's arms. He tried not to let his hands touch her, afraid they were still too hot.

"Can you walk?" he said, keenly aware of Lyssa closing her eyes and swaying, her lips stretched in a grimace.

Lethe gave her mother a venomous look. "Absolutely."

She pushed away from Eddie and ran to Lannes. She hugged him hard, pressing her cheek against his chest—but he remained frozen in place, grimacing with frustration and pain.

"Sweetheart," he whispered.

Lethe kissed his chest and swung around to face her mother. No words. The betrayal in her eyes was enough—as well as the hate.

Ursula sighed. "Let him go, Morgana. You lost. You lost more than you had to."

The woman stared at her daughter and swallowed hard as her pale, bony hands trembled. "You can't be sure the baby will survive. There has never been a human and gargoyle hybrid. And if you *do* carry it to term, what then? What if the birth . . . kills you?"

Lannes sucked in his breath. Tears glittered in Lethe's eyes.

"Let him go," she whispered.

"Let him go," Lyssa said, flexing her claws. "Or I'll make you."

Morgana flashed her a hard look, one filled with fear and hate—but Lannes sagged forward with a grunt, reaching for Lethe in that same heartbeat of freedom. The desperate relief on his face hit Eddie in the gut.

After today—after so much violence and pain—it was like a star of hope, shining for one lost moment.

He looked at Lyssa and found her watching them, too. He reached for her left hand. She flinched when he touched her—and then relaxed—giving him soft, grim eyes.

It was as if she was reaching for him with just her gaze—and he felt himself reaching back, with all the cold broken pieces of his heart.

"Alice," whispered Morgana, but her daughter deliberately turned her back and grabbed her husband's arm in a white-knuckled grip.

Eddie couldn't see her face or hear more than the murmur of her voice, but Lannes dipped his head, silver hair falling past his broad shoulders—and his eyes were hard and full of love as he whispered, "Yes."

He looked past her at Morgana and the rest of the witches.

"If you come after us," he said quietly, "it will be war."

Eddie felt a shiver course through the room.

"War," murmured Morgana, glancing at Lyssa. "I believe you."

Lyssa did not move a muscle, but the sense of menace that had been growing around her seemed to spark and intensify, until it was as though actual doom was descending: a hard dread that was physical and cold as ice. Eddie felt it, but the sensation slid off him like water.

It did not slide off the rest of the room, though. He saw pale faces, hollow eyes, and fear. Fear that was sharp, biting.

"You damn well better believe it," whispered Lyssa. "You go after any gargoyle, or your daughter—*or* their child—and there will be a storm that comes down on your head that you won't rise from, ever. Do you understand me?"

Only an idiot wouldn't understand. Eddie didn't know if it was Estefan's murder that made her so angry now, or if she had always been this full of purpose and intensity. What he *was* certain of, though, was that he wanted to bow his head from the odd, dark pleasure that filled him when he listened to her. He squeezed her hand, and though she did not look away from Morgana, her fingers tightened around his. Fire between their palms.

The witch trembled and looked at her daughter. "Don't do this. Don't go with that monster."

"I love him," Lethe hissed.

"Not him," she replied. "*Her.*"

Lyssa started laughing again, but it was a strangled sound that put even Eddie on edge. Not with fear, but concern. He remembered how she had tasted her own blood—and the aftermath. Like a drug user coming down from a high.

He wasn't sure he wanted to know the consequences of tasting someone *else's* blood, if there were any. He didn't understand magic or witches, or how any of this was supposed to work . . . just that his job was to make things right and safe. Somehow.

Almost every witch in that room seemed to shrink from Lyssa's voice.

"*I'm* the monster?" she asked softly, eyes glowing with golden light. Morgana stepped back, burying her hands against her long skirts. A tremor raced through her.

Ursula stepped toward Lethe and Lannes and made a shooing motion. "Go on, now. Quick."

Lethe glanced back at the old woman, tears spilling down her cheeks. Lannes barely looked at her. His focus was on Lyssa. Eddie didn't like what was in his eyes. Too much bad news. Like he'd just discovered that you could catch a terminal disease from breathing the air.

"We're gone." Lannes wrapped his arms around his wife and gave Eddie a haunted look. "Eddie—"

But he didn't finish.

Lannes staggered forward, grunting in pain, nearly taking Lethe to the ground as he went down on one knee.

He was big. His body had been blocking the entire doorway. But when he moved, Eddie saw that someone else had been standing behind him.

Betty. Pale, beautiful, and smiling. Seeing her was like being slapped in the face by a nightmare that Eddie had, until that moment, forgotten.

She held a curved obsidian blade in her hand, which was dripping blood from the shallow cut that she'd made across Lannes's back.

"A gargoyle, a dragon, and a roomful of witches," she murmured. "What a perfect day."

CHAPTER THIRTEEN

I
T was the knife. Lyssa looked at it, and for one precious moment, lost herself to memory. It was night, and she could hear the *drip, drip, drip* of blood on snow, and the rasp of sobs, and her mother's quiet breathing as she begged, with dignity, for her daughter's life.

And then the memory died, she blinked, and said, "Kill her. Quick."

Eddie gave her a startled look, but Lyssa didn't hesitate. She couldn't. If Betty got away and told the *Cruor Venator* what she'd found, there would be another bloodbath. Lannes and his wife would never be safe. Neither would the witches, though frankly, Lyssa was a hell of a lot less worried about *them*.

She lunged toward Betty, claws out. An entire room separated them. Betty had time to blink, and raise her knife—

—and then Lyssa was on her, claws slashing downward as she aimed a blow at the witch's perfect, startled face.

Betty moved aside at the last moment, graceful and inhumanly quick. Her empty hand turned into a blur as she tried to punch Lyssa in the gut—but her dragon reflexes saved Lyssa, and she blocked the blow.

Betty lashed out again in a series of precise kicks and hand-strikes. She did not use the blade. No permission. The first cut, and every cut after, would belong to the *Cruor Venator*.

She had training, though. Her fighting style was too polished. Time in a gym or dojo, no doubt at the encouragement of the *Cruor Venator*. Lyssa knew within moments that she was outmatched.

Betty's fist caught her across the face—the blow hard enough to knock her back. She would have fallen if Eddie hadn't caught her. His hands were strong and hot as hell, and his gaze was furious.

As he helped her stand, Lyssa caught a glimpse of the rest of the room. Lannes had dragged Lethe away from the door, holding her out of sight behind him. She could smell the stink of his fear—though it was a little less strong than the stink rolling off every other witch in that room, who stared at Betty like she was Satan personified: evil, *more* evil, and *shitting in the pants* evil.

It was just the projection—the infection of fear—but it was as potent as a death ray. Morgana was already sinking to her knees, sweat pouring off her face as she trembled so violently her teeth chattered.

Eddie, though, stepped in front of Lyssa. His hands were on fire.

"You," he said a deadly soft voice. "Will never touch her again."

Betty stared at him with total, unaffected calm, her gaze thoughtful, and assessing. "I told her about you. The *Cruor Venator* wants to know what makes you tick. Why you're not afraid of us."

Lyssa pushed past him, fire pulsing at her fingertips. "She'll never find out."

Betty frowned. "Lizard. Do you even know what she is? What *I* am?"

Prey, whispered the dragon, coming awake.

And Lyssa whispered, "Dead."

Betty snarled, raising the obsidian blade. Lyssa stepped forward, ready. There was a sour taste in her mouth, bitter and metallic. A thread of power. The aftereffects of tasting Lethe's blood.

She wanted more. More blood. More power. More than just a taste. It was like the lightest brush of an ice cube on her tongue after dying of thirst in a desert.

In other words, torture.

And here was Betty, served up on a platter. It was almost too easy.

It is *too easy,* she realized.

"Where's your friend?" Lyssa asked, but Betty had already begun her attack in a frenzied blur of deadly movement. She braced herself, ready to block those blows—

—but they never came. Eddie stepped in front of her, fire still raging around his hands, and rained down one single blow that sent Betty to her knees. He was unbelievably fast—as if he were a shifter himself, or fueled with the same blood magic that infused Betty's muscles.

The witch hit the floor, stunned, nearly unconscious. Lyssa heard, behind her, a deep release of breath—everyone in the room freed from that infection of paralyzing fear.

Do it, she told herself. *Right now. End it. Betty can't go free.*

But once again, she was too slow.

Lyssa got knocked into Eddie's side as Lannes stormed past and grabbed Betty off the floor.

His hands were massive around her throat, and she was limp as a rag doll, almost swinging from his grip. Half her face was burned. Her eyes cracked open, and she gave him a slack, half-conscious stare—just before he snapped—and then crushed—her neck.

The sound was loud, crunchy, and final. Lannes dropped Betty and backed away, staring at her body. Pure silence filled the apartment.

"Oh, my God," someone whispered.

And then Lethe said, "Lannes."

The gargoyle exhaled and looked at his wife. Gaze terrible, and haunted. He reached out to her with a trembling hand.

She went to him without hesitation. Lyssa released her own breath—realizing that Eddie did the same.

Without a word, Lannes picked Lethe off her feet and carried her over Betty's dead body—which blocked the doorway. In a heartbeat, they were gone.

Eddie moved close. Fire gone from his hands, though his eyes were filled with the same haunted remorse that she had glimpsed on the gargoyle's face.

"I was going to kill her," he whispered, as if he couldn't quite believe it.

"So was I," Lyssa told him, just as softly—still able to taste the resolve that would have kept her fighting until the bitter end. A tremor raced through her, and she swallowed hard, feeling nauseated. Part of her was disappointed she hadn't been the one to make the killing blow—but mostly, she was relieved.

Lyssa turned in a slow circle to study the witches behind her. The girls who seemed to be sisters had fled down the hall, and the woman seated beside the old man was helping him to his feet. Both looked pale, shaken. A heart attack, perhaps imminent.

Morgana had gotten off her knees. Ursula seemed

surprisingly calm, except for the fine sheen of sweat on her wrinkled face. It was rare to see a witch who was physically old. Which meant Ursula was very, *very*, old, and accepting of it—enough, so that she felt no need to cast an illusion of youth.

Old witches usually also had balls of steel.

"We'll take care of the body," she said. "Thank you. Thank you so much."

"Come on." Eddie touched Lyssa's hand, something in his voice and movements undeniably shaken. "We should leave."

But she remained still. Morgana gave her a grim, wary, look. "What now?"

Cutting Betty and tasting her blood would only expose Lyssa to every murder Betty had ever committed. Unlike Lethe's blood, which was easily read, the *Cruor Venator*'s woman would carry only one message in her veins: death.

And that would tell Lyssa nothing she didn't already know.

"I need to find out where the *Cruor Venator* is taking her kills," said Lyssa. "Have you heard anything? Even rumors?"

Morgana pointed. "Maybe you should have asked. As if you don't already know."

"Ma'am," said Eddie. "Go to hell."

Ursula touched Morgana's arm. "You and the others should leave this room. Right now."

For a moment, Lyssa thought there would be an argument. But Morgana took another look at Betty's corpse—her gaze lingering on the obsidian knife—and she backed away, jaw tight, eyes slightly unfocused. The old man and his companion had already left the living room. Morgana turned, and staggered down the hall—leaning heavily on the wall.

Ursula sighed and rubbed her face. "My God. No wonder we are a dying race."

"Because you're cruel and stupid?" said Lyssa wearily. "Yes, that's a problem."

The old woman gave her a look that made her feel small and slightly ashamed.

Eddie flexed his hands. "I see suitcases lining that wall. You planned on running."

"Of course. The *Cruor Venator* prefers to kill witches and those with power. It was only a matter of time before we became targets. We would have left already, except Alice . . . Lethe . . . chose today to visit, and it became clear after spending some time with her that she was with child. We could . . . feel it . . . even though she couldn't."

Lyssa didn't want to be here anymore, and she *really* didn't want to be near a dead body. Especially this one.

"Do you know where the *Cruor Venator* is?" she asked again, in a sharper voice.

"No," said Ursula. "I have something else to discuss with you."

"What?"

"Kara. Your mother."

"MY LAST NAME IS HADRADA," SHE SAID. "IS THAT familiar to you?"

Lyssa shook her head, unable to find her voice. Hearing this woman mention her mother by name had formed a knot in her throat that seeing Betty, fighting Betty, and standing over Betty's dead body couldn't come close to touching.

She seemed disappointed. "Ah."

"How . . ." Lyssa stopped, wetting her lips. "How did you know her?"

"Kara saved my life." Ursula smiled. "Much too long a story for a time like this. But you have her face. When I saw you . . . I thought at first it was her."

Again, it was difficult to speak. "She's dead."

Ursula's visible surprise—and regret—did painful things to Lyssa's heart. No one had ever been sorry her mother was dead. Quite the opposite.

"I'm sorry," whispered the old woman. "She was . . . a good person. Few understood that, and she was unfairly treated because of it. As you are, I suspect."

"She understood why." Lyssa looked deep into her eyes, memorizing them. Some rainy day, when or if anyone ever disparaged her mother's memory, she would recall this old woman, and her compassion. "So do I."

"And yet, you haven't fully embraced . . ." Ursula stopped and looked past her at Eddie. "Never mind. I wanted to know if there's anything I can do for you." She looked down at Betty. "You're here because of the *Cruor Venator*, aren't you?"

Eddie's shoulder brushed against hers, hard and warm. "She's hunting Lyssa."

"And so you become the hunter," said Ursula softly, glancing down at Lyssa's gleaming claws. "A formidable one, I expect."

She pulled the jacket sleeve over her hand. "Not formidable enough to keep them from killing my friends, and . . . tracking me."

"Tracking you." Ursula paled. "Ah."

Lyssa thought about Estefan and closed her eyes. "I'm sorry. That's how Betty found this place. We should leave, and so should you. Right now. Before anyone else comes."

"We will," said the old woman firmly. "But how are they tracking you? It shouldn't be possible."

Lyssa was keenly aware of Eddie listening, and was afraid of how much he might hear that would damn her. But the truth had to be told, because she sensed Ursula might be able to help. She had nothing to lose, at this point.

And, Ursula had spoken her mother's name. She had looked Lyssa in the eyes, without fear. No other witch in that room had been able to do the same.

That had to mean something.

Lyssa swallowed hard, and looked at Eddie. "Can you . . . bring out the . . ."

Skin, she could not say. *Estefan's skin.*

Compassion filled his eyes. He slid off the backpack and pulled out the paper parcel. When he began to hand it to her, she shook her head and backed away.

Tight-lipped, Eddie unwrapped the brown paper and revealed the leopard hide.

Ursula leaned forward but did not touch.

"A shape-shifter," she said, after a moment. "And so are you. I understand now. That's the blood they're sniffing."

"I need to break the link. I'm not sure how."

"If you're Kara's daughter, you know how. But I think you know the medicine will be worse than the disease."

"What does *that* mean?" Eddie asked.

Lyssa finally reached for the parcel. "It means I can't just grieve like a normal person."

He hesitated, holding it back. "You know what you're doing?"

"No." She tried to smile for him, but the burning had already begun in her throat and eyes. "I don't want any more knocks on the door, though. Do you?"

Eddie gave Lyssa a sharp look but handed her the parcel. She sat down on the couch, just as his cell phone began ringing. He answered tersely, his gaze never leaving hers. She was dimly aware of him speaking to Lannes, but her focus was mostly on Estefan's skin.

Betty's body was a surreal exclamation point on the floor, but it was easier to ignore her—or feel nothing at all but relief. Especially while holding part of her friend's corpse.

Ursula murmured, "If you need blood . . ."

Lyssa gave her a sharp look. Eddie hung up his cell phone, and said, "If she needs blood, she can have mine."

It was like offering cocaine to a drug addict. He had no idea what that meant to her. She closed her eyes and shook her head. The remnants of Lethe's blood would have to be enough. Before she could change her mind, she placed her hands on Estefan's skin and opened her mind.

Images slammed like a hurricane, stealing her breath and squeezing her heart until her world was reduced to nothing but endless suffering—a life teetering on the edge of death.

From this maelstrom rose the memories of two women: one of them tall, lithe, and dressed in crimson; and the other, whose pale face was surrounded by a tumbling mass of glossy black hair. Betty and Nikola.

Both held curved obsidian blades in their hands. Their eyes glittered, and their smiles were white and sharp.

"*I wish you had a child,*" said the black woman, Nikola. "*I've never had the blood of a shifter-baby. It must be sweet. So . . . succulent.*"

Betty rose from her couch, and glided across the floor. "*Would it taste like spring?*"

In her memories, Estefan trembled. Lyssa trembled with him, lost in his skin, lost in the pounding fear that fell upon him in throbbing waves. A primitive, violent fear, overwhelming, paralyzing—and dehumanizing.

No fear could match it. No fear could be as powerful. No one but a *Cruor Venator* and her women could tear a brave heart to pieces with nothing but a look.

Estefan was untied in her memories, but still helpless, wearing his leopard body as he pressed his belly to a concrete floor and groveled. Frightened into paralysis.

Betty and Nikola surrounded him, obsidian knives flashing.

The first cut was shallow, across his side. The second cut deeper, over his heart. Betty sank to her knees, licking his blood off her blade. Nikola did the same, throwing back her head with a shuddering sigh. Lyssa hated them with a terrible fury.

From behind Estefan a familiar, leathery voice whispered, "*I will wear your skin as my own, leopard. I will hunt your kind and make them live as animals until I am ready for their blood. I will take their power, and my empire will stretch into the fire when the new world comes.*"

His terror sank like a sick root into his soul. It did not matter that it was out of his control, nothing but an illusion induced by evil. Being forced to endure such a violation of emotion was the same as rape.

Her friend, tortured to death. Estefan, whose only crime had been showing kindness to a lost girl with no home, no family, and a lot of loneliness.

Leave these memories, whispered the dragon, finally stirring. *Do what you came to do and let it be over. Find the link. Sever it.*

Whatever spell the *Cruor Venator* had cast would be linked to Estefan's skin. Not the physical skin, because otherwise, burning it to ashes would be enough. The spell was linked to the essence, to the spirit and blood.

Shifting magic was a unique magic. All shifters could sense one another if close enough. The *Cruor*

Venator would now have the same ability, simply augmented by her own power.

Guide me, she said to the dragon. *Please.*

A wing stretched through her soul, gathering her close. *Here. Follow.*

Lyssa flew through a vast darkness dotted with golden stars.

Each star is a shifter, whispered the dragon. *There are not many stars, but that could yet change.*

How?

Time, replied the dragon. *And those like your mate, who are their allies.*

He is not my mate.

You will have babies with him.

Focus, she growled, and the dragon laughed with a sibilant hiss, before her voice dropped again to a whisper.

We cannot shield all these shifters from the Cruor Venator, *but we can hide you.*

That wasn't good enough. No one could be allowed to suffer.

Then you will kill her, said the dragon, sensing her thought. *And no one will suffer.*

Lyssa ignored her, focusing on her own light. *How do I shield myself?*

Like this, it murmured, and spread its wings around her.

Darkness fell down. She fell with it.

And heard, on the other side of those wings, a pounding fist. It had to be the *Cruor Venator.* The witch knew she had lost the link and was trying to find her again.

Fear laced through Lyssa's heart but lasted only long enough for her anger to consume it.

I want to see her, she told the dragon, and without

a word of argument, warning, or caution, those wings pulled back—and let the *Cruor Venator* in.

Lyssa was ready for her, and attacked.

It was like trying to tangle with the breeze off a garbage dump. The witch's spirit smelled like it was rotting. Except Lyssa was the wind, too, made of claws and fire, and she wrapped around that unclean spirit with a power born from grief, fury.

The *Cruor Venator* snarled, but before the witch could react, Lyssa bit her soul—and tasted a different kind of blood.

She drank, and a maelstrom blasted through her like dynamite exploding. Images flashed, forests and mountains, men in Nazi uniforms, a strange woman with black eyes and blood on her teeth . . . Lyssa's mother, except younger, much younger . . .

Lyssa didn't want to see any more. She tried to wrench herself away, but the *Cruor Venator* held tight with frightening resolve.

Your mother was so very pretty, whispered the witch, with satisfaction. *As are you, I'm sure. After all these years, Lyssa . . . what took us so long to find one another?*

Go to hell, she snarled, but her heart was thundering, and hearing that smug voice reminded her too much of that night in the woods, when the witch had murdered her parents. Snow and moonlight flashed, the forest in a blur—

Suddenly, unexpectedly, she heard another voice inside her mind.

This voice was stronger than the *Cruor Venator* . . . and surrounded her in a burst of fire and blazing light that cracked the shell of darkness.

Eddie.

Lyssa, she heard him think, as the connection bloomed between them. It was just her name, but that was enough.

His voice sounded like home.

Lyssa slammed the *Cruor Venator,* knocking herself free—and the dragon did the rest, tearing the witch away and tossing her beyond the protective circle of its wings.

Silence fell. A soft darkness.

Then the world returned.

She blinked, and suddenly there was a couch beneath her.

She was not alone. Eddie cradled her against his chest. A shimmering cocoon of heat surrounded them, making her feel safe, protected. As if nothing could hurt her while he was close.

Not pain, not loss. Not evil.

Blood dripped down her nose. Eddie pressed his sleeve against her nostrils. Lyssa pushed him away, gently.

"I'm okay," she lied.

He gave her a haunted look. "You started to convulse."

"I was fighting the *Cruor Venator,*" she whispered. "I don't think she can track me anymore."

"Good. Because we're leaving this city. We're gone."

"No."

He looked at Betty with her crushed neck and half-staring eyes. "Yes, Lyssa. Right now."

She fought free of his arms, half-falling off the couch. "I'm finishing this. One way or another. I have to."

"I won't let you. I can't. I don't know if I can protect you, Lyssa."

"I never asked you to."

His gaze darkened, and those strong hands tightened with bruising strength. "Don't. Not this again."

"I'm not yours," she snapped. "And you're hurting me."

Eddie stiffened.

Lyssa wished instantly she could take back those words. But she couldn't even speak when he stood up and walked away from her.

Ursula swayed close, bangles chiming. Watching him, then her, with inscrutable eyes. She held the parcel with Estefan's skin, having wrapped the paper around his remains.

"You dropped this," she said, as Eddie stood at the darkened window, staring at Central Park. Smoke rose off his back.

Lyssa slipped her glove over her right hand, trying to keep her voice from shaking. "Your suitcases are packed. I wouldn't let that go to waste."

Ursula handed her the parcel but didn't let go. "Your mother once told me she was afraid of herself."

Lyssa stared. The old woman gave her a soft, sad look.

"She said it was always a struggle. But it was a struggle she mastered. Do you understand?" Ursula stepped closer, cupping her cheek with a soft, trembling hand. "You are her daughter. If your face hadn't convinced me, your actions here today most certainly did."

Lyssa tilted sideways, light-headed. Eddie turned, saw her swaying, and strode toward her with quick, urgent steps. His scent was dangerous. Angry.

His hand, though, was gentle when it found hers. Lyssa was a little surprised he even wanted to hold her hand, especially when he couldn't even meet her gaze.

Ursula scrutinized him. "You . . . are another mystery entirely."

Eddie made no reply, but he didn't need to. Nothing about him was soft, in that moment—or afraid. The old woman, who was a witch and held a hard power about her, had to look away first.

They had to walk over Betty's body. Lyssa made a point to stare at the dead woman's face, memorizing the emptiness of her eyes. Eddie waited beside her, silent. When she chanced a glance at him, he was also studying Betty . . . but with no emotion, just a flat, cold remoteness that transformed him into different man entirely.

The obsidian blade lay on the floor. Lyssa did not touch it. Too much death.

Ursula did not follow them. Out in the hall, Lyssa gave her a last, lingering look. The old woman stood alone, a wrinkled hand held over her heart.

Lyssa was surprised at how reluctant she felt to leave her. If the old woman had known her mother . . .

One day, she thought. *One day, if I live through this.* Another thing to do, on an already long list. A list she hadn't realized she was keeping until now.

They did not take the elevator. Eddie waited for her just inside the stairwell. Lyssa's head began to throb, and so did her right arm, down to the tips of her claws.

"Are you okay?" he asked, but his voice was distant, and he barely looked at her. His distance felt personal—and was at direct odds with everything she thought she knew about him. It bewildered her. It hurt.

"I'm fine," she said, wondering how it had all gone wrong. And why it felt as though her heart was crumbling to pieces.

Lyssa pushed past Eddie to walk down the stairs. He followed, staying close. Silent, though the waves of wild heat flowing off his body said more than words.

Outside, the evening breeze off Central Park tasted sweet, and she glimpsed a handful of stars. Lyssa stood for a moment, soaking it all in. Their cab was gone. Eddie strode to the street to hail another. His movements were powerful, confident—not at all like the damage in his scent, the fear and anger. Lyssa didn't realize she was holding her breath until there was some distance between them.

"I don't want to ask this," she said, speaking to his back. "But what the hell is wrong with you?"

"Nothing."

"Is it because I don't want to give up?"

"I'm not asking you to."

"Yes, you are, if you ask me to leave. I'm terrified, Eddie. I'm scared out of my wits. But if I break now . . . if I let myself run . . ."

I'll never stop, she wanted to say. *I'll run forever, until I die. Like a cornered animal.*

"Safe isn't the same as giving in," he said in a low, hard voice. "Safe is buying time, coming up with a plan."

"The plan is now," she said, but even as those words left her mouth, the sidewalk began spinning. Sweat broke out, and so did nausea. She tilted sideways, lights dancing in her eyes—and something wet bubbled inside her nostril.

She touched the spot. Her fingers came away red.

"Damn it," Eddie muttered, covering the distance between them in moments. "Hold on to me."

Lyssa closed her eyes, dizzy. "I'm not an invalid."

"You're an Amazon," he replied. "Here's a cab. Get in."

She tried to pull away. "No, I don't think so."

He didn't say a word—just grabbed the front of her jacket, holding her still. But he didn't need to touch her to do that. All it took was the look in his eyes. All the gentleness gone, replaced by a cold that sank through her, into her heart. It bruised her feelings and frightened her.

She stared at him, knowing full well she could hide nothing of what she felt—and as he stared back, a terrible darkness entered his eyes.

With what seemed to be a great deal of effort, he let go of the jacket. Lyssa let out her breath. Stepped back, and climbed into the cab.

After a moment, Eddie followed.

"Bayard and Elizabeth Street," he told the driver, then glanced sideways. "We're meeting Lannes and Lethe in Chinatown."

The cab accelerated into traffic. Lyssa leaned against the door, aching and tired. "Can I talk about this without you freaking out?"

"Yes," he said tightly.

"I've been hunted for ten years," she told him. "Since I was twelve years old. I always knew I would be found. And I knew when it happened, I'd have to make a choice. Run . . . or stand my ground and fight."

The cabbie glanced in his rearview mirror.

"World of Warcraft," Lyssa told him. "It's a gaming thing. We're very melodramatic."

She turned back to Eddie, expecting him to say something . . . anything . . . but it was as if he hadn't heard a word. He remained silent, staring at his hands, which were resting flat on his thighs. Lyssa stared, too—at his scars.

The cab driver rolled down the window, fussing with his heater. "Turning into an oven in here."

She hadn't noticed the heat rising off Eddie, but when the cab driver spoke, she felt an invisible flame wrap around her, from head to toe. It felt good, and she didn't like that. Right now, she wanted to feel cold, resolved.

She tried to move away from him, but came up against the door. Eddie turned his head, and watched her. She looked away from him, out the window.

The cab ride seemed to take forever. Traffic was bad. Lyssa heard sirens all around them, far away and close, wailing through her until the noise was in her spine, and her heart beat to the rise and fall of that ominous sound.

Chinatown was run-down and gritty. Even the cover of night and neon lights couldn't hide the dirty awnings and sidewalks. Five- and six-story walk-ups lined Bayard Street, those brick faces crowded with fire escapes, and cheap, glowing signs covered in a funky mix of English names and Chinese characters. There was hardly enough room to drive. Everything from delivery trucks to minivans parked on both sides of the narrow one-way street.

The cab dropped them off at the intersection of Elizabeth and Bayard. Lyssa got out first and put her face to the cold wind, inhaling exhaust and grease scents, and an undercurrent of sewage, slime. She smelled blood, too, but realized—as she pushed back her hair—that it was from her hand.

Nauseating twirling sensations hit her, as though she were going to vomit and spin at the same time. Eyes closed, she breathed even deeper, ignoring the tingle of power that rode up her right arm.

Before today, she would never have contemplated casting a spell—let alone three. *I knew the price,* she thought, with dread.

"Lyssa," Eddie said, and she made room for him to exit the cab.

It was difficult not to limp along as she walked, hunched over and nauseated. Even her heart pounded too hard. For some reason, that made her think of Mandy, dying alone in the park. She felt like the same thing was happening to her.

Eddie slid his arm through hers. She tried to pull away, but even with her inhuman edge of strength, he didn't budge.

"Lean on me," he said.

"I don't want to." *I'm afraid to. You'll let me down.*

He didn't say anything or let go. Lyssa had no choice but to keep up, but it was easier than she expected to fall in at his side. Natural, as though she'd been doing it all her life. Heat flowed between them. Her heart began to slow. Breathing was easier.

Don't be tricked, she told herself. *This doesn't mean anything.*

Of course it does, replied the dragon, as the muscles of her right arm twitched. *What would* you *say? Oh, yes.* Loosen up.

Loosen up. She hadn't been loose in ten years. She hadn't even been flexible. Her heart was so stiff and brittle, it would break if anyone touched it.

Especially him.

They stopped in front of a narrow metal door crammed beneath the awning of a magazine store. Teen girls filled the small, well-lit clothing shop next door. One of them looked up, saw Eddie, and began nudging the others. She didn't think he noticed until he turned slightly to put his back to them.

Lyssa peered around his shoulder. The girls were giggling, biting their bottom lips as they checked out his ass.

"They think you're cute," she told him. "Not a criminal."

"It's amazing how fine a line that can be," he replied, unlocking the door.

They entered a dark corridor. The cracks in the walls were wide enough to stick her fingers into, and the pea green linoleum on the floor had been spray-painted with obscenities—as well as one giant heart decorated with a skull and crossbones.

Mold tickled her nose, but so did the dry, salt-breeze scent of the gargoyle—accompanied by notes of jasmine, vanilla.

"Lannes and Lethe are here," she said.

They began climbing a narrow staircase so steep it was almost a ladder. Lyssa had to stop halfway up, breathless. Worn-out.

For the briefest, most terrible moment—she thought about cutting herself again. Just a little cut, a little blood, to give herself energy. Enough to get through this day.

Or I could cut Eddie.

Revulsion filled her. Lyssa leaned hard on the cracked wall and pressed her fist against her mouth. Memories trickled—memories of power, and being inside the *Cruor Venator*'s rotting mind.

Other memories strained: her mother's smiling eyes, a splash of blood on snow. Her father's scream of rage.

Both of them murdered. Estefan killed, and many others. All because power had become someone else's addiction. Power and revenge. What had she said to those guys studying *Macbeth*?

Once you decide to use violence to get power, it's difficult to stop.

Eddie hung back, two steps down—and leaned on the wall opposite her.

Silence fell. Just their breathing and the creak of the building. Muffled voices from outside, and the honk of a car horn. Her heartbeat. Her terrible thoughts.

Lyssa closed her eyes. "Something you want to say to me?"

She heard him climb the steps separating them. The stairwell was barely wide enough for her shoulders, let alone two people. His leg touched hers, and his hand slid past her arm to rest against the wall. Heat poured off him. Fire. Fire in her own skin, licking down to bone, and blood.

"Is it easier not to look at me?" he asked, in a soft voice.

"Yes," said Lyssa.

"Okay," he replied. "It's about what you said in the cab."

"I didn't think you heard me."

"I was listening." His thumb brushed against her mouth, and she flinched, opening her eyes . . . and meeting his. "I understand fighting. I understand the choice to run . . . or hold your ground. I respect you for it."

"So what's the problem?"

His expression was so severe. "Lyssa. Don't play dumb."

She pushed against his chest. "Fine. *Of course* I'll get hurt. There's no win in this situation. I'm *already* hurt. I'm just not dead."

"That's not good enough. I want you safe, alive, and happy." He caught her hand and held it against him, unmoving. "Is it such a bad thing for someone to care what the hell happens to you?"

Yes, she thought, suddenly exhausted. *Yes, if I lose them.*

Heavy footsteps on the landing. Heavy as a gargoyle. Lyssa sagged against the wall, heart sinking into her stomach as she looked away from Lannes and Eddie—staring down the stairs, desperately fighting for control over her memories, and grief.

Eddie said, in a rough voice, "Give us a minute."

Silence. Then, Lannes replied, mildly, "Is everything okay?"

Lyssa closed her eyes, tears rolling down her cheeks. Eddie made a small sound, deep in his throat, and moved so that he blocked her from Lannes.

"We're fine," he said, in a gentler tone. "We'll be right there."

She couldn't see their faces, but the hush that fell in that stairwell was immense, and charged.

Until, finally, she heard the rustle of wings and the groan of stairs.

Eddie let out his breath. Lyssa chanced a look and found his back turned to her. He stood one step above her, staring up at the landing. His hands curled in loose fists. Strong, broad, steady.

"I'll be honest," she murmured, closing her eyes again. "I didn't like it when you were angry with me, back at the apartment building. And I don't like it that I even cared."

Eddie turned and sat on the steps. Then he held out his hand to her.

His hand looked so large and warm. Lyssa couldn't help herself, and let him draw her down to the same step: crammed together, side by side, in that narrow space, cocooned in cracking walls and heat, and shadow.

He held her hand in a loose grip. "You know my worst nightmare? Losing my temper. I did that once, and it ended . . . so badly. And, oddly, not as bad as I wanted it to."

The wounds in her heart bled a little more. "Is that why you ran from home?"

"Yes." Eddie looked down at their hands, turning them over so his scars were hidden. "And I wasn't mad at you."

"Yes, you were."

He closed his eyes. "I'll go insane if I can't protect you. But . . . I'm afraid I won't be strong enough. I hesitated, with Betty, at the end. I knew what I had to do, but taking that last step . . ."

"I know," she said softly. "Part of the reason I've been running all these years is that I don't *want* to kill." Lyssa held up her right hand, oddly shaped inside the glove. "I was so close to taking Betty's life. And then, when Lannes finished her . . ."

"I felt relieved," he said, and they shared a long look.

"Well," Lyssa told him, finally. "I'm glad."

The corner of his mouth softened. "That so?"

"I hate movies where the heroes just go around shooting people like it's nothing. You know, bang-bang, right in the face—and then they get off some funny line and keep on going like it's just another day, and oh—it's time for lunch."

His smile grew a fraction more. "But some people find that sexy."

Lyssa struck a pose, aiming a gun with her fingers. *"Pew-pew."*

A snort escaped him, and his eyes warmed.

"You're right," she said, blowing on her finger, concentrating on making actual smoke trickle from the tip of her glove. "It's totally hot."

Eddie laughed outright and covered her hand with his. His smile faded, though, and he bowed his head . . . drawing her hand close to his chest, holding it with heart-stopping gentleness. Lyssa leaned in and kissed the top of his head.

Above them, the ceiling creaked. Someone big was pacing.

"Your friends are waiting," she said.

"You're my friend, too." Eddie glanced up at the ceiling. "You saved Lannes and Lethe today."

"It wasn't that simple."

"You saved them," he said firmly. "You didn't have to come with me, and you didn't have to help them, but you did. I know it cost you something."

Lyssa remembered the taste of Lethe's blood . . . and how good it had felt when she frightened those witches. Knowing she could own them, if she really wanted it.

She sighed. "I would do it again in a heartbeat."

"But?"

"You're right. It cost me."

Maybe my soul, she thought.

CHAPTER FOURTEEN

DIRK & Steele owned the entire building—five stories filled with a handful of individual apartments that remained locked and unused, except for times like these, when people needed a place to go.

Eddie found Lannes on the second floor, inside the first apartment on the left. Hardly any furniture: two chairs and a battered folding table, and a small dingy lamp on the floor in the corner. Illusion-clad, he stood in the middle of the apartment with his arms folded over his massive chest. Unhappiness and unease were written all over his face, and his frown only deepened when he saw Lyssa.

"We shouldn't have left you," Lannes said, when they walked in. "I'm sorry. I wasn't thinking."

"You did the right thing," Eddie told him. "Don't doubt it for a minute."

"The woman . . ." He looked down, staring at his big hands. "Is she really dead?"

"She was only the servant of a *Cruor Venator*," Lyssa said, quietly. "So yes, she's dead."

"Just a servant?" Lannes gave her a haunted look. "The way she made me feel . . . the fear . . . I was certain she was one of them."

"Close enough. If you hadn't killed her, she would have reported your existence to the witch. The *Cruor Venator* would have certainly hunted you and your family."

Eddie thought of the gleam in Betty's eye and the blood that had dripped from her knife. Estefan had been skinned alive, drained, partially eaten . . . what would they do to a gargoyle, who would be even harder to kill?

He swallowed hard. "Lethe's people will . . . get rid of the body. We didn't ask how."

"I don't want to know." Lannes raked his hands through his illusory hair though his hands hitched upward—as though hitting his horns. "What a day."

No kidding. Eddie fought to keep his feelings in check: more anger and fear, and something deeper, more disturbing. "You both have to leave the city."

"Obviously." For a moment, pain eased in the gargoyle's face . . . and his mouth twitched into a smile that was wild and tremulous. "I'm going to be a father."

Warmth spread through Eddie's chest, accompanied by an odd longing that made him glance at Lyssa. She was looking at him, too, though her gaze flew instantly away. Her cheeks reddened.

He cleared his throat. "Congratulations."

"It's impossible," whispered the gargoyle, as if he didn't hear him. "I'm terrified. What if her mother was right? I'm not human. The baby could be . . . deformed, or sick . . ."

"Lannes," he said quietly. "It's a miracle. Don't overthink it."

"I know." He flexed his fingers and looked at Lyssa. "You and I need to talk."

She gave him wary look. "Okay."

Lannes fidgeted. "I'll never be able to thank you enough for what you did today. You saved my wife and me. You saved my child."

She was silent a moment. "But?"

But nothing, thought Eddie, disturbed at the regret that filled Lannes's eyes . . . as though bad news was coming . . . and he was the bearer. Suspicious, already feeling defensive, he stepped closer.

Lannes gave him a slight frown but focused in on Lyssa . . . and in a voice so low, so quiet it was difficult to hear him, he said, "I know what you are now. So forgive me . . . but I don't feel comfortable with your presence. I respectfully ask that you stay away." His gaze flickered back to Eddie. "From all of us."

Eddie felt stunned. Lyssa's shoulders sank, but she showed no surprise. Just acceptance. As if she expected nothing less.

Seeing *that* was almost as terrible as hearing Lannes reject her.

Anger settled hard in his chest like a cold, iron ball. "How can you say that, Lannes? After *everything* she did for you and Lethe? She *saved* you both."

Lyssa wrapped her hands around his arm. "He's trying to be your friend. It's not personal."

"Of course it's personal."

"No, he's right."

"Listen to her," Lannes said. "You don't understand what she is."

"I know what matters."

"No," he said, grim. "And what you don't know might kill you."

Lyssa flinched. Eddie stepped in front of her. "We're not having this conversation."

"We *have* to."

"You can go to hell."

"*Stop*," Lyssa cried, and the strangled grief in her voice made both men go quiet and stare.

"Stop," she said again, and looked at Eddie, then Lannes, with tortured eyes. "Please, stop this. I'll go. I promise, I'll go . . . and I will never come near your family again. Just don't . . . don't lose your friendship over this. I'm not worth it."

But it was too late. He remembered what the old woman, Ursula, had said to Lyssa about her mother—how she had been treated unfairly. He recalled her bitterness about Long Nu, her confession that friends and family had rejected her parents.

He had the horrible suspicion that this was how she had lived her life—pushed away, for no reason. Pushed away for some reason that couldn't possibly matter.

Every protective instinct railed against that—everything in him, battling the urge to sink his fist in Lannes's face.

That wasn't him, though. Fighting was not *him*. But being with Lyssa, seeing her pain, turned his entire sense of self upside down.

He wasn't sure he could trust his own heart or the blood in his veins, or his instincts—but he also knew he didn't have a choice. Everything in him was pulling toward *her*. Even now, all he wanted to do was put her behind him, against him, and protect her. With his last breath.

Eddie covered her hand, and squeezed. Lyssa stared at him, still and pale, lost in his jacket.

"You're worth it," he told her. "You're worth it to me."

A hush fell between them. Nothing else mattered but the way she looked at him, but there were no words for what he saw in her eyes. Maybe grief. Maybe joy.

Maybe anguish. He felt as though he were dangling from a cliff by his fingertips, ready to fall—or be caught.

Lyssa pulled her hand from his arm and stepped back. Eddie didn't move a muscle or breathe, though his heart felt as though needles were jabbing and cutting it free of its moorings.

Falling. He was falling, and no one was going to catch him.

He watched her turn and face Lannes, who observed her with unease.

"I never asked to be found," she told him. "And while I know *exactly* why I make you uneasy . . . don't you *dare* take that out on him. Don't be that small-hearted. He doesn't deserve it." Her voice broke a little. "You're lucky he cares about you. If you throw that away, because of *me* . . ."

Warmth pooled in Eddie's chest. Suddenly, he could breathe again.

Lannes unfolded his arms and made a slashing motion with his hand. The illusion surrounding him flowed away in tendrils of light, revealing silver skin and hard muscle, and folds of wings that fell around his massive arms.

"I don't toss out friends," he rumbled. "But I do protect them. You know why he's not safe with you."

Fire rolled off Eddie's hands. Actual flames, throwing off sparks that hissed and crackled in the air.

"Lannes," he warned, just as someone else said the gargoyle's name—even more sharply, with *real* annoyance.

Lethe emerged from the hall, pale, hair mussed, with shadows under her eyes. Maybe she had been resting, or making a call . . . but she walked up to her husband and craned her neck to stare at him. Then, she poked his chest.

"This isn't you," she said. "Lyssa Andreanos saved our lives. You owe her *more* than the benefit of the doubt. And if you won't bend on this, I will."

Lannes looked away. "Call me a hypocrite if you want, but—"

"You're a hypocrite. My family called you a monster and told you to get lost. Now you're going to do the same thing? You're going to be a father. Not a maniac."

"Is there a difference?" he asked, with some exasperation.

Lethe walked to Lyssa, and before anyone could react, reached out and hugged her, hard. Lannes cursed to himself. Lyssa tensed, surprise flickering over her face. But finally, she patted the other woman's back, awkwardly.

"I'm not a hugger, just so you know," Lethe told her, pulling back. "You're welcome in our home, anytime you want."

"Er," said Lyssa, glancing at the gargoyle. "I don't know if that would be a good idea."

Lethe set her jaw. "I mean it. I just spoke with Ursula."

"What?" Lannes said.

His wife ignored him. "Thank you. For everything."

Lyssa looked uncomfortable. "It was nothing."

Lethe's smile held real warmth, and compassion. "We both know that's not true." She glanced at Eddie, then Lannes. "Both of you, out. I want to speak with Lyssa alone."

"No," Lannes said. "She's—"

"Get over it," Eddie interrupted, and shot Lyssa a quick look. "You okay with this?"

She hesitated a heartbeat too long. "Yes."

Eddie stepped in front of her, blocking the others from sight. Making it just the two of them. Searching her gaze. Letting her search his. Waiting.

Lyssa relaxed a little and gave him a faint smile.

"I'm sure," she said, to his unasked question.

"Okay." Eddie backed away and glanced at Lannes. "Come on."

The gargoyle hesitated, but his wife pushed him to the door. Eddie paused just outside the apartment and gave Lyssa one last look. She stood alone in the center of the room, hugging her right arm against her body, her gaze lost and distant, and filled with sadness.

Lannes waited at the bottom of the stairs, illusion firmly in place. Eddie stopped several steps above. A full minute passed in silence.

Finally, Lannes sighed. "I repair antique books, Eddie. It's quiet work, and I don't go searching out trouble. I used to do that, and you know what happened." He looked him dead in the eyes. "Do you know what you're doing?"

Eddie set his jaw. "Yes."

"Do you know why you're suddenly immune to magic?"

No answer for that. Lannes sighed. "No, you don't know what you're doing."

"You said you wanted to help this girl who was being hunted by witches."

"She *is* a witch."

"So is your wife."

Lannes grimaced. "Fine. But it's worse than that."

Eddie looked down at the scars on his hand. "What is it?"

"Do you know what gargoyles used to do, back in the ancient days? Did my brother ever tell you?"

A chill filled him. "He said your kind hunted demons."

"No more of those around. Not the way there used to be. But they bred with humans, and every now and then . . . you run across some of those descendants. Humans, with a flick of demon in them. We've got a sixth sense for that sort of thing."

Eddie steeled himself. "And?"

Lannes gave him a hard look. "I thought it was just the witch vibe I was picking up. But it was more than that. Lyssa Andreanos is not just a shape-shifter, and she's not only a witch.

"She's part demon, too."

LETHE CAME DOWNSTAIRS FIRST, BUT SHE WOULD not tell them what they had discussed. Instead, she leaned against her husband, o1e of his massive arms slung around her waist, and closed her eyes with a sigh that seemed to travel through her body and his at the same time.

"I like her," she said to Lannes. "Give her a chance."

He grunted, but his tone was softer than it had been up in the apartment. Eddie had spoken his mind, just between the two of them—and so had Lannes.

He looked away and found Lyssa coming down the stairs, taking each step with slow, careful grace—and some wariness. Eddie walked up the stairs to meet her. She stopped, teetering, searching his eyes.

"You okay?" he asked.

She gave him an uncertain look. "Fine. You?"

He brushed his lips over her cheek.

"Better now," he whispered, in her ear. Lyssa let out her breath, tension flowing from her shoulders.

She wasn't certain I'd still be here, he thought, watching her peer around him at the gargoyle.

Lannes looked at her, as well. And then Eddie.

"We're done here," Lethe said, and pushed open the door to walk outside, letting in a blast of sound. "We're going to the airport and taking a flight back to Maine."

The stairwell had been quiet, musty, and dark. The city on the other side of the door hurt his eyes: too many headlights, so many people. He thought about fire, and skinned shape-shifters, witches and demons. Danger, everywhere. No place could possibly be safe.

Not even *his* home. Not where Matthew Swint still walked.

Hopelessness slipped over him, but he pushed it away. *Was this why Lyssa's parents lived in Montana?* Eddie wondered, thinking about what Lannes had told him. *Not just because their friends rejected them but because living in the middle of nowhere gave them the illusion of safety?*

Lannes glanced down at Eddie. "You coming with us?" And then he amended that, by saying, "Both of you are welcome."

Lyssa shook her head. "I can't go. But thank you."

"I'm staying with her," Eddie said.

The illusion hid none of the gargoyle's emotions: His mouth flattened into a grim line, and his gaze was all flint and shadows. "Despite everything I said, I was *not* going to abandon you."

"This isn't abandonment. This is a matter of priorities." Eddie held out his hand, and Lannes clasped it in a firm grip.

Instead of letting go, however, the gargoyle pulled him close, and in his ear, whispered, "Remember what I told you. Just in case."

Eddie tensed. Lannes glanced past him at Lyssa— who was holding back from them, hands shoved in her pockets.

"You," he said. "Whatever happens . . . keep him safe."

She remained silent. Eddie pulled back his hand. "Give my best to your brothers."

Lannes hesitated, giving Lyssa another long, assessing look. Lethe stepped in front of him and patted his face until he looked down at her.

"Save the death stare for someone who deserves it," she said dryly, and drew him away. He went reluctantly, scowling when his wife waggled her fingers at Lyssa.

Lannes shot Eddie a glare, mouthed, "Watch yourself," then turned and strode down the sidewalk with Lethe at his side. At the end of the block, they flagged a cab.

"Well," said Lyssa, in a mild voice. "That was interesting."

Eddie's brow arched. "What happened with Lethe?"

"She's afraid her family will tell someone about her pregnancy—by accident, or not. If the child is a true hybrid between a human witch and a gargoyle . . ."

She didn't have to finish that sentence. Eddie understood, and it made him afraid for his friends. If someone decided their child was valuable enough to steal . . .

"That's not all you talked about with her," he said.

"I'm sure Lannes gave you an earful." Lyssa sighed, and rubbed her neck. "You sure you want to stick around?"

Eddie stared at her. She gave him a weary smile.

"Okay," she said. "Come on. It's been a long day, and we need to rest. I'll take you home."

CHAPTER FIFTEEN

A N hour later they stood on a dark, quiet street ten
blocks from Central Park, in a tree-lined neighborhood that felt removed, and cocooned, from the
rush of the city around it. All the buildings were old
and made of stone and brick, with little identity to dif-
ferentiate one from the other.

Lyssa led him up the stairs to a wooden door and
dialed an access code.

"You live here?" he asked, as she led him inside,
down a narrow hall.

"It's complicated," she said. "I have a studio upstairs, but that's not where we're going. There's a safer
spot I know."

She yanked open a door that led to the basement.
Faint gouge marks were in the wood—the same shape
as her claws. "This place was built almost a hundred
years ago. Most of the inside has been gutted and re-
built about a dozen times over, but some things never
changed."

They clattered down the stairs. The lights were on,
and Eddie saw a laundry room off to the right, set in
the only well-lit spot in the basement. The door was

partially closed, but he heard washing machines rumbling, and a radio playing a slow love song. A man and woman were laughing.

The air smelled like detergent and rust, and wet concrete. Thick pipes ran along the ceiling. Ahead of them was a crudely built chain-link wall that blocked off a makeshift mechanical room.

Lyssa ignored it all and headed to a pitch-black corridor that ran to the left between the foundation wall and a slab of stone. Maintenance had hung a rope across the entrance, and attached was a sign that read: DO NOT ENTER UNLESS YOU WANT TO DIE.

Lyssa took off her backpack and slipped under the rope. Eddie paused. "Anything I should know?"

"Don't pet the rats," she said. "Come on. I do this all the time."

Eddie frowned but followed her into the tunnel. Several feet in, she stopped and crouched.

"The tunnel keeps going into the next building's basement," she whispered. "But it got walled off a couple years ago. Management keeps threatening to do the same with this one."

Her right hand scrabbled at an ancient manhole cover set in the stone floor. Eddie said, "Let me help you."

"I got it," muttered Lyssa, as her clawed fingers slipped through the tiny holes. Grunting, she hauled backward and lifted out the thick metal disc.

Eddie stared. Lyssa blinked at him. "What?"

"Remind me never to arm wrestle you."

Her mouth twitched. "Get in. There's a ladder."

"You sure this isn't a dirty trick?"

"Well, it'll be dirty."

He smiled and lowered himself into the hole. Lyssa followed, clinging to the ladder to pull the manhole cover back into place—plunging Eddie into blinding darkness. It wasn't the same as being in a dark room. This was a sightlessness that carried its own oppressive weight: claustrophobic and immense.

Dizzy, he swayed into a set of warm hands.

"Sorry," he said, hoarse. "I'm blind down here."

"I won't let you get hurt," she said.

Words that made an unwanted memory surface.

She's part demon. And there's something else. I knew it the moment I saw her taste that blood.

Eddie didn't want to think about what Lannes had said. He fumbled until he found Lyssa's arm, then her shoulder. It was her right arm. Right shoulder. He forgot that until she flinched.

"Er," she muttered. "I'm twitchy."

Eddie didn't want her to feel embarrassed. "For years I didn't like to be touched."

"You didn't like it . . . or you were afraid of it?"

"I was afraid. For a variety of reasons."

Lyssa pressed her hand against his chest. He shied away from the unexpectedness of contact—and the heat that exploded from it, inside him.

Eddie caught his breath. "I guess I'm . . . twitchy, too."

"Does it ever go away?"

"I don't know."

"Tell me if it does." The wistfulness in her voice made his heart ache, and so did her hand, capturing his. "Come on. You'll have to walk sideways for a while. It's going to get narrow."

"You never answered my question. Where are we going?"

"Down. This city is full of tunnels. Most are old and not on any map. Dug by hand in the early part of the twentieth century, used to run guns and liquor—sometimes men and women who wanted to keep their comings and goings private. Urban legend."

"Fairy tales. A dragon in the middle of them."

She laughed, and the sound sent a frisson of heat through his body. "When I was little, I used to pretend I was a princess. Never the dragon."

"Why not?"

"I didn't realize shape-shifting wasn't normal. Being a princess, though . . . that was magic."

Eddie had believed in magic, as a boy. And then he'd stopped.

The walls were uneven, sometimes jagged and sharp when he touched them. Cut from rock, hacked away, sloping downward at a steep angle. Eddie had to watch his breathing as he walked—not because he was out of shape but because it was too easy to feel buried alive.

He lost track of time. Lyssa never let go of his hand. Once, she pressed down on his head. "Watch yourself."

"I could light a fire to see with."

"Trust me," she replied.

Do I trust you? Eddie wondered, feeling her body tight against his side, guiding him. *What do I risk by trusting you?*

Because with Lyssa, it wasn't like trusting one of the guys. It wasn't the same as trusting Serena to watch his back, or Roland not to stab it. It felt deeper than that, more raw. As though he was asking whether or not he trusted himself.

And he didn't trust himself.

Eddie heard water dripping, and the squeak of rats. "How did you find this place?"

"I was desperate. There's nothing here that burns. I can't . . ." Lyssa paused, and he sensed her weighing words. "I can't sleep . . . in a normal place. I have nightmares, and when I dream . . ."

"Fire," he said. "I have a room for that."

"Really?"

"Why are you surprised?"

"You seem to have your act together."

"No." He thought about his cage in the penthouse. He hated it. But it was heaven compared to this. "My emotions get the better of me, as you've seen. Sometimes . . . I think it would be easier not to feel anything at all."

"Don't say that."

"Why not?"

"Because there are already too many cowards in the world. Myself included."

Eddie didn't know anyone else who could affect him the way she did, just with words. She was right. Not feeling anything was the easy way out. Safe. How many years had he been running from himself?

"You're no coward," he told her. "Just the opposite."

"You have no idea," she replied. "Careful. There's a big hole on your right."

"I'm serious."

"Step sideways."

He stopped walking altogether. "Ten years on your own, surviving. I know what that means, Lyssa. I know the cost."

"Eddie."

"I know what it's like to have *no one*. To spend nights sitting up, hiding in boxes with a piece of glass in your hand because you're afraid someone will sneak up and kill you, or worse. I know hunger, Lyssa. I know every hunger imaginable. I know what it's like, trying to stay alive without becoming the predator."

She broke away, leaving him dizzy and alone in the darkness.

"Lyssa," he called out, before he could stop himself. "I tried to kill myself once."

He was horrified to hear those words come from his mouth—horrified and stunned—and then, just humiliated.

But even in that absolute darkness, he felt the heat of her stare—so he cleared his throat, and said in a hoarse voice, "Some things are too hard to live with. I didn't want to hurt anyone . . . ever again. And I was sick of hiding, of being alone. There was no one to go to. No one I trusted well enough to ask for help."

He was rubbing his hands, their scars, and stopped himself with a deep breath. "I got better. What I am . . . what I did . . . I can live with now. I can say it out loud. I don't have to hide all the time."

Which was a lie. He was still hiding. No one knew the truth of what he'd done, all those years ago. What he *hadn't* done. This was as close to it as he'd ever come to speaking the words . . . and her silence killed him.

His beating heart was louder than the world. For the first time, he saw a glint of golden light in the darkness: two faint sparks, in the shape of eyes.

"I never tried to kill myself," Lyssa said finally, in a soft voice. "But I thought about it sometimes. It frightens me, how close I came."

Her words hit him hard, again. Old wounds suddenly felt fresh, and sharp. Eddie couldn't push down the loneliness, the grief, fast enough. He folded his arms over his chest, bracing himself, holding himself up, keeping his head down—because even in the darkness, he was afraid of what she might see in his eyes.

"Like I said," he whispered, "you're no coward."

"I am. In every way that matters." Her voice broke. "You don't know how easy it would have been for me to leave you and your friends today."

"But you didn't."

"Neither did you."

"No. But I've run, in the past. I've let people get hurt when I could have done something to stop it. I almost let the same thing happen today when I didn't finish off Betty. So whatever you think you've done, or haven't . . ." Eddie stopped, fighting for the right words, wondering why the hell he'd opened his mouth in the first place. What was he trying to tell her? Why had he vomited all these emotions that he'd thought were dead?

That slow-burning glow of her eyes drew near. Eddie looked into that light, and said, "People change. Whatever you think you are, or have done, it's not . . . the end of it."

"My mother used to say that. She'd tell me . . . you make up for your mistakes by *living*. You pay back the bad debts by being worth something, somehow, to someone."

"I like your mother."

"I loved her." Lyssa drew in a shaky breath. "But I don't think I've followed her advice. It's easier to run than to fight."

"I know it is," Eddie said, on the verge of telling her about his sister. It was too easy to talk to Lyssa, to tell the worst parts of himself. Things no one else knew. Things, he realized now, that he was desperate to unburden.

He looked down, blind and lost. Moments later, Lyssa's hand found his. Her touch was warm, soft.

"Life is hard," she murmured.

He squeezed her hand. "It could be worse."

A short, sad laugh escaped her. "Yeah."

And then she sucked in her breath. Eddie knew that sound. Full of pain, shock.

"What is it?" he asked sharply, staggering backward as she hunched over, her shoulder hitting his. Her entire body quaked with terrible violence, and a crawling sensation filled his throat.

Heat exploded against his skin, sparks of flames riding through the air. His left shirtsleeve caught on fire, illuminating the darkness.

Lyssa stood beside him, hugging her right arm against her body. She twisted, shielding her eyes from the light, and snarled.

"Put that out," she said harshly.

"You're hurt."

She tried to knock him back. Eddie ignored the weak blow and moved in close. Fire shone golden and warm on her hair. She kept her face turned away from him.

"Lyssa," he said again.

"It's nothing. My arm. I told you, I have trouble with it, sometimes."

"Let me see."

"No," she said, and shuddered. "All I need is time."

He ripped off the remains of his burning sleeve and held it in his hand. "Are we close to where you were taking me?"

Lyssa nodded tightly. "Just down this tunnel."

Eddie slid his arm around her waist. "Relax. I've got you."

She was silent a moment.

"I'm glad," she said.

ACCORDING TO LYSSA, THE SUBWAY TUNNEL THAT Eddie soon found himself in had been the victim of bad planning, corrupt politics, and a more powerful real-estate developer who had wanted all that underground territory for his own projects. Sealed at both ends some time in the early seventies, it was blocked off from anything functional—except for two very old tunnels, hand-dug, that had been uncovered during the initial excavation.

Eddie and Lyssa emerged from one of those tunnels, dirty and tired, and sweating.

He heard voices in the distance. She bumped him sideways with her hip and steered him across rough, uneven ground. The remains of his sleeve had burned to almost nothing, leaving him nearly blind—again.

Lyssa stopped him. "We're here."

Eddie wasn't sure what that meant—until, unexpectedly, she placed his hand on a steel bar that slanted down and felt like a rail.

"Hold on," she muttered, and he listened to her move away from him, her feet scuffing upward as though climbing stairs. His sleeve turned to ash. Eddie let it fall away from his hand, and waited in the darkness.

Metal rattled. A loud groan filled the air.

Then, light. A flickering flame. Eddie focused on it and sighed.

Lyssa held a candle in her hand. It shed enough light that he could see the stairs beside him.

He joined her at the narrow doorway. She had already taken off his jacket and laid it neatly on the back of a small plastic chair.

"This used to be the workers' station," she told him. "Come in."

It was one small room made of concrete, with a stone floor that had been carefully swept and covered in bright-colored rugs. A plastic table was set against the wall, covered in paper and pens, inks, tin cans full of brushes. Water jugs were on the floor, surrounding a small cooler. In the corner was a sleeping bag.

In his opinion, quite cozy. Surprisingly so. Homey, even.

Except for the scent of smoke, and charred walls.

Eddie walked in, carefully. If he'd been wearing a hat, he would have taken it off. He felt as though he were trespassing, that the ground beneath him was made of glass. He was certain, in his gut, that few people ever came here.

"You're probably wondering how anyone could live like this." Lyssa set the candle on the desk and started lighting others. She used matches, he noticed. Not her own power.

He joined her at the table. "No, I would have been happy for something this good, not so long ago."

Lyssa glanced at him. Eddie said, "I told you I was homeless."

"Yes," she said, with particular gentleness.

"I ended up in Los Angeles. It wasn't an easy place to survive."

"L.A.," she said, staring at him with a compassion that made him want to sit down. "I tried living there when I was thirteen. It was a nightmare. I went to Vegas next, but when you're a kid, alone, there's nothing for you."

"Nothing you want to be part of," he added. "You were younger than me."

"Twelve, when I . . . when I began. I didn't know

anything." Lyssa looked down at the table and scattered paintings. "How'd you survive?"

"I stole," he said, and hated those words, and the memories. "I got odd jobs. I ate from garbage cans. I did everything short of prostituting myself. Sometimes I wonder if I didn't do that anyway, just not with sex."

Lyssa didn't say anything, just ran her fingers over a watercolor filled with flames and an empty white spot. Eddie said, "I've never talked about it."

"How could you? No one would understand." She finally looked at him. "It's not just surviving. It's keeping the secret. It's keeping other people safe from you."

"I don't like to remember." He took a deep breath, then another, and studied the watercolors and sketches in front of him. There were a lot, and each was extraordinary: castles on clouds, and dragons floating on ponds; and women holding spears, with flowers in their hair.

There was fire, too. Fire, in several paintings, and in one, especially, which Lyssa kept staring at.

"These are beautiful," he said, which was inadequate, but he thought she might be embarrassed by too much praise.

"Thanks." Lyssa went to the cooler and flipped it open. Inside was half a loaf of wheat bread, a small bag of apples, and a couple bottles of water. "I'm an illustrator."

"Really?"

"Surprise," she said, with a faint smile. "Mostly children's books, some comic-book covers. I do spreads in magazines, every now and then."

"I . . ." Eddie stopped, and took a water bottle from her outstretched hand. "How?"

"I taught myself. I told you I hung out in libraries. I spent time around the art books, because I liked the pictures . . . and I had done a lot of drawing before my parents died. My dad was a painter. Most of his work . . . burned in the fire." Lyssa cleared her throat. "I'd find old newspaper or scraps of scratch paper around the library . . . pencils, pens . . . and then I'd draw. I drew everything. There was a librarian in Salt Lake City . . . Mrs. Shue . . . who paid special attention to me. She gave me a sketchbook, and I used that to make money. I'd tell people I was in high school, raising cash for charity . . . and then I'd draw portraits for whatever people wanted to donate."

Eddie smiled in admiration. "And then?"

"Luck. I drew a portrait of a woman who ran a local comic-book store, and she liked what I did enough that she had me sketch some superheroes for an event she wanted to advertise. It wasn't much, but it gave me confidence. And then Mrs. Shue started leaving out books on art school. I knew I couldn't go, but I started researching how people make a living at that sort of thing. Building a portfolio, making contacts. It helped that my librarian was having some luck selling her own writing. She started making inroads at children's magazines and recommended me to some editors."

"You did it."

Lyssa shrugged. "It was slow. I didn't have anything better to do. I wasn't in school, so all my time was spent trying to make a living at the only thing I was really good at."

She made it sound as though it were nothing, but Eddie knew better. Brains, determination, talent . . . she'd taken all that, and despite everything else against her . . . had turned it into something beautiful.

"I didn't have aspirations," he told her, "except to survive. I stole cars. I was good at it, but it was dangerous. You had to be careful of the territory you worked, the people you worked *for*. Cops almost caught me more times than I can remember. I never felt safe. And then . . . not long after I got out, I heard that the crew I ran with had gotten in some dispute with a local gang. Most ended up dead, or in jail."

"You seem so straightlaced."

He looked away. "I was a thief. I could still be a thief if I had to be. I saw so many tourists this morning, and there was a part of me coming up with a plan for how to take each one of them. Pick pocket, or short con. Snatch and grab. I used to tell myself that taking personal property didn't really matter. As long as I didn't hurt anyone physically, all that *stuff* could be replaced."

"But that's not how it works," she said softly.

"No," he agreed. "When I was sixteen, I stole a car . . . and at the shop, we found this box that was full of baby pictures and toys, and . . . things you can't replace. There was something about the way it had all been put together . . . it made me wonder if maybe it was more than just someone's cleaning out a closet. As if . . . the baby was dead, or something bad had happened. Just a gut feeling."

"What happened to the box?" Lyssa tilted her head, lips tugging into a faint smile. "Come on. I know you didn't throw it out."

Eddie shrugged, scuffing his foot on the floor. "I found the owner's insurance card in the glove compartment and put it in the box, along with a note. Then I mailed it to the local police department."

Lyssa laughed, quietly. "A note?"

He felt embarrassed. "Yes, a note. I included the make and license-plate number of the car, and said it had been stolen and . . . and that I thought the owner might like those pictures back. I wore gloves when I handled everything," he added, a little defensively.

She held up her hand. "I didn't doubt it."

"It made me rethink some things," he said, then, wanting to change the subject, said, "You're nowhere. Off the grid. Hasn't that been a problem finding work?"

Lyssa tore off a piece of bread. "You can have a whole life now with nothing but an Internet connection. I only communicate with my editors and agent via e-mail. We've never met even though they all live in this city. I have a laptop, and there's wireless everywhere. It's easier than you think."

"Did you use fake identification to open a bank account?"

"Yes. Dead person's social security number, too. I also have reserve cash in post office boxes all over the country. Salt Lake City, Boston, Chicago . . . all the big cities where I've been. I mailed some to each location, just in case."

Just in case you have to run, he thought, noting how she tensed.

"Name a book you illustrated," he said. "I'll find it."

She smiled. "Like you found me?"

"Come on."

"*The Long Glow,*" she said, ducking her head as though embarrassed. "It's about a firefly who wants to glow all the time. I wrote that one, actually."

Eddie stared. "I know that book."

"No."

"I do." He remembered the illustrations: watercolors and inks, flame-rich in reds and oranges. "I bought it last year for a friend's daughter. But the name—"

"Kara Allan," she spoke softly. "Kara was my mother's name. Allan was my father."

"It's a good name."

"They liked books," she said, and sighed. "I don't want to talk about them."

For several minutes they ate in silence. Lyssa found a can of pineapple and some plastic spoons. They passed it back and forth. Eddie began to relax. He understood why she felt safe in this place, so deep underground. Out of sight, out of mind.

When the pineapple was gone, and most of the bread—and a couple apple cores had been tossed into the darkness of the tunnel for the rats to chew on— Lyssa began gathering together her watercolors and drawings, stacking them into a neat pile.

Eddie looked around as she worked. Cans of food lined the wall, and a black garbage bag slouched open near his feet. He saw clothing inside. His gaze slid past to the scorched, blackened walls.

"What precedes an outburst?" he asked.

"Like I said, it happens mostly when I'm asleep. I'm usually having a nightmare."

"You weren't asleep today."

"On the street? No . . . I was angry. When I touched you . . ." Lyssa shook her head. "It hasn't happened like that in a long time. It wasn't even a matter of control. The fire was just . . . there. It had to come out. Does that happen to you?"

"Used to. Now I usually have some warning." Eddie wished he could make this easier for her. "Are you leaving this place for good?"

"I think I have to."

"Where will you go?"

Lyssa gave him a tired smile. "Doesn't matter, does it? I don't think I can run anymore."

"You want to fight."

"I want to live," she said, and sat on the edge of the table. "When did *you* start to live again, Eddie?"

The question made him pause. No one else could have understood, intuitively, that so much of his life had been spent just surviving.

"When I was found by the organization I work for," he told her. "That was when I felt *safe* enough to live."

"Why?"

"I wasn't alone." He found himself rubbing his scars again, and stopped. "I was protected. It's amazing how something that simple can change someone."

"Yeah," she murmured. "So you really trust these people."

Eddie thought about Roland. "Most of the time."

"Do you think they could help me find the *Cruor Venator*?"

He wanted to tell her no. "I don't know. Maybe."

"I have to confront her."

"Lyssa—"

She held up her hand. "I want to run away, more than anything. I want to run so badly, I can't think straight. This is my worst nightmare."

"So let's go. I told you, I can have us out of this city in hours."

"And then what? I live for another ten years on the run, underground, in shit holes where the rats are my only friends?" Lyssa closed her eyes, jaw tight. "Maybe it's enough to just survive. But I don't want to die alone, Eddie. I don't want to die without anyone knowing me, or caring who I am. Or . . . missing me. I want something different than that. But I won't have it, as long as the *Cruor Venator* wants *me*."

He thought about what Lannes had told him and let out his breath. "You're not going to die, Lyssa."

"We all die," she replied. "I'd just prefer it to be of natural causes, and in the very, *very*, distant future."

"Wouldn't we all?" he shot back. "But I'm not going to let anything happen to you."

He half expected her to throw their stairwell conversation right back in his face, but instead she gripped the edge of the table, with smoke beginning to rise from beneath her hands, and said, "You're going to stick with me twenty-four/seven? You're going to spend the rest of your life looking over your shoulder with me? No, I don't think so. Besides, if you got hurt . . ."

She looked down, and the candle flames around her spat and flared, while a wave of heat slammed from her body into his. "I don't want you hurt."

God, you twist me up, he wanted to tell her . . . maybe right after he explained that looking over his shoulder with her for the rest of his life didn't sound so bad.

"At least tell me you have a plan," he said. "It's crazy to go after the *Cruor Venator* without one."

"You're right. It's crazy. *I'm* crazy. Lannes was right. I should never have let you get as close as . . ." Lyssa stopped, grimacing to herself. "I'll show you how to get out of here, but then you leave me alone."

"Lannes is an idiot. And we're well past the point of where you can tell me to get lost every time I ask questions you don't want to answer."

Lyssa pushed away from the table, so hard it slammed back into the wall. Grief and anger filled her eyes, and a terrible desperation. Eddie waited for her to speak, but instead she strode toward the door. He beat her to it, hands outstretched—determined not to let her go.

"Move," she said, in a deadly quiet voice. Heat rose off her body. Eddie found his own power responding, control slipping—consumed by the desolation in her eyes.

"No," he said, just as softly. "You had your chance to walk away. And so did I."

She trembled, and another pulse of heat slammed against him. Eddie took it in, and something inside snapped loose: living and coiled, and hungry.

He tried to stay calm, to push it down, but his heart wouldn't take any more. Fire rose from his stomach, through his blood. Fire, in his skin. Fire in his lungs.

"Lyssa," he whispered.

Her eyes glowed brighter. "I don't have a plan. You can't plan for the *Cruor Venator.*"

"That kind of thinking will get you killed." His voice shook with the strain of controlling the fire skimming beneath his skin. "I won't let that happen."

"You can't stop it."

"I can."

"No. There's a price for stopping the *Cruor Venator,* and you can't pay it. So *you* walk away. Before they catch your scent. Before they feel *this.*"

She slammed her hand against his chest, and Eddie felt the heat of that contact in his bones. He reached up and grabbed her wrist, holding her. Where their skin touched, sparks flew.

Lyssa snarled, trying to pull away. Eddie refused to let go. He grabbed the collar of her sweater and hauled her even closer. Warnings screamed in his head, but the fire buried them, stealing his control, and fear.

"I'm not leaving," he whispered harshly.

"The *Cruor Venator* will kill you," she told him, face contorted with grief. "She'll take everything you are, and drink it while you watch . . . and in the end, just before you die, she'll *own* you. She will own your heart. That's what her kind *do.* All your dreams, all your love . . . it's *shit* to them. It means *nothing* except power."

Her voice shook, and the candle flames sputtered, and exploded. Wax sprayed the table. Her paintings caught on fire.

"Lyssa," he snapped.

"*I won't watch someone else die,*" she snarled, and her teeth were suddenly huge and sharp, her pupils slit, daggered. Sparks of golden light trailed down her face, leaving behind pale skin that darkened and rippled with crimson scales. When she raised her right hand between them, trying to push him away, Eddie grabbed her wrist. Flames rushed over their skin in a roar of heat and power.

"Lyssa!" he shouted, and her face crumpled with misery and fear. She threw back her head, crying out in agony, and Eddie wrapped her in his arms, unmindful of her claws as they pressed deeper into his chest, piercing his shirt, his skin.

She twisted away, but he stayed with her, fire licking at them, fire between them, inside him, pushing outward until he thought his skin would burst like a bad fruit. Lyssa started sobbing. Beneath his hands, her body contorted. Bones cracked. Muscles twisted in ways that should have been impossible. He felt her spine grow jagged and sharp beneath the sweater.

But she did not shift. It was all wrong. Every shapeshifter Eddie knew changed shape in one fluid transition that lasted only seconds at best. Painless. Even beautiful.

This was ripping her apart.

"Don't be afraid," he whispered, holding her tighter. "Listen to my voice, Lyssa. Listen to me."

She screamed. Eddie crushed her to him, digging his hands into her hair. Fire tore through their clothing, flowing from their chests outward, wrapping them in light.

They burned.

CHAPTER SIXTEEN

*D*ON'T *be afraid.*
But she was afraid.

Afraid and broken, from the inside out. Fighting only made the pain worse, but Lyssa fought anyway, terrified and miserable, and in agony. The shift had never come on her so quickly, not for years. She always had warning.

Let me out, whispered the dragon.

But even had she wanted to, she couldn't have. What should have been magic and miracle was a nightmare. Out of her control. Raging through her body. Ripping her apart.

Only this time, she wasn't alone.

Let me go! Lyssa wanted to scream, but her voice wouldn't work, and no matter how hard she tried to push Eddie away, he held on. His arms were so strong. His voice, stronger.

She stopped hearing the words—but the meaning, the spirit inside them, poured into her—and she clung to the whisper of his voice, the throb of each syllable pounding with her heartbeat.

Each heartbeat broke her bones.

Each heartbeat made the fire grow inside her. A pure golden heat that started in her heart, then spread into her veins. Dragon fire, real fire. It shocked her, and she was afraid—until she remembered who was holding her. Eddie would not burn if she lost control.

She had already lost control, and he had survived. Survived, and stayed with her.

Lyssa, whispered Eddie, only this time his voice was within her mind, rolling through her with the fire. His presence filled her, strong and steady and calm.

But it was his compassion that cut through the pain. Lyssa clung with all her strength to that warm empathy, desperate for a taste. It had been so long since anyone had made her feel protected.

The struggle in her body eased. Pain faded.

Lyssa came back to herself, slowly, in increments that were little more than an easing of the tension in her chest. She knelt on the floor, with no idea how she had gotten there. The rugs were burning beneath her. Her clothes were on fire, turning to ash. Eddie crouched with her, also engulfed in flames—his arms tight around her body.

She chanced a look and found him light and golden as the sun, and burning with a sweet heat she felt in her blood. Fire, all around him. Fire, crawling through the air. For a moment, she imagined a set of wings flaring from his shoulders, wings made of fire . . . but that faded in the blink of an eye.

He bowed his head toward hers, large hand cupping her cheek with a gentleness that cut her to the core. "Lyssa. Are you okay?"

She could only nod, voice broken. His fingers tightened, sliding into her hair. "Look at me."

Her gaze found his, and he gave her a smile so kind

it couldn't be real. A smile that was in his eyes . . . those warm, dark eyes that were even more haunting up close.

He didn't say anything . . . but he didn't have to. Lyssa understood what he was telling her with that one look.

I'll take care of you.

Around them, the fire began dying. A terrible weakness stole through her body: skin tingling, heart pounding as her limbs and muscles settled.

She tried to move, anyway. Eddie's arms tightened. "No. Rest."

"I don't think I can," she whispered.

"Yes, you *can*. Just . . . sit here a minute."

Lyssa didn't answer but stayed put as he untangled himself. He was almost naked—the remains of his clothes little more than charred rags. She instinctively averted her eyes, but when he turned his back, she looked.

She had never seen a fully naked man—not in real life, anyway. His muscles were hard and lean, and his shoulders looked even broader without his shirt. Nothing soft about him. His strength, the way he moved . . . was hungry, and coiled.

And he had a fantastic ass. Lyssa had never thought much—at all—about the qualities of a man's backside, but his was—

She looked away, cheeks hot, as he began to turn. Only to realize that she was just as naked as he. Scraps of her jeans clung to her legs, but the sweater was practically gone.

Lyssa wasn't sure what embarrassed her more—that her breasts were exposed or her right arm. She twisted away from him, trying to cover herself—hugging her arm to her body. Dragon scales glinted in the remains of firelight, like rubies pounded into armor.

Something large and heavy fell down around her shoulders. It was her sleeping bag—or what was left. The edges were burning, but Eddie slapped his hand over the small flames, beating them out.

Lyssa chanced another look at him, admiring his focus as he put out the fire. So calm, and intent. Acting as though there was nothing in the last bit odd about what he was doing . . . or who he was doing it with. Not once did he look at her right arm. It wasn't as if he was avoiding it, either. It just didn't seem to matter to him. Not nearly as much as it mattered to her.

It made her feel . . . almost normal. For the first time in ten years, she didn't think of herself as deformed.

Until she glanced down, and noticed his chest.

He was bleeding from five deep slashes above his heart. Claw marks.

She stared, and all those good feelings died. Eddie followed her gaze. "Oh. I didn't even . . . it's fine, Lyssa."

Horror filled her. "No, it's *not*."

"It's just a scratch. I'm tough."

"There's blood. I could have killed you." Lyssa tried to stand. Her legs wouldn't hold her, and Eddie caught her arm.

"What are you doing?" he asked sharply.

She couldn't answer him, staring instead at her golden claws. She saw no blood, but it had to be there.

Her mother had told her that witches once used dragon claws as weapons.

You're a weapon, she'd said, then. *Be careful.*

"Lyssa," Eddie said.

She hated herself. "I drew your blood."

"It was an accident." He forced her to look at him. "You didn't mean to hurt me."

But what if I did?

Again, she tried to stand, clutching the sleeping bag around her. She was weaker than she wanted to admit, and her knees buckled. Eddie forced her to lean on him as he carefully eased her down.

He was so gentle. Lyssa pressed her fist against her throat, finding it hard to breathe. "Listen to me. Please, just go. Please, Eddie."

His quiet laughter surprised her. "If you were anyone else, I would have been long gone."

"You don't understand."

"I want to."

Lyssa bowed her head, unable to look at him. "There's something inside me. Something terrible that wants to come out. I've fought it for my entire life, but after my parents were murdered . . ."

She swallowed hard, feeling ill. "It's an instinct to kill."

For an agonizing moment, he was completely still. And then his hand came up slowly . . . as if he was giving her time to move.

Lyssa did not. She trembled as his palm slid over her cheek. It felt too good. So safe. She remembered the compassion that had filled her—his heart, full of that terrible kindness—and the weight of it bowed her shoulders until she thought she would never breathe again.

She hated herself for not pushing him away.

"One day I'm going to lose," she said. "I'm going to give in, whether I want to or not. And I'll take someone's life. I'll have to if I want to survive the *Cruor Venator*. And when that happens . . ."

You will inherit your birthright, whispered the dragon. *There is no shame in that.*

No, but there was power in it. Awful power.

"I don't trust myself," she told him. "You shouldn't trust me, either. Lannes was right."

The gargoyle knew the truth. She had seen it in his eyes. Surely, he had told Eddie. But if that was the case, then why was he here now, with her? How could he sit here and act as though nothing were wrong?

And why don't I have the courage to tell him myself? To say the words out loud?

Eddie's hand was warm on her cheek. "Look at me."

She did, reluctantly, and found him studying her with those dark eyes, those eyes in her dreams, lost in fire.

"Let me tell you something," he said, in a too-soft voice. "I killed a man when I was a child. And that was nothing more than instinct, and rage. I ran from that murder. I ran from myself. Sometimes, I feel as though I'm still running, not because I think I'll do it again . . . but because I wish I *could* do it again. And kill the right man, this time.

"So whatever is inside you . . . it's inside me, too. I'd say it's inside everyone in this world." He brushed his thumb over her lips. "Don't go acting like you're special."

"Eddie," she began, but that was all she could say before he pressed his mouth over hers in a firm, hard, kiss.

It surprised her—and then she stopped being surprised, and her entire body melted as heat stroked through her, turning her muscles so soft and heavy she could barely sit upright. Lyssa molded herself against him, savoring the brush and stroke of his lips, the slow movements of his hands buried in her hair, the pound of her heart and the deep hum of pleasure rising from his throat, sparking a burst of tenderness inside her that made her glow with even deeper hunger.

Eddie broke off the kiss but did not break from her. His mouth remained pressed against the corner of hers, their breath mingling, harsh and rushed. Their naked bodies touched with every breath, soft and light, and hot.

"Lyssa," he whispered, touching her throat in a way that made her shiver. "Lie down."

Her eyes were almost too heavy to open. "Gonna take advantage of me?"

His quiet laughter made her feel almost as good as his kiss. "Not yet. But you need to rest."

"There's more . . . I need to tell you. About me."

"When you're ready."

She let her eyes close completely. "What did Lannes tell you?"

"Lannes isn't you. What he said doesn't matter."

"You should trust your friends."

"You're my friend."

Slowly, with exquisite care, he folded her against his chest and made her lie down on her side. His entire body spooned around her, pressing against her back, holding her snug and warm, and strong. It might not have been the most intimate touch a person could receive, but it felt like it, on the inside. More than an embrace. Closer than skin. She felt him, alive, all around her.

"Are you okay?" asked Eddie, his voice low and rough.

"Fine," she lied, because having him behind her, holding her, made her feel—against all odds—safe. More safe than she'd felt in years. As though nothing, no one, could hurt her. Ever again.

And that wasn't fine. It was heartbreaking.

I've been alone too long. I never realized how alone until now.

She'd guarded her heart, all these years. For a very good reason. If she let this man in . . . if anything happened to him . . .

Inside, the dragon stirred. Lyssa felt it, and tensed. But the dragon merely sipped the fire burning in her blood and sighed.

You are still afraid to be close to him, it whispered. *Why?*

He'll cause me pain, said Lyssa.

Then you should have killed him when you first saw him. You should kill everyone, then. Everyone is capable of that.

No.

No, echoed the dragon, softly. *Forget what was. Listen to his voice. Listen to his spirit around you. Feel his touch. His heart is made of fire. It is pure, like fire. You know this. You would not let him be with you now if you did not.*

His lips brushed the back of her neck, while his strong fingers kneaded her left shoulder. Tingling sparks of pleasure raced through her, and she drew in an unsteady breath as she arched against him, wanting—*needing*—more.

There were so many risks involved . . . but she couldn't stand not to be touched. Not now, after having such a powerful taste of what she'd been missing, all these years.

Lyssa rolled over in his arms, letting the sleeping bag slip down her shoulder to reveal crimson scales and twisted muscle. Part of her breast was exposed, as well—and that was where his gaze lingered, with a hunger and desire that made the fire in her blood rise, and rise again.

His hand moved. She held her breath as he tugged

down the sleeping bag, revealing her full breast—and when she saw his eyes darken even more, an ache spread through her, slow and heavy, pooling between her thighs.

Eddie's expression was haunted, pained—his voice, little more than a rasp. "You're beautiful."

"No, I'm not—" began Lyssa softly, but once again he stopped her voice, only this time with his lips pressed against the reptilian flesh of her shoulder. He moved before she could stop him—but the tenderness of that kiss made tears spring to her eyes.

"You," he whispered, "are beautiful."

Lyssa sighed, and struggled closer, letting the sleeping bag slide down again. Eddie's breathing roughened, a wave of heat pulsing off his skin—so much heat it could have been fire.

"Where else do you want to kiss me?" she whispered.

His gaze snapped to hers. "Are you sure?"

"You started this."

"I wanted to . . . make you feel safe."

Lyssa brushed her lips over his jaw. "Neither of us is safe. We're going to break each other's hearts, remember?"

Eddie swallowed hard, heartbreak already in his eyes. "Tell me what you need."

"This," she told him. "You."

"Yes," he whispered, and covered her mouth in a searing kiss, his hand sliding beneath the sleeping bag to rest against the full curve of her breast. Pleasure shot through her, and she strained against him, reaching for his hand.

Before she could touch him, his thumb found her nipple, stroking it in sharp flicks that made her cry out in shocked pleasure. He replaced his thumb with his hot mouth, suckling hard, and even as she writhed against him, he cupped her breasts in his large, warm hands, pushing them together and squeezing as he ran his tongue and thumbs over her nipples, caressing them in an unrelenting rhythm that sent wave after wave of pleasure through her body.

She gasped his name, and he slid down her body, one hand lingering on her breast while his other trailed a blazing path against her side until his palm rested lightly between her legs. He kissed her hip, her thigh, then deeper, making her spread her thighs as his finger glided between the wet folds of her body, stroking— lightly at first, then with more pressure, slipping inside her in another kind of rhythm that tore a low moan from her throat.

His fingers pushed deeper, harder, and his mouth pressed hot against the hard nub of her clitoris, making her shake with such intense pleasure that Lyssa thought she'd explode. Her hips moved against his hand and mouth, her moans growing sharper, shorter. Desire built in throbbing waves, and just when she thought she could take no more, he slipped a third finger into her body and scraped his teeth against her.

Lyssa shattered, blind and lost, feeling all the threads of her soul unravel in one moment of pure pleasure.

Even when she came back to herself, it was slow and languid, her entire being focused on those heavy, bliss-ful throbs that continued to wrack her trembling frame. Eddie's fingers remained inside her body, rubbing her gently, and she tightened her thighs around his hand. He chuckled, making her shiver.

"That was . . ." she whispered. "That was . . . incredible."

"Mmm," he said, his voice so deep it was almost a purr. Lyssa hadn't known he could make a sound like that, and she wanted to hear it again.

Slowly, with a great deal of reluctance, she tried to pull away from him. He grabbed her hip, holding her still.

"Not yet," he murmured.

"I want to taste you," she told him, and his eyes darkened.

Breathless, trembling—her heart pounding with dizzying force—she made him roll over on his back. His body was beautiful. Hard muscle, lean lines. His jaw was rigid, and so was the rest of him.

Lyssa wished she could be patient and explore every inch of his body, but right then, all she wanted was one thing.

His shaft was thick and heavy in her hand, and even before her mouth touched the tip of him, his chest started heaving for air. Sparks flew off his skin, along with a wave of terrible heat that only made her burn hotter for him.

Lyssa stroked him with her tongue, pulling away just enough to blow on his wet skin. He cried out, arching his hips, and she took him in her mouth again, more deeply, sucking hard. She kept her right hand balled in a fist, but her left hand touched the base of his shaft, caressing him with a featherlight touch as she ran her tongue up and down his entire length, again and again.

His hips jerked in rhythm to her tongue and hand, and he sat up, burying his fingers in her hair as she tried to move faster, harder. A groan tore from his throat, sharp pants, and when he said her name in his broken voice, it only excited her more.

Fire raced over his skin, flares of light. Lyssa sucked hard on the very tip of him, and at the same moment, squeezed his shaft in a tight, stroking grip.

Eddie fell back flat and let out a wordless cry as his hips bucked upward. Lyssa felt something wet and hot hit her cheek, but she stayed close as he continued to thrust hard against her hand and lips. She wanted very much to know what it would feel like for him to come inside her body.

When he was finally reduced to little more than a twitch, Lyssa crawled up his side and flopped across his body. She felt slick and hot, and wonderful. Especially when he made a low groaning sound that traveled from his chest into hers.

"Oh, my God," he said.

Lyssa began to laugh, and Eddie rolled over on his side, making her do the same. He hooked his leg over her hip and slid his strong arm under her arm across her back, hitching her hard against him.

"Twenty-four/seven," he said, looking into her eyes.

She wasn't sure what she had expected him to say, but it wasn't that. "What?"

Eddie kissed her, slow and gentle.

"Twenty-four/seven," he murmured against her mouth. "I would stick with you. I would look over my shoulder with you. Every day, for the rest of my life."

Her breath caught. "Wow. I really was good."

He laughed and buried her against him. Lyssa melted into his embrace, savoring his heat and strength, and his soft, rumbling voice.

"Rest," he said. "I'll make sure nothing happens."

Well," she mumbled, suddenly shy. "If you're the something that happens, that's okay."

He laughed again, more quietly, and pulled the sleeping bag over their bodies. She knew he didn't feel the cold, and neither did she, but it felt like a cocoon, a nest, a real bed . . . and she liked that.

Twenty-four/seven, she thought, closing her eyes and listening to his heartbeat.

I could love that.

—

FOR ONCE, LYSSA DID NOT DREAM. SHE DIDN'T EVEN know she slept until she opened her eyes, and found herself in an entirely different position than the one she'd started in.

She lay on her back, sleeping bag partially tugged down. Eddie was on his side beside her, propped up on his elbow. At first she thought he had been watching her sleep, but his other hand was stroking her right arm. Just his fingertips, light and easy, tracing circles against her crimson scales.

Lyssa's first instinct was to pull away, but his gaze was thoughtful and soft, and she forced herself to remain still.

"I'm sorry I woke you up," he said.

"I'm not sure you did," she replied. "What are you . . . thinking?"

He pressed his palm flat against her muscled forearm, and the contrast between human skin and her scales was stark. "I was wondering how this happened."

She was distracted a moment by the round burn scars on the back of his hand. "I've never had an easy time shape-shifting. For some, it's as simple as breathing. But . . . stress : . . at the moment of a shift can . . . make some aspects permanent."

Eddie went quiet. "Did this happen when your parents died?"

"Yes," she whispered, and looked away from him. "I was trying to fight."

He kissed her shoulder. "At least you tried."

Something in his voice made her turn back to face him. He was looking at his scarred hand.

Round, dime-sized scars. Dark, slightly ridged on the edges. At least five of them, but some were bunched close together, so it was hard to be certain.

Sorrow filled her, and horror. "Why would anyone do that to you?"

Eddie stilled . . . and then slowly, carefully, pulled away from her. Lyssa watched him, recognizing the sudden flatness of his gaze, the tightness of his mouth. How many times had she given him the same look when he asked her questions she didn't want to answer?

He rolled over on his back and stared at the ceiling. Lyssa, after a moment, relaxed on her side, cushioning her head on her arm as she watched his jaw flex and his eyes go dark with memory.

"When my mother called . . . do you remember that man I mentioned?" Eddie held up his hand. "He did this."

"No one stopped him?"

"No one knew. I would bandage up my hand and say I hurt it at school. He made me promise not to tell. He said he would . . . hurt my mother and sister."

Lyssa let out her breath. "Does this have to do with the man you killed?"

A grim, bitter smile touched his mouth. "Shoe's on the other foot now. Next time you don't want to answer my questions, I'll remember this moment."

"I'm sorry."

"Don't be. I've never talked about this."

"It hurts too much."

"Don't forget the shame." Lyssa saw the glitter of unshed tears in his eyes. "I could have . . . done things so differently, if I'd just been braver."

Lyssa's heart broke for him—and for herself. "I understand."

He turned his head, finally looking at her—grief in his eyes, such terrible pain. "I know you do."

CHAPTER SEVENTEEN

M Y dad died when I was ten," Eddie said, feeling hollow when he said those words. "He was a really good guy, but cancer got him. He was a little older than my mom. I guess, in his late forties, or early fifties. She adored him, but . . . a couple years after that, she got lonely. She started going out with some guys from the bank where she worked. And then she met Matthew Swint."

Lyssa shifted closer, and Eddie wrapped his arm around her, taking comfort in her presence. He couldn't believe he had told her this much already, but it felt okay. For the first time, safe. He could say the words without his throat locking up. He wanted to say them.

I'm going to spend the rest of my life telling you my secrets, he thought, but instead of being filled with fear or unease, all he felt was relief.

"Matthew was big, like my dad, and a little older. I guess there were some other physical similarities. He was a good mechanic. He owned a garage north of San Francisco. I liked going there at first. He taught me about cars, which . . . came in handy later."

Eddie covered his eyes with his other hand. "He

began molesting my sister about three months after my mom started dating him."

Lyssa sucked in her breath but said nothing. For which he was very grateful.

"She didn't tell anyone," he said, his voice finally breaking. "Maybe for the same reason I didn't tell anyone about the cigarette burns, or the . . . the humiliations. I don't know. We never got a chance to talk about that."

"Your mother . . ." she said.

All he could do was shake his head, as grief knotted his throat. Tears burned, too many to hold in. He shut his eyes and felt them break free, rolling hot down the sides of his face.

Lyssa made a soft sound, and her lips brushed his skin. Kissing away his tears.

It was too much. Too gentle. Too tender. Eddie turned over on his side, away from her—curling into a tight ball as despair shuddered through him. Lyssa immediately pressed against his back, her arms sliding under his, over his chest. Between them, heat, fire . . . soothing away the worst of the tremors.

He found her hand, and held it tightly. "She never noticed. I really don't think she had a clue. She was at work so much, and she . . . trusted him."

"But there must have been signs with the two of you."

"I don't know." Eddie bowed his head even more. "My mom and I have never discussed it."

Another scar. Another resentment. Unfair, maybe, because he could have pushed the issue and opened up . . . but then, so could she. And both he and his mother had always danced around her failure to protect them. And his failure, as well, to protect Daphne.

Lyssa kissed his shoulder. "Did your sister tell you?"

"No. I walked in on . . ." He stopped, as memories burned through him, so offensive and terrible that he remembered, too, why he never talked about this.

"I'm sorry," he murmured, feeling ill. "I can't . . ."

"It's okay," she whispered.

He dragged down a deep breath. "I loved my sister, but knowing that *I* knew what was happening . . . humiliated her. She couldn't look me in the eye after that. And I . . . promised myself that I wouldn't let it happen again. But before I could come up with a plan, Matthew . . . strangled her to death. I found him and his brother trying to hide her body."

"Eddie."

"Something . . . snapped inside me. I can't even tell you. I've never . . . never felt anything like that. I mean, I always ran hotter than other kids, and sometimes I'd get these fevers. When Matthew would hurt me . . . my skin would tingle, pins and needles. I blamed it on the abuse, but now I know differently. It was all just building.

"But right then . . ." He shook his head, heart beginning to pound. "The fire broke inside me. And Matthew's brother, who was standing closest . . . he went up in flames."

Eddie could still hear the man's screams. He would *always* hear his screams.

"Matthew couldn't put his brother out," he whispered. "He stayed, trying—and that's what got him arrested. A neighbor heard the screams and called the police. When they arrived, they found my sister's body and . . . other evidence of the murder. At trial, it was revealed that she was pregnant. That's why he killed her."

Lyssa was so quiet behind him. Then, softly: "What was her name?"

"Daphne," he breathed.

"Daphne," she repeated.

Eddie closed his eyes. "That's the first time in years I've heard anyone say her name."

She propped herself up on her elbow and slid her hand beneath her cheek. She didn't try to make him look at her, but he did, anyway. It was difficult. He was afraid of what he'd see in her eyes.

What he found, however, were tears . . . and a compassion that was raw and grim, and solely for him.

"Don't look at me like that," he whispered.

"Like what?"

"Like I did nothing wrong. If I'd talked . . . if I had told my mother, or *someone* . . . if I hadn't been so afraid of making it worse . . ." Eddie choked on those words and dug his palms into his damp eyes. "How could it have been worse? *I was so stupid.*"

"You were a kid."

"My father taught me better."

Lyssa pressed her lips to his cheek. "Okay."

"Okay?"

"My mother taught me not to be a coward. But what have I done? Spent ten years running, tail between my legs."

"You were just a kid when you lost your family. No could have expected you to start a war."

Lyssa's mouth softened. "Yeah?"

He shook his head. "Don't use logic on me."

"Logic doesn't exist, times like these. You react from the gut, then pay for life." She lay back down again, snug against his side, naked and warm. "So. Based on the way you spoke to your mom on the phone . . . that man, Matthew Swint . . ."

"Is out of prison."

"And you're here with me. Jesus. I'm sorry."

"Don't be. If I had stayed . . . I think I might have killed him. It could still happen."

"You'd be justified."

His smile felt crooked. "No warnings to be a better man?"

"No." Lyssa stared him dead in the eyes. "You're already the best man I know. You can take a dent and still be the best."

Her words almost killed him. A hot bolt of tenderness and wonderment shot straight through his raw, broken heart.

"But I'm the only man you know," he said.

Lips quirked. "Don't get uppity."

Eddie leaned down and kissed her—gently at first, then deeper, harder, overcome by desire for this woman who could listen to his darkest secrets and just . . . take them. He could hardly believe, or trust it . . . but when he pulled back just enough to look at her . . .

Lannes can go to hell, he thought fiercely. *She's no demon.*

Lyssa paled. "What?"

He hesitated, taken aback by the shock in her eyes, "I didn't say anything."

But I thought *something,* he realized.

She struggled to sit up, movements jerky, rushed. He held out his hands. "Hey."

Her gaze refused to meet his. "We should probably find some clothes."

Eddie gripped her shoulders. "Can you read my thoughts?"

She tensed and gave him a reluctant look. "Sometimes."

"Well," he said, then stopped, staring at her. "Why didn't you say something?"

"Like what?" Lyssa batted him away with her left hand while keeping her right tucked in a fist against her stomach, a return to her defensive posture. "No one

wants to hear that their mind is . . . exposed. Besides, it
only happened a couple times."

"A moment ago?"

Her mouth tightened.

"Listen," Eddie began, but she stiffened, then swung
around to stare at the partially open door behind them.

"What is it?" he asked.

"Someone's coming."

He pulled away. "Stay here."

"Like hell," Lyssa muttered, standing with him and
searching for clothes. Not much was still intact, except
for his jacket. She slid it on and wrapped the remains
of a charred blanket around her hips.

Eddie didn't bother with clothes at all. He crept to
the door, listening as gravel crunched. Light footsteps,
careful.

But Lyssa suddenly made a small, pained sound—
and ran past him, out the door. Eddie couldn't catch her
in time, and chased her.

Only to find himself staring at Jimmy.

The boy stood at the bottom of the stairs, clutching a flashlight in both hands. Huge eyes, as he stared
at Lyssa. When he saw Eddie, his mouth dropped in
shock—but that lasted only a moment. He was trembling, his hair stuck to his sweat-soaked forehead.
Eddie saw a dark smear on his cheek.

Blood.

Lyssa crouched and grabbed his shoulders. She
didn't seem to notice or care that her right hand was
exposed, and Jimmy fell into her arms, hugging her
with a choked sob. She sat back on the step, holding
him tightly, silent and tense.

"Tell me," she said. "What happened?"

"They took my mother," he whispered.

EDDIE WENT BACK INSIDE TO FIND CLOTHES. HIS options were limited. He jammed his feet into his boots and found another blanket that he wrapped around his waist. While Lyssa went to dress, he sat with Jimmy on the stone steps.

"Details," he said.

"We got to the airport," he whispered, and Eddie heard a whimper beneath the boy's sweatshirt. "Private plane, like you promised. We drove up, and some men were waiting. They had g-guns, and they sh-shot the man dr-driving us. And my dad."

Jimmy's voice choked, and he drew in a shuddering breath. Hands shaking, he fumbled beneath his sweatshirt. He wore a T-shirt underneath, tucked into his jeans, and there was a squirming bulge against his belly.

He pulled his T-shirt free, and Icky tumbled into his lap. Eddie bowed his head, rubbing the back of his neck as the boy hugged the panting dog. Tears streamed down his face.

"Jimmy," he said, as softly as he could. "What else can you tell me?"

"They put us in a car," he said haltingly. "And took us across the river out of the city. There was a big house in the middle of trees, and it was quiet."

Lyssa emerged, dressed in jeans and a long-sleeved shirt. Her left hand was full of a fluttery pale scarf that she wrapped around her neck. On her other hand, a glove—and his jacket.

Jimmy twisted to look at her, and his face crumpled. Lyssa tried to smile for him, but Eddie could see the strain on her face. She sat down beside the boy and wrapped her arm around his shoulders.

"Icky," she rasped, as the dog whined.

"I hid him," he whispered, and dug into his pocket for a piece of paper. "I was told to give you this."

Lyssa hesitated before she took it. "You were telling Eddie about a house?"

"Some ladies were there." Jimmy stopped, swallowing hard. "They were scary. They separated me from my mom, then c-cut me."

Eddie watched rage flit across Lyssa's face, quickly swallowed into a flat mask. "Show me."

The boy pulled up his sleeve, revealing a thick white bandage wrapped around his forearm.

"They used a black knife." Jimmy shuddered again, and gave Eddie a desperate look. "Then licked off my blood. It was . . . g-gross. They said they'd kill my mom if I didn't find you."

"Those women knew you would," Lyssa said, her eyes glowing faintly in the darkness. "It's okay, baby. We're going to get your mom back."

She pushed off the step, fingering the still-unread note. "Eddie, wait here. I'll get you some clothes."

Without another word, she walked into the darkness of the subway tunnel and was swallowed up almost immediately by the endless shadows. He couldn't even hear her feet on the gravel.

"How did you get here?" Eddie asked.

"Two men drove me back into the city. They're waiting above."

"And because those ladies have your mother . . . they don't think you'll go to the police?"

Jimmy looked scared. "It was the police who drove me."

Cold sweat broke out over Eddie's body. "They took orders from the women?"

"Yes."

"Do they know how to get down here?"

"I don't think so."

He stood and stared into the darkness of the subway

tunnel. "I need you to be brave again, Jimmy. Can you stay here?"

The boy hugged his dog tighter. "No. I need to help."

"You are."

"No," he said again, more firmly, rubbing tears from his eyes. "I have to be there."

Eddie stared at him. "How old are you?"

Jimmy straightened. "Twelve."

Twelve was still a kid. Twelve years old meant he should be *nowhere near* this kind of danger.

But he was also old enough for heartbreak. Old enough to start living with regret. Making a kid feel helpless was another kind of crime.

"Lyssa's word is final," he said. "You know that, right?"

The boy nodded. Eddie walked back inside the workers' station for his backpack. All he needed was his wallet and cell phone.

"Come on," he told Jimmy. "Let's go find her."

They walked fast across the uneven ground, flashlight beam swinging wildly across the shadows. Squeaks echoed off the walls, and the air smelled like rotting garbage, accompanied by the occasional whiff of feces.

Jimmy gave Eddie a sidelong look. "Are you Lyssa's boyfriend?"

His heart squeezed. "I hope so."

"You don't know?"

"Do I have to go through you first?"

"Maybe. I like her."

Eddie smiled to himself. "I'll arm wrestle you for her heart."

"You're bigger. That's cheating."

"Can you blame me?" He heard voices ahead of

them, and saw the reflected flicker of fire against the tunnel walls. "Wait."

"It's okay. I know them." Jimmy began to lurch ahead, but Eddie grabbed the back of the boy's sweatshirt.

"Wait," he said again, firmly. "Give me the flashlight, and stay back."

The boy's scowl wasn't quite lost in the beam's glow, but he lingered in the shadows as Eddie strode across the rough gravel. He listened for Lyssa's voice, but all he heard were men laughing coarsely, and the hum of a radio.

"Jimmy," he said, over his shoulder. "What did that note say? The one you gave her?"

The boy hesitated. "No message. Just a piece of fur stapled to the paper."

"Dammit," Eddie muttered, and began running—right into a tent city that reminded him of some apocalyptic way station for humanity. When and if the end of the world came, this would be what it looked like: homes made of cardboard and trash, and broken furniture that held up nothing but air. Fires burned in barrels, and a few men were huddled around them.

They stared at Eddie with surprise and wariness as he approached, clutching that blanket around his waist.

"Lyssa," he said sharply. "Did she pass through here?"

A tall black man blinked heavily at Eddie. "Like a bat out of hell. She mentioned a naked man might come this way. Left money for clothes, but there's not much to give you."

Eddie gritted his teeth. "I'd appreciate anything you can spare, sir. I can pay, as well."

"Hmm," he said, just as another old man saw Jimmy and bared his teeth in a brutal hiss that sounded like the death throes of a decrepit snake.

"Fucking little thieves," he muttered, coughing on a snarl. "I'm ready for you *and* that dog."

The boy sputtered. Eddie stepped in front of him. "You touch this kid, and I'll break your arms off."

"Hey, now," said the black man, holding up his hands. "No need for bad feelings. Mack, maybe you should go sit down. Take a load off your bad back."

The old man, whose skin was the color of snow and ash, made a wet grunting noise and gave them all a dirty look. He didn't leave the circle of heat but looked down at the flames with a stubborn jut of his chin.

Two minutes later, Eddie was forty dollars poorer, and dressed in jeans that were loose in the ass and short in the leg. His red sweatshirt smelled like mildew and concrete and made his skin itch.

"Lyssa said to tell you not to follow," said the black man, rubbing his knee with a wince. "But that she knew you *would*, and that she was sorry for trying to get a head start."

"I bet," Eddie replied.

"Women," he added. "They're killers."

CHAPTER EIGHTEEN

HANDCUFFS were cold, even on dragon skin. Lyssa's glove was still in place, but the soft portion covering her wrist had ridden down just enough for the metal to rub against her scales. She ignored the sensation, watching red taillights and the two police officers riding up front, who did not speak to her or talk with each other.

It was still night, which surprised her. Time never meant much underground, but this day had been one hammerblow after another.

Life hates the complacent, her mother had told her. *Almost as much as the complacent hate living.*

Are you talking about me? Lyssa's father had asked, grabbing his wife around the waist. *If I'd been complacent, I'd never have caught you, darlin'.*

Her mother had a beautiful laugh. Sometimes it was hard to remember what it sounded like.

You knew this would happen, thought Lyssa, wishing her mother were here. *You knew you weren't the last of your kind.*

You knew someone would come for you, one day.

And if not you, then me.

Lyssa wore Eddie's jacket, and it felt like a suit of

armor. His warm, smoky scent still clung to it—and
her—and she breathed deep as she listened to the radio
crackle, and the squeak of the vinyl beneath her, and
the jangle of handcuffs.

Eddie, she thought. *Eddie, don't look for me. Jimmy,
don't tell him anything.*

Stay away. Please, stay away.

The two police officers had done their best not to
show her their faces. Only during that initial approach
on the sidewalk had she gotten a good look at them.
The driver was middle-aged, white, with a downturned
mouth and milky blue eyes. His partner was Latino,
young and handsome, and six inches shorter than
Lyssa. He kept giving the other man nervous looks.

Both had been waiting outside the neighborhood
Laundromat, a nondescript hole-in-the-wall between
an Italian deli and a convenience store that sold more
comic books and cigarettes than milk and bread.

The building that housed the laundry—and, to some
degree, the deli and convenience store—had been built
over the second entrance to the abandoned subway
tunnel. Or rather, there was a door in the laundry's
basement, which descended into a mechanical room
that held another door that opened into a corridor filled
with pipes—leading to yet *another* hall that had a
metal grille in the floor—which, when lifted, revealed
a ladder that descended into a hand-dug corridor that
spilled out into the subway tunnel.

One had to be very brave or very stupid—and
sometimes lucky—to find certain secret places. It also
helped that the owner of the Laundromat was sympa-
thetic to folks who lived underground. Mostly because
they washed all their clothes at his place.

Lyssa had not felt brave, stupid, or lucky when the
cops pointed guns at her. She felt no surprise, either,

not even when a tall, African-American woman in a red jacket glided from the shadows.

Nikola.

The men handcuffed Lyssa while she watched, and their scents washed over her in a wave of body odor and sweat, and nauseating fear.

No rights read. But why would they? Rights didn't exist. Not here, not now.

All that mattered was power.

"Lyssa Andreanos," said Nikola, and the police officers flinched at the sound of her voice.

"That's me," she said, staring the woman in the eyes. "Sorry about Betty."

Nikola punched her in the stomach, then grabbed her hair, yanking back her head.

"You *will* be sorry," she whispered, then frowned when Lyssa's only response was a quiet laugh.

Nikola drove a red Corvette. During the ride over the Hudson, she pulled alongside the police sedan and looked into the backseat at Lyssa—who stared back, straight into her eyes, with a smile.

You can't make me afraid of you, she thought. *Not unless I choose to be afraid.*

The witch's frown deepened, and she gunned her Corvette ahead of them. Lyssa kept smiling but for a different reason.

Five minutes after crossing the bridge that spanned the Hudson, the police took an exit off the freeway and cruised down a series of twisting streets that carried them into a quiet riverside neighborhood filled with expensive homes nestled in expensive gardens, where a person could smell the money in the breeze, and the breeze smelled good.

At the end of the street, the police pulled into a long, curving driveway that wound up an increasingly steep hill. Delicate lights illuminated the way. Lyssa didn't see guards or security cameras, but it was night, and there were a lot of trees. Anything could be out there.

The house was too big to take in at one glance. It seemed to sprawl over the hill in climbing layers of glass and stone, and the light from within shone in the night with a warmth that would have been, in another life, comforting.

The Corvette was parked in the driveway. Nikola leaned on the hood and watched, unmoving, as the police helped Lyssa from the back of the sedan. The men did not speak as they unlocked her handcuffs. Both kept their gazes down, and oozed sweat.

Nikola sauntered close. The men trembled, cowering like abused dogs. Lyssa knew they had no control over their reactions. It would have hit them like a bomb in their heart. If the witch asked them to, they would crawl on their bellies into the river and never come out.

Nikola, however, did not look at them. Her focus remained on Lyssa.

She stared back, her gaze flat and calm, and unflinching. It wasn't difficult. Rage might have had something to do with it. Maybe she should have snapped before this, but discovering that Jimmy and his mother had been kidnapped, his body cut, blood consumed . . . that he could have been subjected to emotional torture . . . put her on a whole new level that transcended anything she had felt since her parents' murder.

And then, there was that scrap of fur stapled to the note in her pocket. Another reminder of what Estefan had suffered—as if she hadn't already seen enough.

"You're not afraid," Nikola said to her, trailing an elegant hand over the younger police officer's shoulders. He squeezed shut his eyes, shaking violently as her fingers stroked his hair.

Lyssa gritted her teeth because she was very afraid and determined not to show it. "Why would I be?"

Nikola frowned. "Just like the young man who saved you from the fire. I don't like mysteries."

She pushed the police officer away from her, and he stumbled against the car, one hand on his weapon, the other clutching his chest as he panted for air. Lyssa felt the break in the air around them, a release of tension— the witch pulling back her influence.

The difference in the men was immediate—as if the hands squeezing them to death relaxed enough to let them breathe.

"You can go," Nikola said to the officers. "You *should* go. Now."

No hesitation. No questions. Lyssa had not heard those men make a single sound the entire time she'd been in their presence, and nothing changed when they left.

Leaving her alone with Nikola.

The night was very quiet. Lyssa felt reminded of another evening, ten years in the past, when she had stood bound and captured. The memory made her heart quicken, but she thought of Jimmy and his mother. Estefan.

Eddie.

She was not bait this time. She was not a kid.

"You're wasting time," she said. "I want to see Georgene."

A muscle twitched in Nikola's right cheek, and deep in her eyes there was a glint of unease. Defiance—and simple knowledge—unsettled her. Made her uncertain how to proceed. This woman—likely any who served the *Cruor Venator*—had relied on power too long and forgotten what it was to be vulnerable. If she had ever known.

Nikola reached inside her jacket and pulled free an obsidian blade. "How do you know the *Cruor Venator*'s name?"

"Easy," she replied, ignoring the weapon. "We're cousins."

The witch blinked. It would have made Lyssa smile, under different circumstances.

Or maybe not. It wasn't really that funny. Over the years, when she'd let herself think too much about the truth, it all seemed rather disgusting.

"She didn't tell you much of anything, did she?" Lyssa said. "How many surprises can you handle?"

Nikola's face hardened. "Don't talk to me like that."

"Or what? You'll kill me? You'll scare me to death?" Her stiff lips curved into a cold smile. "You have no power over me. Betty found that out the hard way."

The witch edged forward. "Are you stupid?"

"Are you? Who do you think you are?" asked Lyssa, feeling the night air warm around her body. "What has Georgene told you? That you're a *Cruor Venator,* like her? That you can *be* like her if you continue to serve her?"

Nikola said nothing, but she didn't have to. Lyssa felt a terrible sense of déjà vu, as though she was living inside her mother's skin—ten years in the past. Her words, so similar to her mother's as she had stood in the snow and confronted a woman just like Nikola.

"You're nothing," she whispered to the witch. "Do you think Georgene would keep you so close if you had the ability to kill her?"

Nikola tensed. Lyssa said, "Go on. Try and take her life. See the truth for yourself."

"You're only a dragon," she said, but the obsidian blade wavered. "You're just a shape-shifter. You cannot be her cousin."

"But if I am?" Lyssa stepped toward her, and Nikola swayed. "You know what that makes me."

Conflict filled her eyes. "No. We watched you for

weeks. You live in a hole. You have nothing. If you possessed that power, you would never deny it. No one would."

Lyssa barely heard her. Her blood was tingling.

Your mate is close, whispered the dragon. *He is terrified for you.*

She tried to bury her unease. *How do you know what he's feeling?*

How do you not?

The idea of Eddie being here, witness to what she was, what she was capable of becoming, made her insides turn to rubber.

"Is Georgene in that house?" Lyssa asked, proud her voice sounded sharp, strong.

Nikola's jaw flexed. "Yes. She is waiting for you."

"How many people are imprisoned?"

No response. Lyssa pulled off her glove, flexing her clawed hand and savoring the pull of the contorted muscles in her arm. The witch's gaze settled on her hand and stayed there.

Lyssa wished she had Eddie's skill with fire—to summon a flame and have it burn in her hand—but all she could do was let the woman look, and imagine.

"That knife doesn't mean anything to me," she said softly. "Tell me how many people are there."

Nikola gave her a hateful look, but there was caution in it, too. "Go and find out for yourself."

As the tingling in her blood intensified, Lyssa turned on her heel and strode toward the house.

You could not run forever, whispered the dragon, as pain throbbed down her arm. *You must fly or die, little sister.*

Just as she reached the front steps, twin beams of light swung and bounced off the house. Lyssa listened to the low rumble of a car engine—watching as headlights flickered through the trees that lined the winding driveway. The vehicle that appeared was an older Cadillac, built like a tank. Lyssa couldn't see the driver, but she knew who it was.

Eddie left the engine running as he climbed from the car, keeping his hands in plain sight. No sign of Jimmy.

"Lyssa," he said, watching the witch.

"Get away," she told him, heart in her throat, dying a little on the inside even as another part of her thrilled that he was here, with her.

Nikola tightened her grip on the knife. "Hello, puppy."

Lyssa felt the power in her voice—an attempt to spread her infection of fear. But beneath that was a tremor.

Weakness. Uncertainty. Lyssa thought about the memories she had seen from Estefan's death—this woman, slashing him with that blade. Torturing him simply because she could.

Eddie gave the witch another lingering glance, full of disdain. It made him seem decades older—those searing eyes in that young, hard face. He didn't need some magical hoodoo to make someone feel uneasy. Just a look.

He walked right up to Lyssa and she braced herself, cut to the quick by the flash of concern and disappointment in his eyes.

"Of course I ran," she said to him, before he could say a word. "That's what I do."

"You ran in the wrong direction. And you forgot someone." Eddie took her hand, entwining their fingers. "Why do I get the feeling I'll be chasing you for the rest of my life?"

"You wish."

"You're trouble."

"I won't change."

"I'll just have to run faster to keep up," he said, and squeezed her hand. "If you dislike me, that's one thing. But if you're trying to keep me safe, don't bother."

She started to shake her head, but before she could say a word he leaned in and pressed his mouth to her ear. A smoky scent washed over her—real smoke, drifting off his clothes, accompanied by sparks. The tremendous heat that flowed from his body into hers felt like a balm on her soul, stealing the worst of her fear and misgivings, and self-hatred.

"Being safe alone holds no appeal," he whispered. "We haven't known each other long . . . but trust me. I'd rather have no chance, with you."

"You," she said, but couldn't speak all those words inside her. Eddie kissed her hand.

"I know," he said.

Lyssa dragged down a deep breath and looked at Nikola, who was watching them with hollow eyes.

"You have a choice to make," she told the witch. "Accept the truth that you've been lied to and that your friend is dead because of it . . . or continue to serve the lie. This"—and she waved to Eddie and herself—"is no illusion. If Georgene told you that I am merely a shape-shifter, then she did so thinking, perhaps hoping, it would get you killed."

Nikola swayed. "She would not do that."

"Then you really don't know the heart of a *Cruor Venator*," said Lyssa.

The witch's gaze darkened, and she glided past them to the house to open the front door.

Lyssa and Eddie shared a quick look, then followed.

Hands tightly clasped, fingers knotted. Inseparable. Her heart pounded too hard, and she forced herself to breathe through her nose. Blood scents crowded, though. Too much blood, bitter and rusty, mixed with perfume.

She saw a dark red footprint on the hardwood floor. Red, as in blood.

More than one print. A rusty trail, leading across the foyer to the front door where Nikola stood. Nearby, a bloodstained towel.

"I was busy, earlier this evening," she said, and slipped off her shoes. Traces of dried blood covered her feet.

Lyssa's knuckles cracked as her hand curled into a fist. Eddie quivered.

Tracks covered the floor, leading through a home that would have fit nicely in the architectural magazines she sometimes bought for reference and daydreams. Big open rooms, huge windows, dark slabs of stone and wood fitting into the walls and floors, creating a space that felt as much outdoors as in: rustic, rough, rich.

She caught the cool clean scent of freshwater—and clung to it as something better than blood. She heard water, too—a low gurgle that seemed to come from below, and in front of her.

A few more steps revealed an actual creek running through the house, surrounded by artisan-laid rock. In some spots, thick glass sheeting that had been laid on top as a clear floor, but other areas were exposed.

Blood covered the glass, too. Fresh drops. A normal person might not have noticed, but it practically glowed in her vision. It seemed different, somehow, than the blood on Nikola's feet. Golden, even.

She glanced at the witch, but her gaze was almost immediately drawn back to the blood on the floor.

"What is it?" Eddie asked, also watching Nikola, who studied them with thoughtful, uncertain eyes. The front door stood open. Lyssa wondered, with enough motivation, whether Nikola would walk out into the night and abandon her *Cruor Venator.*

"This blood," she told him. "It's not human."

Nikola's gaze sharpened. "You know that?"

"I know the blood on your feet is human," she snapped, anger making her throat thick. "But this . . . this right here is not."

"Whose blood is this?" Eddie demanded.

Nikola was silent a moment. "I don't know. I was given a vial and told to scatter it."

Lyssa wanted to walk away from that blood. She feared it with a cold desperation that made her break into a nauseated sweat.

But when she tried to take that step back . . .

"Lyssa," Eddie said quietly, and a reckless hopelessness rose inside her.

Still holding his hand, she knelt and swiped her finger over the blood. A quick glance showed Nikola watching her with a deep frown.

"Eddie," she whispered, hoarse.

"I have you," he replied, and she licked the blood off her finger.

A blast of heat hit her, and then a sharper sensation, focused behind her eyes. Her psychic connection with Eddie bloomed, allowing her to feel his concern.

Then, in almost the same instant, she felt three dull blows inside her head—like a hammer striking softly, without pain.

On the third strike, a door opened.

And Lyssa found herself in her mother's memories, breathing her mother's last breaths.

This was her blood.

CHAPTER NINETEEN

THREE knocks inside his skull. Eddie felt them like knuckles made of thunder as he struggled to watch Nikola through that terrible distraction.

But it was impossible. His vision wavered, cut with threads of crimson light, and inside his head he heard a sinuous voice whisper:

Do not be afraid. You are in her blood. You are of us now, forever. Dragon bound.

And there are things you must see.

Eddie choked, trying to breathe, but the air was sucked out of his lungs with terrifying force. He found himself falling into a terrible darkness. The only thing he could feel was Lyssa's hand in his, but even that became fluid and hard to hold.

Until, suddenly, the world shifted again—

—and he found himself kneeling in snow, naked and bleeding, staring at a sobbing girl with golden eyes. Her hands and feet were bound, two obsidian blades digging into her throat. Two women, holding her down, laughing and nuzzling her soft hair as she stared at him with eyes that showed a blistered, burning soul.

Lyssa, he thought, fighting to reach her—but he was bound in place, an iron collar around his throat.

"Let her go," he said, but it was a woman's voice that left his mouth, low and quivering with fury. "Let her go. You promised."

"I lied," murmured a soft voice. "Blood murders blood. That is how it works. You know this better than anyone."

"Your mother deserved to die," Eddie said. "She was a monster."

"But she was mine." Pain flashed against his back, making him stiffen with a gasp. In almost the same instant, a hot tongue raced across the wound—and he felt part of himself drift away as though tugged by a string. "Just as you will be mine . . . and your daughter and husband, as well."

"No," he said, just as the blade sunk through his back, barely missing his heart.

The pain was beyond words—but not as terrible as seeing Lyssa's tortured gaze—or hearing her scream for him.

For her mother, he realized, and suddenly he could feel her hand again in his, clutched so tight he barely knew where one began and the other ended. Lyssa's scream clawed through him, changing in pitch from young girl to woman, and in his mind Eddie squeezed her hand until he thought it would break, pulling with all his strength until a hard, warm presence slammed against him—and fire exploded behind his eyes.

When he could see again, he was back in his own body, crouched on the floor beside Lyssa. Hands clutched, white-knuckled, fingernails drawing blood from one another. His head throbbed, lights dancing in his vision, but when he looked up, he saw Nikola staring with hunger and fear.

I'm on fire, he realized dimly, noting the flames crawling up his arms as though far away, distant as a star. Lyssa was burning, too, the claws of her right hand flickering with a golden light that licked the air with threads of hungry fire.

Eddie tried to stand, dragging her with him. From the corner of his eye, he sensed Nikola take a step toward them—and without thinking, he set her jacket on fire.

She screamed, twisting wildly to tear off the burning red leather. Eddie hauled Lyssa across the room, following bloodstained tracks on the floor—guessing, hoping, that it would lead them where they needed to go.

Namely, to where Jimmy's mother was being held. Though he hoped fervently that the blood wasn't hers.

Lyssa choked down sobs as they ran. Part of Eddie was still inside that vision, and each time her voice broke inside her throat, some of his heart broke with her. Fire skipped down her body, crossing their joined hands and riding up his arm. Fire shimmered in the air. Fire, in his blood. Rising, rising into an explosion. Not yet, but soon. His control was fraying. No calm. Nothing but thunder in his head and the feeling of a knife stabbing his back.

His life, licked away by a hungry tongue.

No, not his life, he reminded himself. Lyssa's mother.

"Down," whispered Lyssa, surprising him. Her tears still flowed, but there was a look in her eyes that was a pure stubbornness, and that eased some of the tightness in his chest that was making it so difficult to breathe.

"Basement?" he asked.

"Yes," she said, and gave him a searing look. "You were there in my mind. I could feel you."

He knew what she was referring to. "Yes."

She looked away, wiping her running nose. "I'm sorry."

"For what?"

"My mother was a good person," she replied, which under different circumstances might have seemed like a random response—but in this case made sense. Especially given what he knew: truths he had figured out for himself, on top of what Lannes had told him.

"She loved you," he said.

"She gave herself up for me. And my father." Lyssa shot him a pained look. "I couldn't save her."

Eddie knew there was more to it than that, but there was nothing he could say to comfort her. He hadn't saved his sister. No words or sympathy would ever lessen the pain.

Ahead of them, the blood-sticky tracks led to a massive oak door that stood partially open. Stairs on the other side. Lyssa inhaled deeply, closing her eyes. Light leaked from beneath her lids.

"This is it," she said, trembling. "I need to tell you something. About what I am."

"No," he replied, nudging her aside as he peered down the stairs. "You really don't."

Empty stairwell. No sounds. Eddie didn't trust it. This had been a trap from the start, and nothing would change that. On the other hand, he had the feeling that both of them were wanted alive. No one went to this much trouble to play mind games—literal and otherwise—just to put a bullet in someone's head.

Down the stairs, silently. Breathing controlled, and soft. Lyssa stayed behind him, her back pressed to the wall. No more tears. Nothing but cold, sharp stone in her eyes.

They still held hands: wrapped together, anchored. Heat between their palms. Fire, building in their tangled fingers. Eddie wasn't certain he could have let go, even had he wanted.

Bloody footprints covered the stairs. A trail that

led to a dark hall with a stone floor and rough rock in the walls, lit in intervals by track lights that hung from the ceiling. The air was cool and held a scent that reminded Eddie of caves he had explored with his friends: a vein inside a hill always had its own scent, like air was blood and the earth the flesh.

Lyssa pulled back on his hand. "I hear pain."

Pain. Eddie studied the hall ahead of them, which curved. "What kind of pain?"

"The cutting kind," she murmured, and edged ahead of him with her right hand held up, palm out, clawed fingers flexing as though she was feeling the air.

It wasn't until they were around the curve in the hall that he heard the whimpers.

There was a door in front of him, standing ajar. It was as if seeing it opened his other senses: He could hear pain, he could smell blood. He didn't want Lyssa anywhere near those things.

Not up to you, he told himself, beginning to sweat. *She needs to do this.*

And he needed to watch her back. No blade was going to touch her. Not while he was breathing. Her mother's stabbing still made his shoulders tingle, and the idea of anyone doing that to her—

Eddie tugged on Lyssa's hand and made her look at him. Before she could say anything, he leaned in and kissed her—with all his strength, every ounce of passion he could muster, throwing open his heart.

She leaned into him, her lips soft and hot as she grabbed the front of his sweatshirt. Desperate longing filled his chest—swelling, rising, until it was hard to breathe. He had never felt so lost in another person. He hadn't thought it could happen to him—not so fast, with such intensity.

Alone, for so long. Alone, with friends. Alone, in a crowd. Alone, in his heart, because some pain couldn't be shared, much less spoken out loud.

"Remember," he murmured. "Whatever happens in there, you're not alone."

Lyssa loosened her fingers from his sweatshirt. "When you say things like that . . ."

But she stopped, and a hard look flickered in her eyes as she looked at that door at the end of the hall. For a moment, Eddie lost himself in memories not his own, and saw knives pressed to her twelve-year-old throat. A chill raced over him.

He heard a low groan, thick and heavy with pain. Dread prickled, a sickening anticipation. The bloodstains on the floor caught his eye. Nikola's feet had been red and sticky. Walking through that much blood . . .

Lyssa took a deep breath and strode toward the door. Eddie followed.

A cold rush of power rolled over him just before they reached the end of the hall. Like water, a river, flowing against his skin. Lyssa glanced at him and pushed open the door.

Blood, everywhere. For a moment, it was all he could see. A small circular room, made of stone, and a floor that was crimson and wet, and reeking of death. He saw lumps in the blood-pool. It took several seconds for his mind to register them as bodies.

Horror wasn't big enough for what he felt in that moment. Some primal, primitive force clawed through him, tearing at his heart, ripping his soul. He wanted to scream, but his voice wouldn't work. He wanted to run, but he couldn't move. Part of him died, looking at that room.

Something moved, on his right.

It was a leopard.

Again, shock filled him. The cat was huge, sitting on its haunches and grooming its massive, blood-soaked paw. Blood covered its entire coat, crimson streaks obscuring its spots. Its tongue made a low rasping sound—though it stopped, once, to stare at him with black eyes.

Lyssa stepped past him, her shoes making squelching sounds.

"How dare you," she said to the leopard, in a deadly soft voice. "How dare you wear his skin."

The leopard blinked, and its mouth opened in a panting grin.

Eddie heard another groan, turned—and his heart collapsed.

Jimmy's mother was slumped against the wall. Head hanging, chest rising and falling. Unconscious, but alive. Seated in blood, though it didn't seem as if any of it were hers. Hard to tell if that was the truth.

"You've grown," said a rough voice, behind him. "I suppose I imagined you as a child, all these years."

Eddie turned, and watched as that leopard shifted shape: fur disappearing into flesh, bones lengthening, human features becoming prominent in a feline face.

Lyssa stood beside him, very still, tense, as the leopard became a brown-haired woman: pale and slender, with small breasts and narrow hips, and deep scars across her torso that looked like claw marks.

She seemed very young, hardly eighteen—until he saw her eyes. The pits of her eyes were black as a winter lake, bottomless and cold with death. He was afraid to look too long into that gaze, as if it would consume him—starting with his heart—swallowing his dreams, down to the last drop.

He had managed to push away the crippling fear that Nikola and Betty had tried to infect him with, but Lyssa was right: the *Cruor Venator* was something else entirely.

Her presence felt like a vacuum, sucking away on the edges of his soul—nibbling and tearing, and tugging with sharp teeth all the bits of himself that mattered. He wanted to scratch his skin and twitch. His heart pounded. Cold waves of power rushed over him, tendrils breaking through his immunity.

It made him sick. Fear crept. He wanted to cringe.

Instead, Eddie forced his spine even straighter and met her gaze. This woman, he told himself, was nothing but another Matthew Swint—a monster hiding in a human shell—and he was *not* going to be a coward again.

He was not going to be cowed.

The *Cruor Venator* smiled faintly. "You have balls, young man."

"Don't look at him," Lyssa whispered.

"If I were not too old to breed," replied the witch, ignoring her, "you would tempt me. I like how you stare into my eyes, as though it is a challenge."

An imaginary tongue raced across an imaginary wound in Eddie's back, and he fought down the shudder that crawled up his spine into his throat.

Lyssa stepped in front of him. "You found me. I'm here. I got your messages."

The *Cruor Venator* rolled her shoulders, dark eyes glittering. "You're here, but you're hardly ripe. Or perhaps you're far more coldhearted than I gave you credit for being."

Lyssa quivered. "Ripe."

"You haven't killed. I can see it in your eyes. You

have not yet embraced your blood," said the *Cruor Venator*, giving her a look filled with curiosity and disdain. "Your mother was never so stupid, but we were from a different age. Death was once a quiet thing, as accepted as water and air. To kill was to survive."

"I survive," she whispered.

"But you do not live. How many excuses do you need, little one? I show you the wounded body of someone you know. I kill your friend. I threaten the lives of others in your care. I practically give you Nikola and Betty, whom I know you could have killed with just a thought. Indeed, I thought you might have taken Betty's life . . . but alas, no."

The *Cruor Venator* smiled. "I murdered your mother and your father. And yet, you still pretend. You refrain from death." Her gaze ticked left, to Eddie. "Perhaps you are ashamed. Does *he* know what you are?"

Lyssa tensed. Eddie placed his hands on her shoulders, heat spreading from his palms as he summoned all his strength to make his voice sound steady, and calm.

"She is a *Cruor Venator*," he said, too gently. "And she knows she has nothing to be ashamed of with me."

Beneath his hands, Lyssa stilled.

Then, in a voice that trembled, said, "Why are you doing this, Georgene? Why bait me? Why try to force my hand?"

"Because we're family," she said, which didn't surprise Eddie nearly as much as it should have. "And it has occurred to me, over the years, that it is a sad thing to be the last of one's kind. I will make no pacts with a demon for immortality. And likewise, no fae would grant it to me. So when I die . . ."

"You should have thought of that before you killed my mother," said Lyssa.

"Your mother," replied the woman, "had it coming. And if your father hadn't stolen her from me before I was done—"

The *Cruor Venator* never finished that sentence. Fire roared off Lyssa, a blast so furious the blood began boiling beneath their feet. Flames engulfed the witch, whose skin crackled and peeled, her hair lifting up as hot air slammed her face.

But all she did was bare her teeth and smile.

"Not yet," she said, her voice almost lost beneath the hiss of fire. "You're no *Cruor Venator* to kill *me*. Not until you take a life of your own."

The witch pointed behind them. Tina was still unconscious

"Kill her," whispered the *Cruor Venator*, holding Lyssa's gaze. "Take her blood, then neither of us will be alone. You will be a true *Cruor Venator*."

"And me, as well?" asked a soft voice from the door.

Eddie turned and found Nikola just outside, watching them. A blade in her hand. Gaze steady and cold.

"Darling," said the *Cruor Venator* softly. "Of course, you."

Nikola smiled, her feet making sticky sounds with each slow step. "And am I too late?"

"For the killing?" murmured the witch. "No, dear. Not too late for that."

"Good," Nikola said, and threw her dagger at the *Cruor Venator*. The blade sank hilt deep into her throat.

Eddie moved in almost the same instant, grabbing Lyssa around the waist and swinging her away from the witch. He didn't have to worry, though. Nikola snarled, leaping across the blood-soaked floor to slam fists into the *Cruor Venator*'s chest.

"Tina," Lyssa gasped.

Fire filled his hands, racing up his arms as she squirmed away from him, slipping and sliding across the slick floor to Jimmy's mother. The woman was unbound. Lyssa grabbed her arms and began dragging her to the door. Eddie moved to help her, just as a cold wave of power slammed into him.

It was from the witches, who were engaged in an eerily silent contest of blood and wills. The *Cruor Venator* made not a sound as Nikola stabbed her, but he knew in his gut that no matter what damage they did . . . she would survive.

And then this would begin again.

Without looking back, he went to Lyssa—picked up Tina in his arms—and they ran like hell from the nightmare.

CHAPTER TWENTY

A NOTHER world, outside: a river breeze and starlight and the faintest hint of morning. No scent of blood. Lyssa shuddered when they ran from the house, full of her mother and the memory of that death-drenched room.

A scream had been building from that first taste of her mother's blood—a scream caught in her throat, growing with each moment spent in Georgene's presence. But now, away from her, that silent scream was becoming something else—and the moment Lyssa stepped onto the driveway, she fell to one knee, burning up. Her skin split open in seams of golden light. Bones cracked. Her heart thundered so hard she clutched her chest.

She was going to explode.

"Lyssa," Eddie said urgently, but she shook her head and stumbled sideways, away from him. He stood too close, and Tina was in his arms. The poor woman would burn and die if Lyssa lost control.

A small, young voice rang out. Lyssa looked up, and saw Jimmy running down the driveway toward them.

"No," she croaked, backing away. "Jesus."

"Jimmy!" shouted Eddie. "Stay there!"

The boy did not stop. Lyssa turned, fleeing back inside the house, trying to put walls between herself and the boy. Fire erupted over her skin, burning through her clothing—rising in her throat, filling that buried scream with terrible power.

She heard a screech, far away—twisting into an inhuman note of agony. Nikola, dying. Blood-prints on the floor, stinking up her nose with death.

Lyssa detonated.

Fire slammed outward in a pulse so strong the walls exploded, and furniture splintered into toothpicks. The inferno enveloped the foyer and living room in a shimmering, unending blaze—turning the hardwood floors to crumbling ash.

She watched, unable to move. Staring, lost, feeling fire swarm through the house like a long tongue, licking the air with blistering, explosive heat. Down, down the stairs into the basement, sucking out the air . . .

Hands grabbed her shoulders, dragging her backward. With that contact, a new fire rose in her blood, and she turned to find Eddie—staring into her eyes—surrounded in his own golden light.

Fire in his gaze, fire on his skin, fire burning all around him—consuming them, together. In that moment, a choking ache rose from her heart, a hunger for him that ran deeper than her need to breathe.

Somewhere distant, she heard more screams—filtered through the sizzling crackle of the burning house. Eddie's mouth moved, but she couldn't hear his voice. Just those twisted, strangled cries. None of them sounded like Georgene, but she couldn't be sure.

Eddie dragged her through the blaze. The floor groaned beneath them, half-broken, burning. Stone slabs glowed.

Cool air blasted her face as they stumbled outside. Lyssa carried the fire with her, flames dancing over her naked skin. Not a stitch of clothing left, except for the stubborn remains of Eddie's jacket.

Eddie also burned, but some of his clothes were still intact. Lyssa tried to beat out the flames. It was a losing battle. He tore off the remains of his sweatshirt.

Jimmy sat in the car, face pressed to the glass. Engine running, headlights blazing. Lyssa locked gazes with him, taking in his horror and shock, suffering the same emotions as the heat of the burning house rushed over her naked body.

"Come on," Eddie said in a rough voice.

"I'll frighten him," she mumbled, trying to pull away.

His grip on her arm tightened. "No. He worships you."

"He shouldn't be here. What were you thinking?"

"I was thinking that it hurts more to be useless." Eddie leaned in, his gaze terrible with concern. "I know how he feels."

Jimmy shoved open the car door, half-tumbling out before stopping, staring.

"Shit," he squeaked.

Lyssa tore her gaze from Eddie. "Watch your mouth. And get back in the car."

He cringed. "You're *burning*."

Mustering all her strength, she focused on the fire flowing over her skin and took a deep breath, fighting to draw it down. Light sputtered, gasping in puffs and spurts—but after a long moment, the flames receded. The effort stole more strength than the explosion. Lyssa hunched over, barely able to stay upright. A chill punctured her bones.

Somehow, Eddie got her to the car and pushed her

into the backseat. Lyssa blinked blearily at the flames engulfing the house, feeling very distant from the blaze.

An immense cracking sound filled the air.

The burning house tilted sideways: roof sinking, collapsing, as the entire structure slid down the hill, burning chunks of wreckage breaking apart to tumble toward the river. Immense, ridiculous, as though from some movie.

Except it was real. Her fault. She knew that. But nothing in her seemed to care. Instead, all she felt was a sense of deep satisfaction and *rightness*.

Her mother had once said that dragon fire was pure. Pure enough to kill a shadow.

Lyssa hoped that was true.

AT THE FIRST GAS STATION THEY FOUND, EDDIE asked Jimmy to get out and use the pay phone to make a collect call. His phone had burned, along with his wallet. He parked the stolen car on the outskirts of the lot. The sky was growing lighter. Lyssa hoped no one could see them from the road. She was naked. Eddie a little less so, but this wasn't a beach in Hawaii.

Lyssa slouched in the back with her arms crossed over her breasts. Tina took up the rest of the seat. She was still unconscious and smelled like blood. The bitter scent made Lyssa sick, and she had the window rolled partially down. Even the nearby Dumpster smelled good in comparison.

Icky sat in the front seat, whining. Eddie scratched his ears. There was a line between his eyes that hadn't been there when Lyssa first met him. She wondered how her own face had aged. She felt older by a hundred years—mostly on the inside, in her heart.

"I had my chance," she murmured. "I looked Georgene in the face—and still wasn't able to do what was required."

"You act as though *not killing* was a bad thing," Eddie said softly.

"She won't stop. We're back to square one. I told myself I was done running, that I'd finish it, once and for all."

"So, what? You would have killed a friend in cold blood? That would make things better?"

She shuddered, unable to look at Tina. "No."

"Exactly. We'll find another way."

"It makes me feel weak."

"I know," he said. "But you're not."

Lyssa leaned around to watch Jimmy at the pay phone. "How long do you think it will take him?"

"Why?"

"I want to erase Tina's memories."

Eddie turned to look at her. "You can do that?"

"It's like cutting threads, then absorbing them. It's what a *Cruor Venator* does when she kills. She absorbs and steals, until, at the last moment of death, the victim doesn't even remember his or her own name. Everything is gone." Lyssa had trouble meeting his gaze. "Does that bother you?"

"Be more specific," he replied. "What you want to know is whether or not it bothers me that you're a *Cruor Venator*."

"Okay, yes. Does it?"

Eddie gave her an incredulous look. "Seriously? Get real."

Lyssa stared, then leaned forward to kiss him. She couldn't quite reach his mouth, so she had to settle for a spot between his nose and cheek. Their breath mingled, rich and warm—and his sigh as she kissed him again, this time beneath his eye, was more healing than anything she could have imagined.

"Thank you," she whispered. "Thank you, for being my dream come true."

"I'm no one's dream," he murmured gruffly.

She tugged his ear, gently. "You're mine."

Before he could say anything, she leaned back into the seat—heart pounding, cheeks flushed. "Do I have time?"

He touched his face where she had kissed him. "A few minutes. Have you ever . . ."

"No. I'm not sure I should start now, but . . . Tina deserves a second chance. So does Jimmy."

"You won't erase his memory, will you?"

"He can keep a secret."

Eddie smiled. "Every good detective can."

Lyssa rubbed away her own smile with the back of her hand. "I think he can handle what he saw. Even the fire and my arm. But Tina was down in that room, with the blood . . ."

She stopped, unable to finish, and reached out to cut the unconscious woman's hand. Blood welled, tipping a claw. But instead of licking it off, she pressed her mouth directly to the wound.

Power filled her, but it was easier somehow to accept it into her body. That, and the fact that Tina was only human, and the taste was different.

Lyssa found the memories quickly: sharp, bright, floating on the surface of her mind. She felt Tina's horror, her fear for her son . . .

. . . she saw Flo's face, covered in blood . . .

. . . and heard the *Cruor Venator* whisper, *"What I am . . . is what will survive the world. I will grow fat on death and fear . . ."*

Right before she slammed the blade into Flo's chest.

Lyssa tore those memories loose from Tina's mind and ate them. Then, she went looking for more.

Two minutes later, she was done.

Tina still slept, but the lines in her face had smoothed, and her breathing was easier. Lyssa wished she could say the same for herself.

Eddie reached back to wrap his fingers around her hand. "Okay?"

"Okay," she told him wearily, "but *I'd* like to forget the things I saw in her mind."

"I'm sorry."

She shook her head. "My mother did this, sometimes. Before she met my father, anyway. When she lived in Europe after the First and Second World Wars, people would come to her . . . knowing she had a peculiar gift . . . and beg her to steal their memories of the war. To just . . . erase it all . . . so they could move on with their lives."

"She didn't think it was better to remember?"

"She refused some people. Others, no. She also believed in second chances, for obvious reasons."

"But she had to live with *their* nightmares."

Lyssa closed her eyes. "I asked her about that once. She said it was nothing compared to what she had to live with after killing the other *Cruor Venator. That* woman's mind . . . she said . . . was too vile to comprehend. That *trying* would be enough to make a person unclean."

"You mother was tough."

"I will never be as strong as her."

"I doubt she would agree."

Lyssa's mouth softened into a smile. "You're probably right. But she'd be biased. And so are you."

"No," he said, kissing her hand. "Not even a little."

Jimmy ran back, his sweatshirt sleeves flopping wildly over his hands. Breathless when he got back into the car, he scooped Icky into his lap.

"I got her," he said, with a hint of pride. "Serena? She said that someone named Roland called her, and she flew into New York an hour ago. She'll be here soon."

"Huh. What else?"

"I asked her if she was with the FBI, and she said it was better than that."

Eddie gave him a wary look. "What *did* she tell you?"

"Mercenary." Jimmy seemed totally fine with that and looked back at his mom. "Is she okay?"

"Better." Lyssa wondered who Serena was. "She woke up for just a minute while you were gone, but didn't remember anything about what happened. When you talk to her . . ."

"I'll be careful," said the boy. "I don't want her to be more scared."

But a moment later, he gave Lyssa a hesitant look. "You didn't really see a drug deal . . . did you?"

Lyssa chewed the inside of her cheek. "Because of my arm, you mean?"

"It looks real. Can I touch it?"

Eddie's mouth twitched. She took a breath and extended her right hand.

Jimmy's eyes got big as he stared at her reptilian scales and sharp golden claws. He grazed them, lightly, with his fingertips. It tickled.

"Wow," he breathed. "Did someone do experiments on you? Is that why they were really after you? Like, the cops were part of a conspiracy?"

What a kid, Eddie thought.

Lyssa said, "Yes. You won't tell anyone, will you?"

"No way." Jimmy hugged Icky tighter. "Are we safe now?"

No, she thought. *I haven't killed the Cruor Venator.* She met Eddie's gaze and saw his concern.

"Yes," she lied again. "You're safe."

SERENA MCGILLIS WAS TALL, LEAN, AND WORE dark clothing that hugged her body like a glove. Red hair, threaded with golden highlights, fell to her chin. Ageless face. Feline scent. An eye patch that Jimmy thought was just too cool for words.

He didn't seem to notice that her other eye wasn't quite human, but Lyssa did, and it made her feel less awkward when Serena openly studied her right arm.

"Does it ache?" she asked.

"Yes."

Serena nodded and tossed her a shopping bag full of clothing. "I didn't know your size, so I went big."

Large jogging pants and a sweatshirt. There were gloves, too. Warm and roomy. Lyssa liked them all. Eddie received something similar. They dressed inside the car, while Serena and Jimmy moved Tina to the Humvee idling beside them. Icky sat in the big front seat, wagging his tail and panting.

"Do you need to wipe down the car for prints?" Lyssa asked Eddie.

He shook his head. "I'm going to burn it. Safer, that way. We've been in it for too long, and there's blood in the backseat."

He waited, though, until they were in the Humvee and on the road. Serena pulled over. Eddie looked through the back window at the stolen Cadillac, which was parked several hundred feet away. A safe distance from them and the gas station.

Lyssa saw flames flicker inside the car. Small, at

first—then larger, licking the windows and spreading through the interior.

When Serena pulled back onto the road, Lyssa didn't look back. Neither did Eddie. She sat snug against his side, warm and drifting, trying not to think too hard. It was all so surreal. All the blood, and violence . . . floating away, detaching from her as though some ghost was absorbing *her* memories. Softening them, if nothing else.

Is that you? Lyssa asked her dragon. *If so, thank you.*

You are welcome. Rest, sister. You will need your strength.

The war, it added, *is not done yet.*

CHAPTER TWENTY-ONE

SERENA parted ways with them at LaGuardia, to— as she put it, go and clean some things up. Tina and Jimmy were already aboard the private jet, and the pilot was a familiar face. Eddie felt safe enough, though he kept scanning the hangar for anything that might be a witch or gun.

"Lannes and Lethe are back in Maine," Serena said to him. "I met them at the airport, along with his two brothers. I've never seen gargoyles armed with *guns*, but they were. And they seemed especially protective of Lethe. Care to explain?"

"No," Eddie replied. "It's their business."

"Huh." Serena looked at Lyssa with a hard glint in her eye. "Lannes explained what you did for him and his wife. He also told me what you are."

"And?"

"Did you kill the witch?"

"Not yet. I don't recommend you go near that burned house for a while, either. Just in case you'd planned to."

Serena hesitated, her single eye narrowing. "You're not what I expected. Eddie and I were both told that we'd be searching for a lost lamb, a damaged little girl. A *shape-shifter,* and nothing more."

Lyssa tensed. "Is that what Long Nu said?"

Serena's gaze hardened. "You know her."

"Of course. And Long Nu knows *me* . . . which is why she didn't come herself . . . if she ever truly was worried about my welfare." Bitterness touched her mouth. "Makes you wonder, doesn't it?"

The implications were very disturbing. Eddie and Serena shared a long look.

"Will you call Roland?" he asked her.

"Of course." She began to turn away, but stopped and looked back at Lyssa. "What are your intentions?"

"Hey," he said.

"She has a right to ask." Lyssa looked her dead in the eyes. "I just want to be left alone."

"You carry the blood of a dragon and a *Cruor Venator,*" replied Serena, and for the first time, Eddie heard a trace of unease in her voice.

"Being bothered," she said, edging away, "will be the least of your problems."

SEVEN HOURS LATER, THEY ARRIVED IN SAN FRAN-cisco.

A rental car was waiting. Eddie drove them to a quiet neighborhood in a nice part of the city, where he had the keys to an elegant Tudor built at the end of a cul-de-sac.

"My friend, Amiri, owns this home," he said, as Jimmy helped his mother from the car. "But he and his wife are in Africa at the moment. He won't mind guests."

Eddie hoped that was true, anyway—but he didn't want Jimmy and Tina in a hotel, not anymore. They needed a private, quiet setting to heal . . . not someplace downtown where people would be coming and going.

Lights came on in the house, which smelled faintly like lemon oil. Tina looked around with careful appreciation, stepping lightly over the floors as if she were afraid to touch anything. "How long can we stay here?"

"Several months," Eddie told him. "Or until we find something else."

"We'll be very careful to leave it as we found it," Tina said, and disappeared into the kitchen.

Jimmy was uncharacteristically quiet as he clutched Icky to his chest. His eyes were so old, reminding Eddie a bit of himself. "You're not really going away for good, are you?"

"I live in this city," he said, gently. "We'll practically be neighbors. You'll be sick of me."

Jimmy nodded, but the worry in his eyes didn't go away. Lyssa crouched and smoothed back his hair.

"You'll be sick of me, too," she said. "I'm staying here."

Eddie's heart leapt. Jimmy peered at her. "Promise?"

"Shhh," said Tina, coming up behind him with a weary, sweet smile. "Don't be a pest."

She said it kindly, with a teasing note in her voice. Jimmy grinned, leaning against her as she wrapped a slender arm over his shoulders.

They had stuck with the Bolivian-drug-lord story. Even Jimmy thought that was better than human experimentation, kidnapping, and fire—and the boy, to give credit where it was due, knew how to tell a very convincing lie.

Tina didn't even remember Aaron Roacher finding her at work, so they'd had to blame her bruises and cuts on a car accident. Memory loss because she'd hit her head. If she was suspicious, she didn't show it. Confused, yes . . . and concerned . . . but willing to take the leap of faith that they had needed to leave New York, fast. She trusted Lyssa and her son *that* much.

And she was used to running, too, he thought.

Of course, telling lies wasn't a fair burden to put on Jimmy . . . but short of taking his memories, all they could do was promise to be there if he needed to talk. And he *would* need someone. Probably every day for a long time to come.

Eddie knew that the boy's smile was deceptive. Nothing could hide the shadows in his eyes. He had seen too much violence.

But Jimmy won. He beat the monsters and helped save his mother. It'll help him heal.

That, and knowing he's still protecting Lyssa by keeping her secret.

It was amazing what helping a beautiful woman could do for a boy's—or a man's—sense of purpose.

Eddie pointed to Jimmy's suitcase. "Serena was able to retrieve your case files. When I see you tomorrow, we'll talk detective work, okay?"

Tina reached for Lyssa's hand. "Thank you. For everything."

"Don't," she said, looking uncomfortable. "I up-ended your life."

She shook her head and gave Eddie a knowing smile. "I can tell that *you* understand."

"She's a little slow when it comes to these things," Eddie agreed, jumping away when Lyssa gasped and tried to poke him.

They left an hour later. One block from the house, Lyssa said, "Pull over."

"Is there something wrong?" he asked, concerned.

"No." She rolled down the window, closing her eyes as a cool breeze filled the car. It was mid-afternoon and sunny, with that clean California light that felt different here, compared to anywhere else. The street was quiet, empty, and even though it was the middle of the day, Eddie felt as though it was just the two of them in the world.

"I want to make this moment last," she said. "I haven't felt so . . . normal . . . in a long time."

"Normal," he echoed, running his hands over the steering wheel.

"Out, with people. Doing things that people take for granted. I've never been on a plane before today. I've ridden in buses and cabs; but before I met Estefan, I never sat inside a personal vehicle. It's strange. How am I going to live now?"

With me, he wanted to tell her. Instead, he said, "It took me a long time to adjust to living off the street, like regular people. You know, with money and a job. It still feels new, even strange, sometimes."

Lyssa studied him with soft, gentle eyes. "You always surprise me when you say things like that. When I'm with you . . . I can't imagine you ever *not* having your life in order."

"Order doesn't mean normal. The job I do . . . it's often violent. I'm always on the outskirts of things. Watching backs. Making sure everything is okay."

"You protect."

Eddie hesitated. "I try. If I can keep someone safe . . . that's important to me. You know why."

Lyssa leaned over and kissed his cheek. Eddie turned his head before she could pull away, capturing her mouth, sinking into her sweet taste and heat. Just being near her was comforting *and* erotic—like, even *thinking* about holding her hand gave him a hard-on— but *kissing* her was something else entirely.

Eddie pulled back. Lyssa gave him a dreamy smile that made him want to drag her into the backseat.

He couldn't help himself. His hand slipped under her sweatshirt, tracing a path up her side until he touched her heavy, full breast. She shivered, pushing against him, and in a voice too rough to possibly belong to him, he said, "Put down your seat."

Amazingly, she didn't argue, fumbling until her chair reclined all the way down. Eddie stared at her, heart pounding, overcome with lust and hunger, and— and *love*—and it drove him a little insane, realizing that the moment belonged to them.

That somehow, in his crazy, lonely life, he had finally gotten touched with luck beyond his wildest dreams.

Lyssa smiled. "Hi, over there."

Eddie grinned, leaning over her. "Hi."

His lips met hers, soft at first, then hard, tongues slipping together as pleasure stormed through him in a hard, throbbing ache. His hand slipped beneath the band of her sweatpants. He knew she wasn't wearing underwear, and he loved the sigh and whimper that drifted from her mouth as his fingers pressed and rubbed between her shifting legs.

"Eddie," she whispered, tugging down his own sweatpants. "I really want you inside me."

He groaned as her hand wrapped around him, and bit back a deeper, louder cry when her fingers squeezed. If anyone walked or drove past, they would be seen . . . but right then, he didn't care.

He kissed her harder, slipping his fingers inside her body and rotating them in a deep, circular motion. Lyssa rubbed against his hand, moaning against his mouth. Her grip on his penis loosened, but only enough to drag her fingers to his sensitive head, caressing him so perfectly in that one, fleeting touch, he almost came in her palm.

"Your breasts," Eddie said in a ragged voice, and Lyssa pulled up her sweatshirt, exposing herself to him. He dipped his head, drawing her hard nipple into his mouth and suckling. Lyssa's back arched, sharp nails digging into his scalp.

He pulled his fingers from the slick, wet heat of her body, and started flicking the hard nub of her clitoris.

Lyssa's hips jerked, and her soft grunts of pleasure were so sexy he thought he could climax just as easily from listening to her. He rubbed her harder, faster, taking her cries into his mouth with long, breathless kisses—and when she finally came, he muffled her scream, and her eyes glowed golden hot.

"Eddie," she whispered raggedly, sagging against the seat. "Take me someplace where there's a bed, please."

He laughed, but it turned into a groan when her hand found his penis again. Her fingers kneaded his shaft in light movements that stole every coherent thought from his head.

Lyssa leaned over the gearshift and licked him. Her tongue was so hot. Eddie couldn't breathe.

"Did you mean it? About not leaving San Francisco?" His voice was hoarse, and broken.

Her smile turned serious. "Yes. Was that . . . should I have asked you first?"

"No." Eddie thought for a moment about what to say next. It was difficult, given that she was still touching him. "If you want to stay in a hotel, I—"

She started laughing and clapped her hand over her mouth.

"Okay," he said, smiling. "I'll take you to my place."

CHAPTER TWENTY-TWO

LYSSA was surprised when Eddie drove to the waterfront and parked in the underground lot of what had to be a very expensive apartment building.

"You're rich?" she said to him.

Eddie shrugged as if embarrassed and rubbed the back of his neck. "I get paid well. It's nice."

She smiled, shaking her head.

They stood close, holding hands, as the elevator took them up the fifteenth floor. Lyssa was suddenly too nervous to look at him, but she kept her cheek pressed against his shoulder, her other hand buried in his sweatshirt. His body radiated heat. So did hers, she realized. The air around them shimmered with it, like an oven.

"Are we going to set off fire alarms?" she asked, with real concern.

"Uh," he said, and laughed. "I hope not."

His apartment was a roomy studio with large windows that overlooked the Bay Bridge. Tidy, without much furniture. Just a bed, a couple soft chairs, and a small table near the kitchen.

"I'm not here a lot," he said.

"Do you travel all the time?"

"I'm gone a week or two or a month, typically. But sometimes I need that . . . room. The one I told you about. Where I can burn."

Lyssa nodded, chewing the inside of her cheek. "I don't know . . . how I fit into your life, exactly. Being with me won't be easy, you know. Your friends . . ."

Eddie had been standing by the door, watching her, but he crossed the distance in moments. He didn't touch her, but instead he loomed, holding her gaze with a dangerous intensity that made her feel like she was the only person in the world who mattered.

"If they can't accept you," he said quietly, "they are not my friends."

Lyssa backed away. "Don't say that. My father lost all his friends because he felt the same way. It hurt him, and my mother."

"But it didn't damage the two of them *together,* did it?"

"No," she said, after a moment. "No, it didn't. They loved each other very much."

Eddie's eyes softened. "Would you believe me if I said I loved you?"

Her breath caught. "If you say it . . . I'll believe."

"I love you," he whispered, in a low, rough voice. "I love you."

I love you. Words that resonated, and flowed. Words that she had been feeling, and holding in her own heart, afraid to think them because it was more than she had imagined ever feeling. More than she had imagined anyone feeling about *her.*

But she *did* believe him. He was too much in her blood, not to believe.

Lyssa swallowed hard, burning up with a fever.

"You know . . . there's this thing about shape-shifters," she said, slowly. "We sort of . . . stick with one person for our entire lives. So it means something when we love. We don't . . . take that lightly." She raised a trembling hand to touch his cheek. "When I'm with you . . . everything inside me says *yes*."

Eddie captured her hand. "Is that instinct or love?"

Lyssa smiled. "It's like . . . feeling as though every sappy love song I've ever heard is my theme song."

His nose crinkled, and he laughed. "Choose one."

She tangled her fingers in his sweatshirt. "Take off your clothes, and maybe I will."

His cheeks turned red, but he stripped. Lyssa stood back, biting back a smile that felt full and rich, and heavy with her heart.

Eddie's body was lean and broad with muscle, and he had an erection. Her scratch marks on his chest were healing, and only caused her a moment's consternation.

Giving her a bold look, he said, "A song, please."

Lyssa hesitated, thinking about her arm—and then pulled her sweatshirt over her head, and tossed it at him. " 'Can't Help Falling in Love.' "

His smile warmed though his eyes darkened with hunger. She noticed that he did not look at her breasts or dragon scales. Just her eyes.

"I want to hear you say it, Lyssa."

"I love you," she told him. "I love you, and it's not instinct. It's me. It's my heart. My heart loves you, and I don't how it happened. But it did, and it's crazy. *You're* crazy to love *me*."

"If you're not the one for me, then I *am* crazy." Eddie took a deep breath and hooked his fingers beneath the waistband of her sweats. "May I?"

She laughed and covered his hands—her right hand, so careful—helping him push the sweats down off her hips. He knelt as he undressed her, trailing kisses against her stomach. Lyssa closed her eyes, savoring the heat of his mouth.

He drew her to the bed. The late afternoon light cast a soft glow over their skins as they made love. Nothing mattered but his touch and smile and kiss, and she strained against him, wanting so badly to take him into her body.

"Lyssa," he gasped, as she guided him to the right spot.

"Please," she begged, breathless.

His eyes darkened, and he grabbed her hip, pushing into her slowly. Lyssa gasped as her body stretched around him. Eddie made a similar sound, squeezing shut his eyes as a tremor wracked him.

"You're so tight," he whispered. "Am I hurting you?"

"No," she breathed, arching her hips so that he had no choice but to sink deeper. "Hard and fast, Eddie. Please."

He groaned and thrust forward. Lyssa felt a sharp pain, but that disappeared in moments. He pulled out, then thrust again, and again, grinding into her with hard, long strokes. She clung to him, matching his rhythm, heat racing through her body into his. Smoke rose from his back, fire licking across his skin. Lyssa covered those flames with her hands—human and dragon—drawing them into herself as her muscles tightened around him.

His large hand covered her breast, squeezing, and he gathered up her leg and hitched it higher, deepening his penetration. His thrusts quickened. Lyssa gasped his name—losing control as a wild, cresting pleasure exploded through her body in one long, throbbing wave.

Eddie came with her, crying out and covering her mouth in a soul-deep kiss as his hips jerked and thrust, nearly sending her over the edge a second time.

He collapsed on top of her, both of them tangled and sweating, breathing so hard Lyssa was afraid their lungs would burst. The sheets were smoking around them.

We almost set the bed on fire. It was too ridiculous—and wonderful.

She started to giggle. A foreign sound. It had been ten years since she'd made a noise like that, but it bubbled out of her from a place of pure joy. Eddie lifted his head, staring, and she pointed at the smoke, breath hitching as she struggled not to laugh. He grinned and began laughing with her.

Their laughter faded, though, as they stared into each other's eyes.

"I'm scared," she told him, softly. "Love didn't save my parents."

"You're such a downer. They loved each other. Focus on that." Eddie bit his lip until it bled. "Kiss me, Lyssa."

She hesitated. "Eddie."

But she didn't stop him when he dipped his head, brushing his lips over hers. She tasted his blood.

The power that flowed from him was different than any other. Before, when taking her own blood or Lethe's, it had felt as though a wall were slamming into her. Disruptive. Painful. Overwhelming.

The energy that flowed from Eddie's blood was just the opposite. It moved into her, through her, wrapping her in a cocoon of fire that was strong and gentle and filled with love. It was power, but a deeper power than any other she had felt, and instead of ripping her apart . . . it filled her up.

Memories flashed through her mind: his pleasure, making love to her, his comfort at holding her in his arms . . . his fear of not being able to protect her.

And deeper than that, she saw a little girl's face: pale and beautiful, with long dark hair and shadowy eyes filled with mystery.

Daphne.

Lyssa sighed into that memory and began to pull away. Except, something nagged at her. Something about Eddie's blood.

The dragon stirred, stretching its wings with a satisfied purr.

Ah, it whispered. *Now his fire makes sense.*

What? Lyssa asked.

She heard a low, raspy chuckle.

Somewhere, not so long ago, one of his ancestors was a dragon.

"Whoa," she said, opening her eyes.

Eddie blinked. "What?"

She told him.

"Oh," he said, staring. "Whoa."

EDDIE HAD NEVER REALLY QUESTIONED WHERE HIS ability with fire came from, though some years back, he had finally asked his mother and grandmother if there were any truly unusual family stories . . . like, anything that verged on the supernatural.

"No," both of them had said, which was either true, or meant that someone had been very good at hiding what they were.

Of course, he'd had to accept that this gift could have come from his father's side. But given that his father had no living relatives, except a distant cousin who lived in Spain, there really wasn't much way to find out.

Except now he knew he had shape-shifter blood inside him. And that was odd . . . but also comforting. The fire was not random. The fire was in him for a reason.

That, and Lyssa, occupied all his thoughts.

They lay tangled, talking, half-sleeping, touching each other and making out, and making love, and just . . . *being*. It was the most miraculous few hours of his life. More healing than anything he could have imagined. Waking up with Lyssa warm and naked in his arms . . .

If he lived forever, he would never forget, never take for granted, *never never never* let go of how deep a blessing it was that he had found her and that she was with him.

His stomach started rumbling, though. And then, so did hers.

"Rwar," she said, scraping her teeth against his shoulder. "*Fooood*."

He laughed, smoothing back her hair. "What do you want?"

"No one's asked me that in ten years," she said, blinking at him. And then she grinned. "What do you have?"

"I don't even know. I usually eat out."

Lyssa looked away from the bed, at the floor where she'd left her clothes. "All my money is in New York. I never used a debit card, but I could call and try to wire—"

"No," said Eddie, and when she arched her brow at him, he added, "What I mean is, don't worry about that yet." Then, feeling even more awkward, he started to say, "That is, it's not . . . I've got . . ."

"Money," she said, dryly. "We really are going to have to figure out how this works."

"Let me take care of you," he replied. "At least for now."

"Mmm." Lyssa tapped her finger against his shoulder. "Just as long as you don't ask me to call you Big Daddy."

Eddie laughed and squeezed her backside. "Deal."

She squirmed, giggling breathlessly, and rolled off the bed. "This is unreal."

He pushed himself up on his elbows, admiring the view. "Tell me about it."

Shyness entered her eyes, and she hugged her right arm against her body, backing away from him. Eddie pushed aside the sheets, and slid from the bed—following her. An appreciative smile touched her mouth as her gaze roved down his body, and desire filled him, again. He couldn't imagine ever *not* wanting her.

"Never wear clothes," she murmured. "I'll call you Big Daddy all you want. And it will be *well deserved*."

He bit back a smile. "Do you know how beautiful you are? Do you have any idea how crazy I am for you?"

"Crazy, yes," she said, and gave him a self-conscious shrug. "I don't know about beautiful. I've got this quirky appendage, don't forget."

"Beautiful," he said again. "You're the bestest-looking government experiment ever."

She laughed, slapping a hand over her mouth. "Oh, that poor kid."

"He has a bright future," Eddie told her, and meant it. "Let's eat and get you some new clothes."

"Yo," she said, holding up her clawed right hand. "I know this is San Francisco, but people here have to have *some* limits for strange, right? Maybe we should shop online."

"Please. If you show off all that dragon, the tourists

will love you, and the locals will give you an award for cool."

"They'll think it's some makeup job?"

Eddie smiled, feeling lighter and more unburdened than he had in had years. "Let's go find out."

Lyssa growled at him and went to explore his closet. He followed, and found her digging through his long-sleeved shirts.

"Take anything," he said.

"I will," she replied, pulling a soft, battered, long-sleeved shirt off the hanger. It was black, like a lot of his clothes.

Before she slipped on his shirt, he couldn't help but reach out and stroke his finger down her smooth back. Lyssa shivered, giving him a half smile that was warm and knowing. His erection was instant, and throbbing.

"I can't believe it," he said. "I want you again. Right now."

She laughed. "Do you have any jeans I can borrow?"

"They'll be huge on you."

"I like wearing your things." Lyssa bent over to dig through his folded pants.

He either needed to touch himself or find his way inside her body. "You're doing this on purpose."

"I'm wet for you," she said bluntly. "Of course I am."

His breath exhaled in a rush, and he reached for her hips. Lyssa leaned forward, bracing her hands on the wall and looking over her shoulder with glowing golden eyes.

"I've always wondered," she said, "what it would feel like to be taken from behind."

"God," he said, and showed her.

HIS CELL PHONE RANG SEVERAL TIMES, BUT HE WAS too busy exhausting himself—and Lyssa—to even think about answering. It wasn't until after a fairly vigorous shower that he finally checked his messages.

All of them were from Roland.

"What is it?" asked Lyssa, rubbing a towel through her hair.

"My boss," said Eddie, reluctantly. "He wants us to come over. Are you comfortable with that?"

"More than you are, I think."

Eddie smiled, grim. "Yeah."

Lyssa dressed in his jeans and a long-sleeved shirt. She had to wear a belt and roll up the legs, but she still managed to look cute, even with a winter scarf wrapped around her neck and gloves on her hands.

His apartment was within walking distance to the office. Lyssa ventured outside with hesitation, touching the scarf, checking her gloves.

"I feel like I'm in a different world," she told him. "I know that sounds stupid, but I'm a creature of certain habits. I've had to be. I familiarized myself with every city I lived in. I studied the people, how to behave . . ."

"You feel out of place here."

"More than usual," she admitted. "Off-balance. Part of that is you, though. It feels strange . . . being with someone. I'm so used to doing everything on my own."

Eddie hesitated. "Do you feel stifled?"

"No." Lyssa smiled. "No. I'm thinking about what to illustrate for my next job assignment."

He ducked his head, pleased—and tucked her hand in his.

It was early evening, and the sun was setting. Scattered clouds covered the darkening sky, and seagulls cried. Eddie bought Lyssa hot chocolate, and he sipped coffee as they walked. It felt natural to have her beside him. As right as anything he had ever experienced. It made him feel . . . like a normal man.

Scattered memories filled him, flashes of his child-hood, his life on the streets. He thought about the cage, and the fire that had wracked him so deeply he had expected his life would never be his again to control.

Out of control. Fighting for control. Stifling his life for control. That described so much of how he had ex-isted.

But with Lyssa . . . he could just *be*.

"I think Estefan might have mentioned Dirk & Steele," she said, when they reached the building and he undid the locks on the narrow front door. "But I wasn't really paying attention, and it was just in pass-ing. All I can remember is an impression of his voice saying the name."

"He knew enough to contact us."

Lyssa forced a sad smile. "Yeah."

During the elevator ride up to the top floor, she began to fidget. Eddie felt the same. He wasn't looking forward to seeing Roland.

But it was Long Nu who greeted them when the el-evator doors opened.

CHAPTER TWENTY-THREE

THE first shape-shifter Lyssa had ever met, besides her father, was an old woman with sharp teeth and a sharper heart. Nothing soft inside her. No compassion for anyone who strayed past a certain line.

A line her father had crossed in marrying her mother.

A line, said the old woman, with a price.

Exile, for starters. And one day, perhaps, death.

The threat of death was a bluff, she realized later.

Long Nu would not have dared cross Lyssa's mother.

Even dragons were scared of the dark.

THE OLD SHAPE-SHIFTER HAD NOT CHANGED AT all. Same wrinkles, same coiffed hair, old, knowing eyes, and a half smile that was cold as ice.

"You," Lyssa said.

Long Nu drew in a deep breath. A man appeared at the end of the hall, big in the shoulders and tall. He had a craggy face, and brown hair that needed a cut. He smelled like the inside of a liquor cabinet, but his eyes were sharp with intelligence.

Roland, she thought. *Eddie's boss.*

Lyssa had wanted to make a good impression, but with Long Nu present . . . she gave up on that plan. Things were going to get ugly.

"Is there a problem?" Roland asked gruffly, striding toward them.

"I don't know," Eddie said, watching Long Nu. "Is there?"

"Yes," replied Lyssa, stepping off the elevator, taking some small pleasure in making the dragon-woman back up. "We've got a problem."

"I'm here," Long Nu said stiffly. "I'm facing you."

Lyssa slapped her. Right hand. With all her strength.

"Fuck," said Roland, while Eddie let out a muffled sound of surprise.

Long Nu did not go down, but almost. Holding her face, she stared at Lyssa with contempt—but also a hint of fear. "Is that all?"

Rage flowed. Pounding, throbbing, fury. The dragon inside Lyssa unfurled its wings, and a terrible ache raced down her right arm. Her vision faded into a golden haze.

"Don't tempt me," she whispered . . . and, finally, Long Nu averted her eyes. Lyssa stepped closer. "Show me your hands."

"Hey," snapped Roland. "What the hell is this?"

"Lyssa," murmured Eddie.

"I want to make sure she's not holding a weapon," she told the men, her gaze never leaving Long Nu. "Do it."

Stiff, chin raised, the old woman held out her hands—palms up.

"Now back away," Lyssa told her.

"You're a stupid child," whispered Long Nu. "I never tried to kill you."

"You promised my father that you'd try," she shot

back. "What was it you said? *'Monsters shouldn't breed'*? I remember that like it was yesterday."

Eddie stiffened. The big man, Roland, stared at the back of Long Nu's head as though he could see right through it. A scowl tugged at his mouth.

The old woman backed away. Lyssa's clawed right hand ached to strike another blow, but she fought down the urge with the same strength and desperation that she used to fight her hunger for blood. If she started fighting Long Nu, she would not stop.

And she would win. She knew that, sure as she was breathing.

It would be worth it, whispered the dragon.

Eddie touched her back, placing himself between her and Long Nu. "Come on."

The old woman's nostrils flared as Eddie and Lyssa walked past her.

Lyssa saw that the apartment was huge once they reached the end of the long corridor. Floor-to-ceiling windows stretched from one end of the room to the other, and the entire space was filled with comfortable chairs, and long antique tables laden with newspapers and books.

She didn't let herself admire the view, instead putting her back to the window so that she could face Long Nu.

The woman was as graceful as ever, but Lyssa had the benefit now of being older, with ten years of hard living behind her. She was no longer scared of the old dragon. Or as naïve about her own power.

Eddie stood very close: an anchor, her broad shoulder to lean on. His presence helped her focus.

"Be honest," said Lyssa. "You hoped I was dead, all these years."

"Not exactly," replied Long Nu in a cold, flat voice. "I found your parents after their murders. When I realized your mother had not killed the other *Cruor Venator,* I was upset. I was even more upset, though, when I didn't find *your* body. I thought, maybe, if you lived . . . that the witch who killed your family was raising you. Which, frankly, was a bomb waiting to go off that I did *not* look forward to dealing with."

"Fuck," said Roland, staring at her.

Eddie said nothing, but heat throbbed off his body, making the air shimmer around them. Lyssa basked in that warmth, breathing deep of it, making herself calm.

"I always suspected," she said, "that you led the *Cruor Venator* to my family."

Long Nu shook her head. "No, I did not do that. I promise you, I did not. But you cannot blame me for wishing that your mother had been strong enough to kill the witch."

"My mother was strong enough . . . but she gave her life to protect mine." Fury thickened her voice, as did grief. "And yes, I wish she had killed Georgene. But only because I *loved* her. *Not* like you . . . who only wanted to see the lesser of two monsters *gone.*"

Eddie's hand curled around hers. "Maybe we should go."

"No," Roland said gruffly, staring at Long Nu. "Not you."

Lyssa stepped closer to the old woman, ignoring both men. Power filled her, born from her own blood and spirit, and the dragon waking inside her. She could feel, on the edge of her spirit, the ability to make Long Nu afraid. Afraid, as Nikola and Betty had made others afraid.

But just before she accessed that power, she thought of Estefan, and pulled back.

"Why now, after all these years?" she asked softly.

Long Nu swayed, golden eyes gleaming. "Because the other *Cruor Venator* began killing. She took the life of a shape-shifter in Florida, one who knew you . . . and I realized that she did not have you and that you were alive. And that maybe, just maybe, *you* might be the one to kill the lesser of two monsters."

Anger filled Lyssa, and disdain. But after a moment, confusion crept upon her, as well.

Lyssa stared. "You knew she killed Estefan?"

"We discovered his murder just before we started looking for you in New York," Roland said.

She took those words in . . . and turned to look at Eddie. Searching, stunned. He did not hide from her gaze, but his eyes were filled with regret.

"How could I tell you?" he said softly. "How, when we first met, could I have said those words?"

"You could have," she whispered, even though she knew he was right. It stung, though, that he had kept something so large and important from her. It hurt worse than she could have imagined. Tears threatened, but she pushed them down—and shook her head at him when he moved to touch her.

Eddie stilled. Lyssa summoned up all her strength and met Long Nu's cool gaze.

"You," she said in a hoarse voice. "I know how much you value your own skin. I suppose that's why you didn't come looking for me yourself. You always had such little faith in my mother . . . and in me."

Lyssa glanced at Eddie. "She sent you . . . someone who would be a temptation if I'd gone bad. If you lived, she'd know I wasn't entirely dangerous. If you died, she would have had another answer."

His jaw tensed. Roland spun away to stare out the window.

Long Nu smoothed down her sleeves. "It was the only way to be sure about you. Perhaps you don't remember the days of the old *Cruor Venator,* but *I* do. I would do anything to make certain that we not live through another genocide."

"I would, too," Lyssa whispered.

The old woman gave her a mirthless smile. "Then kill the other *Cruor Venator.* Do it fast, as you should have when you had the chance. And then never have children. So when you die . . . finally . . . it will be over. *All of you* will be gone."

Lyssa stared, stunned to hear the vicious clarity of those words.

Eddie stepped forward, his eyes consumed with fury. Flames erupted over his arms, hot and crackling. The firelight reflected off his eyes, turning them briefly golden.

He reminded her, in that split second, of Lannes—when the witches had threatened his wife's unborn baby.

Her belly clenched. No condoms this morning. She'd known what she was doing and hadn't cared. She still didn't. If she was pregnant . . .

I'll do what my mother did. I'll love my baby. I'll teach her love.

That was all anyone could do. And she would protect that child with her last breath.

"Stay the hell away from her," growled Eddie.

"Yes, I made a mistake with you," murmured Long Nu, unflinching as she met his enraged gaze. "I had no idea you would bond as mates. A *Cruor Venator* shares her protection with her blood match. It happens upon first meeting. I could feel it on you like slime when I saw you together in that elevator."

Roland stepped in front of her. "Stop talking and get out. Get the fuck out, and don't come back. I mean it. You're no longer welcome here."

She seemed truly surprised. "We have an alliance."

"We don't have shit now." Roland leaned in, his big frame rigid and strained. Lyssa smelled whiskey on his breath and noted his rumpled, slept-in, clothes. "You manipulated me and people I care about."

He stabbed his finger at Eddie. "This boy is like my son. He is one of the finest people I know. That's a line no one crosses. And if *he* vouches for Lyssa Andreanos . . . then I don't care if she has *flying fucking monkeys* coming out of her ass. You leave her *alone*."

Lyssa raised her brow. Eddie stared at Roland with a look in his eyes that was heartbreakingly vulnerable.

Long Nu backed away. "You've made an odd decision today, Roland. Not entirely practical. Or wise." She gave Lyssa a long hard look. "*Your* father was equally foolish."

She started forward, but Eddie held her back. "Go to hell. He loved us."

"Love is rarely enough," replied the old dragon.

Without another word, she turned and walked down the corridor. The elevator opened for her, she stepped forward . . . and in moments was gone.

Lyssa let out a shaky breath and collapsed into the nearest chair. Eddie sat beside her, with a wildness in his eyes that felt too familiar.

Roland bowed his head, rubbing his neck.

"Both of you," he said gruffly. "Tell me everything."

EDDIE FOUND LYSSA ON THE ROOF OF THE OLD building, watching the city come alive in light.

A fire burned in the copper pit, and her feet were

propped up on a wooden bench. She held a bottle of water in her left hand, and her right—ungloved, exposed—hung loose off the arm of her chair.

The wind was sweet. Eddie took a moment, watching her, soaking in the miracle all over again.

I hope I never screw it up.

He ventured close. Lyssa did not turn around but she set down her water. "I smell pizza."

"There's an Italian restaurant downstairs. Roland has them on speed dial." Eddie sat beside her, sliding a box across the small table between them. "Meat. A lot of it."

Lyssa's mouth quirked, but she looked away at the city. "This has been a strange couple days."

He stared at his hands. "I'm sorry I didn't tell you about Estefan."

She sighed. "If you had . . . I would have run like hell. I wasn't ready to hear that news. You were right."

"Still," he said. "It bothered me, keeping that from you."

"I called his wife." Lyssa glanced at him, and tears glittered in her eyes. "Josie was glad to hear from me, I think. But she didn't know who killed her husband."

"Did you tell her?"

"I told her . . . I took care of it. That it was a shape-shifter thing. And she believed me." She rubbed her eyes "I don't want to be a good liar about things like that."

Eddie stared at the city, then the burning fire. Without quite realizing what he was doing, he found himself reaching out—sticking his hand into the flames.

He felt nothing. Just a tickle. Movement of air over his skin.

"What Long Nu said," he murmured, "about children."

Lyssa tensed. "I want them. I didn't before . . . but I do now."

She sounded defensive, but Eddie breathed a sigh of relief. "I do, too."

"With me?"

"Of course. Who else?"

She smiled, but it was tremulous. "You looked at me as if I were an idiot for asking. I like that."

"Good."

"But I had to ask. This has all been so fast. We didn't . . . talk about that."

"No, we didn't. Like I told you, though . . . I like surprises."

"I like *you*," she said, and all that good heat spread through him like the sun was blooming in his bones.

Eddie pulled his hand from the fire and reached for her. Lyssa met him halfway, and he could see in her eyes the weight of the day bearing down on her. This was his home, not hers. She had been wrenched across the country, away from what she was used to—forced to deal with people she hated, people who were grieving—just as she was grieving.

He hauled her into his lap, holding her tight in his arms. The sky was darker, the city brighter. Her hair smelled like woodsmoke and something sweetly indefinable . . . maybe his shampoo.

She buried her face in his neck, and her body slowly began to relax. His did, too, and after a short, very comfortable, time . . . he began to drift off.

Until his cell phone rang.

Lyssa flinched. Eddie briefly considered not answering until he looked at the screen.

"Mom," he answered.

"Matthew Swint," she said, and dread splashed him cold. "He was here."

"I'm coming," he said.

CHAPTER TWENTY-FOUR

EDDIE's mother was a short, slender woman with an elfin face and long dark hair streaked with silver. She wore jeans and a white blouse with chunky turquoise jewelry—but the bright clean colors only seemed to enhance the sadness in her eyes.

Especially, thought Eddie, when she looked at *him*.

She met them at the door and seemed only a little surprised to find that he had brought someone with him. Lyssa was calm and polite, and her smile was warm. But she walked to the windows as Eddie spoke to his mother, and he knew her good eyes were scanning the shadows outside the house for any unwelcome observers.

Roland still had some clothes that had belonged to an old girlfriend, a woman Eddie knew well. Soria was shorter than Lyssa, but her style was the same: long-sleeved flowing blouses and equally long skirts. A silken scarf embroidered with turquoise beads covered her throat, but she'd kept the cream-colored knit gloves Serena had given her in New York. It didn't look all that odd, put together.

"Where is he?" asked Eddie.

"I don't know," said his mother, rubbing a shaking hand through her hair. "I happened to look out the kitchen window, and he was in the backyard, staring at the house. I called you as soon as it happened."

Fear and loathing touched her eyes. "He was thinner, and his skin sagged. He looked . . . sick."

Eddie *felt* sick. "We'll find him."

"No, you stay away from him."

"I can't. You know I can't."

"You have to." His mother's voice broke. "Edward—"

"No."

"I can't lose you."

"You should have thought—" Eddie stopped, but too late. His mother stared at him, no doubt hearing the rest of that sentence in her head.

You should have thought of that.

All the color drained from her face. He looked away, shame rolling off him like a bitter cloud.

"Mom," he said, softly. "Keep the doors locked. Call Grandma and tell her to do the same."

She didn't say a word.

Outside, Eddie strode down the front walk, past the rental car, and down the street. His hands were in his hair, partially covering his face. Every inch of him was strained and rigid.

Lyssa followed, allowing him his silence—until even *he* couldn't take it anymore.

"I hate him," Eddie snapped. "Come on. There's a park nearby."

A small park, filled with trees and a several wide paths. It was empty except for two joggers in black pants and sweatshirts who ran past them with a large golden retriever. The dog shied from Lyssa with a whimper.

They found a bench and sat down. It all seemed too

normal, far away from the disgusting horror of the previous night.

But not sufficiently far away from the horror of his childhood, years and years in the past.

"I'll never be able to talk with her about this," he said. "It'll kill her. It might kill me."

Lyssa leaned against him. "Some things can't be talked about. Anyone who says differently has never lived through a truly horrible event."

"And saying the words doesn't heal anything unless you're saying them to the right person, at the right time." Eddie bowed his head, kneading his brow. "You were the right person, the right time. My mom . . . isn't."

"If you told her that you forgive her—"

"I don't," he interrupted, then softened his voice. "One day, maybe. Not yet."

"Then wait," Lyssa said gently. "Wait until you're ready. If you force it . . . she'll know you're lying. And you'll resent her for making you feel as though you have to say something you don't mean."

Eddie drew in a shaky breath. "Maybe you should be a therapist instead of an artist."

"The artist *is* a therapist." Her lips brushed his cheek with great tenderness. "But I'm better at dishing out advice than taking it."

He took her hand and kissed it. "I want to introduce you a little better to my mom. Do you feel comfortable going back there?"

"Do you?"

When he hesitated, she said, "Let's wait."

"You must think I'm a coward."

"No." Lyssa rested her cheek on his shoulder. "When you returned home for the first time . . . what was it like?"

"Horrible," he whispered. "She was so happy to see

me . . . but she was angry, too, that I'd run away. Angry and hurt. She needed me after my sister died, and I abandoned her. I had a good reason—good, from my point of view—but she didn't know any of that, and maybe it didn't matter. Maybe I should have just stayed and fought it out—the fire, the guilt. All of it."

"Early on, did you have trouble controlling the fire?"

"Yeah. It would just . . . come on me. I spent a lot of time alone. I'm surprised I didn't die from starvation or loneliness in those first few years."

"I almost did," she said. "And I'm surprised I didn't accidentally murder anyone. I was a girl, alone. Men would . . . men would try to take advantage of that. I'd fight them off, or they would see my right hand and freak. Or maybe they'd catch fire, and I would run like hell."

He held her tightly against him. "I'm sorry."

"Did that happen to you? You know . . . with men who liked boys?"

"Yes." Eddie closed his eyes, burying his nose in her hair. "I fought like you did, but it made me think of Matthew, and that was . . . one more horrible thing."

"He didn't molest you, did he?"

"Not like that, but . . ."

"You don't have to talk about it," she said quickly.

"No, it's . . . he would look at me. Me, naked. And . . . say things."

Lyssa gripped his hand so tightly it hurt. But he welcomed the pain.

"That's all," he whispered. "You want to walk now?"

"Yes," she said.

EDDIE WAS GOING TO DRIVE THEM BACK TO HIS apartment, but he could tell that Lyssa was still thinking about what he'd told her—and that wasn't the memory he wanted to end her night on.

So he took her to the Kosmo Klub.

Built underground, the bar was accessible via a narrow stairwell so nondescript and unadorned, the only way to know it existed was by the long line of people waiting to get in.

Fortunately, it was the favorite haunt of Dirk & Steele's agents—and the owner, an endearingly eccentric elderly woman named Dame Rose—loved all those men and women. Like, she *really* loved them.

Eddie walked Lyssa to the front of the line, and she gave all the waiting people an uncertain look. He slipped a protective arm around her waist, aware of the women glaring—and the men checking out her flawless face.

"You sure about this?" she asked, checking her scarf.

"You'll love it. Only the best musicians come here, and the food is great."

"Mmm," she said, peering at the diminutive, old-fashioned sign nailed above the entrance.

"Kosmo Klub," she read out loud, and smiled. "For a kosmic good time."

The bouncer recognized him, and was just beginning to unhook the velvet rope when a musical voice cried, "Eddie!"

An elderly woman hobbled up the stairwell, face lit up in a broad smile. She was dressed in emerald green sequins, with a matching feather in her silver hair. Her skin was very dark and fine, her bones delicate as a bird's. But when she hugged Eddie, her fingers pinched his ass with unerring precision, and she pulled his face down for a hearty kiss on the mouth.

"Lord, you make me lusty," she announced loudly, and turned her sparkling gaze on Lyssa. "And who is this lovely? Don't tell me you finally have a girl?"

Lyssa grinned, and held out her gloved left hand. "My name is Lyssa."

"And yes, Rose," Eddie said proudly. "She's my girl."

"Well," she said, hooking her arms around them. "This calls for free drinks and dancing. You, sweets, are my special guests tonight."

"Be gentle," Lyssa said, and Rose roared with laughter.

The bar was packed, and so was the cleared space in front of the stage, where a small band played. A tall, lanky black man in a T-shirt, jeans, and a suit jacket held the microphone like a lover, and sounded so much like Otis Redding that Eddie had to take a moment to make sure he wasn't seeing the impossible.

"He's something," said Rose with a sigh, and led them to a small empty table on the edge of the dance floor. She plucked away its RESERVED sign, and as Eddie pulled out Lyssa's chair, she said, "Some big-time movie star said he wanted dinner tonight, but he can just stand at the bar and drink his supper standing up. This, babies, is for you."

"Oh," Lyssa said, staring. "Are you sure . . ."

Rose smiled and patted her cheek. "You are sweet. But you should know now that I take care of Eddie and his friends. And his ladies . . . well, you're the first I've seen, so I know it's special. You're always welcome here, Lyssa. Don't forget it."

Before Lyssa could say a word, the old woman spun and disappeared into the crowd.

Eddie caught her hand, smiling. "See?"

"I . . ." she began, and gave him a peculiar look that was full of wonderment. "I've never . . ."

"I know," he said. "But this is your home now. All of this. Everything I have is your home, Lyssa. I want you to know that."

She blinked hard and swallowed. "If she knew what I am, what I could do . . ."

"You do good," he said. "You help people and save lives. You're an artist, a writer. A great one. You're the finest, bravest person I know."

She exhaled, slowly, her eyes beginning to glow. The small candle burning on the table sputtered, and flared like a firecracker. A grin touched her mouth, and Eddie laughed.

"Miracles," she murmured, looking at him with a heat that made him feel his soul was burning in light. "I love you."

The man onstage launched into a stirring rendition of "Try a Little Tenderness." Eddie stood and tugged on Lyssa's hand. "Let's dance."

"No," she said, laughing. "I've never."

"Then you have to, with me."

"You're going to regret this."

"Only if you say no," he said, pulling her off the chair with a flex of one strong arm. Lyssa's laugh became a gasp as she slammed against him, his one arm sliding instantly around her waist and holding her so tightly he could feel every curve of her lush body. She held him just as closely, her right hand clasped in his left. He turned them slowly, swaying to that soulful voice singing about love and tenderness.

And then he looked past her, into the crowd—and saw a man watching them.

Time slowed down. Details stood out in the shadows. Every part of the man was sharp, jutting, hard.

Maybe because he was so skinny, as if every ounce of fat had melted off him, stretching his skin tight as a drum across his chest and face. His eyes bulged, and his mouth was thick, making a long slashing line across his face.

Matthew Swint. It was him.

The world came unhinged around him, tilting sideways. Nothing seemed real. He was suddenly a kid again, heart pounding, crushed with fear.

The *Cruor Venator* couldn't touch him, but Matthew Swint . . . seeing him again was a greasy, sweaty nightmare filled with cigarette burns, and his pants pulled down so Matthew could make fun of his penis and threaten to set it on fire. It was seeing him kiss Eddie's mother, and follow her into her bedroom, and seeing him in that same bedroom with his sobbing sister . . .

A strong, warm hand grabbed his, holding tight. Fire flowed through that touch, sinking into his skin.

Lyssa. He was not alone.

She stared at him with concern, but Eddie didn't wait to explain. He let go of her, and ran toward Matthew—plowing through the crowd with hot, wild, determination. Matthew ran, too—fast, darting. Eddie glimpsed his back just before he disappeared up the stairs to the Kosmo Klub's front door.

Lyssa caught up just as he hit the sidewalk. Matthew was already at the end of the block, and Eddie took off after him—heart pounding, fury fueling his muscles, lending so much speed that he caught up with the older man as he swerved down an alley.

Matthew spun, nearly tripping, and his hand flashed inside his jacket. He pulled out a gun, pointing it at Eddie—just as Lyssa staggered into the alley with them.

Dammit.

"Edward," said Matthew, breathlessly. "I wish you hadn't seen me just now."

"Following me? Visiting my mother's home?" Eddie edged in front of Lyssa. "What did you think would happen?"

Matthew was still breathing hard, one hand holding his chest. He really did look sick, even frail, but there was a wiry strength about him, too—and something quietly frenzied about the way he looked at Eddie that was totally unnerving.

But not as frightening as knowing Lyssa was just behind him, in range of a bullet.

Eddie edged closer. "You should have died in jail. Isn't that what happens to child molesters?"

Matthew's mouth stretched into a ghastly smile. "When they're lucky. Let's just say . . . I wasn't. But it gave me plenty of time to think about you." The gun wavered. "You're the reason I went to jail. You killed my brother. Everyone thought *I* set him on fire, but I knew it was you. I saw the look in your eyes when he went up. Sort of like the look you're giving me now."

His finger began to squeeze the trigger—and the world slowed down with agonizing force. Eddie stopped thinking. His heart and body took over, and he raised his hand at the man.

Fire erupted, consuming him in a spire of flames. But even as Matthew burned, he fired the gun.

Pain lanced across Eddie's arm, spinning him. Just a flesh wound.

But then he heard Lyssa scream.

CHAPTER TWENTY-FIVE

EVERYTHING happened too fast, up until the moment Eddie got shot. But when he spun, hit—the world dropped away.

Lyssa screamed in rage and lunged toward Matthew Swint. She heard shouts behind her, but those were lost beneath the roar in her ears. It didn't matter that he was already dying, that she could feel his blood boiling beneath his skin as the fire licked up his legs. A terrible fury clawed up her throat when she thought about him hurting Eddie—and a sister that she would never know.

Children, abused. And now he was back, trying to kill . . . to murder . . .

Your mate, whispered the dragon, in a voice crackling with rage.

Flames burned through the glove of her right hand, turning it to ash as she plowed into Matthew's burning body. Her claws gleamed with fire.

She barely felt the first blow or the second, but when the blood sprayed from his throat and hit her face, the heat and scent of it flooded her with terrible pleasure. For the first time in her life, violence did not frighten her. It felt righteous.

Matthew Swint screamed, but his voice choked as Lyssa pressed her mouth to his throat wound and drank—deep and long, lips tight as her dragon teeth sharpened and bit into his flesh.

His blood was not sweet. It was terrible. She realized in that moment why a *Cruor Venator* chose victims so carefully: only good people with good lives, because when drinking a soul—drinking memories—it was only sweetness that a *Cruor Venator* would want inside her mind.

Matthew tasted like shit. And the images in his head . . .

Lyssa finally broke off, gagging—but it was already too late. She felt the cigarette between her fingers as she burned a young boy's hand—*a beautiful child who disgusts me because he is weak, a fag, a piece of shit*—and then the memories shifted, and she saw a lovely teen girl with long dark hair and huge eyes, and—

—Lyssa lashed out, unthinking, desperate to kill what was flowing through her mind—

—realizing too late that it was Matthew receiving her final, killing, blow. She saw him drop, half his throat missing, eyes rolled back in his head as the fire turned his skin black.

Strong arms wrapped around her body, pulling her backward. Eddie's voice broke through the roar in her head, and she clung to him—staring in horror at Matthew's body.

She had killed him. Consumed his dying blood.

Power ripped through her, tearing through her veins. Lyssa gasped, clutching her head, throat cracking with a soundless scream as a thousand, a million prickling needles dug into her soul.

And then, just as a abruptly, the pain faded . . . leaving nothing behind but a floating sensation that was cold and sharp as a knife's edge.

Birthright, whispered the dragon, with pride and pleasure. *Finally.*

"No," she said, horrified.

"Lyssa," said Eddie sharply, and she staggered from him, holding up her hands—which were covered in blood.

Eddie chased her, grabbing her wrists. "Come on. We have to go."

Lyssa stared at Matthew's charred, blackened remains. Cars drove past the alley entrance, but she thought she heard shouts, coming close.

"No," she said again, and Eddie pulled ruthlessly away, making her run.

When they reached the end of the alley, he slowed them to a walk and slung his arm over her shoulders. Lyssa staggered against him, clutching his shirt. Power still flowed through her, and it was sweeter than she wanted to admit.

"I killed him," she murmured.

Eddie said nothing, wincing as he reached into his coat for his cell phone. Lyssa sucked in her breath. "He shot you."

"I'm fine," he said.

Lyssa closed her eyes, nauseated. "Be honest."

"I am." His hand tightened around hers. "I've had much worse, I promise you."

Sirens filled the night air. Eddie made them walk faster, and Lyssa finally straightened, trying to pull herself together.

"I didn't mean to kill him," she said, as he dialed his phone. "Actually, I take that back. I really wanted him dead for hurting you."

"Good," he replied, flashing her a quick hard look—and then regret hit his eyes. "I didn't mean . . . I know how you feel about . . ."

"Don't." Lyssa took a deep breath, steadying herself. "He's not worth second thoughts. Trust me . . . when I drank his blood, I saw . . ."

Eddie blinked, and his breath caught. "Oh."

"I'm sorry," she whispered, haunted. He swallowed hard and gave her a sharp nod. Then, with visible effort, he turned his focus back on making his call.

"Roland's not answering," he muttered, moments later. "We're close, though. We should go there. Lay low. I don't know how much anyone saw back there."

"You think . . . ?"

"I don't know," he said grimly. "But Dirk & Steele has too many connections to let any of us go to jail for taking the life of a child molester."

"You make it sound like the mob."

"Feels like that, sometimes."

It was a ten-minute walk. Both of them silent, focused. San Francisco, which Lyssa had been falling in love with, suddenly felt like some glittering, alien cage that might collapse its bars around her at any moment.

Except I'm the monster now, she thought. *I am a Cruor Venator, and if I chose, if I wanted to . . .*

You could control the world, whispered the dragon. *There has never been one like you. Demon blood, mixed with dragon? There is a reason Georgene wants you, either to control or to consume.*

They reached the building, but Lyssa grabbed Eddie's hand as he began to unlock the narrow glass door. A scent curled around and through her—impossible, wicked, and muscular.

It couldn't be . . . not so quickly. It had only been a day.

But then Lyssa remembered that Estefan had known how to contact Dirk & Steele, where they were located, that it was filled with people who could help her . . . people like Eddie.

And what Estefan knew . . .

"Georgene is here," she told him, and deep inside, the dragon began to purr.

THEY TOOK THE STAIRS. EDDIE MOVED ON LIGHT feet, fire sparking off his hair and shimmering over his hands. Lyssa followed, using the climb to mentally prepare—as if such a thing was possible. Being a *Cruor Venator* would not be enough to kill Georgene. For witches who were unaffected by magic, it would come down to hand-to-hand combat.

But this time, there was no small child to use as bait. No mother forced to choose her life over the life of her daughter. No father, away on business, coming home to find his wife being slowly murdered, her body too far gone to save.

When they reached the ninth floor, it was all very quiet. But Lyssa smelled Georgene's scent . . . as well as blood. She grabbed Eddie's shoulder, holding him back.

"She's here," she breathed.

His jaw flexed, and he pulled her close. "My arm. It's bleeding."

Lyssa stared, confused . . . until he swiped some of his own blood and placed his hot, wet fingers on her lips. She recoiled instinctively . . . but the scent filled her, and so did the trace of blood that he left on her mouth. Her tongue licked it off, and his love coursed through, as well as golden light. It chased away the stink and sourness of Matthew Swint . . . and the next time he held up his hand, she did not resist.

She licked his blood off his fingers, then did the same to the wound on his arm—soaking in his strength and goodness, feeling her heart grow, and her spirit.

Eddie's breath quickened. Between them, that mental link bloomed. It did not last, but there was enough time to feel his mind touch hers in a blossoming shower of concern and affection that was not in the least bit dimmed by her lapping his blood away with her tongue.

Which, frankly, she wouldn't have blamed him for finding disgusting. That he didn't . . . was just another miracle. Her miracle. Her man.

I understand, Lyssa wished she could tell her mother. *I understand now.*

"Ready?" Eddie whispered.

Lyssa nodded, jaw set . . . and moved in front of him to stride down the dark corridor to the living room. The lights were off, but the city gleamed through the windows, shedding a glow. Close, the scent of blood intensified . . . and so did the sound of harsh, pained, breathing.

It was Roland, she discovered. Bound hand and foot, and shivering as he lay sprawled on the floor near an overturned table. An obsidian dagger jutted from his shoulder, but he had suffered cuts all over. Blood soaked his clothes.

When he saw Lyssa and Eddie, his eyes widened and a low, pained rumble escaped his throat. He had been gagged, too.

She smelled his fear. The room stank with it, and the stench of his blood.

"Interesting man," said Georgene, moving in the shadows on the other end of the room. "Stronger than I expected. Still not able to resist me, but he fought the fear. He still fights. And his mind . . ."

She made a hissing sound, filled with pleasure. "Such unexpected power. Everyone he loves is filled with power. I could harvest them all and rule this world."

Lyssa didn't look away from Georgene, not even when Eddie slipped past her to crouch beside Roland.

"I'm ripe," she said. "Are you ready for me?"

The witch strode toward her. "I offered you a chance."

"No."

"I meant it, you know. Both of us, together. Yes, you would have tried to kill me eventually, but two *Cruor Venators* working in tandem? That has not been seen in a thousand years."

"I can think of better dreams."

"I can't," said Georgene, with an oddly regretful smile. "There is nothing sweeter than drinking a life and riding that power. I took Nikola with me, and now she rests in here." Her hand pressed against her heart. "Forever."

"You won't take me," Lyssa whispered. "Or Eddie, or anyone else."

"Ah," she whispered, dark eyes glittering. "You are untrained. You are young, and have not fed on a full life. I can feel that. You have no chance, Lyssa. And yet . . . when I take your life, it will be the life of a full blood *Cruor Venator* . . . which is far more powerful than if I had just killed you before your first murder."

Eddie rose from helping Roland, and stepped forward. "You won't touch her."

She smiled. "You'll be next. And when I'm done, you won't remember Lyssa. You won't remember yourself."

That threat. That promise.

For a moment, Lyssa remembered her mother, chained and bleeding. Her father, descending in a cloud of fire.

Fire burned in her hands. Inside, the dragon simmered with such terrible rage she forgot everything but the need, and hunger, to protect the man behind her.

My mate.

Lyssa took one powerful, bounding stride—and grabbed Georgene's head between her hands. Claws pierced her scalp, drawing blood. Blood that Lyssa scraped across her tongue.

The reaction was immediate, and overwhelming. Power roared through her veins with such force she thought her skin would split—like a cocoon, split—or the skin of a snake—revealing her, transformed. Unrecognizable. Alien.

She didn't care. Nothing mattered but that taste of power, which felt like the purest form of infinity—like heaven after a hard death. Impossible and eternal.

I will never give this up, came the unbidden thought. *I will kill to keep it.*

And, just like that, the moment ended. One terrible thought was all it took to snap Lyssa free and send her slamming back to earth in a tumble of fear and hunger, and determination.

The *Cruor Venator* snarled and shifted shape into a leopard. The transformation took a heartbeat, and suddenly Lyssa was on her back, fighting to fend off an enraged 150-pound cat with hate and hunger in its black eyes. Claws gouged her stomach.

Eddie appeared behind the leopard—and in a burst of raw strength, slid his arms around its neck and hauled backward. Lyssa scrambled forward instead of away, slashing her own claws across the leopard's belly, screaming in fury and disgust as she tried to gut the *Cruor Venator.*

The leopard twisted, knocking Eddie on his side.

Lyssa grabbed her tail, yanking the beast away from
him—and barely jumped back in time to keep from
being cut across the throat. Instead of pressing the
attack, the *Cruor Venator* turned again on Eddie.

She's going to kill him first.

Ruthless resolve shot straight into Lyssa's heart.
Pain ate at her right arm, muscles contorting with
power, but this time she embraced it, opening her soul
to the dragon, accepting that other half of her without
hesitation.

Golden light flooded her vision. Hot as the sun, and
bright.

Lyssa's body contorted, expanding, her skin stretching until she thought she would explode from the force
of the dragon fighting to emerge. Everything twisted—
muscles and bone, the shape of the world—even the
slant of light.

Wings erupted against her back. Bursting with fire.

Furniture scattered around her. The floor burned.
She looked down, as though from very far away, and
saw Eddie staring at her, his body surrounded in
flames. Admiration and wonderment filled his eyes.

The *Cruor Venator* still wore her stolen leopard skin.
But her gaze was human and dark . . . and full of fear.

Not that it mattered. She was hardly a mouthful, for
a dragon.

Which Lyssa discovered. When she ate her in one
bite.

Blood flooded her mouth, bone crunching. The taste
was awful, and not because she was eating another
person. The rot of Georgene's spirit was thick and
slimy, coating the inside of her mouth and throat—and
then her soul—in such filth that Lyssa thought eating
shit from a sewer would have been better.

And then the power hit her—memories soaked from blood—and the world went black.

"FUCK ME," MUTTERED ROLAND, AS THE DRAGON ate the witch. Eddie, who had never much cared for swearing, had to agree.

Fuck me was an appropriate response, along with *Oh, my God.*

Lyssa's transforming into a dragon had been awe-inspiring: golden and hot, a shimmer of light that clung to her skin as scales erupted, and her body stretched with furious power.

But Lyssa as a dragon . . . was the stuff of fairy tales and children's dreams on starry nights. A dragon, who in older days, would inspire quests and long journeys—searching for gold, when the only treasure worth finding would be the dragon's heart itself. Living, beating, and full of love.

God, he loved her.

The ceiling cracked above her head. Eddie had to dance backward as her wings nearly knocked him into the window. Roland stayed on the floor, breathing hard, weak from blood loss. Eddie crawled close, thinking about how stupid he'd been to stay so angry at the older man, these last few years. Seeing Roland wounded, tied up, in pain—felt too much like watching his father die for a second time. Making him realize just how much he still cared. He tried instinctively not to feel anything at all, to bury those emotions, but the well was already too full with Lyssa. The cap he tried to screw on wouldn't fit.

"Hey," Eddie said to the hurt man, just as Lyssa let out a strangled roar. Blood dripped from between her long white teeth—

—and then she collapsed.

Eddie dragged Roland out of the way before her long, scaled neck would have crushed him. He kept moving, half-carrying the older man as fire shimmered along her skin. Fortunately, she began to shift shape—and in moments had returned to her human body: naked and on fire.

"Roland," he said.

"Go," he snapped, sagging against the wall. "Hurry."

Eddie raced to Lyssa's side and threw her over his shoulder. The fire intensified when he touched her, and he felt his own power rise as he ran down the stairs to the cage.

He had barely closed the door behind them when she exploded. Moments later, he followed—and in those first few seconds his mind opened to hers, and a rush of emotion not his own flowed through him: fear and longing, and anger.

So much anger. Lyssa's anger. He glimpsed memories—blood and death, snow and a forest in moonlight—and he knew that she was experiencing the murders of her parents all over again, this time in the body and mind of the *Cruor Venator*. From the perspective of the murderer.

He fought to reach her through their bond, struggling against a morass of spiritual slime that tugged at him with sticky tentacles. Lyssa huddled in front of him, a beacon of light amidst disease, and when he finally reached her, it was like touching the sun on a summer morning, clean and white-hot, and full of promise.

I'm here, he told her. *Hold on to me.*

He wrapped wings around her, wings of fire, and held her within the flames. Lyssa held him, as well, with a close, hard strength that bound their spirits together—closer than flesh, closer than blood—bound in spirit, together, as one.

Around them, the *Cruor Venator*'s dying soul thrashed and oozed with murder and filth—but that stain did not touch them.

We're forever, whispered Lyssa's voice.

And ever after, murmured Eddie.

Then, together, their souls consumed the last dark remnants of the *Cruor Venator* . . . erasing even her memory.

Until it was as if she had never existed.

EPILOGUE

THERE was nothing prettier than New York City in the winter, especially around Christmas.

It was especially nice, Lyssa thought, when you had someone to share it with.

Eddie's arm was warm around her waist as they slogged up Fifth Avenue to Central Park. It had snowed the night before, a massive, record dump—and. the city felt quieter, a brief reprieve that would only last a couple hours. Or maybe longer . . . since it was supposed to snow again that afternoon.

"Let me carry that for you," Eddie said, taking her backpack and portfolio. They had returned to her old underground haunt to see if any of her paintings had survived—and to look for her laptop, if it was still there.

Amazingly, it was. Her wallet was gone ("Call it rent," Eddie had said), but Albert had stashed her computer amongst his things, just in case she came back. He'd done the same with the paintings that hadn't burned, stacking them carefully in a neat pile away from anything that dripped.

"You sure you don't want to meet your editors?" Eddie asked her for the hundredth time.

"I'm sure," she told him, exasperated by his persistence. "Baby steps, right? Besides, e-mail's been fine this long."

He flashed her a quick grin, and she shook her head at him.

San Francisco was now home for Lyssa, but she and Eddie were looking for someplace with a little more privacy, where they could build a room that would hold a raging fire. Because that sort of thing had a life of its own . . . and not even a lot of love could chase away every nightmare.

New York City, however, was a nice getaway. They were staying at the Four Seasons, which, for a girl who had lived in a tunnel for three years, was odd and cool in the best way possible.

Lannes and Lethe had told them they could use their home in Greenwich Village, but Lyssa knew that the gargoyle still had reservations about her trustworthiness. Never mind that he and his wife were up in Maine. She didn't want him to feel as though she'd gotten her *Cruor Venator* cooties over everything.

It would serve him right, whispered the dragon. *Gargoyles are so self-righteous.*

Hush, replied Lyssa, and said out loud, "How much time before we meet Ursula for lunch?"

"We still have two hours," Eddie said. "Do we need to shop for Jimmy and Tina?"

She bit back a smile. "That sounds so normal. Shopping for Christmas presents."

"I know," he replied, and kissed her left hand, which didn't have a glove because she liked feeling his skin on hers.

A golden ring glinted around her finger, a match to the one on his left hand. Simple. Nothing fancy. No ceremony, except something on paper to make it official and legal. Not that they needed that, but it felt good. Married for little over one month.

"Tomorrow," she told him, tugging him closer. "Right now, let's walk through Central Park."

No one was out. The snow was too deep, and the paths hadn't been cleaned. Drifts, however, melted easily around them—and they didn't mind getting a little wet. Deeper and deeper they went, into the woods, getting lost in the middle of the city.

Finally, when it seemed as though the tangle had become part of a fairy tale, and the trees were thick and loomed like stark soldiers, they stopped and put down their things and lay together in the snow.

"Life is strange," said Lyssa, pulling off the glove of her right hand. Golden claws gleamed, and her scales were blood red. Even regaining the ability to shapeshift had not healed that part of her body. She would always be caught.

But that was okay. *She* was okay. The last of the *Cruor Venator*, for now. Watchful, ready, waiting. Because one day, she knew, it would not be enough simply to leave her alone. Someone would come. Perhaps Long Nu. Maybe another witch. And she would have to fight again.

Not to save *her* life . . . but to save the lives of the children she planned to have . . . and to keep her mate, her husband, safe. Just as he kept her safe, in so many ways.

"I'd rather have it strange," replied Eddie, in that low, thoughtful voice that she loved so much. "It would hurt just as much. But this way, there's magic. And you."

She rolled over and kissed him, hard. Then, she laughed, and began to strip.

Eddie sat up in the melting snow. "What are you doing?"

"Magic," she said, as golden light danced across her skin and mixed with threads of fire. "Has there ever been a dragon in Central Park?"

"I don't know," he said, catching her clothes and grinning. "But there's one now."